Tomo

Friendship Through Fiction—
An Anthology of Japan Teen Stories

Edited and with a Foreword by Holly Thompson

Stone Bridge Press • Berkeley, California

Published by
Stone Bridge Press
P.O. Box 8208
Berkeley, CA 94707
TEL 510-524-8732 • sbp@stonebridge.com • www. stonebridge.com

Cover and part-title illustrations by John Shelley.

Cover and text design by Linda Ronan.

"Be Not Defeated by the Rain" by Kenji Miyazawa, translated by David Sulz, online in *The World of Kenji Miyazawa*. "Bad Day for Baseball" by Graham Salisbury in *Shattered: Stories of Children and War*, edited by Jennifer Armstrong, Laurel Leaf, 2003. "Blue Shells" by Naoko Awa, translated by Toshiya Kamei, in *The Fox's Window and Other Stories* by Naoko Awa, U.N.O. Press, 2009, and online in Moulin Review. "House of Trust" by Sachiko Kashiwaba, in Japanese as *"Shinyodo" no shinyo* in *Onigashima Tsushin* 22 (December 1993) and in *Mirakuru famirii* (Miracle Family) by Sachiko Kashiwaba, Kodansha Bunko, 2010. "Yamada-san's Toaster" by Kelly Luce in *Ms. Yamada's Toaster* by Kelly Luce, University of Tampa Press, 2008. "Hachiro" by Ryusuke Saito, in Japanese as *Hachiro* by Ryusuke Saito, ©Keiko Saito 1967, Fukuinkan Shoten Publishers, Inc., Tokyo, Japan, 1967, All Rights Reserved. "Anton and Kiyohime" by Fumio Takano, in Japanese as "Anton to Kiyohime" in *SF Magazine* (September 2010), Hayakawa Shobo. "Fleecy Clouds" by Arie Nashiya, in Japanese as "Fleecy Love" in *Suki, data: hajimete no shitsuren, nanatsu no hanashi*, Media Factory Bunko DaVinci, 2010. "Love Letter" by Megumi Fujino, in Japanese as "Rabu rettaa" in *Shukan shosetsu* (March 5, 1999), Jitsugyo no Nihon Sha. "Wings on the Wind" by Yuichi Kimura, in Japanese as *Kaze kiru tsubasa* by Yuichi Kimura, ©Yuichi Kimura/Seitaro Kuroda, Kodansha Ltd., 2002.

First edition 2012.

Printed in the United States of America.

2016 2015 2014 2013 2012   10 9 8 7 6 5 4 3 2 1

LIBRARY OF CONGRESS CATALOGING-IN-PUBLICATION DATA
Tomo : friendship through fiction : an anthology of Japan teen stories / edited by Holly Thompson ; [cover and part-title illustrations by John Shelley].—1st ed.
    v. cm.
    Summary: "One year after the tsunami, this benefit fiction anthology helps teens learn about Japan and contribute to long-term recovery efforts"—Provided by publisher.
    Contents: Shocks and tremors — Friends and enemies—Ghosts and spirits—Powers and feats—Talents and curses—Insiders and outsiders—Families and connections.
    ISBN 978-1-61172-006-8 (pbk.); ISBN 978-1-61172-518-6 (e-book)
    1. Children's stories, Japanese. 2. Japan—Juvenile fiction. [1. Short stories. 2. Japan—Fiction.] I. Thompson, Holly. II. Shelley, John, 1959–ill. III. Title: Friendship through fiction.
    PZ5.T615 2012
    [Fic]—dc23
                        2011051530

In memory of all those lost in the Great East Japan
Earthquake and Tsunami of March 11, 2011

and dedicated to all the young people of Tohoku

Be not defeated by the rain,
Nor let the wind prove your better.
Succumb not to the snows of winter.
Nor be bested by the heat of summer.
Be strong in body.
Unfettered by desire.
Not enticed to anger.
Cultivate a quiet joy.

*Excerpted from David Sulz's
translation of the Kenji Miyazawa poem
"Be Not Defeated by the Rain"*
(Ame ni mo makezu)

Contents

Talents and Curses

Insiders and Outsiders

Families and Connections

Foreword: One Year After

by Holly Thompson

For many years I've lived in the seaside town of Kamakura, where in 1498 a powerful tsunami destroyed the temple building surrounding the huge thirteenth-century bronze statue of the Great Buddha. The foundation stones remain, and the Buddha still sits there serenely, though now in the open, exposed to the elements season after season. Until March 11, 2011, it had always seemed impossible to me that a tsunami could reach so far inland—a full kilometer—with such force. Now, of course, post Great East Japan Earthquake, I know better.

Watching video footage of the March 11th tsunami blasting away towns so similar to the one in Japan that I call home—towns nestled between rolling hills and the sea—left me shocked and distraught. It could have been our town, I knew. It could have been us racing to reach high ground. The suffering and loss in Tohoku were immediately palpable. I ached. Yet in an odd twist of timing, I was in the United States that week. While many were fleeing Japan, I wanted desperately to return.

Like others, I donated goods, I donated money, I donated my writing. And once I returned to Japan, I immediately signed up for an eight-day volunteer tsunami cleanup trip with the NGO Peace Boat. I felt the need to do something physical to battle back the damage the tsunami had done.

In Tohoku, I camped out with other teams of volunteers—volunteers from Japan and from countries around the world—and together we shoveled tsunami sludge, bagged debris, scrubbed away mud from shops and homes, cleared drainage gutters, and picked up eighteen tons of rotting fish scattered from coastal markets. It was sobering work; seemingly endless swaths of cities and towns had been destroyed, and even far inland from the coast, homes and businesses were ruined. The stunned yet stoic locals we met were coping with layer upon layer of loss.

As a writer whose work is often focused on young adults, I surveyed the scenes around me in Tohoku, and my thoughts turned to teens. This trauma would follow them through their lives. I wanted to find a way to support the teen survivors as they navigate the rough months and years ahead—through grief and frustration, recovery and hope. I began to formulate a plan.

I envisioned collecting young adult short fiction from authors and translators with a connection to Japan by heritage or experience. The resulting anthology would be read by teens worldwide, enabling them to "visit" Japan through these stories. Proceeds from the sales of the book would support teens in quake- and tsunami-affected areas of Tohoku. It seemed a far-fetched idea in the exhausting and unpredictable spring of 2011, but thanks to the unwavering support of Stone Bridge Press and the hard work of so many phenomenal Japan-connected authors and translators, *Tomo* has become a reality.

The thirty-six stories collected in this anthology range from contemporary to historical, fantasy to realistic, folk tales to ghost stories, and from prose to graphic narrative to stories in verse. Most of the stories are set in Japan or within Japanese families or communities outside of Japan. One story, *Wings on the Wind*, originally written post 9/11, seems an apt parable post 3/11 as survivors struggle with guilt over those they weren't able to save from the tsunami. Nine stories in this anthology are translated from Japanese, and one story is a translation of the Japanese transcription of an Ainu *yukar*. Five contributors from or with strong connections to Tohoku have been included.

A few days before the six-month anniversary of the earthquake and tsunami, I was in Tohoku volunteering again, this time helping a community on the Oshika Peninsula clean and prepare a shrine in order to hold annual festival rites. The community was a fraction of its previous numbers, but the volunteers and the locals together helped ready the shrine grounds and shoulder the *mikoshi* (portable shrine) through the harborside rubble. Together we boarded several fishing boats and took the *mikoshi* out into the pristine harbor. Flags waved from tall stalks of bamboo in the bows of the boats. The sea was calm and sparkling. The sun was brilliant. The mountains all around us were undulating rolls of lush green from recent rains. The March 11th tsunami's immensity was again impossible to grasp, too cruel to fathom. Kenji Miyazawa's poem

"Be Not Defeated by the Rain" (*Ame ni mo makezu*), about being strong in the face of adversity and compassionate toward others who may be struggling, repeated over and over in my head.

May the hard-hit communities of northern Japan find the strength to move forward. May the young people of Japan cultivate a spirit of compassion and play key roles in reviving Tohoku. *Tomo* 友 means "friend," and I am profoundly grateful to everyone who joins me in saying to the people of Tohoku: We are with you, we will help you, we will cheer you as you take your steps to recover.

Shocks and Tremors

Lost

by Andrew Fukuda

It is night and then it is not. I feel myself rising out of the murky depths of my subconscious, surfacing, an opaque light shimmering above. And then I am through, my eyelids lifting, heavy, my body wrung out and spent.

Everything is white, a bleached glare made manageable only by squinting. White bedsheets, white walls, even the linoleum floor is white. An air-conditioning unit, humming with exertion, billows the white curtains against the closed windows back and forth, back and forth, like the resigned gills of a beached fish. I do not recognize anything about this room. From behind, I hear the electronic ping-ping of a monitor.

An elderly woman lies in a bed on the other side of the room, upright metal handrails flanking her, a tangle of bedsheets kicked to the foot of the bed. She is on her side, staring at me, but her eyes are blank. Blank as the white emptiness of the room. Her chest draws in quick, shallow breaths. Like my dog, Tito-chan, after a walk on a hot summer day, flopped in the shade of the tree, panting hard and hot.

I pull myself up, feel an unexpected heft and weight about my chest. There's a tube in my arm; wires connect somewhere against my ribs.

I am in a hospital. I have no idea how I got here.

For a minute, as my head spins, I stare out the window. Only slivers of scenery slip through the shifting gap between the billowing curtains. What I see confuses me: my head is not clear, I think to myself. It is seeing things not there. It is seeing unimaginable things.

I swing my legs to the floor. I'm expecting weakness in them, but not erosion. I fall to the floor with a cry. The white linoleum flings itself at me and smacks me hard, like a vicious slap.

I lie on the ground, wait for the arrival of nurses, those quick shoes clip-clopping along the corridor and into this room. But no one arrives.

When the pain subsides, I pick myself up, holding up my weight by leaning against the bed. Better now, my legs feeling more like they occupy actual physical space, strength returning to them. I make my way to the bathroom, one slow meter at a time, hands pressed against the mattress, then along the wall, until they grip the bathroom sink. An automatic sensor, slightly delayed, turns the light on. The fluorescent lamp flickers above me, then holds fast. Too much light in my eyes; I shut them, then open them slowly.

The reflection before me. It is me. And it is not me.

I seem older than I should be. My hair, even though tussled and unkempt, falls below my shoulder. How did it grow—

No, something is wrong. I touch my hair, distrusting it. It feels coarse and wiry in my hands, but it is mine. And there are other changes about my face.

My cheek fat is diminished, my face sallow. Cheekbones I never thought I possessed protrude out. Acne scars litter my forehead. I lean forward, needing to look closer. Warily, I reach out and touch the acne lightly with my fingertips. I feel the slight rise of them against my skin. I blink. I have never had a single pimple in my life.

And then my eyes course down, past my face, past my neck, to my chest. I see under my loose hospital gown two soft mounds of breasts I've never seen before, never possessed. When I last fell asleep, my chest was flat. My reflection before me now blinks as I blink; yet it is an alien body.

Footsteps entering the room. A gasp, a short cry. Then the figure of a person walks into view. My mother, her hair uncharacteristically frowzy, her face more lined than I remember. A slight bend to her back, of fatigue and of a weight deeper than that of physical tiredness.

"Mother?" I whisper.

She turns around, sees me. Her hand rises to her mouth, trembling. My mother's hand, the curtains behind her: both shaking together.

"Noriko?" Her eyes are shining now, flooding with tears that never fall.

"Mother."

And she comes to me, clasping me in her arms. Her body is skinnier than I remember, frailer; yet there is a desperate strength to her arms as well. And she is so much shorter than I remember, as if she has shrunk. My head used to reach only her neck; now we stand eye to eye.

And then I think: No, it is not her, it is me. I have changed.

"What happened, mother? What happened to me?"

And she does not say anything, only strokes my hair, my long, long hair, over and over, as if hidden in those strands are those words that elude her, the answers that hover just out of her reach.

⌒

There is something wrong with me. Not with my body, which has seemingly ripened overnight. But with my mind. Days after I come to, I see the doctors conferring over MRI scans, brows furrowed and fingers pointing, then jabbing at the scans. Then, their opinions apparently consolidated (or their patience run out), they stream out of the office. All except for one, who calls Mother and me into the office. He pulls on sagging, pockmarked cheeks, his tired eyes refusing to meet ours as he points to the illuminated scans, my brain, my soul lighted up for all the world to see: here, here, and here. Dark spots, gray spots.

"What do they mean?" my mother asks.

"Amnesia," the doctor says. "During the . . ." His voice fades, his eyes shift. Then: "Your daughter must have hit her head against something. She has lost her memory."

"How much of it?"

"It appears she has lost the memory of the past two years. From what we've been able to gather, her last memory was when she was twelve."

"She's lost two years?" my mother says.

The doctor continues speaking as if I'm not in the room, as if I'm not hearing every word. His beady eyes resist shooting down to his watch. He searches for a silver lining to end this conversation. After awaking days ago, I've picked up on a few of the doctors' tricks. No matter how devastating the news, end on a positive. Leave the patients with something. It makes the getaway that much easier.

"Well, at least she does not remember."

My mother whispers, "The earthquake?"

He nods, slides away.

My mother looks at me. Envy seems to cross her face. Then her head swivels to look out the window at the wreckage that lies outside. She does not speak. As if she is still trying to absorb those words, the full weight of their implications. *She does not remember. She does not remember. She does not remember.*

~

I do not remember.

The truth is explained to me very, very slowly. Over the next few days, little by little, another layer removed, another drop of knowledge crashing down, rippling the wavering surface of my consciousness. So slowly, until I have begun to piece things together even before they tell me. Their words, hushed like a dark secret, draped over me as gently as possible.

The earthquake struck on January 17, 1995, at 5:46 a.m., with a magnitude of 7.3 on the Shindo scale; the shaking lasted for about twenty seconds. These are just numbers to me. I do not feel the raw violence of them, the devastation that they must represent. I only see the trembling of my mother's fingers, the quivering of her lips as she utters these numbers, as if she still, so many weeks after the quake, experiences the aftershocks internally, in her bones and muscle and heart and lungs and lips and fingers. The violence suffered by her, by this land, is unimaginable, I think.

But it is imaginable. When I gaze outside the window of my hospital room during those endless hours of unbroken solitude, at the flattened homes crushed like discarded, folded cardboard boxes; at the concrete slabs of government buildings that rise up like gray tombstones; in those moments, it is imaginable. And where there are gaps in my imagination, they are more than adequately filled in by images that flash from the TV screen. Eventually, I shut off the television and never turn it back on.

Over the next few days, my mother tells me what I need to know. Bit by bit. Her voice is polished as she speaks, smooth like a fragile vase. She says, "Our home is gone."

A day after that, she finally whispers my younger sister's name. This is how she says it: "Keiko is gone."

And this, although I had already suspected it days ago, still jars. I keel over, crumpling the bedsheets in my lap. I stare at the creases in the sheets, incoherent calligraphy, jumbled and jangled. A warm hand on my back, tears falling into the grooves of the wrinkled sheets. Not my tears, not yet; they belong to my mother, her eyes squeezed shut, hand over mouth, her head bobbing up and down, her grief inconsolable. The vase broken, shattered. I shut my eyes.

The next day: "What of Father?" I ask only because she has not mentioned him, and does not appear to be intending to.

She stiffens and turns her back to me as she picks up her handbag. "He is still trying to visit. But it is . . . difficult for him."

She sees the confusion on my face, my lack of comprehension.

Then she remembers. That I don't.

"He lives in Hokkaido Prefecture now."

"He was transferred?"

She does not answer.

"Since when?"

She is quiet for a moment. Then: "Your father moved to Sapporo about eighteen months ago."

"Why?"

Again, she does not answer. She stands perfectly stationary, as if stillness will make this moment, that question, simply fade away. Only her hands move, trembling like a weeping willow tree in the breeze. I gaze at the pale alabaster skin of her hand, still unbroken by wrinkles. She has always taken care of her hands, meticulously lathering on hand cream late every night in the silence and darkness of the living room as she waited for Father to return from work. Even the skin of her fingers is perfectly smooth. And then my throat catches. Where her wedding band once was, now there is the white of emptiness.

Her lips tighten, stretch out in grim white lines, like the laundry lines that used to hang outside the bedroom windows. Before she leaves the room, her head nods once to confirm my unspoken suspicion, quickly, as if something has suddenly snapped in her neck.

‿

At night, when the darkness outside seeps inside the hospital, when the scurry of footsteps in the corridor outside fades to silence, my mind gets itchy, my hands restless. All my life I have written at night, in a secret journal I have never allowed anyone to read. I don't even allow myself to read it, except once a year, on the last day of December. That is how

I always spend New Year's Eve Day—rereading my entries, reminiscing about the year gone by.

When I ask my mother if she would buy a new journal for me, her fingers twitch.

"A journal? That may be hard to come by right now," she tells me.

"Just scrounge up some blank pages, then. I'll steal a pen from the clipboard the doctors bring in." I say this unkindly, a terseness in my voice. It surprises me, this rancor, a tone with which I have never spoken to my mother. But that it does not surprise my mother—she does not flinch or even blink—surprises me even more. She does not reprove me but merely takes in my harsh tone quietly.

When she leaves, her footsteps clipping down the corridor, a nudge of guilt nestles into my ribs. My curtains are undrawn, and I stare at my dim reflection. Beyond my reflection, the city lies dormant and blackened; only a scattering of lights outside breaks the canvas of darkness. But it is my reflection I gaze at, diminished in color and definition. I used to be always on the move, my short hair perpetually swinging back and forth past my ears. But now I am only a gray stillness. I breathe; it breathes. Darkness encages us.

⌐

I am passed from doctor to doctor, each one progressively younger. The latest is a baby-faced man in his late twenties, nose hair jutting out of his left nostril. It is not until the fourth session that I realize that it is not nostril hair but a stretched mole. At the end of that session, I ask him for some sheets of paper, and his pen.

"For my journal," I tell him, when he looks at me quizzically.

"A journal," he mumbles to himself, as if not understanding the word.

At the next session, the doctor seems unusually animated. He asks more questions about the journal, and I tell him everything: that I have written an entry every day since I was ten.

"Including the last two years?" he asks. "The years you do not remember?"

I pause. "I don't know," I tell him. "I don't remember."

But he is already nodding his head. "But you probably did?" he says, and it is not a question.

"I probably did."

"It will be good if you could read your journal. All your entries over the past two forgotten years. It might jog your memory. "Yes," he says, nodding vigorously as if to assure himself, "it will help. Do you know where it might be? The journal."

"I always kept it in my bedroom. In my desk."

He nods. "Then you must do it," he says, looking at his watch.

"Do what?"

"Visit your home, if it's still there. Go find your journal."

I stare at him blankly.

⌒

Two days later, I step out of the hospital for the first time in months. Despite the daily physical therapy regiments, my legs are still weak and I walk with a wobble through the hospital exit doors. Outside, my mother waits for me, sitting on a scooter, an extra helmet in hand. Two minutes later, we are rolling down the street, zigzagging our way through the sea of debris. I do not recognize the terrain, the leveled destruction lying around us. I have been dropped in the middle of Hollywood disaster movie. It is the small things I see, and not the utter vastness of devastation, that gain traction in my mind: a baseball glove caught in the upper branches of a tree; a *salariman*'s attaché case placed upright on top of an upturned car, as if a kind stranger has left it there for the owner to retrieve; an elementary school backpack, face down in a large puddle, its bright red nearly completely smeared over with mud.

⌒

Our neighborhood, I see as we wind our way in, is devastated. Only here and there does a house still stand, its empty, glassless window frames blank and wide as if still shell-shocked. But not ours; our home has been crushed to the ground, as if an angry hand has smacked it down. It is utterly leveled into the overlapping wreckage of other pulverized houses. Shards of wooden beams lie scattered like matches out of a matchbox, the blue roof tiles strewn about. A washing machine—not ours—juts out from the debris. My mother and I stand in front of where our house once stood, leaning against the concrete wall that once ran along the front side of the house. Now there is nothing to do but to run my fingers along the engraving of our family name carved into marble at the end of the wall.

Finally, I step forward.

"Noriko, don't," she whispers, but I ignore her. I step onto a beam of wood, testing it, then another, and now I stand atop of what used to be our home. I turn my eyes downward, searching for something, any remnant of the past. I hope to find my desk, the smallest trace of it, but there is none. I will not find my journals. All those forgotten pages of my lived life, never to be retrieved.

I speak, with a deepness of voice that still feels alien to me. "The journals are gone, I'll never find them." I turn to look at my mother. "What should I do?"

She slowly walks over to the scooter. For a second, I think she wants to leave, needs to leave. But then she lifts up the scooter seat. From the compartment underneath, she takes out a white grocery bag and walks back to me. I step down, off the ruins of my home, my upper body swaying with a top-heaviness I am still unaccustomed to. She takes something out of the bag.

A brand-new journal. The cover is a splish-splash of glossy red and hot pink, the bright sheen startling amidst the drab gray and brown of the fallen neighborhood. She holds it out to me, her ceramic white hands speckled by mud.

"Start a new one," she says.

Shuya's Commute

by Liza Dalby

It was March. His first year of high school was almost over. Shuya had thought he wouldn't be able to bear the hour-long commute to Rikkyo High School from his house in Meguro. Two hours every day wasted going back and forth to Saitama on the train! But lots of businessmen did that and more, his mother reminded him. And his friends too. An hour commute each way was nothing to complain about. Even if he had to change trains four times.

"Read a book," they said. "You like to read—here's your chance."

Shuya did like to read. And he had discovered he liked to write too. His favorite after-school activity was the Literature Club. Members spent a month composing numerous haiku, a month on short stories, two months for screenplays, and a semester on novel writing. The novel part was daunting. But everything up till then had been fun.

Too bad Rikkyo had moved out to the suburbs in 1960. Before that it had been located in Ikebukuro—Shuya could have gotten there in no time. Rikkyo was one of the first Western high schools in Japan. Originally it had been built in Tsukiji, near the big fish market, but those buildings were destroyed in the Great Earthquake of 1923, which had devastated most of Tokyo. Each time it relocated, the campus expanded.

Spring break was coming up. Then in April there would be a new crop of wide-eyed freshmen to start the school year. Shuya was looking forward to being one of the experienced students. By now he had established a routine for his commute. There were never any seats on the Yamanote loop train, but the ride was quick. Shuya usually got a seat on the following leg. Then he could settle in and for the next 13 minutes read a mini-novel on his cell phone. Shuya had a turquoise blue Docomo phone with a black plastic rat dangling from the strap. He had gotten the phone in junior high—the rat was a present from his sister, because Shuya had been born in the year of the Rat.

Today was Friday, a little chilly, but clear. Tomorrow would likely be the same. Shuya shivered a little on the platform. Wished he'd brought his jacket today, hoped he would remember tomorrow. But once pressed inside a standing crowd on the loop train, he forgot being chilly. Ah, Sunday he could stay home and his mother would let him sleep until eleven. Now, though, get off at Ebisu, snag a seat on the train to Ikebukuro. Shuya pulled out his cell phone and flipped it open. What to read? Most cell phone novelettes were stupid romance tales. Shuya liked ghost stories and science fiction. Those were a little harder to find. But he came across one that looked interesting:

The Butt Jewel

Deep in the mountains the rivers are green as jade. Clean, too. The carp that swim here don't taste muddy at all, people say. In early June the fireflies glimmer over the banks in a blinking cloud. Not too many places left now where the streams are this pure and the fireflies still hatch into phosphorescent stars. They're not hard to catch. You can trap one in the cup of a bellflower and make a tiny lantern. The girls like to do this.

There was something else that used to live in these rivers too, I know. I saw one once. A kappa. Green as the river, with bumpy skin like a cucumber and wild hair like riverweeds. Scrawny, about as tall as a three-year-old human child, it was squatting on the bank, washing something and muttering. So intent on its task, it didn't notice me staring from across the river. The sun shone fitfully through white patches of mist that were rising from the water. It glinted off whatever it was the kappa was carefully washing.

What could be so precious? I wondered. I pretended to wiggle my fingers in the water, as if scaring tadpoles and not at all concerned about anything on the opposite bank. Could the kappa tell that I had seen it? I hoped not. Just the day before, my friend's cousin, who had been visiting from the city and not familiar with the currents and rocks of the river, hit his head on a boulder and drowned. They found him downstream later that day. I looked up again. The kappa *was gone.*

A kappa *has no soul, but it yearns for one. Which is why it is always looking for an unwary person it can drag down to the bottom of the river. When the person stops struggling and thrashing, finally going limp, the* kappa *reaches its skinny green hand up inside the person's anus and pulls out the butt jewel. People may think their soul resides in their heart or possibly their head, but in fact, it is found in their intestines. The* kappa *knows this. This is the precious butt jewel, and while you are alive, this is where the soul is found.*

I have no doubt that on that day I had come across a kappa *washing a just-removed butt jewel. I hope it was satisfied. I hope it was able to keep it for its own and not feel the need to grab another one. But perhaps, like humans,* kappa *are not satisfied with just one thing if another chance arises. I don't know what satisfies a* kappa. *Maybe they just like the taste. . . . Still, I don't ever swim in the clear jade green river. Nor do I eat the fat carp or even, really, enjoy the faint glimmerings of the fireflies anymore.*

Shuya snapped his phone shut. He had never seen a firefly in Tokyo. Lots of people always got on at the Shibuya station. They were squashed in like sardines in a tin. The announcement came on as usual.

"Please set your phones to silent mode."

Why did they even bother to say that, thought Shuya. The car was completely silent. No one ever talked to another person, let alone on their cell phone. So many people in such a small tight space. Practically all were reading, though. Shuya scrolled through more stories. And he found:

The Hole

The freak tornado faded into the distance, leaving the village a twisted morass of destroyed fields, shredded trees, and smashed houses. Clothing, cars, books, bottles, chairs, shoes, and pictures stewed together in a mash-up of detritus. Nothing remained that wasn't now garbage. As people trickled back to what had been their homes, the mayor urged everyone to take heart that at least they were still alive.

"Tomorrow we'll start the cleanup. . . ."

And so they did. For weeks thereafter the people sifted through the remains of their village. Roads were cleared, property lines redrawn. One day someone noticed a hole that hadn't been there before. At least, nobody could remember anything like it in that location. They decided to push the bulldozed waste from the ruined buildings into the hole. Down it went. After this, the cleanup went much faster. Everything that was dumped into the hole simply disappeared.

One day, a voice came floating out of the sky. You couldn't tell from which direction exactly, only that it was from somewhere above.

"Hey! Whatcha doin' down there?"

Some pebbles rattled to the ground. The only one who heard was a construction worker who had just at that moment removed his hard hat to wipe the sweat off his forehead. He looked around to see who had spoken. His companions were busy running their bulldozers. He shrugged and went back to shoveling.

"Ikebukuro . . . Ikebukuro . . . Don't forget your belongings. . . ."

Shuya shut his phone and struggled into the crowd surging for the doors. He had to catch a train to Saitama from here. He sprinted to make the connection. From this point on, he would be going against the crowds, as most people were coming *into* Tokyo from the suburbs. He never had a problem getting a seat. Settling in, he reopened his phone.

After a while, neighboring villages that had also suffered tornado damage heard about the seemingly bottomless hole, and asked if they could dump their rubbish in it too. The villagers saw an opportunity, and began to charge for the service of using the hole. Pretty soon, the regional reconstruction office heard about it and they contracted to throw all the waste from the renewal projects into the hole. Of course the central govern-

ment was bound to find out, and before long all the politicians were dumping documents they preferred the newspapers not to see into the hole. Down it all went without a trace. A chemical factory had an accident that created mounds of contaminated waste. Why not put it in the hole? Not everyone thought this was such a good idea, though.

One day a teenage boy from the village was walking by the hole. He picked up a handful of rocks and made as if to throw them in.

"You better not do that," his friends warned.

"Why not?" He threw the pebbles hard into the hole.

"Hey! Whatcha doin' down there?" he called out as he did.

That was it.

What the . . . ? Shuya closed one eye. He had forgotten the beginning so he scrolled back to the top of the story. Oh. Right. Ha ha, pretty good.

Who wrote this? The name was unfamiliar. Shuya was pretty sure it was a fake name in any case. Few cell phone authors posted their real names. He thought about one of the girls in his class who was indignant when she found out her favorite romance had been written by a middle-aged man. In the story, the narrator's voice was that of a teenage girl, and she had identified with it completely.

"Eeeew—that's disgusting!" she exclaimed.

"Why?" Shuya asked.

"It just is . . . plus, it's a lie."

Shuya thought about this. You could say that all fiction is a lie, after all. Did it matter if a middle-aged guy wrote as a teenage girl? They had debated this very question in the Literature Club. Did you need to know the author to appreciate the story? Or, once the thing was written, did it float free from its creator? In Shuya's opinion you had to admire an old guy who could write like a girl. That's being creative! In fact, more so than a girl writing like a girl—which was, by and large, pretty boring.

The train was almost at his next stop, Asagiridai. Seven minutes to walk to the north side of the station to catch his last connection. Time for one more story. He already had it picked out:

New Voyage to Space

Back in the 1960s it seemed not unreasonable to suppose that in fifty years' time, we could all honeymoon on the moon if we wished. Certainly, we expected that by 2010 humans would have pushed on to Mars at least, or possibly beyond.

But as it turned out, humans were the problem. The frailty of the human body and mind subjected to the fierce radiation outside of our cocoon of atmosphere . . . we were the weak link. So a team of geneticists teamed up with NASA to develop humans with characteristics drawn from animals—behaviors that would give them advantages in space.

I am a science reporter, writing this now as I am on my way to visit this secret lab to report on their progress. I am ushered into the office of one Dr. Koda, the lab director. He takes me on a tour of what the team has done. Genetic serums have been created. They can be ingested in varied doses, depending on how long their effects are meant to last. In the first room we enter, a group of young people are crouched on the floor. They spring up as the door opens—but not as you would expect. Their powerful legs carry them almost to the ceiling.

"Frog genes," says the doctor. "That will allow them to easily reach any part of a spacecraft to make repairs."

In another room a large man stands quietly in a corner. I can't tell what he has been given.

"The strength of an ox," I am told. "Useful for building colonies once a mission has landed."

In yet another room a woman is curled up, sleeping on a couch. Her eyes barely open as we enter.

"Sloth," says the doctor. "For much of the travel time, the explorers should be able to slow their metabolism and just sleep. Plus," he added, "a sloth doesn't get bored. . . ."

One after another I am shown various subjects who had been given the genetic essence of different animals. Impressed, I ask Dr. Koda if there had been any failures.

"We tried fish," the doctor replies, "because it would have

*been useful for humans to be able to breathe in water. But all
that happened was the subjects developed scales. . . ."*

I was diligently taking notes on everything.

*"Is it possible," I ask, "for me to observe one of these trans-
formations taking place? Nothing terribly complicated . . . the
simplest example would do."*

*"Well, let's see. . . . I have a vial of the monkey essence here.
That was the first one we developed, since it's closest to the human genome."*

*"Great!" I say, as the doctor reaches for a small tube on a
shelf. "How long will the effect last?"*

*"Oh, about ten minutes," he replies, opening the tube and
swallowing the contents.*

*Quickly the monkey essence manifests itself. The doctor
jumps onto his desk and stretches his face in a rubbery grin.
The spectacle is so funny I can't help laughing. And my laughing just encourages his monkey nature to make more silly faces.
I am laughing so hard I drop my pen. Gasping, I look around
for a water fountain. All this laughing has made me thirsty. The
monkey-doctor sees immediately what I want and bounds out of
the room. He comes back in a few minutes with a tall glass mug
of yellow frothy liquid.*

"Thanks!" Thinking it is beer, I take a big sip. . . .

Shuya couldn't help a quick snort of laughter. Monkey tricks . . .
that was not what he was expecting from the portentous beginning of
a sci-fi scenario. Still smiling, he switched off the silent function on his
phone as he got off the train and called his friend Ryu to meet him at the
school gate.

Literature Club was meeting at 2:30 this afternoon for its last session of the school year. Shuya was going to propose that they all try their
hand at writing cell phone novelettes over spring break, and then upload
them as authored by the club at the beginning of next term. He mentioned the idea to Ryu.

"So we'd all be anonymous, right? Wouldn't show who wrote what?"

"Right."

"What are you going to write?"

"Don't know yet," said Shuya. "I just came up with this idea."

Ryu was doubtful. "My life is too boring. I don't have anything to write about."

"Use your imagination. You don't have to write about yourself, you know."

⌐

Classes ended and everyone who was in a club headed for their meeting place. People brought juice and snacks to celebrate. As Shuya stood up to announce his suggestion for spring break, the room suddenly began to sway. Cups were dashed to the floor even as people grabbed onto the edges of the table. Lights flickered and books tumbled out of shelves.

"Earthquake!" students were shrieking.

"Under the tables!" someone shouted.

They had done this drill numerous times. Automatically, students moved away from the windows, crouching under the tables. Every five minutes or so another tremor caused buildings to rumble. Several students pulled out their cell phones to call home, but the system was down.

After the swaying stopped, a few walked to the train station in Niiza, but the trains weren't running, either. They came back to campus. Most students, especially the commuters, decided to stay at school. The principal walked around with a bullhorn, reminding people to stay with their classmates and not go back in the buildings. Food would be distributed, as would blankets from the school's emergency supplies. The quake had been centered north of here, off Tohoku, and there had also been a huge tsunami. . . . This was all he knew at present.

It was getting chilly. Shuya again wished he had his jacket. He sat with his back propped against Ryu, who was sniffling quietly.

Shuya pulled a notebook out of his backpack. The science teacher had been talking about earthquakes and catfish last week. He mentioned the myth of the monster catfish—people used to believe that there was a giant catfish who lived underground, and when it thrashed, this caused the earth to shake. Recently, scientists had noticed that catfish are particularly sensitive to changes in the electrical field of the atmosphere. And along with this, in fact, just before an earthquake occurs, they get agitated.

This seemed like a good seed for a science fiction story, thought Shuya. But why stick to catfish? A monster living underground, quietly sleeping until something provokes it. . . .

Just then an aftershock rippled through the school grounds. Ryu began to whimper, so Shuya punched him lightly on the shoulder.

"Remember the catfish story?" He asked. "Underground?"

Ryu nodded.

"Well, maybe it's not a catfish at all. Maybe it's a dinosaur, or . . . you know, like Godzilla or something. . . ."

Ryu stopped sniffling.

"And maybe there's a special stone that has to be positioned just right to make it quiet again. . . ."

Ryu was listening. Shuya saw the stone in his mind's eye. It was dark gray and smooth, just like an ordinary rock. "You have to have superior abilities to sense its power," he told Ryu.

"What kind of abilities?" Ryu wanted to know.

"Power of observation," declared Shuya. "To see things ordinary people don't notice."

He decided the rock would be mostly buried in the earth, so that what looked like a simple stone sitting on the ground would be the iceberg-like tip of a massive boulder. Immediately, that suggested the twist of how the story would end.

Inspired, Shuya opened his notebook and began furiously to write.

Half Life
by Deni Y. Béchard

The alarm wakes me at 3:00 a.m. The window to our garden is black, the streetlights extinguished. Since the disaster, Tokyo has been getting darker and darker.

I slip out of bed and follow the instructions I read online. I googled "how to walk quietly." Dad taught me to use the Internet for research, but he didn't expect me to learn these techniques: how to move my foot in a circular motion out and forward, then slightly across, to keep my pant legs from rubbing; how to shift my weight onto the ball of my foot in increments; how to walk on the side of a step to keep it from creaking.

The stairs end in a rectangle of space with three doors: my parents' bedroom, their bathroom, and his study, where, every night for the last week, he's been shut up, the house so dark that the light beneath the door blazes. The one time I knocked, pretending I needed help with homework, he was sitting there, a single lamp burning down on a stack of yellowed papers. He told me he was working, but I recognized the papers. They were Grandpa's, from when he passed away a year ago. I'm certain they will help me understand the mystery of my parents' distance, the silence that has taken over our house.

I listen. The band of light no longer shines beneath his door. He must have finally gone to bed, but he isn't even snoring.

This is the hard part. Normally, his study hinges screech like something from a horror film. When I googled "how to open a squeaky door silently," I doubted that I'd find anything useful, but websites explained every technique.

I put the end of a large screwdriver just beneath, on the side with the hinges, then, holding my breath, lift slowly. After a moment, I feel the door shift upward, and I take the knob with my free hand, wrapping my fingers around it as if touching a skittish cat. I turn it as gradually as possible, and ease it back. With the weight off the hinges, there's not a sound. I gently return the handle to its resting position so that it won't snap back. I repeat the procedure from the other side, drawing the door shut, all in perfect silence. I've brought a folded towel, draped across my shoulder, and I lay it along the base of the door, then switch on the lights.

I almost shout with fear and have to grit my teeth not to.

Dad sprawls in his desk chair, mouth open, face paper-pale, red hair standing straight up, glasses lopsided on his nose, as if he's been punched. His small green eyes open. He smacks his lips and groans and rubs his face, then pushes his glasses into place.

"Yes, Kenji," he says, "what is it?"

By then I've grabbed up the towel and I hold it to my cheek.

"I had a nightmare," I tell him. "I'm sorry. I couldn't sleep."

⌒

When I was little, I used to think my parents were the most beautiful people on earth. They laughed and danced in the kitchen. He was huge, and she was tiny. He'd pick me up, then take her under his arm and press us all together, so I could smell her perfume and his aftershave, feel the beating of their hearts and mine, inside my breathless ribs.

But a few years ago, one night I stayed with Obaachan when my aunt Michiko was over. They thought I was sleeping. I was twelve then, and I liked to listen to other people's conversations, often surprised at how different they spoke when they weren't speaking to me.

"It's amazing," my aunt said in a low voice, "how two people like them can make a boy like him."

"I always worried," Obaachan admitted, "that Yumiko would never find a husband. When your father was alive, we discussed some older men we knew who might be willing to marry her. But then she brought Ed home. If you had, I would have been angry, but to see her with someone—with anyone—was such a relief."

Aunt Michiko laughed quietly. "I've heard people say that mixed children take the best from both parents, so we should be happy."

"I just think that foreign men can't always tell which Japanese women are beautiful. Maybe Ed thinks he's lucky. Maybe for an American, Yumiko is pretty."

After hearing that conversation, I started to see things differently. Each passing day deteriorated the world I'd known. My parents began to look ridiculous. He towered over her, his white face splotched red from the heat. He panted and sweated when he walked. In the subway, his head brushed hanging advertisements for makeup and coffee, and everyone pulled back while they looked from him to me. Mom barely came up to his chest, with large breasts for a Japanese woman, a round butt, and very short legs, and she had crooked teeth until he paid for her to get braces.

After the earthquake came and the tsunami crashed down on Tohoku, we watched the TV reports. He held her in one arm, me in the other, though I didn't like this anymore and sensed that he was comforting himself, not me. Then, with the disaster at the nuclear reactor, the news of meltdowns and radioactive particles in the air and water, they changed. He spent his nights in his study, reading Grandpa's old papers. He and Mom avoided each other. I heard them arguing once, in the bedroom, but they told me nothing. They simply stopped speaking.

〜

Miho sits next to me, head lowered as she checks the answers to her exam with the same focus that she gives me when we talk. Afterward, during recess, we play each other our favorite songs from our iPods while the boys in my class watch jealously. A few times, because I'm half, they've asked where I learned Japanese, but I'm one of the best soccer players, so they don't get mean the way they can with other half kids. I've also done my research. Dad used to spend hours on the computer, learning everything about whatever his new passion was, usually something to do with outer space: black holes or quasars or nebulae. He'd call me into his study and explain that light from the creation of solar systems was reaching us billions of years after the systems had been made, and that we could look at that light and see how things had been when the universe was born, just after the big bang.

Though I liked these ideas, I saw that google could help me with more important things, like "how to be popular," "how to be good at soccer," and "how to practice so you improve quickly." The information was endless, and the answers worked. I had good grades and got into a competitive soccer club, and at school, I chose my words carefully. Being liked wasn't always easy with MacDonald for a last name and a polar bear-size father, his hair so red I feared the other kids would ask if we were descended from Ronald McDonald. Though sometimes I worried about being a fake, I had no choice. Besides, what was wrong with learning the best ways to be liked? Everyone wants to be popular. Miho talks to me every day. She didn't used to. I've read wikihow and ehow articles on ways to make girls like you. Maybe I am an *otaku*—a nerd, no different from Dad, but if the other kids don't know, and she likes me, what difference does it make?

After school, when I say good-bye to Miho on the sidewalk, Dad pulls up. Since he teaches at the university nearby, he likes to stop on his way home and drive me to soccer club across the city.

"Is that your girlfriend?" he asks, motioning his head toward Miho.

"No. She's just a friend."

He laughs and says, "Ah, first love."

"Stop it, Dad," I tell him. I hate how he always makes everything sound dramatic.

"I've seen you talking to her before," he says. "She's beautiful."

I've worried that he'd notice. Aside from being obsessed with outer space, he writes embarrassing poetry. When he used to read it to Mom, I pretended not to hear. I do the same now.

"Enjoy the way it feels," he tells me. "When love's new, it's amazing. It's all so fresh. Then everything changes, though you have a ways to go before that happens." He tries to muss my hair as he accelerates, and I yank my head to the side, dodging his hand, which he drops back to the wheel, not seeming to have noticed.

"Listen," he says, and immediately, from his tone, I know that he's going to discuss something important. He does this when he drives, maybe because if he's busy with the traffic, our conversations seem less personal.

"Your mother and I, we've come to a difficult point. We really love each other, but before we married, she told me that she didn't want to leave Japan. Her English isn't very good. I was the one who'd made the choice to move here and study Japanese, and we met here. Except now things have changed."

He sighs and rubs his face, massaging his jaw and cheeks, his glasses knocked at an angle. I say nothing, afraid that if I ask questions he might stop speaking. He's always talked about problems when I least expect it, his words seeming incidental.

"You're young," he says, "and there's a lot of radiation coming down to Tokyo from the north. People are acting as if it's not a big deal, but this stuff is going to be in the food and water in some places for a long time. For your mother and me, it's not as serious as it is for you. You're growing. The half life of some of these particles is thirty years, and if your body absorbs them, it can't get rid of all of them. They could really affect your health."

"How?" I ask. He's begun to sweat, his face flushed, as if he is suddenly afraid.

"Well, you could get cancer down the road. Leukemia is a real threat. The particles emit waves that damage your DNA, and the effects take time to show up."

I just nod. The disaster has been on the TV often, the three meltdowns, but nothing has really changed. Until now I thought it was a danger only farther north.

"Anyway," he says, "your mother doesn't want to go, but I think that staying is a real mistake. Our old agreement didn't take this into account. The government is finally telling the truth—or some of it—and it seems there's been more radiation in Tokyo than they've admitted. I'm pretty angry about it, but we can't agree. So we've come to a decision. It's your choice. You're old enough that your opinion matters. If you want to go, we'll go. We'll move to the US. If you want to stay, we'll stay."

Cars rush past in the opposite lane, sunlight slanting from the clouds, flashing against their windshields. No one has ever asked me to make a choice like this. The blue, cloudless sky outlines the tops of buildings with gold. Nothing looks dangerous.

When Dad glances at me, he doesn't seem angry but afraid.

"What do you think?" he asks.

"I don't know," I say, but before I can tell him that I don't understand radiation enough to decide, he keeps talking.

"It's a shame what's happening in this country. The nuclear plant has those workers out there under awful conditions, in all that radiation. Those men are giving up their lives. But not everyone has to. I want you to think about what's best for you. This is serious. It's okay to be selfish."

No words come to me, other than a question that I can't bring myself to ask: how can he expect me to make this decision when he doesn't trust me with everything *he* knows? He reads his papers every night, and I'm certain they must have something to do with the meltdowns and radiation. He showed no interest in them before.

The sun has fallen lower, shining between buildings and over rooftops, and I consider all that I don't understand—how this light was created, what it carries, and that everything, the air, the sky, holds tiny particles that are determining my life. But if we leave Tokyo, who will we be, and will we even stay together? I miss how he was when I used to think my parents were beautiful. Together, they seemed perfect, and remembering that, I am so sad I can think of nothing else, of no decisions. I stare into the sunlight, wishing I could see into it, into the past, to before these problems began.

⌣

That night, Dad sleeps in the bedroom with Mom, as though talking to me resolved a question for him, or maybe because he believes I will choose to leave and he wants to be close to her, to reassure her, so that she will go with us.

I am already at the top of the stairs. He snores loudly, as if things are back to normal. I slip the screwdriver under the door and lift, then palm the handle and turn. Once inside, with the door closed, I lay the towel on the floor and turn on the light.

The papers are in the bottom desk drawer, and I take them and begin to read.

> *My Dearest Ellen,*
>
> *This isn't easy to tell you. It is shameful. I don't know what has happened to me. I am not the man you saw six months ago. My hair has fallen out. I have lost two teeth. I thought*

they would all fall out, but they've firmed up again. My hair
is gone, though, and I don't think it will grow back. . . .

I can't make sense of this. Is it Grandpa's writing? I met him only a few times, a man bigger even than Dad, but stern. Dad once told me, off-handedly as usual, that they never got along. His father was of another generation, "like your mother's father," he said. "They were like samurai, not afraid of anything. They'd gone to war and done what they had to. They didn't complain. Men like that couldn't understand change. I was the youngest in the family. We weren't the same generation, and your grandpa wanted me to join the military, but I didn't have the stomach for it. When he refused to pay for me to study literature, we agreed on phys-ics, so I went to college for that, then moved to Japan. I didn't marry until late because my memories of family weren't very good."

Though Dad told me all this, I never considered it too seriously. He'd also put the idea of not being fake in my head, saying that if he'd lived the life his father had wanted for him, he'd just have been faking; he'd have hated himself.

I turn the pages, first letters to Grandma from when Grandpa was stationed in New Mexico, then government documents about radiation at a place called Los Alamos. Most involve a court case. In a testimony, he explains how he and other Navy men, all in the desert to run trials on ballistics, worked while the atomic bomb was tested. Hot wind gusted over them, dust everywhere, and then, within a few days, they began to sweat horribly. They took their helmets off, their hair plastered inside. Their teeth became loose. Overnight, he looked decades older. Later, when he'd started to recover, he was transferred to a ship in the Pacific, off the coast of Japan.

All of the men knew something was going to happen, but I
had a pretty good idea of what it really was. There was mist
on the ocean, and we were waiting. We'd been told to wait.
That was the day they dropped the bomb on Hiroshima.

The papers seem endless, interspersed with articles cut from maga-zines, about the effects of radiation poisoning. Gradually, I realize that the decades of documentation span the period from his time in the desert to his involvement in a long court case against the American government. He and other soldiers tried to sue for compensation, but the government denied responsibility. Is this why Dad is so worried about me? He's been reading what radiation did to his father, a lifetime of small cancers, night sweats, endless health problems.

It is almost 4:00 a.m. I have to go to school soon. He and Mom will wake up. But I can only sit here, staring at the papers. I'm no longer afraid. If he catches me, I'll tell him that I have the right to know. He is asking me to decide. I have to see for myself.

～

Normally, math is my best subject, but the numbers jumble on the blackboard. I haven't slept. After I left Dad's study, I read online about the Daiichi reactor, the release of radioactive cesium that loses half its charge in thirty years. If you breathe or ingest it, it enters the blood, then the cells. Mistaken for potassium, it remains, pulsing with energy.

As the teacher lectures, my mouth becomes dry. My stomach gurgles and rumbles. Kids glance at me, but Miho doesn't. She sits perfectly focused, as always.

During recess, she and I walk as clouds press in from the horizon, the wind buffeting us, whipping her hair against her cheeks.

"Is your family planning on doing anything because of the radiation?" I ask.

"What do you mean?" she says, very softly, lowering her head and tilting it to look at my eyes, as if shielding her face from the gusts.

"The . . . the radiation," I tell her, "it's dangerous. It's really bad, right?"

She nods once and gazes straight ahead. "I don't know. Maybe."

"So . . . so is your family thinking about leaving Japan?"

"Leaving," she says softly. "Where would we go? This is our home."

I begin to insist on my question but hesitate. Her face is expressionless, its skin a hard, cold mask, and I realize—with a suddenness like the moment you gasp after holding your breath beneath water—what I hadn't understood. All this time I have done everything to fit in, but I can leave. I have that choice. My father has told me how difficult and expensive it is to move to a country, to learn a language, to get residency and a job. Not everyone can do this, even if they want to.

"I'm sorry," I tell her, softly, but she stares straight ahead, wind blowing against her hair, and she says nothing.

∽

Sometimes, in the mirror, I see the black hair and eyes, the neat features of Mom's family; at others, it's the American, the faint curls, the open gaze and fleshiness of Dad's face. And sometimes, at soccer practice, when boys joke, I don't get it and feel that I'm missing something. Other days, when I make my own joke and they say nothing, I have the sense that there's too much of me. If I stay here or move to America, how long before the traces of the other half fade and I no longer have to try so hard?

"Dad," I ask as he drives me to soccer club, "did you move to Japan only to get away from Grandpa?"

He sighs. "I guess so. He couldn't believe it. For him, the Japanese were still the enemy. He didn't take it lightly that I decided to make my life here."

"Are you happy here?" I ask, wondering if that's why he likes outer space. He wanted to leave the planet Earth, but Japan was as far from home as he could get.

"Until now," he says. "It's not an easy country to fit in, but I've found my place. It's been good to me. The people I know who aren't happy in Japan are the ones who want to be totally accepted. The Japanese are a kind people. They'll leave you alone. But I don't know if they ever really accept foreigners. We'll never fit in the way they do. They have a harmony that's hard for us to understand."

His words echo my thoughts. It's what I'm beginning to see. I've always sensed the unity of my classmates, even if I didn't fully grasp it. I understood that to live within it was like learning to swim in the ocean, to merge with the waves, to forget who you are and move with all that surrounds you.

But talking to Miho, I saw how different I am. The shock felt physical, as if I'd driven the ball to the goal and been knocked down.

I want to go home and sleep, to forget that I'm not fully one of them, that maybe I'm like those particles that slip into a place that belongs to something else. Then, gradually, a thought comes to me. What will Mom be in the United States? Are Americans so different? Dad has been here over twenty years. I was born here. If he and I struggle, will she ever feel at home? I don't know why this hasn't occurred to me until now.

Dad clears his throat, and I realize that he's waiting for an answer. The shock has worn off. Yes, after all of the effort with which I've learned to live in Japan, I feel that I'm on the outside. But I'm not special. Is it possible that I have the least to lose?

⌒

That afternoon into evening, I stay in my room and work through everything I know. The Fukushima-Daiichi nuclear reactor isn't close to Tokyo, and though it might be like Los Alamos to those living there, for me, how dangerous is it really? And how can Father be so angry at Japan when the American government behaved no differently?

I read online that over forty million people live in the region around Tokyo. We can't all leave, and I wonder if Dad is easily frightened. He came here to get away from Grandpa, so maybe for him leaving is the obvious solution. But this is where I've wanted to belong, studying others, doing everything to be one of them. And I have been, I realize, most of the time, except now, when I'm thinking about this.

I open my laptop and type into google, "how to lie to your parents." Though I have made my decision, it's hard not to have doubts, and I don't want them to show. I get up and leave my room, and go into the kitchen. Dinner is almost ready, Mom finishing up, her movements brisk and precise, her eyes calm. It's impossible to know, from seeing her, that she might be on the verge of the biggest change in her life.

"I've made up my mind," I say when Dad sits down. "I don't want to leave. I guess I just don't want to change schools. All of my friends are here."

He shakes his head. "That's not a good reason," he tells me, his voice so low and breathy I can barely make out his words.

"I don't want to go," I insist, keeping my tone even.

Mom says nothing. She glances from Dad to me, lets her gaze linger, then looks down and nods once.

"Okay," he says and swallows. "But you're certain?"

"I'm certain," I tell him. I don't say that everything will be perfect. That's too much of a lie. But they'll be together, and with time, we'll all find our harmony again.

IF YOUR **LITTLE BROTHER** WERE IN DANGER, WOULD YOU BE WORRIED?

OF COURSE.

YOUR PARENTS **BOTH** HAVE BROTHERS **AND** SISTERS IN DANGER.

HIEVE

SO *THAT'S* WHY THEY WERE BEING WEIRD THIS MORNING.

SAM, THAT'S **YOUR FAMILY** IN JAPAN. YOU SHOULD HELP THEM.

Aftershocks

by Ann Tashi Slater

If you want to know a few facts about me, here they are: I'm a teenage girl living in Tokyo with my parents, in a two-story house next to a graveyard. My dad's Japanese and my mom's American, from California. He's a mystery writer and she's an editor. They met on the old streetcar that goes to Waseda when they were each on their way to a dinner date, exchanged numbers, and a year later I was born at my grandparents' house in western Japan. I want to be an architect, I make amazing miso soup, and yes, we were here for the big one on March 11th. I think we survived it, though I can't say for sure.

March is never a good month in Tokyo. It's cold and rainy and long. The cherry blossoms are pretty nice when they start blooming at the end of the month, but it's usually, you know, still cold and rainy. And anyway, this year people aren't having their usual *hanami* cherry blossom parties in the neighborhood park. No one really wants to after the earthquake and all.

I heard my parents arguing over our *hanami* one evening about a week after the disaster, when school was closed and I was lying on the landing in the dark with our dachshund, Momo. I'd considered going for a run in case the track meet that got canceled because of the quake was rescheduled, but didn't feel like it. I didn't even feel like checking Facebook—I was sick of all the stuff about the earthquake, everyone here posting about how they're taking off for a while to Singapore or Hawaii because of the radiation, my relatives in the States asking fifty times a day what's happening, how dangerous are the aftershocks, aren't we thinking about leaving. So I was just lying there with Momo, listening to my parents' voices float up from the kitchen.

"We should have our *hanami*," my dad was saying. "Invite people in the neighborhood, as a show of community. *Joshiki da yo.*" Which sort of freaked me out—he's pretty American, because he lived in Ohio for about ten years when his dad was transferred there; he usually only says things to my mom in Japanese when he's about to go off the deep end. To tell the truth, ever since March 11th he's been kind of a head case: he keeps humming "*La vie en rose*," which means "Life in Pink" and is a super-romantic French song with lyrics like *It's you for me, me for you, in this life* . . . , and a couple nights ago I heard noises at two a.m. and found him downstairs typing in the living room, his face like a ghost's in the pale glow of the computer screen. I asked him what he was working on and he said it was his latest mystery, but I could have sworn he'd already sent that off to the publisher.

"It's *not* common sense!" my mother insisted. "If we have a party, it'll look as if we don't care about what's happened."

Then they just kept on arguing, the way you quarrel over who forgot to put the milk away when it's really about some other minor thing like *I have terminal cancer* or *I'm leaving you*. Not that they never used to argue, but since the quake they fight all the time and never make up; they're two galaxies speeding away from each other in deep space.

I knew what my mom was doing while they were fighting: she was tidying up, her red hair loose around her shoulders, her mascara smudged and her blue eyes tired. She's always been laissez-faire about domestic things, but since March 11th, the house has been so clean I wouldn't be surprised if she started scrubbing the roof tiles. When she arrived home from her office the day of the disaster, after walking for five hours from Yokohama because the trains were out of service—not that five hours is such a big deal; some people walked like *ten*, and even though the bus ride back from our international school is normally forty-five minutes, it took me seven hours—she and my dad got to work putting away all the books and stuff that had been thrown from the shelves. And she just hasn't stopped. Yesterday I saw her taking down the living room curtains to wash them.

The other thing is that even though she hates grocery shopping and always gets our stuff online, she's started going to the store every day. And twice when I've been out walking Momo, I've seen her in front of the supermarket talking to this man. I want to ask her who he is but get the feeling I shouldn't.

⤳

"What's he like?" Hana asks, her ponytail swinging as she looks up from playing Tetris on her phone.

A couple of weeks since the quake and we're at the Harajuku Starbucks having our usual mocha lattes. *That's* usual, but the rest is freaky: the streets are deserted, like we're on an abandoned movie set, and shops and restaurants are dim because the power plants have been damaged and now everyone has to save energy.

"Twentyish, Japanese, jeans."

Hana considers. "Is he hot? Maybe your mom's seeing someone. You know, a cougar kind of thing."

We burst out laughing. I can imagine my dad having an affair since, being a mystery writer and all, he probably has secrets. But my mom's the straightest arrow on the planet.

"Still, you never know," Hana says and then starts telling me all these things about people we're friends with at school, people whose parents everyone thought were happily married. Like Alessandro, a Japanese-Italian guy in our history class. After the radiation started, Alessandro's mom picked up and moved back to her hometown in Italy with the younger brother. And this Japanese-American girl named Risa, who went with her parents to Texas, where her mom's from, right after the quake and since her mom doesn't want to return, her dad just took Risa and flew back to Tokyo. Her mom can't do anything about it because the law here sides with whichever parent is Japanese.

I push away my mocha latte and Hana and I stare out the window at the moon floating over the huddled buildings. Fat drops of rain splatter against the window, then trickle down the glass in a hundred rivers. And even though dogs in Tokyo are always on a leash, a black terrier emerges alone from one of the side streets and trots past, all perky ears and jaunty tail, like it hasn't heard the news about real life.

⤳

The next evening, my dad and I are on the back veranda eating takeout ramen because even though my mom's always home to make dinner, she called to say she'd be working late.

"*Itsu made tsuzuku no?*" I ask my dad. *Is this ever going to be over?* Snatches of a broadcast on the rising radiation levels drift from the TV in my parents' bedroom.

He glances at me, chopsticks in midair, eyes bloodshot. "*Eh? Nan no koto?*"

I can't believe he's asking what I'm talking about. "When are they going to get things under control?"

"Don't worry. Everything is okay." He goes back to slurping his ramen. Then, trying to change the subject, he says, "Why haven't you been running, Katie? The track meet will be rescheduled."

I shrug. "Even if it is, I might not run in it."

"Why?"

"I just might not." The truth is, I don't feel like doing anything.

"But the team needs—"

"Why don't we get on a plane and fly away somewhere? Half my friends are already gone." I watch a crow swoop down onto the stone wall of the house next door.

He raises his eyebrows. "Where do you want to go?"

"Anywhere but here."

"We should not leave your mother." His face is distorted in the shadowy light, like in a funhouse mirror.

"Who said anything about leaving Mom?" The ramen is heavy and oily in my stomach, and this thing starts cartwheeling through my mind: Maybe my dad isn't working on his book in the middle of the night. Maybe he's going to pull something like Risa's dad and is making a plan for just the two of us to go away.

He coughs. "What I'm saying is, there's nothing to worry about. The reactors are 150 miles from Tokyo, the aftershocks are going down—"

"Like you guys are really getting used to them." Every time one hits, he screams at me to get under a table and my mom runs and grabs the earthquake kit from the entryway, as if that little backpack filled with rope and band-aids can save us.

"We live here," he says. "We can't just leave."

The blooms on the jasmine vines along the railing look blue and cold in the twilight. "But they said on the news that a really big quake could hit Tokyo."

"That's always been true. It's not news."

"What if there's a nuclear meltdown?"

"If that happens, we'll have time to evacuate." He's drumming his fingers on his leg, like when he's about to blow. "*Papa ni makasenasai.*"

"Leave it to you? Which means we're just going to stay here and wait for the next aftershock to crush us?" I brace myself for the explosion, but something much worse happens: he only rubs his forehead and stares at the floor. His shoulders are slumped and his shaggy hair is more gray than I've ever seen it.

What's going on? I feel like shouting. He always knows what to do—why doesn't he *do* something?

Cats start yowling from the alley next to the house and a siren whines somewhere close by. My dad stands up and goes inside.

⌐

That night, I lie in bed with Momo, staring at the bamboo drawn by moonlight on the *shoji* screens over my windows. The leaves and budding shoots and branches are all tangled up in a design so complicated it's exhausting.

I try to stay awake because I've been having nightmares. Last night I dreamed of a big wave, like in Hiroshige's woodblock prints, or in a sculpture I saw a couple of years ago at the Rodin museum when we took a trip to Paris for my parents' fifteenth wedding anniversary. In the sculpture, there's this huge green wave about to crash down on three people. In the dream, I was watching the wave crest over me and I could feel the tug of the ocean, the salt spray on my face. I heard the ocean breathing, like when you hold a shell to your ear, and it sounded like the sighs of all those people in Tohoku as their bodies were washed out to sea and their spirits went right to heaven.

Now I hear what sounds like someone crying in the kitchen. I sneak down, holding Momo so her toenails on the stairs won't give us away, but no one's there. Just the fridge humming, the sink so clean it sparkles in the moonlight, the dish towels folded neatly on the counter.

Back upstairs, I take out the photo of me and my parents in Montmartre that I stuck under my mattress when the glass in the frame broke in the quake. It's a sunny day and we're standing in front of Sacré Cœur, the white church on top of a hill looking out over Paris. Behind us you can see couples kissing and staring all lovey-dovey into each other's eyes (PDA is big in Paris). I look at my parents' smiling faces, their arms around one another, me in the middle with my arms around them. If I look long enough the three of us will turn to shapes and colors, and then, like these special papers in a spy kit I used to have, the shapes and colors will turn into a secret code. If only this photo held a message for me from the universe, some answer or clue to how my parents could be so happy then and not now.

↬

School finally opens again the first week of April. Some students still aren't back—and some have left for good—but most of us are here. Every day we bring in canned food, diapers, towels, and blankets for Tohoku. And we're making a thousand origami cranes to send to students at one of the high schools—like that will help them. Getting more OCD by the day, my mom forces me to carry an emergency kit that takes up my whole backpack: a copy of my passport, water, chocolate, a radio. I'm surprised she hasn't thrown in a tent, just in case.

In science class, we talk about tectonic plates and fault lines.

"I get that there are deeply buried places where one plate meets another and all this pressure builds up," I say to Ms. Belsky, our teacher. "And they might slip in our lifetime or not. But what I don't get is why the world has to be so sketchy. Couldn't we all have managed just fine without fault lines?"

Everyone laughs, but the thing is, I'm not joking. They should have put me on the Committee. I'd have designed a world without earthquakes. And while I was at it, without volcanoes, floods, tornadoes, droughts. Why couldn't the Earth just be one big, smooth round ball, turning forever and ever in harmony with the heavens?

↬

My parents send me to a shrink. Which is a pretty major thing to do in Japan, where usually people who go to shrinks are considered to have lost it. I figure with my parents it's a transference thing, like when you're

mad at someone so you kick the dog. Instead of going to therapy themselves, they're sending me.

"I'm basically fine," I tell the shrink, a sixtyish Japanese woman who
keeps doing watch checks she thinks I don't notice.

She nods. "I imagine things have been quite stressful for you?"

What a genius. "Nothing really happened to us here in Tokyo. It's
the people in Tohoku who have it bad."

"Do you feel guilty in some way about that?"

"I don't know." I should just say yes. Then she'll think she's figured
out my problem and we can wrap this up.

The conversation lags, so I tell her about some research I've been
doing, that plate tectonics came from continental drift theory, which is
about how places like Africa and South America once fit together but
then drifted apart.

She says some stuff about trying to relax, letting things take their
course, blah, blah, blah.

If this is what they teach you in psychiatry school, I can start seeing
clients next week.

Everything seems really pointless and I feel like crying, but I don't
say anything else and neither does she. We sit for a while without talking,
a Japanese thing that normally drives me crazy, but today it's nice to just
look at the plum trees in the garden.

⌒

When I get home, my dad's gone somewhere and my mom's in her study
off the kitchen. I never see them together anymore, like in this Spanish
movie my parents and I watched once where it's the Spanish Civil War
and the mom and dad don't get along so they're never on screen at the
same time.

"How did it go, Katydid?" my mom asks, taking off her reading
glasses. Her desk usually looks like a hurricane hit it but now everything's perfectly straight: a row of sharpened pencils, a stapler and ruler;
a silver Eiffel Tower paperweight she bought one morning from a souvenir shop by the Seine.

"Okay," I say, a small happiness flitting through me—she only uses my pet name when she's in a good mood. "The therapist told me that I shouldn't keep things inside. That I should tell people what's going on."

"Well, she's right." But she doesn't say anything else, just looks at me with this faraway expression. "Did you put your lunch bag by the sink when you came in?"

"*Yes*. Quit asking me, okay?" I'm so sick of her tidiness campaign— if it's not my lunch bag, it's putting away my clothes or straightening the books on my shelf. Yesterday, she even made me brush Momo's teeth. But I'm also a little worried: you hear about people with OCD who just flip out.

I sit on the floor and rest the back of my head against her knees. "Mom? Is everything okay with you and Dad?"

"What is this, the Inquisition?" she says teasingly, mimicking what I say to her when she asks about my personal life. Then she sighs and tilts my chin up toward her. "Your father and I are . . . just going through a bit of a difficult time. Nothing for you to worry about, baby."

Which sounds totally lame, like: *Don't worry, we've just hit a bit of an iceberg.*

Her cell phone rings and she digs it out of her pocket, squints at the caller ID. "I've got to take this, okay?"

I know who it is: the guy from the supermarket. I stand up to leave because now she's going to want some privacy, but she says, "No, stay. I'll just be a minute."

She answers the call and I realize I was totally wrong—it's someone from her office. And I wonder if there are other things I might be wrong about.

While she's talking, I look at the papers on her desk: she's editing the English version of a script for a bilingual documentary about adventurers. In the part she's working on, there's an interview with the author of a book about Edmund Hillary, who with a Sherpa climber named Tenzing Norgay was the first to reach the top of Everest.

"Looks like an interesting show, don't you think?" my mother says after she finishes her call. "It's important to attempt something big in life."

"Maybe, but think about all the people who don't make it. What's the point if you end up dying of altitude sickness or being swept away in an avalanche?"

She smiles. "Well, I'll tell you, one thing I'm learning from all this earthquake stuff is that there are no guarantees. Things happen that we don't always have control over. But even though they do, we have to keep trying, right? Whether it's climbing Everest or anything else."

There's something I don't exactly get about what she's saying, like when you look directly at an object in the dark and can't see it, but if you look just to the side of it, you can.

⌒

It comes to me that evening. Even though I still don't feel like running, I lace up my shoes before dinner and force myself to go. I walk for a few minutes, break into a slow jog, and then I'm on my way, energy starting to flow through my body. A new moon is rising over the canal, the houses and apartment buildings, the old wooden shrine next to the neighborhood park, just like in the books I loved when I was little, stories of towns where everyone lived happily ever after. I stop to ring the shrine bell and wake the gods so they can hear my prayer: *Please help the people in Tohoku. Please let my parents stay together.* And then I keep on running—through the park, past shops and restaurants, up a steep street of more houses and apartments. As my feet pound the earth, I think about adventurers walking along paths, crossing ice fields, sailing ocean routes to new worlds. My mom's right: even though you don't always know what's going to happen, or why, you have to keep going. And I guess it's like that with lots of things, including earthquakes and marriages.

When I reach the top of the street, I stop to catch my breath. The cold spring air is sharp in my nostrils and the lights of the dim city spread out below like a quilt of fireflies. Maybe, just maybe, the universe isn't designed so badly after all. Maybe it had to be designed the way it is because if there weren't any obstacles in our path, we'd be like . . . rocks or plants, with no chance of becoming anything more than what we already are. I mean, it's this chance that makes us human. Rocks can't push themselves to become better rocks; plants can't decide not to give up on themselves or other people.

When I get back to the house, my mom's study light is on but the room is empty. On her desk is a legal pad covered with my dad's scrawl. I'm surprised to see it's an evacuation plan for the three of us (four including Momo): if necessary, we'll go to my grandparents' place in Okinawa, or if we have to leave Japan, we'll go see my other grandparents in San Francisco.

As I climb the stairs, I hear voices from the veranda. I tiptoe toward the sliding door in my parents' bedroom and see two figures on a blanket: my mother, with her head on someone's lap. It's the guy from the supermarket. No—edging closer, I see it's my father. He and my mother are looking up at the sky, Momo at their feet. I step outside and they don't say anything, just shift position so I can sit between them, then put their arms around me. And now I notice there are all these leaves on the veranda—my mom didn't sweep today—and I realize something was different about her study tonight: The desk was a mess. A wonderful mess! Especially with my dad's family evacuation plan sitting right there in the middle of it all.

An aftershock rattles the house and we jump. But amazingly, my dad doesn't shout at me to get under a table and my mom doesn't run for the earthquake kit. When the house stops shaking, we sit quietly, looking at the stars, and then we talk a little, my dad asking how school's going, my mom telling a funny story about a colleague. We stay out on the veranda for a long time, all of us together on this beautiful night.

Friends and Enemies

Bad Day for Baseball

by Graham Salisbury

Someone's hand was on my shoulder. I was dreaming of clinging to the mast of a boat in a storm with lots of thunder. The sounds were so real.

I peeked open an eye.

"Tomio," Mama said. "Telephone."

I bolted up and fumbled for the clock. Not even eight o'clock yet. Jeez. Scared me. I thought I was late. I flopped back down and rubbed my eyes. I could sleep another hour. The game was at ten.

My brown and white mixed-breed mutt, Zippy, jumped up on my bed and licked my face. I shoved him away, but he thought it was a game and grabbed my wrist in his teeth. "Jeez, dog, you got bad breath."

"It's Butchie," Mama said. "He said get up and come to the phone. It's important."

"What's all that noise?"

"Army or something. Maneuvers. I don't know."

"It's loud."

"Come on. Get up. Daddy's outside watching the planes."

"What planes?"

"The army. Come on, Butchie's waiting."

Butchie was my cousin, and two years older than me. We were like brothers. Me, him, and Zippy went everywhere together. I stumbled out to the phone in the kitchen. "What?" I said.

"Get dressed. I'm coming to get you. And don't bring that mutt."

"What are you talking about? I can't go anywhere. I got a game to-day. And anyway, why I can't bring Zippy?"

"I telling you, he can't go where we're going."

"Where we going?"

"Just get dressed. Hurry it up."

"But—"

"Wear your Rotsie uniform if you got one. You got one?" He said *Rotsie*, not the letters *ROTC*. Anyway, what was he talking about, ROTC?

"Only the shirt. Why?"

"Put it on if that's all you got. But hurry. This is an emergency. I'm not kidding, Tomio. Don't you see all that smoke?"

"Wait," I said.

I glanced out the window. The sky was pockmarked with small dirty black clouds. Mama was right. It was maneuvers. But probably navy, since it was so close to Honolulu harbor. "Yeah, but that's just—"

"No, no, no. I telling you, Tomio, this is for real. The Japanese are bombing us. The radio said for all Rotsie guys go UH, now! So get ready. I'm coming to get you."

"But Butchie—"

He hung up.

I peeked out at the dirty clouds one more time, then ran into my room and dug up my Rotsie shirt. I tore off my T-shirt and put it on, all wrinkled up like a rag.

"I gotta go somewhere, Mama," I said, hurrying back out to the kitchen. I didn't want to be the one to tell her what was happening. Anyway, I wasn't sure Butchie wasn't joking. "Where's Daddy now?"

Mama pointed toward the front room window with her chin. Out on the street Daddy was standing with his hands on his hips, eyes to the sky. Mits Yumoto was standing next to him, also looking up.

Zippy was leaping at the door, ready to go. He knows when I'm going to leave, every time. "You gotta stay home this time, Zip. Sorry."

I opened the door a crack and squeezed out.

Zippy started scratching the back of the door like crazy. Scratch, scratch, scratch, scratch.

"Come on, Zip. Shhhh! I be back soon. No worry."

I stuck my fingers under the door so he could smell me one last time, his paws scraping the floor. I hated leaving him. He always went with me. I could carry him on Butchie's putt-putt like always. But Butchie said no.

"Daddy, what's going on?"

Daddy kept on staring at the sky.

Mr. Yumoto turned to look at me. He didn't smile.

Daddy said, "I never seen the army make it look so real. They even painted the planes to look like Japanese."

There were planes all over the place, circling, diving, shooting, and roaring back up. "It's not the army, Daddy. It's real. Butchie just called. Those really *are* Japanese planes. He said they bombing us. Can't you hear it?"

Daddy turned and frowned at me. He didn't say anything. I think he already figured it out but didn't want to believe it.

"I gotta go with Butchie. They calling for Rotsie guys to go UH. He's coming over now. Where's Leonard?" I asked Mr. Yumoto.

"Fishing. Down the harbor. He went early this morning."

Leonard was his son. He was first year at UH, and also he was in ROTC. "You gotta tell him the army wants all Rotsie guys to go to the university."

Mr. Yumoto nodded and left. Two minutes later Butchie zoomed up on his smoky putt-putt motorbike. The explosions were getting louder now, and the sky was dirtier, and it wasn't just from the small smokes. Now there were huge stacks of black clouds boiling up from somewhere on the other side of downtown. How could it be real? It was impossible. Japan was too far away. But I could see them with my own eyes, hundreds of fighters with red suns on the wings. And they were bombing us.

Daddy looked back up, frozen where he stood.

"He thinks it's maneuvers," I whispered to Butchie.

"Hurry up. Get on. We gotta go."

I slid on the back and grabbed hold of the belt loops on Butchie's khaki uniform pants.

"Uncle," Butchie said, calling to Daddy.

Butchie's father and mine are brothers.

Daddy didn't move, stiff as a pipe.

The smoke filling the sky was looking bad, real bad.

Butchie shrugged, gunned it, and buzzed out of there.

As we drove to a higher elevation you could see the smoke billowing up from Pearl Harbor, ugly fat black funnels of it with giant red flames spurting out at the bottom. More people flowed out into the streets. Some stayed in their yards, and a few even climbed up on top of their cars, everyone watching the planes circling around Pearl Harbor.

There was an explosion on the hillside near us, and I knew then that the navy was shooting back now. And missing. People scattered back into their cars and houses.

Me and Butchie leaned forward on the putt-putt. I peeked around him, the wind making me squint. He had the motorbike on all out.

"What we going do?" I yelled above the whining engine.

"Just what the radio said," he shouted back. "They just want us at UH. That's all I know."

"But I'm only high school Rotsie."

"Yeah, but Rotsie is Rotsie, right? Anyway, it don't matter. Nobody cares right now. This is an emergency."

We roared uphill, higher and higher, past Roosevelt High School and across to Punahou, where we turned and took a shortcut through the rich houses in Manoa. It was spooky seeing those big homes like that, all peaceful with every kind of flower you can think of growing in the yards when the sky was filled with warplanes and ugly black smoke. Even up here people stood on their porches looking up. Through the plate glass windows behind them I could see big mirrors and paintings on the walls, and vases stuffed with flowers.

I held tight onto Butchie. His uniform was clean and pressed sharp as brand-new. Mine was a mess. At least it wasn't dirty. I had on my Rotsie shirt, some old pants with no belt, and nothing on my feet.

At the university there were guys all over, hurrying down from cars and bikes parked any which way under the trees and on the grass. We got off and leaned the putt-putt against a tree, and jogged down to the football field where everyone was assembling. Looked like there were hundreds of us.

Five real army guys with grim faces were quickly inserting firing pins into the old Springfield rifles. They handed them out with live ammunition.

"Hey you!" One guy called. "Over here!"

Me and Butchie ran over. The guy threw us rifles and four clips of bullets each. He didn't even ask who I was or if I even knew how to use the rifle. Which I didn't.

I looked at the Springfield.

"Here," Butchie said, showing me his. "That's where the clip goes. And this is the safety. You can't use the rifle with the safety on. But don't take it off until you need to shoot."

I fumbled with the clips, stuffing three in my pocket. I dropped the other one in the dirt, picked it up and blew off the dust, then managed to cram it in place. Forget the safety. I didn't want to touch it. What was I supposed to shoot, anyway? The planes?

They were gone now, I noticed. I couldn't hear the engines anymore.

When everyone had rifles and bullets the top army guy told us to line up. I was only five feet tall, the shortest guy there. The rifle was almost as big as me. And it was heavy.

"Listen up," the army guy said. His nameplate read *Capt. Smith*. "We are under attack. We don't know what will come next. Anything can happen. We've received word that paratroopers have landed in the mountains and are working their way down. They're somewhere up there."

He turned and swept his hand toward the jagged ridgeline above St. Louis Heights. My stomach suddenly knotted up, like a fist closing. This was getting too real. A sour taste rose in my throat. I felt like I was going to throw up.

"We're going to keep them from advancing. Understand? That's our job. Is that clear?"

"Yes sir!" all us guys said at the same time. Just like in Rotsie at school. Only now nobody was laughing or joking around or whispering how stupid it was. At school, Rotsie was a joke. But not now.

"And make sure you don't shoot each other."

I peeked over at Butchie. His face was tight, looking like he just lost his girlfriend or somebody stole his putt-putt. He kept his eyes on the army guy.

Captain Smith broke us up and sent us toward the jungled ridge, groups of us jogging off in different directions. Luckily I got to stay with Butchie. Ten other guys were with us, twelve in our group, all of us Japanese, except for one *haole* guy.

We ran into the woods beyond Manoa Stream. The valley was dense, a jungle of green. Me and Butchie and our gang of friends played up in there plenty times as kids. We knew the place well, the jungle, the stream. I loved being there, back then.

But now my mouth was so dry my tongue felt like twice its size. It was hot, the sun blasting down through the trees. The guy in front of me was sweating. Had big dark splotches on the back of his shirt.

"What if we see them?" I whispered to Butchie.

"That's when you take off that safety."

"Then what?"

"What'choo think?"

We hiked single file, bushes and tall grass lying down as we crushed them. All around us vines like snakes crawled up into the trees. I didn't see any paratroopers or even any abandoned parachutes. Maybe they buried them and crept down the other side of the ridge. Or maybe they were hiding in the jungle, waiting for us to come in the open so they could shoot us.

I hit the ground like a stone when someone fired a shot. It wasn't one of us. Maybe someone in one of the other groups. I dug deeper into the grass, its smell warm and sweet. Ants crawled on the stems inches from my face. I clutched the Springfield close; its oil reminded me of school.

"Hey. Up front. You see anything?" someone called to the point man, who wasn't really a man, but a boy like the rest of us.

"Nothing."

Nobody moved.

When there were no more shots, we slowly got up and inched ahead. Butchie was in front of me, and I was the second to last guy, the haole behind me. Every few steps I turned around to check if anyone was behind us. The haole never said a word.

"Butchie," I whispered. "What if I have to shoot this thing? I never did that. And how can I shoot somebody."

Butchie said over his shoulder, "Listen to me, Tomio. You don't shoot them, they going shoot you. You got to shoot, you hear me? You got to."

My fingers were gripping the Springfield so tight somebody would have to pry them off with a screwdriver after this day was done. Every part of my body felt electric. Little jolts charging through me. Everything about me was wide awake. My eyes prob'ly looked as big as a cow's. I could have spotted a centipede in the grass ten feet away.

The stream was close. I could hear the rushing water, but couldn't see it. I could even smell it, tangy like mud and iron. In my mind it was flowing down over mossy round stones and half-submerged boulders, still and quiet in the deep pools and hissing in the shallow rapids. The sun through the trees crawled up my back. Sweat crept down my temples. The higher we went the thicker the jungle got, everything green and brown. Mosquitoes buzzed in my ears. Muddy muck bubbled up between my toes in the wet parts of the trail.

Nobody spoke.

We walked kind of hunched over, ready to drop again if we had to. Single file, like real army. I didn't like taking up the rear, but it was better than being first.

I wondered if Leonard got the news yet. Prob'ly. And the guys on my team. I guess the game got canceled. Jeez. How can you think about that at a time like this?

"Down!" somebody shouted.

A shot rang out. *Bam!*

And again, and again and again.

Bam! Bam! Bam! Bam! Bam!

We hit the ground, the mud. I clutched my rifle in one hand and covered my head with the other. Muddy wetness crept into my chest, seeping into my shirt.

Sounded like the whole world was shooting, and they were shooting at us. I could hear bullets thwacking into the trees right above my head.

Branches above me burst apart. Splinters rained down. Leaves shattered and evaporated.

Then it stopped, a momentary lull, a sweet smell of gunpowder in the air.

I slowly peeked up.

Our point man crawled to a tree and stood up on his knees, peeking around it. He saw something and fired, his rifle jerking. Four, five, six shots.

A couple of other guys in our group started shooting. At what, I don't know. I couldn't see anything but jungle.

Then the other side started blasting us again.

Our point man drew back his rifle. "Wait!" he yelled. "Stop!"

Still hiding behind the tree, he screamed to whoever was shooting at us. "Cease fire! Cease fire! We're American!"

The shooting slowed, one, two shots more.

Then nothing.

Then silence.

"Identify yourself," someone off in the trees shouted.

"ROTC group two! Who are you?"

There was the longest, eeriest silence.

Then they called back. "ROTC group one . . . did we hit anyone?"

Our point guy glanced back at us.

We all waved, okay.

"No, but if you do that again I'm going to tear your damn heart out with my bare hands!"

They went their way and we went ours.

We never even saw them.

My shirt was messed up, mud all over the front and on my arms and face. Butchie's eyes were dark and deep as lava pits. He looked like he'd seen a ghost. I felt it too. Somebody could have been killed!

We hiked up the ridge and found nothing.

Not one thing. Not even a muddy footprint.

Nobody but pigs and wild dogs had been up there.

We hiked back down into the valley and stopped at a bend in the stream. Shady tree branches met in the middle out over the water. Sparkles of sunlight broke through in some places and glinted on the water, reminding me that there was a world out there.

Somewhere.

"What time is it?" I asked Butchie.

He shrugged.

"Twelve-thirty," the haole guy said.

Me and Butchie both looked at him. It was the first thing he'd said all day.

I nodded, thanks.

Twelve-thirty. If we'd played the game it would still be going.

I stuck my mud-crusted feet in the water. So good, so cool and clean. I lay back in the grass and nearly fell asleep.

"Hey, Butchie," I said.

"What?"

"I was going to play baseball today."

Butchie said nothing for a long time.

I slapped at a mosquito in my ear.

"Kind of a bad day for baseball, Tomio," Butchie finally said.

I laughed. But it wasn't funny. Nothing about this day was funny.

"Okay guys, we gotta get moving," our lead guy said.

Nobody complained. We just got up. I brushed off my pants.

"We're going to break up into groups of two and head back down to campus. If there's anyone in this jungle we'll see them."

He started counting off, one two, one two.

"I can't believe they did it," Butchie said, shaking his head at some thought. I figured he meant the guys who shot at us.

"No kidding," I said. "They could have killed somebody."

"Not them, Tomio . . . Japan."

"Oh."

"What if they land guys on the beaches?" Butchie went on. "Or come bomb us again?"

I nodded.

The lead guy told me to go with the haole.

"But—"

"Get moving. You two head that way."

Me and the haole left. I glanced back at Butchie, but he was already gone. Everyone was gone.

Me and the haole pushed through the jungle, me in the front and him a couple of steps behind. It was getting drier, so I knew we were close to campus.

"If we find them, Jap," the haole guy said. "Who are you going to shoot? Them or me?"

I stopped and turned around. I gave him a small laugh, thinking this is no time to be joking around like that. But he wasn't joking. His face was like a rock.

We stared at each other.

He really *did* mean it.

I reached out and took the barrel of his Springfield and pointed it right at my chest. "If we find them, who *you* going shoot? Them or me?"

He kept his eyes on me.

Then he nodded once and motioned to move on.

When we got back to the university, Captain Smith said, "It was a mistake. A rumor. Someone saw a sheet blowing on a clothesline, is all. There were no parachutes." He shook his head. "You all okay? I heard a lot of gunfire."

"We thought we saw something, sir," one guy said.

Captain Smith studied him. He looked like he wanted to say something, but didn't.

"It was nothing," the guy added. "False alarm."

My jaw dropped. Nothing?

They could have *killed* us.
But we were all still here.
Still here.
For now.

Half a Heart

by Mariko Nagai

October 1941

The house is surrounded by roses
of all names: Bride's Dream, Chicago
Peace, Mister Lincoln, Timeless, Touch
of Class. The house is surrounded by hues
of red and white: red like an azure sun,
red like the sunset over the Pacific Ocean,
red like Grandpa's fingertips,
white so transparent they call it Tineke,
the kind of white that looks like Seattle on a rainy day.

The living room is a mixture of east
and west: Grandpa packed a little of Japan
when he came here across the sea—a sword,
a photograph of himself as a small boy,
dolls for future daughters he never had—
memories of his once-ago life.

Grandpa is a rose breeder.
He calls roses *bara*; he calls them his *kodomo*—children.
My father sometimes helps out Grandpa,
though most of the time, he works in an office
downtown writing articles for a newspaper.

Mother sits in the kitchen, always singing.
My room upstairs is All American: a bed,

an old desk, white lace curtains my mother sewed,
pictures of Jamie and me on the wall.

My brother Nick's room next to mine is filled
with trophies he won in track races.
Grandpa calls me by my middle name, *Masako*,
and he calls Nick *Toshio*. He never speaks
English; says that he lived longer in Japan
than he has in America, and that there's no more
space for another language or culture.

He speaks to us in Japanese, my parents speak
to him in Japanese, and Nick and I speak
some words in Japanese, but mostly in English.
Just like our breakfast, rice and pickled
plums with milk and potatoes, they all go together.

December 1941

I was singing with the Sunday School
choir, practicing our Christmas carols,

all our mouths opening and closing as one
to sing the next note.

We were singing "Silent Night, Holy
Night," and just as the boys hit

their lowest key, the door burst
open like a startled cat dashing.

The next note lay waiting
under Mrs. Gilbert's finger; our mouths kept

the *O* shape, when a man yelled, *the Japs bombed
Pearl Harbor*. The world stopped.

The next words got lost. *Oh, oh, oh,*
someone wailed, until I realized that it was

coming out of my mouth,
my body shaking, trembling.

And the world started again
but we were no longer singing as one.

December 1941

Jap, Jap, Jap, the word bounces
around the walls of the hall.

Jamie, my best friend, yells out, "Shut your
mouth!" but the word keeps

bouncing like a ball in my head.
As soon as I get to my Language

Arts class, the entire class gets quiet.
Mrs. Smith looks down

like she's been talking about me,
or maybe she doesn't see me.

She clears her voice; she calls
out our names, one by one; she pauses

right after Marcus Springfield.
She clears her throat, calls out *Mina Tagawa.*

And instead of calling out Joshua
Thomas, she starts to talk

about what happened yesterday.
My face becomes hot and heavy; I look

at my hands, then at the swirling
pattern on the desk. I look at my hands again,

yellowish against the dark brown
desk, and Jamie's hair, golden,

right near it. *Jap-nese*, Mrs. Smith
starts. *Jap-nese* have attacked Pearl

Harbor. *Jap-nese* have broken
the treaty. *Jap-nese* have started the war.

Even the newspaper that Father works for screams in
bold letter headlines: *Japs. Japs. Japs.*

I feel everyone's eyes on me. I hear
Chris Adams snickering behind me, whispering

Jap Mina. I'm not Japanese, I want to yell.

I am an American, I scream
in my head, but my mouth is stuffed

with rocks; my body is a stone, like the statue
of a little Buddha Grandpa prays to

every morning, and every night. My body is heavy.
I don't know how to speak anymore.

December 1941

We are not Americans, the eyes tell us.
We do not belong, the mouths curl up.

We are the enemy aliens, the Japs,
the ones who have bombed

Pearl Harbor, killing so many soldiers
who were enjoying their Sunday

morning in Hawaii, who were waking
up to their breakfasts of oatmeal and toast.

Death to Japs, they say. The voice
from the radio says *Jap-nese,*

a pause between *Jap*
and *nese,* just like Mrs. Smith.

Mother walks down Main Street with her head
up, her back straight, though

men spit at her and women hiss
at her. *Masa-chan, onnanoko rashiku*

sesuji o nobashinasai. (Masako,
keep your back straight like a

good girl), Mother says as she pulls
on the whitest kid gloves,

one by one, stretching her fingers
straight to sheathe each finger.

Masa-chan, tebukuro
hamenasai. Amerika-jin wa

saho ni kibishii kara (Masako,
put on your gloves. Americans

are strict with manners), Mother says
as she straightens her jacket.

We pass by stores that sell grains and bread
and instead go to Mr. Fukuyama's shop:

Patriotic Americans, says a sign on the window.
She buys a bag of rice and *umeboshi* and bonito

flakes. If I could, I would keep
only my first name, *Mina*, my American name,

and tear off *Masako Tagawa* like the
pages of journals I tore out when I found

out that Nick Freeman liked Alice
Gorka. I would change my hair color into a honey-

colored blond that changes into lighter
shades of white during the summer,

just like Jamie's. If I could change
my name, if I could change my parents,

if I could change my life: I would be an American.
But I already am.

December 1941

We're best friends, no matter what, Jamie
              says as we sit under the Christmas

tree together. *We're best friends until
       we die*, I say.

She hands me a small packet wrapped
              in a crinkled wrapping paper.

Open it, open it, she urges. Mr. Gilmore's humming
              drifts in from his workshop in the

backyard, and Mrs. Gilmore's baking
              smells of cinnamon and nutmeg.

We sit under a big Christmas tree lit by small twinkling
    lights like lost fireflies late in summer.

A package the size of my palm, so light like a butterfly;
    Jamie chanting, *Open it, open it!*

I undo the ribbon, gingerly, then unfold the red
    paper, one corner at a time. In the middle,

a jagged half of a heart. She pulls her sweater
    down, *See, I have half a heart, too.*

And whenever we are together, we have a whole heart.
    Only then do the two halves become one.

December 1941

When I come home, the house is quiet.
    Basho is outside, looking confused.

Mother is not home, where she always is,
    waiting with a cup of green tea between

her hands and a glass of milk for me.
    Everything is turned inside

out, rice scattered all over the kitchen
    floor, all the drawers wide open

with cloth strewn all over the floors
    like garbage the day after the circus

left town. A note, *I will be back soon,*
    in Mother's beautiful and careful handwriting

pinned to the door like a dead butterfly.
    It is only later, too late for dinner,

too late for a glass of milk and cup of tea,
    when Mother and Grandpa come home

looking like they are carrying the night
    on their backs, their bodies heavy

from the weight they drag through
    the door. "Men came this afternoon,

they said they are from the government;
    your father had to go with them so he can

answer some questions," Mother says quietly
    as she sits down on the sofa, heavily

throwing her weight down. "When is he coming home?"
    I ask. Basho mewls, climbs next

to Grandpa, pressing his body so close that his tail
    curls around the bend in Grandpa's

skinny body. "I'm not sure, honey, I'm just
    not sure," Mother says quietly.

Grandpa takes his owl-like glasses off slowly,
    presses his eyes with the palms

of his hand like he was pressing down the dirt
    around his rose trees, and leans back

on his rocking chair. Mother leans back, too.
    I sit, the word *war* ringing

through my head, forgetting about milk,
    forgetting about dinner, forgetting about

history homework, thinking only about Father
    in prison.

January 1942

This year, there wasn't a
Christmas tree, or dinner with
our neighbors.
There weren't any New Year's
festivities this year,
no mochi—sticky rice—
no giving of money or playing games.
Without Father's face red as a beet
from *sake*, and Grandpa
singing as he plays
the *shamisen*—the three-
stringed lyre made out
of the belly-skin of a cat—
there is no laughter, no joy.
Mother hurries from the dining
room to the kitchen,
sleeves of her kimono
fluttering
like a hummingbird's
wings. All is quiet in this
house, with its small
ornament of bamboo
and pine branches
Grandpa left hanging
on my door.
Happy New Year it is not.

January 1942

Father looks small
sitting behind the bars,
surrounded by
soldiers towering
over him. He smiles,

then coughs, once,
twice. He asks me
how I am, whether
I've been a good girl,
and have obeyed my elders.
He squints his eyes,
his eyes bigger without
his glasses.
Mother gives him *onigiri*—
rice balls—and he smiles,
saying that the food
they serve him is too oily,
too *American*. I ask him
how he is, a stupid question,
I know, but he looks so small,
and so tired,
that's the only thing
I can think to ask him. *Fine*, he whispers.
Everything is going to be fine,
they'll figure out, soon, that this
is unconstitutional.
We are led away
only thirty minutes later,
our footsteps echoing in the hallway,
the door behind us banging
behind us, then locked,
my father left alone
in prison like a caged bird.

January 1942

Every time I walk down the hall
at school, kids hiss *Jap*
Jap. Every time I walk home
from school, I feel eyes as heavy
as handcuffs around my wrists and ankles.

Every time Mother and I go downtown
in our Ford to shop at Mr. Fukuyama's
grocery store, every time Mother says
Konnichiwa, I look away.
Every time I see the word *Jap* in newspapers,
I become hot. Every time Mother cooks
miso soup and rice for dinner, suddenly
I am not hungry. Every time I see
myself in the mirror, I see a slant-eyed
Jap, just like they say, my teeth protruding
like a rat's. Every time I look away,
Jamie holds my hand.

February 1942

Dear Father, I hope
everything is okay
and that you are
doing well.
From the letters
you sent us,
from what we can read
that hasn't been
lined out, it seems
that they are treating
you well. Here, at home,
Grandpa's been
pulling us together,
saying now that you are
in Montana (or North
Dakota, or wherever
they took you), we have
to listen to him.
Don't tell Nick I told
you this, but a week ago,
Grandpa found out Nick's been

breaking the curfew,
and without saying a word,
as soon as Nick came home,
Grandpa raised his cane
and hit him hard, once,
twice, over the head.
Nick just stood there,
angry, with his fists raised,
but he didn't say or do anything
as Grandpa kept hitting him
again and again with his cane.
Mom was crying, and shouting,
Otosan, yamete, yamete
(Father, stop it, stop it), and
I was frozen, right there.
I've never seen this
Grandpa, who was like a stranger, angry
and spiteful. But as soon
as Nick apologized (for what?),
Grandpa stopped.
Don't give them more reason to punish us, Grandpa shouted.
But we didn't do anything wrong, Nick shouted back.
We're American, just like everyone else.
Grandpa shook his head,
Ware ware wa Nippon-jin demo naishi,
America-jin demo nai—we are neither
Japanese nor American. His words stung me,
stronger than bee stings, even stronger
than the news of Pearl Harbor.
Most of the time, we are
doing okay, but Seattle's changed.
Chinese kids walk around with buttons
that say, "I am Chinese."
Then there are all these signs:
We don't serve Japs. Japs go home.
The entire country hates
Japan. And they hate us.

No one seems to like us
anymore, except for Jamie
and her family next
door. Nick doesn't say
it, but he's having a really
hard time, I can tell.
He comes home with bruises
and cuts, and when Mother asks
him what happened, he only says
that he fell. I know he's lying,
I know he knows that I know,
but we don't talk about it.
Mother tells me not to go out
by myself. It's hard to walk
down the street, being different.
I hope the new glasses Mother sent
you are the kind you like.
I miss you very much. I hope they are
treating you well. Father, I hope
you can come home soon so we can
all be together. I miss you.
Your daughter, Masako

February 1942

President Roosevelt
signed Executive
Order 9066 today. Nick says
that Germans and Italians
aren't arrested like
Japanese men have been all over
the West Coast. *Mina,*
he whispered in the back
yard, *they'll put us
all in prisons.*
I don't want to believe him,

but I see, with Grandpa
and Mother worrying over our
frozen bank accounts and
curfews and blackouts
and the five-mile radius, I know
we will probably be put in
prison like the Germans were put in
concentration camps.

March 1942

Grandpa sits on his favorite chair right near the rose
garden. His face, from where I stand, is as big as the

roses all around him, roses of bright red, deep red,
blood red, all kinds of red only he knows the names

of. "Masako, *chotto kinasai*," he calls me over as he hears
the gate opening. He does not turn around. He does

not look at me, but keeps looking ahead, at his roses,
at the sky, at everything but me. Basho stretches

his body on Grandpa's lap, saunters over to me, and says
hello by twirling his tail around my legs.

Grandpa, without moving his mouth, says, "We have
been asked to leave. We need to pack up

everything: the house, the nursery. We can only take two
pieces of luggage per person. We need to leave soon. And

I'm sorry, we can't take Basho." I am not hearing him right,
I tell myself. Why do we need to move, is it called

to *evacuate*? "They say that they are doing this for our
safety. They say that we will be taken care of. They say

that it's for our own good," Grandpa says quietly in
Japanese. He reaches over, then taking a pair of scissors,

snips off a bud near the middle of the rose stem. "They say
that it's for our own good," he repeats again. I know

that's a lie. I know they are doing this to hurt us. But I
do not say anything at all.

April 1942

We have one week
to get ready.
It's only been one week
since Mother and Grandpa
went to the Japanese
American Citizens League
Office and registered us
to be evacuated
to a place called Camp
Puyallup somewhere
not far away.
We are to leave
on Thursday, April
30th. Not a single Japanese
is to stay in Seattle
after May 1.
Mother and Grandpa
told us we are not
selling the house
or the garden
like other families,
but that we'll board it up,
and that we'll be back.
We have a week to say
good-bye, a week

to pack everything up.
It's a week that
seems not long
enough,
but forever.

April 1942

What I can take:
>the Bible that Mother gave me for my 12th birthday
>my journals
>Jamie's Christmas present
>homework assignments for the rest of the semester
>(in case I return to Garfield next September)
>clothes for autumn (maybe for winter, too)
>the things that the WRA has ordered us to take:
>blankets and linen; a toothbrush, soap,
>also knives, forks, spoons, plates, bowls and cups.

What I cannot take:
>Basho
>our house
>Jamie
>the choir
>Grandpa's rose garden
>Seattle and its sea-smell

What my grandfather packs:
>a potted rose

April 1942

Basho is old.
The mangy

orange kitten
with a broken tail
came to the front
steps on a rainy
day and no matter
how much Grandpa shooed
it away, the cat kept
mewling until
Grandpa got sick
of it and pulled him
from under the porch
by the scuff
of its neck
and stuffed him
into the bed
next to him.
Fleas got
Grandpa, but Basho got
Grandpa. Basho came
before I was born.
See that scar
on his cheek?
He got it fighting
Kuro from four
houses down; he won.
See how his left
ear is torn? He got
it fighting
crows that were in the roses.
Basho brings gifts;
don't be surprised.
Birds. Squirrels. Baby
moles. Basho likes
to get his ears
pulled gently.
He'll show you
his belly if you do

that. He doesn't understand
English; he grew
up around us, listening to
Japanese. He doesn't drink
milk. He grew up drinking
miso soup and eating bonito
flakes and rice.
He is a good cat.
Please take care
of him. He'll love
you, like he loves us,
like we love
him, like I love you, Jamie.

April 1942

Mother stands
in the middle
of the room,
our sofas
and table
and chairs
covered in
white sheets
looking like Halloween
ghosts.
She walks,
the sound of
her bare footsteps
across
the bare floor
empty, until
she pulls my hands
up the bare steps
to my room,
where she puts me to sleep

on a blanket
on the floor.
It is cold;
I never knew
our house could
be so cold.

April 1942

The nursery is dismantled,
each glass pane taken off
from the frame. All the windows
of our house are boarded up;
the car's inside the garage.
Everything has been put into
boxes and crates and stored
in the garage or with our neighbors.
My room is bare except
for the naked bed and an empty
dresser draped in white; it's
my very own ghost.
Mr. Gilmore shakes his head
as Mother gives him the keys,
"I don't know what the world
is coming to, but don't worry,
we'll take care of everything.
They'll realize how silly all this
is, and you'll be back here
before you know it." Mother bows
deeply, her shoulders trembling
like a feather, and Mrs. Gilmore
puts her arm around Mother, she, too,
shaking. Mr. Gilmore opens
the door to his truck
where the back is filled
with our bags. Grandpa stands

in front of our house, feeling
the bark of the cherry blossom
tree he had planted when I was
born, feeling it, stroking it,
gently, as he looks at the house,
at the space where the nursery
used to be, then he raises his hat,
tips it gently, saying good-bye
to everything, to the house, to the wintering
roses left behind that will probably die
without his care, and to the tree
that has begun to bud.

April 1942

Chinatown,
where all the
Japanese stores
used to be, is
boarded up.
It's a ghost town;
no one's about so early
in the morning.
It's a ghost town
now and maybe will forever be.
A sign:
Thank you for your patronage,
it was a pleasure to serve you
for the past twenty years.
Then it gets smaller and smaller
and finally disappears
as we drive
quickly
toward the junction
of Beacon Avenue

and Alaska Street
at the southern end
of Jackson Park.

April 1942

We are all tagged like parcels,
        our bags, our suitcases,
        my mother, me, Nick, Grandpa.
        Tagged with numbers, we become
        numbers, faceless, meaningless.

We were told to come to Jackson Park
        just two suitcases each,
        no more names, no memories, no Basho,
        only ourselves and what we can carry.

Here we are, waiting for the buses
        to arrive, photographers flashing and clicking,
        other Japanese like us, so many,
        all quietly waiting, wordlessly smiling,
        without resistance,

And we all shiver because it is cold,
        because we do not know where we are going,
        because we are leaving home as the enemy.
        The only thing warm, pressed against my chest,
        is the half-heart Jamie gave me, waiting to be one
        with its other half.

The Bridge to Lillooet

by Trevor Kew

Ken Takahashi was about to cast his fishing line into the current when he heard a splash.

Across the river, no more than twenty yards away, stood two boys, shirtless and barefoot. They were perhaps three or four years younger than Ken.

The taller one hurled a stone. It sailed over Ken's head and clacked against a rock.

"Jap," called the boy. "Jappity-Jap-Jap."

The smaller boy made slanty eyes at Ken with his index fingers.

Although this was Ken's favorite spot for catching rainbow trout, he grabbed his fishing pole and his tin of worms, stood up, and began to walk away.

"*Banzai!*"

Ken spun around. His younger brother Tom was sprinting down the path, holding a large stone in each hand. As he reached the bottom of the hill, he let one fly. It sailed across the river and smacked against the tall boy's arm.

The tall boy roared in pain.

Tom hurled another stone and the boys ran off toward the line of white houses in the distance.

"Sneaky Japs!" screamed the small one. "Filthy yellow rats!"

There were shouts from the iron bridge upstream. Ken knew that two Mounties were on duty at all times, guarding the only route to the town of Lillooet.

"Let's get out of here!" he hissed.

They took off up the path.

By the time they reached the top of the hill, Ken's heart was pounding and his legs ached. Steadying himself, he looked back at the bridge. The Mounties had gone back to their posts.

He grabbed hold of Tom's arm.

"What were you thinking?" he snapped. "Do you know what kind of trouble you could have got us in?"

"But I rescued you," said Tom.

"I didn't need to be rescued," said Ken.

Tom kicked a rock down the hill. His face was flushed with anger.

"Look," said Ken, "Ignore the whites. They have their side of the water and we have ours. Remember what father says—*gaman*. Endure and be patient."

Tom opened his mouth to protest, then changed his mind. "Sorry, *Oniisan*."

"Forget it," said Ken. "Let's go get some dinner."

They turned and began walking toward the little group of shacks huddled in the shadow of an endless wall of mountains.

"I can't believe you yelled *banzai*," laughed Ken. "Our country's fighting a war against Japan and you go hollering the Japanese battle cry at some white kids."

"Samurai yell it in films sometimes," said Tom. "I thought it might scare them."

The streets of the camp were made of packed dirt that ran between rows of small wooden shacks. The one street that had a few shops was known as Ginza-dori, after the famous shopping street in Tokyo. It was full of men walking home, covered in dust from working the fields all day. Tom and Ken exchanged greetings with them.

Thick smoke was flowing from the chimney pots atop the roofs of the shacks. Ken knew the women were all inside, finishing preparations for dinner. Rice would be bubbling away on stoves and grilled fish sizzling in skillets.

But no smoke flowed from the chimney pot atop the shack where Tom and Ken lived.

Ken spotted their father sitting on the woodpile out front, massaging his bad leg. He called to the boys as they approached and they waved back.

"So what happened at the river today, Kentaro?" he asked.

Ken heard Tom gulp a short nervous breath.

"No fish?" said their father.

Ken thought Tom might collapse with relief.

"Not even one bite, Otosan," Ken said.

Their father grabbed his walking stick and levered himself up. He had used that stick for as long as Ken could remember.

An old woman approached, carrying two steaming black metal pots.

"Smells delicious, Kinoshita-san," said Ken. He took the pots and set them down. "Thank you."

"Kinoshita-san—I'm terribly ashamed," said Ken's father, bowing, "but would it be possible to pay you on Monday? I am still waiting for news on the sale of my boat."

Kinoshita-san nodded, then ambled away.

It was such a nice evening that they decided to eat outside. With Tom's help, Ken rolled over three log-ends to sit on and a fourth to act as a table. Tom went into the house and returned with bowls, chopsticks, and a large wooden spoon.

Kinoshita-san's cooking was, as always, bland and overcooked. The slices of daikon radish atop the rice were so mushy that Ken's chopsticks cut right through. The chicken was little more than bits of gristle and fat. But Ken was so hungry that he devoured two bowlfuls.

Back when they'd lived in Vancouver, his mother had been known throughout Little Tokyo for her savory *nabe* stews and delicious *ocha-zuke*. Friends had come over to their house on Powell Street for dinner nearly every Sunday. Even in the early days at the camp, people had loved her food. But that was before she had started coughing during that first terrible winter. Ken didn't want to think about that.

"Takahashi-san—*sumimasen!*"

It was a young man carrying a satchel. He handed a small envelope to Ken's father. "Mail for you from the coast."

Ken's father nodded to the man but his hands shook as he tore the envelope open. He read the letter once then slipped it back into the envelope. He stared down at the dirt.

"What is it, Otosan?" Ken asked.

His father grabbed his walking stick and rose to his feet.

"It's what I should have expected," he said, and went inside the house.

〜

That night, Ken dreamed he was perched on the prow of his father's fishing boat, gazing out over the water to the land across the sea. He looked back at his father, who was standing at the helm.

"Those mountains are in Japan, Kentaro—where your mother and my parents were born, and where everyone looks like us," his father said.

In those dreams, Ken always found himself sailing and sailing over a calm but endless sea. But no matter how much he hoped to reach the land of the great mountains, he could still see the docks of Vancouver when he turned and looked back.

He awoke to the morning light shining through an open window. He glanced over at Tom. Still asleep. From the next room came their father's usual thunderous snores.

Ken put on a pair of sandals and slipped out of the house. He walked the short distance down Ginza-dori to the communal toilet. It was occupied. As he waited, Ken stared off at the mountains that rose behind Lillooet and thought about his dream.

Those mountains he'd seen as a child were not in Japan, of course. They were on Vancouver Island. In first grade he'd told everyone that he had seen Japan from a boat, and his teacher had scolded him for spreading lies. When Ken's father had found out, he'd laughed so hard that he'd sprayed tea onto the kitchen table. Now, his father never laughed. He rarely even smiled.

Once, Japan had sounded like a kind of heaven to Ken—a place where everyone looked like him and no one would call him rat or monkey or stinky little Jap.

But now Japan was a place where no one from Canada could ever go. A place surrounded by walls. Enemy territory.

Ken's gaze shifted down from the mountains to the town of Lillooet. He couldn't go there either. No one in the internment camp was allowed to cross the bridge. He wondered about the people in the town. Did they think of him as their enemy?

On some days, Lillooet seemed as far away as that strange land across the sea.

Because it was Saturday, there was no school, and Ken spent a long hot day working in the apple orchards with his brother.

When they got home, Tom grabbed their baseball gloves down from a shelf and grinned.

"I don't know if I can," said Ken, wiping his brow on his sleeve. He slumped down into a chair.

"Come on, *oyaji*—old man," Tom said.

"I'll show you who's the *oyaji*," said Ken, snatching his glove.

There was an open stretch of ground next to the river where the boys met almost every night to play baseball. Some of the men played too. Others sat on the side and talked about how good they had been when they were younger.

The field was full of holes and rocks. Ground balls took sudden sideways bounces and every now and then someone hit a foul ball into the river. But at least it was baseball, of a sort.

Ken's mother had been the biggest baseball fan in the family. Even when Ken's father had been working on the boat all day, she would drag him and the boys over to Oppenheimer Park to watch the Asahi Tigers, champions of the Vancouver Terminal League.

By the time Ken and Tom arrived at the field, a game was already in full swing.

"Let Kentaro pitch," called a small boy from the outfield.

"Yeah, give him the ball," said someone else.

Ken tried to wave them away, but his friend Ichiro placed the ball in his hand.

"Just one inning," said Ichiro.

"I'll catch," Tom said. He jogged off to crouch behind home plate.

Ken set his feet, his right shoulder facing the plate.

The batter, Kinoshita-san's grandson Shogo, stared back wide-eyed. He didn't even swing at the first pitch.

Thump—the ball landed in Tom's glove.

Thump.

Thump.

"*Out-o!*" called Ichiro's father, who was standing behind Tom.

Ken noticed his own father sitting next to some other men on a log behind third base. He wondered if his father had seen the strikeout.

The next batter went down on four pitches, and the third popped the ball up. Scrambling backward and tumbling to the ground, Tom snagged the ball in his glove.

Tom was a good catcher. Some of the older men had nicknamed him "vacuum cleaner" because of his ability to pull bad pitches out of the dirt. But he was a terrible hitter.

"You're up first, Tomonori," Ichiro's father called out.

Ken watched as Tom swung at three bad pitches and then walked away, swearing under his breath.

Ken was up next. As he walked toward the plate, he noticed someone walking toward the field from the direction of the bridge. It was a Mountie in full uniform.

Sometimes Mounties on duty came to the end of the bridge to watch, but this was the first time one had walked into the middle of a game.

"Good evening," said the Mountie, stopping next to first base. "Who here speaks English?"

At first no one volunteered. Ken wondered if anyone would. Most of the young people in the camp could understand English but many of the older men, including Ken's father, knew very little.

Tom jumped forward.

"I do, sir," he said.

"Very good," said the Mountie. "It's straightforward, really. A group of us junior officers were talking recently about how life in this town can be rather dull. We've noticed you playing baseball and well—we want to challenge you to a game."

He waited for Tom to translate, but Tom just stood there. The Mountie continued. "It would be played tomorrow at the baseball ground—in Lillooet. Will you play?"

A stunned silence hung over the field.

"Yes," agreed Tom, without translating a word.

"Wonderful," said the Mountie. "I'm Officer Dupont. Please be at the bridge tomorrow at one o'clock sharp."

And with that, he turned and walked away.

Everyone seemed to converge on home plate at once. Loud and excited voices filled the air.

"A real game, against the whites—"

"Across the river—"

"I never thought we'd—"

Ken pushed his way out of the crowd. He saw his father hobbling away from the scene, red-faced, heading toward home.

Pushing back through, he found his brother talking to three elderly gentlemen.

"We've got to go," he said. "Otosan's not happy."

They caught up to their father as he reached the front door of their house. He glared at Tom as he wrenched the door open. It slammed hard behind him.

"Come on," said Ken, turning to his brother.

Tom shook his head. "No way am I going in there—"

Ken grabbed him by the arm and pulled him into the house.

Inside, their father was sitting next to the potbellied stove in the center of the room. He held his hands over his face.

"Tomonori," he said. His voice was low but laced with anger. "You had no right to speak for everyone."

Ken looked over at Tom. He expected his brother to utter some sort of apology. But none came.

"You should have let the older men speak to that Mountie," said their father, looking over at Tom. "Did you ever stop to think that we might not agree? Now how do you think it will look if we change our minds?"

Tom glared back at his father. "Why wouldn't we play?"

Slam—their father's fist smashed down on the table. "Play a game—with them?" he roared, eyes blazing. "After everything they've done to us?"

Crash—a bowl shattered on the floor.

Ken stood in the middle of the room between his father and younger brother. He didn't know what to do. Nothing like this had ever happened in his family before.

"I fought for this country," said their father, staring at the wall. "I lived in filthy trenches and had my kneecap shattered by a piece of iron when I was twenty years old. And what did I get for it—a few worthless war medals to wear while they spat on me in the streets and called me a dirty, stinking Jap."

"And then," he continued, "this new war starts and they take my fishing license, the one I inherited from my father. They take our home and all our things. They take my fishing boat. Do you know what they sold that boat for? One hundred dollars."

Ken felt sick to his stomach. Long ago, he had overheard his parents talking. He knew the boat had cost his father close to five thousand dollars.

"And you boys know as well as anyone what that first winter in this camp took away from us—"

Ken noticed that Tom had tears in his eyes.

"At least here in the camp," said their father, "we are with our own kind and away from—those people."

Tom turned and ran out of the house.

"You will not play in that game!" shouted their father.

"I'll go after him," said Ken, unsure what else to say.

He caught up to his brother at the hill overlooking the river. He was sitting on a boulder, chucking pebbles into the water.

"Tom," said Ken, sitting down. He put a hand on his brother's shoulder.

Tom gulped two quick breaths. He wiped his face on his sleeve. "I know I'm only thirteen," he said, "and that I can't understand everything our father has gone through, but he's wrong about this, Ken. He is."

Ken took a deep breath. "It doesn't matter. He's our father. We must obey him."

Tom turned and looked at him. "What are we going to do when we leave this camp—go live in Japan? Japan's not our country. It's the enemy. This is our country." He picked up another pebble and heaved it into the river. "We've been given the chance to cross that bridge. I think we should take it."

⌣

Just past noon the next day, Ken stood in the middle of the room he shared with his brother, staring into the tattered old suitcase lying open on his bed. Inside was a white baseball cap with thin black stripes and a red brim next to a jersey with "ASAHI" emblazoned across the front in bold red letters.

He recalled the day three years ago when the Tigers coach had asked him to come and train with the team. Ken had thought the man was joking. He was only thirteen at the time and the men who played for the Tigers were his heroes. All at once, here was the chance to play alongside them.

He'd been almost too nervous to attend the first practice but his mother had made him go.

"*Ganbare*," she'd told him. "Be brave. One brave person is worth more than a world of cowards."

Ken took the jersey out of the suitcase and slipped it on. He tugged the cap down over his forehead.

Tom burst into the room. "Quick! He's gone to the outhouse!"

They grabbed their baseball gloves and hurried outside. The streets were full of men, women, and children—all walking in the direction of the bridge.

"Come on!" said Tom.

When they reached the bridge, they saw two Mounties standing amidst a sea of people. One of the Mounties was Officer Dupont.

"Are you sure we're allowed to let everyone across?" Ken heard the other Mountie say. "Boss said just ball players."

"They all look like ball players to me," said Dupont. "And anyway, the boss is out of town."

"Okay," said the other officer. "But it's your head on the block when he finds out."

Lillooet was not a big town, but it was larger than the camp. The main street was lined with a great variety of shops, and the houses, while not grand like some Ken remembered in Vancouver, dwarfed the shacks on the opposite side of the river. Some of the houses had front porches, and from every porch and window, townspeople stood watching the spectacle flowing through their streets.

A little girl broke away from her mother and ran over to Ken. She put her hand on his arm and stared up at his face with wide confused eyes. Then, screeching and giggling, she ran back to her mother.

A young boy stepped in front of Tom. Ken recognized him as one of the kids he and Tom had met by the river. "Filthy Jap," the boy said. "You know we're bombing your brothers overseas?"

Officer Dupont, who had followed the crowd, hurried over and cuffed the boy on the back of the head. "You mind your tongue," he snapped and the boy slunk away.

The baseball field had dugouts and fences, and the ground was even and flat. Someone had even raked the dirt in the infield. The other team was already out there, warming up.

"Wow—a real game," said Tom.

In the few minutes that it took the visitors to sort out their team, the fences became lined with spectators. Behind the third base line sat the townspeople of Lillooet and behind the first base line, the people from the camp.

Lillooet batted first.

"*Oniisan, ganbare!*" said Tom, tossing Ken a baseball.

Ken walked to the pitcher's mound. He knew that hundreds of eyes were focused on him. He tried not to think of his father.

A burly man with a thick beard stepped up to the plate, the bat like a chopstick in his hands.

Planting his right foot, Ken wound up and hurled the ball.

The man carved the air with a mighty swing.

"Steee-rike!" called the umpire. Loud cheers from behind the first base line.

Another pitch. Strike.

"Are you watchin' this?" Ken heard a Lillooet fan say. "How can anyone hit a pitch like that?"

Ken tossed a fiery fastball.

The large man lumbered back to his team's dugout, shaking his head.

The next batter struck out on five pitches. Dupont followed. He managed to foul the first two pitches off, but the third zipped past him, right over the plate.

"Not bad, *oyaji*," said Tom, as they sat down in the dugout.

The teams had agreed to play six innings. By the end of the fifth, it was 3-0 to the visitors from the camp and Ken had struck out twelve batters and only allowed two hits. As he took to the mound in the sixth, Tom walked over.

"Some of the Lillooet kids asked me your name," he said, pointing to the fence. Ken looked over and a group of little children waved back at him.

Tom grinned. "I think they're cheering for you, not their fathers."

Ken's thoughts turned to his own father. The game was almost over. Soon they would have to go back and face reality.

Would his father ever forgive him?

He looked over at his own supporters, then at the Lillooet fans.

Of all people, his father deserved to see this.

He threw a bad first pitch and the batter smacked the ball over the shortstop's head for a single. The next man hit a pop fly, but Yujiro dropped it, leaving runners at first and third.

Dupont stepped up to the plate. He missed the first pitch, but the second dipped right into his swing. Ken spun around just in time to watch the ball fly over the fence.

Home run. Tie game.

And then Ken saw his father sitting behind the fence.

Somehow, he struck the next three batters out.

"Last inning," said Tom as they sat down again.

"You see father?" asked Ken.

"I'm trying not to think about it."

The first two batters went down swinging.

Ken stood up and walked toward the plate. He locked eyes with his father, who stared right back at him.

The first pitch was a strike, and so was the second.

Ken closed his eyes and imagined his mother sitting there beside his father, clapping her hands and shouting for him to hit one out of the park. He clenched his teeth and swung hard at the next pitch.

The ball hit the ground hard near first base and skipped into right field. Ken raced down the line, legs pumping.

"He's missed it—go, go, go!" someone yelled in Japanese as he rounded first base. Second base thumped under his foot but Ken didn't stop. He slid into third base hard. Above his head, the ball whacked into a glove.

"Safe," called the umpire.

Ken watched, muscles tensed, as his brother stepped up to the plate. He stared down the third base line at home base. So close. But Tom hadn't hit a ball all day and Ken could see his brother's arms shaking as he faced the first pitch.

Strike.

Ball.

Ball.

Strike.

Ball.

Full count.

And then Ken remembered what he'd taught Tom earlier that summer. It was probably their only hope.

"Tom!" he shouted. He used his finger to write three Japanese *kana* in the air.

Tom squinted. Ken wrote the *kana* again.

The pitcher hurled a fastball.

Tom held out his hands and let the ball hit the bat.

"Bunt!" shouted the third baseman as Ken sprinted away.

He closed his eyes and dove for home, expecting to feel the thump of the catcher's glove. But the tag never came and when he opened his eyes, he was lying facedown in the dirt with his arms wrapped around home plate.

There were wild cheers all around and Ken was slapped on the back and pushed and pulled in all directions.

"That," said a voice behind him in English, "was a great ball game."

Ken knew from the accent that it was Dupont.

He turned around. There stood the young Mountie, the whole Lillooet team behind him.

"You little fellas sure are good ball players," he said.

Ken saw Tom extend his hand. Dupont hesitated, then shook it.

"Let's do this again," said the Mountie.

It was then that Ken realized who the heroes of that day had been. He walked over and shook Dupont's hand too. Then he put an arm around his brother's shoulders and they walked together to the fence behind home plate where their father was standing with a huge smile on his face.

The war was still on. No baseball game would change that. And nothing could bring back their father's boat or their house on Powell Street or their mother's warm embrace.

But they had crossed the bridge to Lillooet. It was a start, if nothing more.

Blue Shells

by Naoko Awa

translated by Toshiya Kamei

I'm going to tell you the story of a mysterious flared skirt I used to own. Sadly, I no longer have it. When I became obsessed with the skirt, my family hid it from me. Shortly later, it was burned in the war.

But I have never forgotten the dazzling blue of the skirt. Even now, when I close my eyes, I can see the color.

The skirt was made of silk, with an amply wide hem, which was rare in those days. During the war, most women wore *monpe* pants. So you can imagine how I attracted attention, how people spoke ill of me.

I was never a stylish girl. As a child, I wore only my sister's hand-me-downs. My looks were homely, and my intelligence was average. I was a quiet, ordinary girl, and there was nothing special about me. This is my story of how I became smitten with the blue skirt.

When I was twelve or thirteen, I was friends with a very beautiful girl named Michiru. The daughter of a foreign father and a Japanese mother, she had eyes as blue as iris flowers. She lived with her mother in an old Western-style residence near my house. No one had seen her father. Rumor had it he was an Italian trader, an American sailor, or a German officer.

"My father is on a ship. He's in the middle of the Pacific Ocean," said Michiru. "He came home late last night and gave me a present." When she opened her palm, a necklace of shells spilled over.

I wanted to meet Michiru's father, just once. But she never invited me to her house. No one had ever been inside the house surrounded by thick shrubs.

Even so, Michiru and I often played together. We went out and bought beautifully patterned *chiyogami* paper, showed each other boxes full of ribbons, and talked about books we read.

I was very fond of Michiru. When we walked together, she made passersby turn their heads. I was secretly proud of having such a beautiful friend.

One day—it was spring or early summer—Michiru came to my house. It was early afternoon, and the scent of thick green leaves wafted from the hedge.

"Michiru-san is in the backyard," Mother said. I ran out the back door and found Michiru, whom I had last seen a few hours earlier. Wearing a new linen dress, she stood still.

The instant she saw me she said, "Yae-chan, can you keep a secret?" Then she whispered, "I've come to say good-bye."

I remained silent, stunned.

"We're going away tonight," she said.

"What? Where are you going?"

"A town by the sea. My mother's home. But don't tell anyone," Michiru said and handed me a small package. "I give you this as a keepsake."

"A keepsake? Is she going away for good?" I thought. Before I could say a word, Michiru fled. I still remember her white feet and her *geta* sandals echoing behind her. I unwrapped the package and found a blue flared skirt inside.

⁓

The next day I went to Michiru's house. A crowd of people had gathered around it. They looked at each other, whispered, and nodded: "Come to think of it, I've heard low clattering sounds at night."

"I see. He must have been using a typewriter."

"That foreigner came out only at night, always hiding. No one had seen him by daylight."

"I never imagined there was a spy in our neighborhood!"

A spy? My heart froze. Fear crept up my legs and spread through my body. "It's a lie! It's not true!" I screamed inside my head, straining my ears to listen to the people in the crowd.

"The foreigner seems to have left early."

"The wife and child followed him."

It was the middle of the war. The neighbors gossiped excitedly about the whereabouts of the foreigner and his family.

"I hope they'll get caught soon!" said the greengrocer's wife, raising her fist into the air.

"Run, Michiru! Run!" Silently, I prayed she and her parents would escape safely.

My knees buckling, I staggered away. I held a secret—Michiru's destination. She had told me not to tell anyone.

As I walked, I kept telling myself not to reveal this secret. Even if the whole world turned against Michiru, I was still her friend.

The neighbors knew she and I were close friends. When they saw me in the street, they asked me all kinds of questions—whether I had met her father, or how her family lived. Every time they asked me a question, I told them I didn't know. After a few days, I no longer felt like going out.

I shut myself up in my room and thought about Michiru all day. Every night I had a nightmare that someone was chasing me.

A town by the sea—these words weighed heavily on my mind, and my heart began to ache as if someone had died. For a twelve-year-old girl, keeping a secret was a daunting task.

⌒

One night I was jolted awake by the recurring nightmare. I slid a drawer of the chest open and took out the blue skirt Michiru had given me.

I put on the skirt. Since she was tall, it was too long for me. "I'll have to raise the hem," I whispered. I opened my workbox, found a blue thread, and passed it through the eye of a needle. I don't know why I started needlework in the middle of night.

At any rate, I decided to raise the hem about five centimeters. But sewing the hem of the flared skirt was a lot of work. The hem was incredibly wide. Besides, the skirt was made of thin silk, and no matter how many times I stitched, I made little progress. The needle seemed to be motionless or moving backward.

As I kept moving the needle slowly, I thought about Michiru. I wondered where she was, how she was doing. After a while, the hem of the skirt began to look like the edge of the sea, like the long, arching shore.

Then I thought I heard Michiru's footsteps from inside the cloth. She was running alone.

For some reason, she had no shoes on and was running barefoot on the beach. I stood on the shore while the waves foamed, making white lace-like patterns on the sand.

"Michiru!" I cried in spite of myself, and began to run. The sand felt soft and wet under my feet. I, too, was shoeless. "Michiru, wait!" I kept calling her, but she didn't look back. She ran faster and faster.

"Why, Michiru? I'm doing everything to keep your secret," I thought. I watched her figure grow smaller and smaller in the distance.

On the verge of tears, I sat down. Then I saw her crouch down in the distance. She seemed to be picking up something. Or had she fallen down and wasn't able to get up? Feeling sad, I stood up and plodded toward her.

I went up to her and called her from behind: "Michiru!"

She finally looked back. "Yae-chan, it's you," she said, flashing a friendly smile. "I'm gathering shells. Look, blue ones," she said. She opened her palm, revealing a shell. It was small and thin as a cherry-blossom shell, but it was blue.

"Beautiful," I mumbled. "I've never seen such a beautiful shell."

Michiru gave a cheerful smile and said, "I'm gathering shells. I want to make a necklace."

"A necklace?" I asked.

"Yes. We once made a necklace with camellias in the temple. Remember?" she said. "I want to make a long one with these shells. But I can't focus on gathering shells. Every time I find one, someone comes after me." She looked up and strained her ears. "Do you hear footsteps?" she said with an edge of fear in her voice. "It's not just one person. There are three or five."

"I don't hear anything. That's the sound of waves," I said, laughing.

Then we went back to picking up shells. After gathering a few, however, Michiru looked up again and said, "I hear footsteps. Not just one person. It's ten or twenty people."

"I don't hear anything except the sound of the wind," I said and laughed again.

Still worried, Michiru nodded and began searching for shells again. But soon she cried, "I hear footsteps. They're after me!"

She got up to run. The shells fell from her skirt, scattering over her feet. They were the same color as the sea. When I held a shell against the sun, it became tinted with purple, filtering the sunlight. Captivated by the beautiful shells, I didn't go after Michiru. I stayed there for a long time.

Before I knew it, she was only a dot in the distance.

"Michiru! Michiru!" I called as a burst of wind scattered my voice. I kept calling her. "Michiru! Michiru!"

A voice called me from beyond the sea: "Yae-chan, Yae-chan." Over the sound of the wind, a familiar voice kept calling me.

But when I glanced back toward the voice, I saw a naked light bulb flicker over my head. The *shoji* door slid open, and my older sister peeked in. "Yae-chan, what's the matter? You were screaming," she said.

Later, she told me I had been pale and shaking; with vacant eyes, I looked as if I'd had a fit.

⤶

A few days later, I heard a rumor about Michiru. In her mother's home-town, she and her mother had thrown themselves into the sea. I won-dered if she, a blue-eyed girl, had met with a cold reception over there. Or if the rumors about her father had already reached the town.

Then I became captivated by Michiru's blue skirt. I wanted to see her again. As my longing to see her grew, I started acting boldly.

After school, I slipped into the skirt, went out shopping, and visited a friend's house. "You shouldn't wear a foreigner's skirt," my friends said. "She looks like one of them," they said behind my back.

But it didn't bother me. As I walked, the hem of the skirt swirled, making me feel cheerful. When I ran through the wind, I felt as if I were floating in the air. When I played jump rope with my friends, I was able to jump higher than before. When I jumped really high, I thought I caught a glimpse of the sea beyond the roofs of houses. Yes, beyond the sea, I saw an island carpeted with evening primroses.

"Yae-chan, you're like a bird," my friends said.

Oh, how I wished I were a bird! I wished I could fly to the beach where Michiru and I had gathered shells. Maybe it was a faraway island. Those beautiful shells weren't found anywhere in Japan.

When I thought about the blue shells, my heart grew tight with yearning, and tears welled up. My family kept an eye on me from a distance. One day when I came home from an errand, I discovered the blue skirt was gone. Maybe my mother had locked it up in a drawer. But no one ever mentioned it again. No matter how many times I asked, I received no answer.

A few years later, the skirt was lost in a fire.

Borne by the Wind

by Charles De Wolf

It was only a modest house, but it stood on a hill, with a fine view of the sea. Sitting in the cramped upstairs study, Toshio let his eye wander to the window, but he was listening nonetheless, as his Uncle Muneo read from a musty volume he had taken off a shelf. Sometimes his uncle would pause, look up at him and continue the story, quite ignoring the text. He spoke in what for Toshio were the familiar and consoling patterns of Tokyo speech.

Toshio had been abruptly taken out of school and sent away from the capital during the last months of the war. His mother had anxiously seen him off, admonishing him to be both brave and obedient, as she looked up at him from the station platform on that late wintry afternoon. He had stood there stiffly, fearing above all that he might weep like a child. "Don't worry. I'll be home soon," he had said, imitating the departing words of his father as he embarked for Manchuria as a soldier.

Wishing to be a man but feeling like a boy, the fourteen-year-old told himself that if he were brave and obedient at least on the outside, all would somehow be well. And so for all his anxiety and loneliness as the train doors closed, it did not cross his mind that this might be the last he would ever see of his mother.

Just before the beginning of spring came the great air raid, and though their remains were never found, it was presumed that she and Toshio's grandparents were among the tens of thousands who perished in the firestorm. Shortly after the war ended in mid-August of that year, his father was captured by invading Russian troops and sent to Siberia, his fate unknown. And so it was that Toshio, perhaps already an orphan, found himself in the care of his uncle and aunt.

For a boy who had known only the urban life of the capital, the small fishing village on the coast of Ishikawa was strange but enchanting. Accompanied by his uncle, he would walk along the shore in the late summer, gazing at the boats bobbing on the waves. The couple had no children of their own, and Toshio could sense that, as kindhearted as his uncle was, it was not easy for a man in his early fifties to relate to an adolescent. His mother had told him that her elder brother had once been a rising scholar, but it was only recently that he had heard his aunt whispering that it had been the dark clouds of militarism that had driven her husband-to-be into exile here on the Sea of Japan.

On their walks, his uncle would sometimes point out landmarks or mention a fact or two from local history, but otherwise he said little. Once Toshio ventured out on a jaunt alone, only to be scolded by his aunt when he returned for supper.

"Don't ya know what happens to boys who wander off by themselves?" she exclaimed. "The Americans'll come and take ya 'way, and that'll be the last anyone'll ever see of ya!"

His uncle in turn had chided her: "No need to frighten the lad with nonsense!" But the words of warning had rung in Toshio's ears. He instantly pictured towering, long-nosed monsters, all in uniform, grimly combing the beach and the rocky inlets.

Toshio's troubles began in earnest when he was sent off to school in the nearby city. In the morning, he had been introduced by the teacher, but then at the noon break, he was approached by a tall boy and four companions.

"So yer the orphan, are ya?" the boy began. He spoke in a thicker form of Ishikawa dialect than Toshio had heard even his aunt speak.

"I am in the care of my relatives here," Toshio replied. "I am grateful for the kindness and consideration of you all."

His words were stiff and formal, as though addressed to adults. Lowering his eyes he added in a half murmur: "I do not know as yet whether I am indeed an orphan."

The boy turned to his companions and in a mockingly mincing tone repeated what Toshio had said. His comrades jeered as he turned again to Toshio, grabbed him by his school uniform, and pushed him against the wall.

"Listen, ya little Tokyo sissy. I am Hiroyuki Maeda, descended from the Maeda clan. You'll do whate'er I or my men tell ya to do. And don't think ya can be runnin' fer help to the teacher or yer uncle and auntie. Understood?"

Toshio returned home in dread. That night, in a dream, he saw an even larger Maeda, now outfitted in an Imperial Army uniform and waving a sword as he chased him along the beach, leading a dozen other boys.

The next day Maeda quite ignored him. Toshio thought the danger had passed but then noticed that when he tried to speak to any of his classmates, they would look away. When the school day was over and he made his way to the bus stop for the first leg of his journey home, the clusters of other pupils heading in the same direction made no move to include him. By the end of the week, he was feeling quite forlorn.

At home, he had kept his distress to himself, but his aunt, seeing him withdrawn and distracted, eventually coaxed him into confiding in her. His uncle had just returned from his usual late-morning walk, as Toshio reluctantly finished his account.

"Hiroyuki Maeda?" his aunt sputtered. "Descended from the old lord of Kaga? My, how ridiculous! That young lout may be the spoiled son of a minor landowner round here, but he's no high and mighty one to be abullyin' my nephew! I'll be off to see the headmaster tomorrow!"

As she returned to the kitchen, Toshio gave his uncle a pleading look, but he only smiled, sipped his tea, and said nothing.

Toshio was in the midst of preparing for Monday lessons, when his uncle came into Toshio's room and motioned for him to follow.

"Do you like stories?" he began, as they sat down in the study.

"Yes," Toshio replied politely, uncertain as to where their awkward conversation was leading.

"Well, this is an old story, a strange story, first recorded in the language of a thousand years ago. It comes from a collection of tales that almost always end with some sort of lesson, a moral of sorts, though I am not sure what it should be in this case. Perhaps that is for you to decide."

↬

"Long ago, when this region was still known as the Province of Kaga, there were seven young men, scarcely older than you, whose misfortune it had been to lose their parents at an early age. Two of them were brothers, the remaining five their distant cousins. Banding together, they vowed to support one another in good times and bad. One afternoon, while wandering a lonely beach in search of clams and crabs, they came upon an abandoned boat and resolved to repair it and make it their own. Seeing them at their work, occasional passersby would gawk and jeer: 'You'll soon be food for the sharks!' But the youths ignored them, determined to learn the hazardous ways of the sea and to earn their livelihood as fishermen. And so they did.

"Now in those days, the peaceful capital to the south was still in its glory, with gentle court nobles wooing their ladies with poetry and song. But in Kaga, life was full of danger, and from more than storms and waves. So whenever the lads set out from shore, they took on board not only their nets but also their bows and arrows, along with seven short swords. Young as they were, these fishermen were also warriors.

"One morning at the crack of dawn they launched their boat and rowed out until all sight of land was gone. Just as they had cast their nets, one of them, whose name was Norimitsu, glanced behind and saw dark clouds swirling toward them. He had barely time to warn the others, before they were caught in a fierce gale, which swiftly bore them ever farther out to sea. Terrified, they shipped their oars, clutched the gunwales, and surrendered to the wind, knowing that at any moment a wave might come crashing down and toss them overboard. But still their tiny boat went skimming and plunging ahead.

"They had cast off at what by their measure of time was halfway through the Hour of the Rabbit. Now it was nearly noon, well into the Hour of the Horse, when at last Norimitsu dared to lift his head and look to the horizon. There in the hazy distance lay what appeared to be an island. 'Land!' he shouted to the others.

"On their present course, they were doomed. Yet suddenly, as if by design, there was a shift in the wind, and soon they saw the island looming before them. Passing through the breakers, they reached the shore and joyfully tumbled out. When they had pulled their boat up onto a rock-strewn beach, they looked warily around.

"Would there be food and water? Were they alone on this island, and, if not, would they be attacked by hostile inhabitants?

"A stream was flowing down a nearby hill, and beyond lay what they thought must surely be fruit trees. Fear having been replaced by hunger, they began walking toward them, when they saw coming from that same direction the figure of a man. As he came closer, they could see that he was scarcely more than a youth himself. Lean and handsome, he smiled at them and exclaimed, 'You are most welcome! We are pleased to know that you have made your way here safe and sound.'

"As they had hardly begun to recover from their ordeal, the young fishermen could only acknowledge his greeting with silent bows, even as they marveled that he seemed to have known of their coming. As though reading their thoughts, he laughed and then asked, 'Do you know that it is I who have brought you here?'

"To these strange words the bewildered youths could only reply, 'How could this be? We went fishing just this morning, when we were caught in a gale and blown into the open sea.'

"'But it was I,' the stranger said softly, 'who sent the wind.'

"Speechless, the lads looked at him, then immediately lowered their eyes, for they now knew that this could be no ordinary man.

"'Do not be afraid,' he assured them. 'Come. You must be weary and hungry.' Turning about, he called out in a loud voice, 'Where are you then? Quickly! We must serve our guests!'

"Suddenly there was the sound of trampling feet, and as though out of nowhere two long chests appeared, carried on the shoulders of men entirely dressed in blue. When the chests had been opened, the youths could see that a splendid feast had been prepared, with varieties of fish and vegetables they had never before seen or tasted, together with soft, steaming rice. Their host promptly urged them to eat, and eat they did.

"There were ample jugs as well, filled with a sweet drink that eased whatever anxiety they still might have felt. When they had eaten their fill, they carefully replaced the remaining food in the chests and leaned back in drowsy satisfaction against a large boulder.

"'Now then,' said their master, sitting down beside the fishermen, 'I must tell you that I have brought you here for a reason.' He paused for a moment, looking at their faces most earnestly.

"'Across these waters lies another island, ruled by a cruel tyrant who would take my life and make this domain his own. For many a year he has sought to carry out his will, but we have always resisted and prevailed. Tomorrow he and I will finally meet in deadly combat. I have summoned you to seek your aid.'

"The lads stared first at him, then at each other. Finally, the oldest of them, whose name was Tadasuke, boldly responded: 'We know nothing of his forces or the size of his fleet. Yet as fate has brought us here, we will fight, though our strength fail us and we perish.' The others all murmured and nodded their agreement.

"When the lord of the island heard this, he threw his head back and laughed in delight, before resuming in a tone of utmost seriousness.

"'You must not be alarmed when I tell you that the enemy we shall meet tomorrow will not appear in human form. Nor shall I.'

"Again the lads exchanged glances, but then they turned again to listen.

"'As he approaches, I shall come down from above. Always in times past, we have driven him back before he could reach the breakers. But tomorrow you will join the fray, so we shall allow him to advance to shore. He will be pleased with that, for his strength is greater on land. Yet leave him to me and watch how the struggle goes. Should I falter, I will give you a sign with my eyes. Then you must loose your arrows, as many and as furiously as you are able.

"'You should begin your preparations in the morning, during the Hour of the Snake, for the battle will begin at midday. Climb to the top of the cliff and stand in waiting. From here the enemy will attempt to rise.'

"Thus having carefully instructed the fishermen, he left them to their preparations and walked back into the heart of the island."

〜

Here Toshio's uncle paused and looked up from his book, seeing an unhappy expression on his nephew's face.

"Is something the matter?" he asked.

"Forgive me, Uncle," Toshio replied. "It is a fine story. Those boys are all strong and brave, but *I'm* not and don't suppose I'll ever be!"

"Ah," said his uncle with a smile. "You can never be so sure. Besides, you have not yet heard the end of the tale."

〜

"The seven young fishermen set about building a hut from the trees that grew on the mountain, diligently sharpened their arrowheads, and inspected their bowstrings. Food had again been brought to them, and so when night had fallen, they sat round their campfire in a festive mood, bolstering each other's courage with jibes and laughter as they recalled their eventful day.

"Norimitsu alone was silent, sitting at some distance with his back to the fire and staring into the darkness. As, one by one, the others crawled into the hut and nodded off to sleep, Tadasuke walked over to join him.

"'What is it, Cousin?' he asked. 'It is not like you to be so quiet.'

"'That is because it all so very strange,' Norimitsu replied. 'This morning we seemed close to death, and yet now we are celebrating, even as we prepare for a battle of which then we knew nothing. We have put our trust in a stranger, one who is clearly as powerful as he is charming. But what do we know of him? What assurance do we have that he means us well or that his enemy is truly evil? And why, if he is in need of help, has he chosen seven poor and fatherless lads from across the sea—and not before terrifying them half out of their wits?'

"As though shocked at his own outburst, Norimitsu gripped his knees and lowered his head. 'I am sorry. You must think me quite a coward.'

"'Not at all,' replied Tadasuke, his hand on his cousin's shoulder. 'I am sure that everyone one of us is thinking the same—only you perhaps more clearly. And if we were not having such thoughts, we should no doubt be fools. I have wondered myself whether I was wrong to have been so bold in speaking for all of us. It is easy enough to boast on a full belly.'

"The two fell silent, and then Tadasuke spoke again.

"'See how dark it is. We must rest and wait for the light. I can only say that I trust there is some purpose in this and that whatever tomorrow's outcome, we'll have acted with honor.'

"Norimitsu glanced at the cousin he had long regarded as a gentle elder brother and nodded. Silently they returned to the others and lay down to sleep.

"All too soon the sun had risen, and now the Hour of the Horse was upon them. They had eaten heartily and were looking out to sea, awaiting a sign of the enemy's approach. A strong wind arose, and even as they watched, they saw the ocean surface, suddenly strange and menacing, begin to glow with a greenish light. Surging out of the water came two immense fireballs. Behind them on the peak the grass swayed, the leaves shook, and then came a low rumbling sound, as two more flaming fireballs appeared.

"Turning again to the sea, they saw coming toward the shore what seemed to be a huge ship, with countless gleaming oars, but as it came closer they saw to their amazement that it was a colossal centipede, twice, no, thrice as long as any beached whale they had ever seen. Its back was a gleaming green and its sides a fiery red. What they had taken for oars, they now realized, were its many legs, as thick as temple pillars.

"Again there was a roar from the peak, and as they looked behind them, they saw descending an immense blue serpent, equal to the centipede in length and broader than the circumference of a grown man's encircled arms. The deadly foes, the one as fearsome as the other, advanced, giant tongues licking the corners of monstrous mouths in eager anticipation of the battle. The serpent halted, his head raised, and, as the youths had been told, allowed the jubilant centipede to come ashore. Now they waited, face to face, each glaring at the other.

"Faithful to their instructions, the fishermen climbed to the craggy ledge and readied their arrows, even as they kept their eyes steadily on the serpent. The centipede came forward, and the struggle began, each slashing and biting the other, so that both were soon drenched in blood. With its many legs, as it churned up the sand, the centipede had the advantage.

"The battle raged all through the long afternoon, the centipede steadily pushing its way ever farther up the beach. At last, the faltering, sorely wounded serpent looked up at the fishermen and gave them the long-awaited sign. 'Now!' cried Tadasuke, and immediately a stream of arrows went flying toward the centipede, the shafts striking up to the notch into the entire length of its body, from head to tail. The monster shuddered but then desperately lunged again at the serpent. Again Tadasuke gave a shout, as he and the others raised their swords and charged down the slope, cutting away at the centipede's legs until, with a loud cracking sound, it collapsed. When the serpent saw that his mortal enemy was dead, he gazed at those who had saved him and nodded wearily before slowly and painfully slithering away into the mountains.

"The seven young warriors watched him go, then dropped their swords and let themselves fall to the sand, where they sat slumped in silence, gazing at the remains of the great centipede. And now in the twilight the young man who had first sought their aid reappeared, and though limping and bleeding, his face and body cut and bruised, he was smiling. Once again, this time in joyful triumph, he commanded that food and drink be brought for a feast more splendid than ever.

"When the chests had again been closed and the last song had been sung, the lord of the island rose and said to the fishermen: 'This day is one that neither I nor my subjects will ever forget, for, thanks to your strength and bravery, I may now rule in peace. And you seven lads must share in that happiness. Here there are both the fruits of the sea and the fruits of the land. Our island is fertile, and life is most pleasant and easy. Will you not settle here yourselves? You may bring your families with you.'

"'Ah, but we have no families,' said Tadasuke ruefully.

"To this the young lord laughed and said, 'When the cold and haughty inhabitants of your native village see the gifts that I intend to bestow, you will soon have family enough!'

"'But how are we to return?' asked Norimitsu.

"'With the same wind that I summoned before. And once you are again in Kaga, you must visit a shrine that is built there in my honor. And then in time I will once again bring you here.'

"The young men nodded their assent, and when they had loaded their boat with the magnificent gifts they had received and were ready to row, a wind arose from the island and soon brought them back to their native land.

"There is only a little more to tell. Most importantly, the once despised and rejected orphans were suddenly the most sought-after men in Kaga. Within two years of their return, each had acquired a wife, and three of them had become fathers."

Toshio's uncle was again looking at him as he spoke these last words but then turned his eyes back to the book and read aloud:

"And now the time came when they knew they should depart. Having once more visited the shrine and worshipped there, they launched the boats and again were borne by the wind to the island.

"The fishermen lived there, cultivating their fields and growing ever more prosperous, with children and grandchildren. There, on the Isle of the Cat, their descendants may still be found.

"It was surely strong karma that brought the seven fishermen to their new home. They say that the island can be seen from Omiya on the Noto Peninsula, and that, when the sky is clear, the higher western side appears in the distance as a solid blue expanse rising out of the sea. It is indeed, says the tradition, a most rich and fertile land. And so the tale has come down to us."

～

Toshio's uncle slowly closed the book and put it back on the shelf.

"Well?" he asked.

"Uncle, have you ever been to the Isle of the Cat?"

"No, I haven't," he replied slowly, "but there is no doubt that there is indeed such a place. Still, you must remember that this is a very old story and that names have changed, along with much else."

He continued to look at Toshio, as though expecting him to continue.

"So the lord of the island was really the serpent god?"

"Yes, so it seems."

"Our teacher tells us that we must put aside old superstitions for the sake of building a new Japan."

"Quite right! But much of the evil that must now be undone is more recent than old, and we mustn't be too hasty to judge all that is past. In our modern world, we are quite sure that men are men and that snakes are snakes. But perhaps at least some of our ancestors thought so too and yet could still enjoy the story."

Toshio did not immediately reply, and his uncle too fell silent until, again seeing a glum expression on his nephew's face, he again urged him to speak.

"Maeda seems to think," he half-mumbled, "that I am like the centipede, an invader who has no place here."

"No, no," his uncle exclaimed, "you're not at all like the centipede!"

"And if Japan is like the serpent god," Toshio continued impulsively, "why have we been brought down by the Americans' arrows and swords?"

"Ah," exclaimed his uncle, "you're more than a match for me!" For an instant Toshio thought he was angry but now could see that he was chuckling.

"I said at the beginning," he resumed, "that I do not know what the moral of the story is. Perhaps it is less about karma than about trust and courage. But even then we are often like Norimitsu and Tadasuke in the night, knowing neither the justice nor the outcome of the battle. All I can say is that you must deal with Maeda in your own way. And I promise to see to it that your loving aunt keeps her peace."

〜

As Toshio entered the classroom the next day, he glanced at Maeda, whose seat was against the right wall at the back. He had turned around and was chatting with his friends before the arrival of the teacher but paused when he saw Toshio.

"Time ya went back to Tokyo," he remarked with a sneer. Toshio did not reply but continued to look at Maeda, who rose and started to move toward him with a threatening swagger.

"Hiyoyuki Maeda," said Toshio quietly, trying desperately to sound calmer than he felt. "I'm a member of this class too. I'm your classmate. But if you grab me or push me again, it'll be a fight. I can't say I'm not afraid of you. You're bigger and taller and can probably give me quite a bashing. But I'll fight you anyway. And then we'll both be punished. Is that what you really want?"

Maeda clenched his fists, took one step forward, then hesitated and looked about, as a girl at the front suddenly stood up and cried, "Stop it!" With his eyes still fixed on Maeda, Toshio could hear the sound of chairs scraping the floor.

"Go ahead, hide behind a girl!" Maeda taunted, but then turned back. At the very moment he took his seat, their teacher came in.

〜

And so the crisis passed, as did the weeks and months. Toshio no longer walked to the bus stop alone, and though former enemies did not become friends, there was now at least no feud between them.

More than a year had gone by when Toshio returned from school one day to hear the news that his father was among those who had survived the Siberian ordeal and would be returning to Japan.

"And now you'll be goin' back to school in Tokyo again," exclaimed his aunt, momentarily sad amidst joy. But such thoughts were still far from Toshio's mind.

That night he dreamed of his father, limping slowly along a long stretch of beach to meet him, and though his face was cut and bruised, he was nonetheless smiling.

Ghosts and Spirits

The Ghost Who Came to Breakfast
by Alan Gratz

One warm morning in July, a ghost came to our breakfast table.

The ghost was a girl, about twelve or thirteen years old. Just a little younger than me. She had long, stringy black hair and a round face, and wore a blue kimono with large white chrysanthemums on it. My mother and father froze when she stepped out of my bedroom. Off in the corner, the people on the television kept talking about weather and politics, but mother and father were quiet while the ghost girl tiptoed across the room, like they didn't want to spook her.

Ha. Trying not to spook the spook.

I held my breath as the ghost girl knelt down beside me at the table. We were all watching her but pretending not to, the way you do with other people on the train. The ghost girl sat and stared at the empty place on the table until my father nudged my mother.

"A bowl," he whispered. "Get a bowl."

My mother bumped the table a little as she stood and hurried into the kitchen. Soon she was back with a bowl of rice and a pair of chopsticks, but when she realized she would have to get close to the ghost girl to set them down, she hesitated. My father nodded impatiently for her to do it. Very slowly, my mother set the bowl down in front of the ghost, like the girl might reach out and grab her.

The ghost girl nodded her thanks without looking up and shoveled rice into her mouth like she hadn't eaten in weeks.

My mother brought her another bowl, and another. None of us ate. We just watched the ghost girl eat while pretending to stare at our own bowls. I don't think any of us breathed until she stuck her chopsticks into what was left of her third bowl of rice, bowed quickly, and scurried back to my room to hide.

"Did you see?" my mother said. "The way her kimono was wrapped right over left? And the way she left her chopsticks sticking up in her rice?"

"Yes, yes," my father said. "It's clear she is a ghost. But is she a *zashiki warashi*?"

It had begun two weeks ago. Little things at first. Pillows stacked in corners. Blankets flung off beds. One day my stereo started playing a Unicorn Lemon song at full blast while I was gone, and the neighbors banged on the wall before my mother could figure out how to turn it off. Mother and father blamed me, of course, even though I hadn't been there.

Then one night I woke to the sound of giggling. Half awake, half asleep, I saw all my stuffed animals piled on top of each other at the foot of my bed in the dark. And then I saw *her*. The ghost girl. She stood in the corner with her hand over her mouth, giggling.

I screamed. I screamed so loud I woke the whole apartment building. Mother and father came running and turned on the light in my room. When you're scared, you always think turning on the light will make the monsters go away and scare off all the ghosts, but she was still there when the lights came on, the girl with the stringy black hair and the blue and white kimono. I pointed to her, still screaming, but my parents couldn't see her. Not yet. They got mad and turned off the lights and made me be quiet and go back to bed, with the ghost girl still standing there watching me.

I stayed awake all night, watching back.

My parents started to believe me when my father woke one night with something invisible pressing on his chest. He cried out, and when I peeked in my parents' room I could see her, sitting on him and giggling. The next night my mother spread ash on the floor, like they did in the old days, she said, and in the morning there were footprints.

They came from my room, but not from my bed.

We had a ghost, my mother announced. Just like I told them before. But of course neither of them apologized for not believing me.

"A *zashiki warashi*, I think," mother said. She had grown up in the snow country, and her mother had read to her and her sisters all the stories of the *yokai* from *The Tales of Tono*. "If it is, we're lucky. A *zashiki warashi* brings good fortune to the house it chooses."

The day the ghost girl came to breakfast, my father got a big surprise promotion at work and my school wrote to say they were moving me into more advanced classes next year. My mother was beside herself.

"A *zashiki warashi*! It must be. As long as we're happy and show respect, it will stay and bring us good luck. We must not anger it though, or show strife. If we do, it will leave and take its good fortune with it."

Mother and father both looked at me then, like I was the only one who would screw that up.

"You must promise to behave," father told me. "For the sake of the family."

"Fine," I said. But *they* were the ones who were always getting upset over nothing and blaming me for everything.

The ghost girl came back to breakfast the next day, and this time mother and father were all smiles, which was creepier than the ghost girl living in my room. Mother and father never smiled.

"Look, Mayumi," mother said. "It seems you have a new friend."

Father nodded at me, his lips pulled back over his yellow teeth like a fox, and I tried my best to smile.

⌒

I tried. I really did. I wore my tamest outfits. I listened to my new Unicorn Lemon album half as loud as I liked. I stayed in my room day and night reading manga when I could have been down in the tunnel under the tracks at the train station hanging out with my friends. All for the sake of the family.

And it worked. Or it seemed to. Father's big promotion came with a big pay raise, and mother's plot in the community garden grew fat with vegetables while everyone else's withered in the heat. Our family quickly became the most successful one in our apartment building, maybe even our whole neighborhood. My mother and father were delighted.

And then, one morning, the ghost girl came to breakfast wearing a school uniform.

My school uniform.

She wore it differently than I did. She had the long sleeves pulled all the way down, which I never did, even in winter, and she had un-rolled the top of the skirt so it went down below her knees, where I never wore it. The neck ribbon was threaded perfectly through the loop on the blouse, and her socks were pulled all the way up her calf, not pushed down loose like I wore them.

"Don't you look nice today!" my mother told her. Mother took one look at what I was wearing—yellow Sumo Sumo babydoll T-shirt, pink tulle miniskirt over pink-and-white-plaid shorts, and pink socks with rainbow cats on them—and pursed her lips. She didn't have to say what she was thinking. I had heard it all before. *You dress like a prostitute, Mayumi! You have no shame!* Before the *zashiki warashi*, she would have told me so to my face; now she held her tongue.

For the sake of the family.

"Did you hear about Nakayama-san? He resigned yesterday in disgrace," father said. Mr. Nakayama lived on the third floor of our apartment building and worked in the same office as father. "There was a flaw in his database program. Hundreds of thousands of medical records were made public. Word has gotten around. He'll never be able to find work now."

"Oh! That's too bad," mother said. "And his wife has taken ill. She's in the hospital with food poisoning. Mrs. Wada says she may not survive. And they have a daughter your age, don't they, Mayumi? What's her name?"

"Hotaru," said the ghost girl. We all jumped. It was the first word she had ever spoken. She stared down at her bowl without moving, the way she had the first morning she'd joined us at breakfast.

"Yes. Yes, I think that's it," mother said.

None of us said anything more all meal. When I was finished, I got up to go back to my room for another day of sitting around reading manga. The ghost girl helped clear the dishes.

"Oh! Aren't you so helpful!" mother said.

All that day while I sat in my room listening to music and reading, the ghost girl worked. She washed the dishes. She swept the floors. She hung the laundry out to dry. When all the housework was done, she pulled out my schoolbooks and sat at the table studying. During summer break!

I turned up my Unicorn Lemon album and hid behind a stack of manga on my bed.

When my father got home from work, the ghost girl brought him beer and massaged his feet.

"Such a wonderful child!" he said. "You could learn a lesson from her," he told me. "Show your parents the same respect."

That night, I dyed my hair pink.

Mother and father cornered me in my room when they saw it, shouting at me.

"What could you be thinking?"

"Why would you disgrace us in this way?"

"We agreed. No trouble. For the sake of the family."

"Do you want the *zashiki warashi* to leave? Do you want us to lose the boons she has brought us?"

"Yes!" I told them. "Yes. I hate her!"

My father raised a hand to strike me, but he froze. The ghost girl stood in the doorway, watching. I didn't know how long she had been there, or how much she had heard. None of us did.

"*No strife*," my mother whispered desperately. "*There must be no strife!*"

My father lowered his hand and smiled his fake yellow smile. "No strife," he said. Together, he and my mother bowed their way out of the room.

The ghost girl stayed where she was in the doorway, staring at me.

The rest of the week, my parents didn't look me in the eyes, and they only spoke to me to tell me to do things. The ghost girl ignored me too. I thought she would be mad at me, or play tricks on me, but she went around the apartment pretending I wasn't there. After a while, my parents stopped talking to me altogether too. Whatever. I didn't want to talk to any of them either. I stayed in my room and listened to my music and read my magazines. For the sake of the family.

On the morning of my fourteenth birthday, I came to breakfast to find only three places set. My heart leaped. Was the *zashiki warashi* finally gone at last?

"Good morning!" my mother said, smiling her fake smile. They were the first words she had spoken to me in days.

"Good morning," said a voice behind me. It was the ghost girl. That's who my mother had been talking to, not me. The ghost girl walked right past me and took her place at the table with my parents, and they all began to eat.

Without me.

I sat down at the table and stared at my parents, waiting for them to notice I had no food.

"Don't think I've forgotten what today is," my father said. He held a silver and gold present out over the table in both hands and bowed. "Happy birthday!"

I was stunned. They had forgotten to give me breakfast, but remembered my birthday? I reached out for the gift, but the ghost girl snatched it and opened it.

"A Monster Island Zero *bento* box!" she said. It was shaped like the turtle in the anime series, with a shell that lifted off to reveal the separate compartments for your lunch. I had wanted one just like it since last school year.

"It's not her birthday, it's mine," I told them.

"Now you can replace your old one," mother told the ghost girl.

"*My* old one, you mean," I said.

"Thank you! Thank you!" the ghost girl said.

"It is nothing," my father told her. "You are the best daughter we could ever wish for."

"*I'm* your daughter!" I said. I slammed my fist on the table, and the bowls and glasses rattled.

"What in the world?" father said. He reached to steady the dishes.

"Is it an earthquake?" the ghost girl said.

"You know it's not an earthquake!" I yelled. "I'm sitting right here! *I'm* your daughter, not her!"

"Maybe it's the downstairs neighbors," mother said. "They're always fighting."

"Why are you doing this?" I asked. "Am I being punished?"

My father stood. "I'll be late at the office again tonight. The vice president has asked me to stay late with him, to prepare for the conference. I think he has me in mind as his replacement when he retires."

"Oh, that's very fortunate indeed," mother said. She smiled at the ghost girl, and they got up to see my father to the door.

I went to my room and turned my stereo up as loud as it would go, blasting Unicorn Lemon so loud my toy figures vibrated off the shelves. Mother and the ghost girl rushed in.

"There! You can't ignore me now!" I said. I stood right in front of the controls. They would have to talk to me or move me out of the way to turn it off.

Mother went right through me instead.

It felt like stepping into a cold water spa after soaking in an *onsen*. I shuddered and staggered away, my skin prickling with goose bumps. My mother must have felt it too. She shivered and pulled her *yukata* close up to her neck.

"Oh! Such a cold draft! There must be a storm coming," she said.

The ghost girl turned off the stereo, and the room was suddenly quiet. I stared at my hands and arms, wondering how mother had been able to pass right through me. I felt like I was dreaming.

"How did the music play when you weren't here?" mother asked.

"I don't know," the ghost girl said. "Perhaps the stereo's defective. We can sell it tomorrow anyway. It only distracts me from my studies."

"Such a good girl," mother said. She kissed the ghost girl on the forehead. "Happy birthday, Mayumi."

I backed away until I hit the corner of the room and slumped to the floor. *She called the ghost girl Mayumi.* But I was Mayumi.

Wasn't I?

The ghost girl climbed onto my bed with a stack of manga. She opened one and started reading. I don't know how long I stared at her before she finally felt my eyes on her and looked up.

"Oh, are you still here?" the ghost girl said. "Go away. Go. You're not welcome here."

That night, mother left the front door open while she took the trash and the recycling downstairs for collection, and I slipped out with the rest of the things my family didn't want anymore.

᠆᠆

It began in the fall after Yumiko went back to school, and it began with little things. Yumiko's manga stacked in a tower as tall as she was. Her father's ties all worked into knots. Every shoe pulled out of the shoe closet by the front door and stuffed into the cat's little house. Yumiko was blamed at first—she was almost thirteen, but her parents still blamed her for *everything*—but soon it was obvious she couldn't be doing it all.

"A *zashiki warashi*, I think," Yumiko's father said. "But we must be sure." His grandmother had once spread ash on the floor to catch a *yokai* in the act, he told them. All they had was flour, but it worked just as well. The next morning there were footprints all through the house. Footprints that came from Yumiko's closet.

A *zashiki warashi* was a good omen, Yumiko's father told them. When a *zashiki warashi* came to live with you, good fortune smiled upon the whole house. And there had already been good fortune, to be sure. Yumiko had made the soccer team at school when another girl broke her leg, and mother had sold six paintings to a gallery in Shibuya.

"But we must always have harmony," father explained. "If we argue or complain or become mad, the *zashiki warashi* will leave, and our good luck will turn to bad luck."

"That means no sneaking out to skateboard with your friends," mother told Yumiko. "And no more talking back to your teachers."

"For the sake of the family," father said.

"Fine," Yumiko said. She would try. For the sake of the family.

The next morning, the ghost girl came to breakfast. She was about Yumiko's age and size, and wore a blue and white kimono. And was that a hint of pink Yumiko saw in her hair? Yumiko's mother and father froze, torn between pretending not to notice the ghost girl and not wanting to offend her. Finally Yumiko's mother put a bowl of miso soup in front of her, and the ghost girl slurped it up like she hadn't eaten in weeks.

"Look, Yumiko," her mother said. "It seems you have a new friend."

Yumiko's mother and father smiled big, fake smiles, pretending to be happy.

"Oh! Did you hear about the Aoki family on the fifth floor?" father said. "Aoki-san is drunk all the time now, and sleeps in the park. It's said he overslept one morning, and failed to bring his boss's presentation to a big conference. He was fired in disgrace."

"That's so sad," Yumiko's mother said. "I hear too that his wife tripped on the vines in her plot in the community garden and broke her neck. Such an irony! Hers was the only garden growing in this heat."

"Didn't they have a daughter?" Yumiko's father asked. "A girl your age, I think, Yumiko. What was her name?"

The ghost girl spoke, startling them all. "Her name," she said, "was Mayumi."

House of Trust

by Sachiko Kashiwaba

translated by Avery Fischer Udagawa

My mother wore a strange frown.

"Hajime, is it true you've been taking kimono fitting classes? Mrs. Tamura from across the street said to me, 'So, I see Hajime-chan goes to the kimono school over by the train station.' I was shocked!"

I nodded. Mom's frown grew deeper.

"Why are you going to a place like that? When did you start?"

"First year of middle school."

"Three years ago . . ." She fell silent.

"I have a good teacher," I told her. "It's this older lady named Tsuki Sasaki. She must be close to seventy. She said that since I'm a guy, the other students and I might be uncomfortable around each other in classes, so she gives me private lessons once a month. My allowance more than covers the fee."

I kept talking to try and wipe the frown from Mom's face, but she was looking at me as if seeing her son of sixteen years for the first time.

"Mrs. Tamura must have seen me when I helped out the other day," I continued. "Whenever there's a big tea ceremony or something and dozens of people have to put on kimono, Tsuki-sensei gets hired and she dresses them. But she's getting on in years, so with a large group of people, she gets tired just tying all the *obi*. So I get pulled in to help. It's a great job. Tsuki-sensei pays me well. And the people like me—they say that when a guy ties the *obi*, they don't come undone. I could get a license to teach kimono fitting if I wanted. Tsuki-sensei says I should. She told me it's always been men who have tied the *obi* for geishas and apprentice geishas."

"Is that the kind of work you want to do, Hajime?"

"Not really."

"Then why? Why do you have to learn kimono fitting? And how could you go off to that place without telling your parents!" She slapped the table, her eyes narrowing.

She acted like I had been going someplace horrible. But the masters of the schools of tea ceremony and traditional flower arrangement are men, and a lot of men study those arts. There are even cooking classes for men only. So why was my taking kimono lessons such a big deal? And I hadn't kept it a secret.

"I told you I wanted to learn kimono fitting."

"When?"

"When I was in sixth grade. Don't you remember?"

"You did?"

"I did. You said you were going to teach me yourself, but then you didn't."

My mother frowned. "Hmm . . . I did help you put on a *yukata* that one winter, didn't I?"

"Exactly. You taught me how do a *yukata* and then nothing else, remember? But I figured out pretty quickly that you go running to the beauty shop whenever you have to wear a kimono, so you were probably the wrong person to ask."

"Nobody needs to know how to put on a kimono without help. If you can wear a *yukata*, that's plenty. Plus you're a boy. Hajime, please tell me you're not doing this because you want to wear a *furi*, a *furi* . . ." Her voice choked and she began to cry with big tears.

I finally understood why she was getting so worked up. *Furisode* are the long-sleeved showpiece kimono worn by young women at coming-of-age ceremonies and weddings. What was my mother thinking? I'm almost five feet ten inches tall and a hundred fifty-five pounds. I guess I'm on the skinny side. But thanks to the swimming I've been doing since grade school, my shoulders at least are broader than average. Just what kind of *furisode* did she think would fit me?

I started laughing.

"There's nothing funny about it!" Mom yelled.

I was wondering what to do about this when the telephone rang.

Having seen that her son was apparently not learning kimono fitting because he wanted to wear a *furisode*, Mom had at least stopped crying. After glaring at me to make sure I stayed put, she picked up the phone.

"It's for you, Hajime. It's your father." She held out the receiver.

"*Hajime, is that you?*" said my father's voice. "*Tomorrow's the day. Get over here quick.*"

I knew immediately what he was talking about.

"Got it. I'm on my way!"

I already had my jacket in my hand.

"Where do you think you're going?" my mother called as I headed out the door. "We're not finished here!"

"To Dad's shop. Look, I'll quit the kimono lessons."

After saying that, I jumped on my bike. The timing could not have been better. The lessons were all for this moment.

↜

Three years ago, my father quit his job at a company and opened a small handyman shop on the outskirts of town.

"Even if you do have to change jobs, why a handyman shop?" Mom was always grumpy in those days.

"Working with my hands is all I'm good at," Dad told her. "Plus I'm not qualified for anything else. Look, if I can just get the customers to trust me, I'll have plenty of work." He named his shop House of Trust. He was so excited he was like a different person.

Mom and I both knew that the corporate world was no fit for Dad, a quiet man who wasn't very good at socializing. In his tiny one-man shop, he was able to work just the way he wanted to and seemed happy. I was thrilled to see my father acting like that and began to hang out at the shop every day after school.

↜

On that particular day three years ago, a light snow was falling just like today. The mountains were already covered in snow.

A bare concrete floor. A kerosene heater. A wooden desk and vinyl couch bought from the secondhand store. My father and I used to sit on that couch and do nothing but play *shogi*. Despite Dad's excitement about starting his business, he only occasionally had jobs, and it was mainly my *shogi* skills that were going somewhere.

It was dark outside already, so I think it was after four o'clock. The glass door to the shop opened briskly and, along with a dusting of snow, a woman came rushing inside. She was tall.

"Is it true a handyman will do whatever job people need?" she asked, almost yelling.

She must have come in a big hurry, because her cheeks were flushed and her whole body was practically steaming. Her hair was very long but tousled, and she wore a slightly dirty down coat over a worn-out sweater. If her hair had been shorter, I swear I would have mistaken her for a man.

My father nodded. "Whatever you need," he said.

"Good. The old fellow I always used to go to died, and I don't know anybody else I can ask. I tried a housekeeping service, but they only list women. I can't work with women." She pulled a piece of paper from her coat pocket. "The address is here. You won't need my name. There's only one house in the area anyway. Please come by tomorrow morning at nine."

She started to leave.

My father hurried to stop her. "What would you like me to do? I'll have to prepare."

"You don't have to bring anything. I want you to clean," the woman said. "And I want you to do my kimono and my hair," she added.

"Kimono and hair . . . ?" My father's words trailed off.

Dad could deftly handle carpentry work, appliance repair, cooking, and even sewing, but he had never even imagined that he would be asked to do a job like this.

"Whatever I need . . . right?" The woman knit her eyebrows.

"Perhaps if you tried a beauty salon . . . ," Dad suggested.

"I can't work with women!" she shouted.

"There are male beauticians."

"The only beauticians who could do kimono were women. I've been running around this whole day searching, and I'm out of time. You told me you would take the job. How can you call this place House of Trust?" The woman stamped her foot like a spoiled child.

It seemed like the flame in the kerosene heater grew smaller all of a sudden. My spine tingled and I scooted closer to Dad. I was sure he was going to turn the job down, but to my surprise he said, "Very well. I'll see what I can do."

He could just have been reacting to those words, "How can you call this place House of Trust?" But looking back, I think he actually accepted the job because, even though she was yelling at him, the woman looked desperate.

"Oh, good," she said. "I actually have a marriage interview tomorrow. It's last-minute and I was in a panic." She laughed a little as if embarrassed.

Her face looked kind of pretty then, even to me. It hit me for the first time that she was young.

The woman left, and my father unfolded the piece of paper with the address on it. "Gentagoya?" he said. He tilted his head quizzically, and then his jaw dropped. "That's the climbers' rest hut clear up on Mount Takamori! I'll have to leave now or there's no way I can even make it there by tomorrow morning." He paused. "But I thought the newspaper said old Mr. Genta died and the hut might be closed now. And it ought to be closed for winter in the first place—has been since he was alive."

"Maybe the person who just came in here was his successor?" I offered.

"Could be. And maybe we're not into true winter yet."

Dad and I both grew convinced of those things.

"Anyway, I'd better get ready. Hajime, I'm going home to prepare for the climb. You go to the bookstore and buy whatever you can find about how to put on a kimono and do hair," my father requested.

I ended up climbing Mount Takamori together with Dad the next day. It was a Sunday, and he seemed nervous about going by himself.

Mount Takamori is one of the taller mountains near my town. It has unusual alpine plants and even a swamp that features in local legend. In the summer it has a lot of climbers, but it's a bit of a tough course in wintertime if you're not really into mountaineering.

We drove as far up Mount Takamori as possible and spent the night in the car. Both my father and I were so focused on getting to Gentagoya—more than two-thirds of the way up the mountain—by nine in the morning, that we completely forgot we were supposed to help put on a kimono and fix a woman's hair once we got there.

We reached the top third of the mountain as the sun was rising. The mountainside was already covered with snow, but the sky was clear and the sun was warm, and we were sweating when we reached Gentagoya just before nine o'clock. It was perfect climbing weather, but we didn't see anybody else on the mountain. Later, I heard that there were severe blizzards on the lower half of the mountain that day.

Gentagoya consisted of nothing but a simple cooking area and a large room with a wooden floor. Both the doors and the windows were flung wide open, and the woman from the day before was unfolding her kimono in the large room. The kimono was the same blush of vermilion red that the sky turns just before sunrise. Even now, I still remember that color.

My father cleaned the hut, and I heated water in the steel barrel bathtub behind the building.

While the woman bathed, Dad and I opened up the books I had bought. We decided to sweep the woman's hair into a high bun called *odango*, and to tie her *obi* into a drum-shaped knot called *otaiko*, since the book said it was the most common style.

Dad and I are both pretty good with our hands. I would like to say we did fairly well for a first attempt, but I couldn't, even to flatter myself. The woman's coil of hair, which was as thick and long as a large snake, ended up towering over her head like a Tibetan temple stupa supported by dozens of pins. Her *obi*, which we somehow managed to tie, stuck flat against her back like a dried squid. And she seemed to find it hard to move, probably because we tied everything too tight.

Still, she was beautiful. It seemed impossible that she could have looked like a man the day before. I'm sure my father thought so too. But still he told her, "There will be no charge."

I agreed with not charging her. This was a matter of trust.

"But you got it done somehow," she said. "I could never have put this on by myself. This is the only nice kimono I have."

The woman seemed happy just to be able to wear the vermilion kimono, and acted so pleased with our inferior effort that we were even more embarrassed.

Just then, I felt strongly that I wanted to arrange the kimono more beautifully for her. I really did. "Allow us to do a better job next time," I said loudly. "I will practice."

I actually said "next time," even though she was meeting a potential groom. . . .

She started to give me a look, but then she chuckled. "Next time," she said as we were leaving, "you'd better tie me a *fukura suzume*."

Back then, I had no idea what that meant. But I found out later from Tsuki-sensei that when someone wears a *furisode*, you tie the *obi* into a "plump sparrow" shape, or *fukura suzume*. It's especially flattering on tall women.

Heading back down the mountain, my father muttered, "That person, she couldn't be possibly be the *kami* of the mountain, could she? Her dislike of women and all?"

I too thought she might be the mountain's *kami*, or spirit, but I didn't say anything.

⌒

I have no idea what happened to Gentagoya after that. A paved hiking course opened up on the other side of the mountain, so everybody began to climb from that direction instead. A new mountain hut was also built on the side opposite Gentagoya.

And my father and I have never spoken about our experience there. Dad never asks me whether I am taking kimono lessons. I never ask him anything either. But I know that he has been going to hairdressing school, because sometimes he comes home smelling like my mother does after she gets a perm.

We haven't said a word, but my father called me today. That's because he trusts me. And together, we are going to put the trust back in House of Trust. I can tie an *obi* into a *fukura suzume*, a *bunko*, you name it. I can even tie *hakama*. As for Dad, I bet he can sweep that long hair up into any hairstyle you could imagine.

I open the door to the shop to find Dad tying the laces on his hiking boots. "Another marriage interview?" I ask.

"Nope. A wedding," he answers.

And he smiles.

Staring at the Haiku

by John Paul Catton

The story goes like this:

A young trainee teacher is patrolling long, empty high school corridors, making sure all students have gone home. His footsteps echo down the halls, and beyond the windows it's already dark, the hot, steamy twilight of a Japanese July. He's nervous; summer is the time for ghost stories, and all kinds of tales are going through his head.

Then he hears crying.

It's coming from the end of the corridor. He walks through pools of shadow to the classroom, opens the door, steps inside. He flicks the switch; the lights don't work. Strange. But in the dark he can make out a girl, in school uniform, sitting at one of the desks. She's turned away from him, her head hanging down, long black hair over her face, and sobbing like her heart's broken.

"Every student should have gone home," he says, trying to keep his voice firm.

The girl doesn't turn around, just keeps on sobbing, her hair masking her face, and the teacher is feeling creeped out by now.

"Are you all right? What are you doing here on your own?"

He walks into the classroom, reaching out a hand, and gently taps the girl on the shoulder. As quick as a striking snake, the girl turns toward him, her hands snatching at the teacher's arm with razor-sharp nails. She flicks back her long hair, and her face . . .

Her face is . . .

Her face, is like . . .

Well, *what do you think it was like?* Welcome to . . .

www.yokai.com

which is the most amazing blog *ever* on Japanese ghosts, written by yours truly Tomoe Kanzaki! In English! I'm seventeen years old and a student in the Global Studies class for returnees, here at Chiyoda High. Now I'll let the other ghostbusting ghostbloggers in the Club introduce themselves—scroll down for the introductions!

> *Hi, I'm Shunsuke Wakita. My birthday's January 27th and my blood type is B. I like PE, and I'm in the baseball club at school. My family lived in Ohio for three years and Frankfurt for two years. My ambition is to get into a good university—or become an F1 racer. Yoroshiku onegai shimasu.*

> *Hi, I'm Xin Yao Liu! I'm an exchange student in Japan for a year, and I'm from Chongqing in southwest China. My strong point is I'm a quick reader—I can finish a novel in less than a day. My ambition? I'm interested in science, so I'd like to be a pharmacist.*

> *I'm Hideaki Sakamoto. I like all sports, but I'm in the* kendo *club. I like animals, pasta, Japanese curry-rice, going to karaoke parties, hanging out in Shibuya. In the future I'd like to travel around the world and then get into male modeling. Or maybe the other way around.*

> *I'm Reiko Bergman. I'm half Japanese, or a* haafu, *as they say here. My father's American and my mother's Japanese, and we lived in New York for eight years. My other nickname is Rekijo, which means "History Girl," but I'm not a geek! I just like stories from long ago, and I've got a good memory.*

And like I said, I'm Tomoe, and this is my blog. I could tell you more about myself, but I won't, because we've got ghost stories to deal with!!

↝

Assignment 1: Staring at the Haiku

The last two weeks of February. The time of year for final exams, graduation ceremony, and then spring break, when every teenager within a hundred kilometers of Tokyo tries to get into Tokyo Disneyland at the same time. It's also the season for Girls' Day, on March 3rd, when families put up a special display of Japanese-style dolls in their houses, and have *hamaguri* clam soup with sweet *sake* to celebrate. For some reason Boys' Day on May 5th is a national holiday but on Girls' Day we still have to go to school. Boys get all the lucky breaks, huh?

So there we were, with the finals done and grades given out, looking forward to a break with no lessons or homework, when—bang! The craziest thing happened! The junior high school girls started talking about a miracle in the Calligraphy Room!

It started just after Valentine's Day, and news spread around the whole school and soon everybody was totally OMG. Except the teachers, of course. The teachers were more concerned with the principal's new toy—a set of antique dolls that he'd put on display in the third floor lobby for Girls' Day. Go figure.

So what kind of miracle was it? The juniors said if you put a blank sheet of calligraphy paper on the wall before you went home, the next morning the first *kanji* character of your future boyfriend's name would be written on it! So if you saw a character pronounced "*ma*"—like, maybe

摩

then your boyfriend could be Masahiro, or Masatoshi, or Masataka! And you know what junior high girls are like—they all believed it!

So, about ten days after this miracle had started, we held the very first Ghost Blogging Club meeting in the Chiyoda Station Starbuck's after school. I was the chairman, and also the note-taker, and I explained in great detail the nature of Assignment 1.

"You are the freakiest person I ever met," Reiko said, after I'd finished.

"Thank you!"

"It wasn't a compliment," she added, shaking her head.

That's just how she is.

"I don't need to find out my boyfriend's name like this!" said Xin Yao.

"Because you've already got a boyfriend?" Hideaki muttered.

"Come on, guys," I said, in my Madam Chairman voice. "Something amazing is going on, right? This is like those stranger-than-fiction TV specials, like those stories of statues that weep blood and drink milk."

"Or statues that drink blood and weep milk," said Hideaki, digging Shunsuke in the ribs.

"Shut up!" Xin Yao yelled, and I thanked her and quickly brought her into the discussion, as our resident calligraphy expert. I asked her if there was anything special about the paper used in the Calligraphy Room. I gave her a few sheets I'd secretly 'borrowed' today and she held them up to the light.

"It looks like just ordinary paper and ink to me," she said. "Smells like it, too."

"Oh, come on," said Hideaki, leaning back in his chair. "It's all a joke, right? Someone steals the key, gets into the Calligraphy Room after school, puts something on the wall, and laughs at the juniors the next day."

"That would be the obvious answer," I said, "and this is my proposal for ruling it out. Hideaki, your mom and dad gave you a little Minoru robot with a stereo webcam inside it, right?"

"Yeah. It was a free sample from one of my dad's clients."

"How about," I said, trying not to grin too much, "if we put it in the Calligraphy Room to monitor what happens, and we do an all-night vigil from our bedrooms?"

"Keep it online all night?" Shunsuke cried. "How much is *that* going to cost?"

"Got a flat monthly rate from J-Com," Hideaki said with a shrug.

"There is no way I'm staying awake all night for this," said Reiko hotly. "I'm up until twelve every night doing homework already!"

"Doesn't have to be all night," I kept on. "We take turns—one hour each, and when the hour's up, we call the next person."

"Spying on the school?" Hideaki nodded slowly. "Yeah, okay! Why not."

"You'd better put the webcam somewhere the teacher won't find it," I said.

"I'll make up some errand and go in early in the morning and take the camera out," said Shunsuke.

"I'll come in with you and distract the teacher so she doesn't notice," said Xin Yao.

"I'll stand in the background and whistle the *Mission: Impossible* theme," said Hideaki.

The first investigation of www.yokai.com *had begun*!!!

∽

The next morning, after a disturbed sleep broken by an hour of staring at a darkened computer monitor, I met the other bloggers in the homeroom, when all the other kids were at the lockers or eating early morning snacks.

"You didn't see *anything*?"

"It was too dark," whined Xin Yao. "I could see the paper's faint outline, but nothing else."

There were slow nods all round.

"Was there anything written on it when you came in?" I asked Shunsuke.

"Yeah, the juniors were all over it. But it wasn't *kanji*. It was the *hiragana* character for '*mo*.'"

"So somebody's going to have a boyfriend called . . . Motoki?" Hideaki asked.

In math, we learned that two negatives make a positive, or something like that; and as I listened to my classmates gripe over the sleep they lost, I suddenly realized—with a big shock of happiness—the negatives they brought to the table added up, in fact, to one big positive. Which is not mathematically sound, but it was lucky for us.

"Guys! Nobody came into the Calligraphy Room, right? So however this is happening, it's not a junior or senior sneaking in to write something as a joke! We've got a genuine case of paranormal activity on our hands!"

Blank looks turned into shifty sidelong glances as everyone tried not to look scared.

"So what do we do now?" asked Shunsuke.

"I think I'll talk to the Calligraphy Club members again," said Xin Yao. "I don't know if they've still got the original papers, but I'd like to know which *kanji* have appeared on the wall."

"Good idea," I said. "While you're doing the legwork, let's find out what happens—if there's no paper on the wall."

So that night, after the latest crowd of giggling juniors had put up a blank sheet of paper in the 'special' place on the wall, Xin Yao and I went in and took it down again.

‿

The next morning the homeroom teacher told us of a special announcement from the principal, broadcast over the PA to every classroom. Uh-oh, we thought, he's found out about the "miracle" and he's going to warn us about impressionable young minds and not believing gossip or whatever.

Nope. Instead of that, he spent the whole ten minutes of homeroom time telling us not to touch the antique dolls. Apparently they'd been moved during the night, although I hadn't noticed anything when I walked right past them that morning.

Men and their dolls. Brrrrr . . .

‿

"Tomoe, Tomoe, you've gotta see this!" Xin Yao said from the door to the Calligraphy Room. She had the keys, so the five of us locked ourselves in, keeping the juniors out.

There was a new *kanji* character. Written *on the wall* in the place where the paper would have been.

読

We got up close and peered at it. It was the verb "to read." It looked kind of gross; it hadn't been drawn with a brush, it was clumps of dark spots and stains that were almost . . . organic.

"What *is* that stuff?"

"Not ink," said Xin Yao. She leaned forward, and recoiled with a face like a lemon. "It smells like . . . *mold*."

"We've gotta clean this off," said Shunsuke.

"But this is *evidence*!" I said.

"Evidence for who? We've seen it, that's enough. I'll take a picture with my cell phone. If the teacher sees it, she'll go crazy."

We had no idea how crazy things were going to get!

↜

I went through the rest of the day in a trance, unable to concentrate on lessons, until Xin Yao came up to me after school and said breathlessly, "I think I've got something."

"What?"

"I've been going through all the *kanji* the Calligraphy Club members gave me. Sen-Botsu-Tai-Sho-Ni and the rest. We thought the characters meant boys' names, like Tsuyoshi or Taishi or Shotaro, but they don't. If you put them together, the whole thing spells a *haiku*!"

She handed me the paper. From top to bottom, and right to left, she'd brushed hasty but elegant *kanji* characters. In English, the poem said:

> *Of our battles lost*
> *Banners speak of fate; Omens read*
> *In death we meet again.*

"And this means?"

"It's a poem from the late Sengoku Civil War period," she said, "composed by one of Shogun Tokugawa's samurai generals. The *kanji* on the wall this morning was *yo*, right? That means the next one tomorrow should be *shin*, beginning the poem's final line."

"The *kanji* for death." My head was spinning, and I felt my skin break out in goosebumps. "Xin Yao—you're a genius! Now, if we could only figure out *how* and *why* this is turning up on our wall. . . ."

↜

Every answer we got was raising more questions. To tell the truth, after school that day I felt like leaving it alone, before things got any weirder, but like my dad always says, "Don't give up."

He also said, "Tomoe, do what you're best at." And as it turns out, that means investigating funky paranormal stuff. Who knew?

Speaking of the old guys, that night I got home and Mom was yakking on the phone to her club cronies. Ballroom dancing—she's off every Sunday with her friends in tacky costumes, but she says that's how she keeps her figure. While we waited for Dad to get home for dinner I went up to my room, put the headphones on and started blasting out Spacecandle so I could concentrate.

Spacecandle. Only the best Japanese rock band *ever*. They helped me get through reviewing for all my exams so far, so they'd help me with this. I lay on the bed, headphones on, staring at the haiku.

Hmmmm. If I ever form a rock band, which is my ambition, I'm going to call the first album "Staring at the Haiku."

Just before Dad called "*Tadaima!*" as he slipped his shoes off in the parlor, the answer hit me.

〰️

"We've been looking at it the wrong way," I told them the next day, when we all gathered in the Calligraphy Room. "It's not the *kanji* themselves."

"So what is it?"

"It's the wall."

Shunsuke made a face. "There's something special about the wall of the Calligraphy Room?"

"Yeah, there is," I told him with pride. "It faces the *kimon*. You know what the *kimon* is?"

"Yeah, sure." Shunsuke threw a sidelong glance at Hideaki. "Not really."

I pointed to the big window running along the wall of the room. "The *kimon*—the demon gate. The old superstition that says spirits enter and exit the world of the living from the northeast; that's why there are so many temples and shrines in northeast Tokyo."

"A line of defense," muttered Reiko, nodding.

"The haiku is a message," said Xin Yao. "It's trying to tell us something."

"A message from who?"

We all moved to the window. Central Tokyo stretched away from us, towers of steel and glass shining in the sharp winter light, and not far away, the tranquil green of the Imperial Palace gardens.

"The flow of spirit energy," I said, "is entering the building from this direction, so it's passing that way." I turned around, and pointed to the door.

"Over there?" Hideaki said. "There's only the staircase."

"And the windows."

"And a janitor's storeroom on the landing. You think the janitor's doing it?"

Reiko opened the door.

"And the *dolls*," we all said at the same time.

〜

Dolls. And not just any dolls.

Usually, Girls' Day dolls were little figures wearing traditional Japanese costumes. A medium-size display had one emperor, one empress, three ladies-in-waiting, three male attendants, and five court musicians. But ours were different. There were eleven male retainers wearing samurai armor from the Sengoku Civil War Period, and one female doll dressed in kimono as the general's wife—but the general's doll was conspicuously missing. According to the plaque on the wall, the dolls had been in school storage for many years, but were brought out especially for this year, the four hundredth anniversary of the Siege of the Kodaira Garrison in western Japan.

"I might have guessed it was dolls," Xin Yao said when we were in Starbuck's again. "Dolls are so freaky."

Hideaki looked up from his café latte. "Why are you so scared of them?"

"There was a doll once. It freaked me out." She glared angrily back at him. "End of story, okay?"

"I'm getting really confused now," said Shunsuke. "This started off as a so-called miracle, but we're now investigating a bunch of spooky *dolls*?"

I turned to Reiko. Or more correctly, I held up my cell phone. This was her night for exam prep at cram school, but she was sending text messages every ten minutes.

"The Kodaira Garrison was about to be overrun by the forces of the invading Shogun Toyotomi Hideyoshi," I said, reading from Reiko's text. "General Hasegawa and his eleven men chose to stay behind and engage the enemy, giving their lord, Tokugawa Ieyasu, time to regroup.

The night before their last battle, Hasegawa composed his suicide poem. The next day, every last man was cut down in combat as the garrison burned around them."

We all sat quietly around the table for a while, just taking it all in.

"But there are only eleven dolls," said Shunsuke eventually. "Where's the leader? Where's the General Hasegawa doll?"

I held up the cell phone again. "This is the clincher, guys. There *was* a doll in the likeness of General Hasegawa, but it was badly damaged in the 1923 Great Kanto Earthquake and laid to rest in Kosenji temple near Roppongi. There's a special part of the grounds where broken toys and dolls are laid to rest."

"You've got to be kidding," said Hideaki.

"The Shinto religion says everything has a soul," Xin Yao mused. "Even dolls."

"So these dolls have been in storage for decades, until the principal puts them on display for the anniversary, " said Hideaki.

"Somehow, it awakens their spirits, and they become . . . aware," said Xin Yao.

"They sense the final thoughts of their dying general, from across Tokyo," said Shunsuke.

"And across the centuries," I added. "Thoughts that take form on the wall of our school where the dolls are displayed."

"And they're going to do what?" said Hideaki, almost as if he was angry. "Follow their general into the great Doll Afterlife?"

"Whatever they're going to do," said Xin Yao, "they'll probably do it three nights from now. That's when the haiku ends. And . . ." She looked at me. "Oh, no. No, Tomoe! We're not going to!"

But of course, we were.

↫

If you want to secretly stay behind in school after the premises have been locked up, it's not impossible. All you have to do is find a nice dark place and be absolutely quiet. Which is maybe impossible for Hideaki, but you know what I mean. The security guards are retired *salarimen* who spend most of the night in their cabin with their TV and boxed dinners, and there are security cameras at the school entrances, but not inside the corridors. In Chiyoda High, students have individual keys to their lockers, but there's no lock on the door to the Locker Room itself on the second floor. So that's where we hid.

We stayed there until six. When we opened the door and crept out, the corridors were in darkness, with white security lights shining out onto the tennis ground and the trees. Hideaki and Shunsuke took up the lead, with the wooden swords borrowed from the *kendo* club. I was behind, and Reiko and Xin Yao took up the rear (holding hands—hah!). We tiptoed down the corridor and got to the stairwell leading to the Calligraphy Room, and then—that's where we saw them.

They weren't dolls.

Not anymore.

Nine tall shadows stood above us, the dim light reflecting from iron and leather masks, battered chest plates, leather gloves covered in nameless stains. The two horns of a crescent moon insignia gleamed upon their helmets, and their swords hung at their sides.

Someone gave a muffled scream; it could have been Reiko or Xin Yao. Or maybe me. Shunsuke and Hideaki huddled together, their wooden swords held up in front of them. Even in semidarkness, I could tell their faces had gone white.

With shaking hands, I flipped open my cell phone, switched on the video camera, and held it up in front of my face like a talisman.

The nine figures moved down the stairs like smoke. Their outlines were misted, almost transparent. The corridor filled with a whispering, like echoes in a cave, and the overpowering smell of forest earth and decaying leaves.

We followed them, because we couldn't stop ourselves. They melted into the glass of the windows and reappeared on the other side, in the courtyard. They marched silently into the trees. We ran to the window and pressed our faces up to the glass, and I saw the last man in the line turn back. He lifted up his head, his great dark mask with horribly blank eyeholes in the battle-scarred metal—and he bowed to us, arms straight by his side, in formal Japanese style.

Then he melted into the Tokyo night like he'd never been there at all.

⌒

The next day the school was pretty quiet.

It wasn't obvious that the police were there; one patrol car was parked discreetly at the back entrance. The principal was trying to keep the lid on the fact that his entire display of dolls had disappeared—but there were no signs of a break-in.

At our post-mission debriefing at Starbuck's, I looked around the café; there were tables of juniors giggling about boys and zit cream and pop idols, student types with their books and their headphones screwed into their ears to shut themselves away, the young *salarimen* with their laptops and schedules taking a break between sales appointments . . . none of them knew. None of them knew what *we* knew.

That there was another world beyond this one.

And my team, my club, my *nakama*—I looked around the table at them, as they looked soberly back at me.

"I'm sorry," I said eventually.

Shunsuke did a double take. "Why?"

I shrugged. "Well, for one thing, the cell phone video didn't come out. We can't put that on the blog because it's too dark to see anything. And I feel kind of bad for getting you into this."

"We voted on staying," said Xin Yao.

"Yeah, but they were all . . ." I made a mask gesture with my hands over my face.

"I think 'they were all dead' is what she's trying to say," put in Hideaki.

"Thanks." I took a deep breath. "Maybe I made a mistake. Maybe we should just forget ghosts and concentrate on the living."

"I don't think so," said Reiko.

We all looked at her.

"Now, we know some happenings are not just coincidences, right? There are things that people never talk about but that doesn't mean they don't exist. I think we should find out how many of these old stories are based on some kind of truth. I think we *should* do it; it's a responsibility."

"A responsibility to a world that can't be seen," said Xin Yao, with a funny look in her eyes.

I raised my Frappuccino in salute. "That was really well put, Reiko. We've got a mission!"

Clink!

That would have been the noise our toast made if we had glasses instead of paper cups. But there it was, our new brotherhood and our first mission, sealed with coffee and juice.

"What the heck," snorted Hideaki. "This is more fun than the *kendo* club."

DAY 2

Woke up dead tired. BIZARRO dreams last night ♪

Visited zillions of shrines + temples today (yes, I counted).

BLA BLAH BLA BORING BLA... *

MRS. TANAKA ("MRS. T") - Resident Chaperone + Tour Guide

(ok, but a little weird)

* Thank god I have my sketchbook!

Amy saw me drawing, asked if she could see my sketchbook. I said NO right away, without thinking. Regretted how I said it a second later but it was too late.

Fine.

Whatever.

Not So Perky Amy

Back at Minaku, Amy got an invite to a room party. She didn't ask me.

<u>LIKE I CARE.</u>

Went to bed early. Woke up in the middle of the night, couldn't get back to sleep. Something made me go over to the window (real quiet, so I didn't wake Amy) + when I looked down, there was a BOY standing there, watching me. As if he was waiting for something. I was so freaked out I ran back to bed. WHO IS HE?!?

Emailed Mom to let her know I was ok. She asked if I had made any friends. I said "yes."

If I had to choose ONE thing to eat for the rest of my life, it would be SUSHI.

DAY 3

As soon as I woke up, I ran over to the window but no one was there, of course. Stupid nightmare.

(It seemed so REAL. What if it wasn't a dream?) Too creepy to think about.

Amy says I missed a fun party last night, that I should have gone. Also that I didn't look so great, & maybe I should get more sleep.

Perfect. Seven more days to go in this trip & it's already

→ ME   vs   THEM

LATER:

Mrs.T took us for a group hike in the forest behind the hostel today. Says it's one of the oldest in the region, warned us to stay close so wouldn't get lost. Others found it creepy but I loved it. So much delicious dark fairy-tale atmosphere.

But thought I saw the boy from last night at one point, following us. (!)
Does that mean last night really HAPPENED?

Day 4 Met Kenji last night! He exists.

Saw him yesterday when we were all out back getting a tea ceremony lesson from Mrs. T (Mrs. T teaching tea - HA, how appropriate).

In our free time after the lesson I found him, accused him of being a creepy stalker-type, said I was going to report him.

He was all apologetic, introduced himself, said he was a groundskeeper for the hostel. Said he found me intriguing. Me. INTRIGUING.

STILL find it hard to get this: Kenji (a cute boy) interested in ME (awkward social outcast type!)

Saw Amy giving us a weird look while we were talking. Jealous, I'm sure. EAT YOUR HEART OUT, A.!

Unbelievable. Amy thinks I'm making Kenji up. Says I was TALKING TO MYSELF this aft, that there was no one with me. She's telling the others I'm pathetic. LIKE I CARE. I've met a boy who's different + cute & fun to talk to, + he finds me INTRIGUING.

We've already made plans to get together tomorrow night (!!)

This may sound lame, but I wish Mom + I hadn't had that stupid fight right before I left. Not sure why I'm thinking of that but here goes. I miss you.

Sooooooo tired.
Nightmares getting worse

DAY 5

Benefit:
Mrs. T worried about me, thinks I'm getting sick, told me to stay at the hostel today & get some rest instead of doing sightseeing with the others.

Going to meet Kenji as soon as everyone's gone. EXCITED!

DAY 6: OMGOMG. Can't believe this is happening to ME. Kenji is - amazing-. Never met anyone like him before. We spent all day yesterday together hiking through the forest, talking about everything imaginable.

ALSO (wait for it): Kenji made me a bracelet! He made it during our walk, weaving it together from vines & leaves. So COOL.

I had my sketchbook with me, of course, & he asked to see it. I've never let anyone see these pages before, mainly because they're so personal, but I trust Kenji completely. I was sort of worried what he'd think of the sketches I did of him but he said he loved them.

DAY 8 (I think ☺ - Days blur together here LOL)
stupid weird nightmares make it hard to sleep. Feel like I'm walking in a daze all the time. Was worried K would notice but he doesn't seem to mind.
Meeting K again tonight, after everyone's asleep. Lucky that Amy wears earplugs.

SO TIRED. HEAD FUZZY. Afraid to close my eyes, or I'll dream again →

DAY ?

Met K's people. They have strange eyes like K but are taller, leaner. Their voices wash over me like music. Next to them, I feel so clumsy + awkward. UGH.

Fell asleep beneath the stars last night. Or was it the night before?

Why is it always THEM vs ME?

Them   Me

What K told me:

"But you ARE beautiful."

Don't want to wake up. Don't.

DAY ??

this place is incredible, filled with endless light & beauty. The trees are taller than any I've seen, reaching up into the sky with long fingers of green + gold.

Kenji's people are so good to me. They bring forest gifts + food, tell me how good I am for Kenji.

I should be happy. Would be happy, if only I could get some real sleep. Too many strange nightmares, dreams of half-familiar faces, a nagging feeling of... ...what? Not sure.

Nightmares are back. ∵ K says it's because the forest knows I don't belong. Story of my life. I tell him, but he says he has a solution. What do you remember, he asks me. And I tell him, I remember you. Truth is, that's all I CAN remember...

I keep forgetting to write in my journal. Have No IDEA how many days have passed. Weeks? K says it doesn't matter.

To NIGHT, K says. The others are prepping everything. I'll finally truly belong. Just one scratch, he says. Only hurts for a second. Then a drink, + my Becoming is complete.

I should be happy
I want to be with Kenji
I will

I

Day 15 = Writing from my
hospital room in Tokyo.

Catching up on sleep in a BIG way

/ / / / / \ \ \ \ in the forest with K for
Turns out I was 3 days. Mrs T & the others at Minaku were
totally freaked out. Everyone was looking
for me. They called Mom, & then SHE
freaked out, caught the next flight here.

From Mom

→ As you might have guessed by now,
I didn't finish the Becoming ritual.

They cut me a little, just like K warned me.
Then he held a wooden bowl up to my lips, & whatever was in it
smelled incredible. Fresh, like sunlight & spring & green.

I could almost taste the
freedom, waiting for me.

But then I thought:
→ FREEDOM FROM WHAT?

Why couldn't I remember? I asked K for my journal,
but he said no, just drink. Saw one of the others trying
to hide my journal then so I grabbed at it. We
both pulled & then a piece of paper slipped out & fell to
the ground.
Stared at it for a sec,
then..... remembered EVERYTHING.

Have a
great trip,
Nikki!
Love Mom ♥

Just a jumble at first, in no particular
order: the fight with Mom, the trip, perky Amy,
not fitting in, the sadness. But then goodstuff as well,
things I'd miss. Like sushi. My hamster, Noodles. My
BOOKS. My room at home. The smell of coffee.

And my mom. Even when she's
nagging me.

(DAY 15, continued)

DRINK, Kenji... time kept saying, louder each time + his face started changing. So did the others. K tried forcing the stuff in the bowl into my mouth, but I yelled & gave him a Perky Amy Kick™ &

RAN!!

K called after me but I kept running. Felt a sharp pain around my wrist — the bracelet he made me was cutting into my skin! Managed to get it off. Kept running. Got lost. Wandered. Ran some more. Walked. Hungry. Exhaustd. Lay down (don't remember this, but that's what the rescue workers who found me (+ later, my journal) said probably happened.

Mrs. T (still weird but not as boring as I thought)

Mrs. T said that Kenji + his people were Kodama, or tree spirits. Everyone else said I had been hallucinating, probably from exhaustion or hunger or who knows what else. Except they can't explain why my eyes have changed. Like Kenji's.

(why do I still miss him? STUPID.)

→ Still too perky but she did smuggle sushi into my hospital room for me so she can't be all bad.

Going back home with my Mom tomorrow. We had another fight (of course) at the hospital, about the usual stupid things. But then Mom got all weird + started crying + hugging me. Go figure.

P.S. Super Secret Factoid: I didn't really mind.

♡

Where the Silver Droplets Fall

transcribed and translated from Ainu into Japanese
by Yukie Chiri
translated and illustrated by Deborah Davidson

"Where the silver droplets fall, where the golden droplets fall . . ."

I was singing my usual song as I rode the wind and followed the river to the sea, when I glanced down at an Ainu village and noticed that those who had once been poor had become rich, and those who had once been rich had become poor.

I watched a group of boys on the beach playing target practice with bows and arrows. As I passed over their heads singing "Where the silver droplets fall, where the golden droplets fall," they ran along the sand below me, calling out, *"iPirka chikappo! Kamui chikappo!* Beautiful bird! Sacred bird!" Then they turned to each other and said, "Come on guys. Let's see who can shoot it down. Let's see which of us is a true hero."

Calling out to one another in this way, those from families that had once been poor but were now rich fixed their golden arrows to their golden bows and released the arrows at me. Many little arrows came flying toward me, but I caused them to veer up or down, and they all missed.

One boy carried a bow and arrow made of plain wood. I saw from his clothing that he was from a poor family. But when I looked into his eyes, I knew he must be either the son or grandson of a great man. There was something in his bearing that made him stand out from the others, like a swan among ducks.

This boy fixed his plain wooden arrow to his plain wooden bow and took aim at me. But as he did so, the boys from families who had once been poor but were now rich laughed at him and said, "Hey, this is really funny! You stupid pauper, that's a sacred bird! It will never accept your rotten wooden arrow when it won't even accept our golden ones. Not in a million years." They kicked him and punched him, but the boy ignored them and carefully aimed his arrow at me. I watched him and was moved.

"Where the silver droplets fall, where the golden droplets fall," I sang, as I slowly drew a circle in the sky. The boy drew one leg back and set it firmly behind him, while setting the other leg firmly in front of him. He bit his lower lip and steadied his aim. The arrow was released in a whoosh of air and sparkled as it came toward me.

Seeing this, I stretched out my claw and plucked that little arrow from the air. I sliced through the wind and fell spinning to the ground. The boys churned up the sand in little storms as they raced one another toward the spot where I had fallen.

I fell to the earth almost at the same moment that the poor boy reached me, ahead of the others. He ran to me and grasped me in his hands. But the boys who had once been poor and were now rich soon caught up with him and began abusing him with harsh words and fists.

"How dare you succeed where we failed!" they shouted at him. And as they thrashed him, the poor boy covered my body with his own, pressing me firmly against his belly. He wriggled and squirmed till he had escaped through a gap between his abusers. Then he leaped away from them and ran as fast as he could.

The boys who had once been poor and were now rich threw stones and pieces of wood at the poor boy, but he paid them no mind. Kicking up a cloud of dust, he continued to run till he came to a tiny, run-down shack.

He passed me through the sacred window on the east side of the house, hastily explaining to someone on the other side what has transpired. Inside the house an elderly couple approached me, framing their eyes to get a better look. They appeared practically destitute. Yet the man had a gentlemanly dignity, and the woman a refined femininity. They were both so surprised to see me that their legs buckled and they fell to the floor.

They adjusted their clothing and bowed before me saying, "*iKamuichikap kamui. Pase kamuy.* Owl God, O Weighty One. Thank you for entering our humble home. There was a time when we were prosperous, but as you can see, we are now destitute. We hardly dare to receive you as our guest. But since it is already late, we offer you lodging for the night. Tomorrow we will only be able to honor you with a single *inau* before we send you back to the land where the gods dwell." So saying they worshipped me over and over again.

The old woman spread a woven grass mat at the base of the sacred window and laid me on it. Then everyone went to bed, and soon they were snoring. I sat quietly between the two ears of my head, but at midnight, I went into action.

"Where the silver droplets fall, where the golden droplets fall," I sang softly as I flew about the tiny room, sending beautiful echoes to the left and to the right. As I flapped my wings, marvelous treasures appeared, also making beautiful echoes as they scattered onto the floor of the room. In moments the tiny house was filled with the most amazing things.

"Where the silver droplets fall, where the golden droplets fall," I sang. In an instant I rebuilt the tiny shack into an impressive metal mansion, with alcoves for storing the treasures and decorated with elegant robes. It was more splendid than any rich man's house. When I was finished, I returned to sit at the place between the two ears of my head.

Then I caused the people of the house to dream. I made them dream about an Ainu gentleman who had become impoverished through unfortunate circumstances, and, as a result, was being scorned by those who had once been poor but were now rich. I revealed to them how I had pitied them and had come to bless them, though I am not a god of ordinary status.

Shortly after this, dawn broke. The people of the house all awoke at the same time. Rubbing the sleep from their eyes, they looked around and were struck dumb with astonishment. The old woman wept loudly with joy and the old man shed large drops of tears. The old man rose from his bed and came toward me, bowing many times. Finally he spoke of the dream that I had given him to explain what I had done.

"I thought I was dreaming an ordinary dream in an ordinary sleep, but it has all turned out to be real! We were honored just to have you come to our miserable dwelling and didn't dare to ask for anything more. But you—sacred guardian of the village—you had pity on us for our bad fortune and blessed us even beyond the blessing of your presence among us." He was weeping as he spoke. When he was finished, the old man took a branch of wood and carved a fine *inau* from it, which he then set next to me.

The old woman attended to her appearance, then had the boy run out for firewood and water so she could make the sacramental *sake*. In no time, she had made six barrels of it and they were lined up at the head of the hearth, the seat of honor. While I watched her work, I talked with Ape-Fuchi Kamuy, the elderly goddess of the hearth fire.

After two days, the delicious smell of *sake*, which we gods so appreciate, filled the house. Now, even though they had been provided with many luxurious garments, the old couple purposely dressed the boy in his old clothing and sent him out to the village. This was to invite to their house those who had once been poor but were now rich. I watched over the boy as he entered each dwelling to relay the invitation.

But the people who had once been poor and were now rich laughed at him saying, "Wonder of wonders. What kind of *sake* can you beggar folk make, and what kind of feast can you prepare for us, that you would dare to invite us?"

Then they said to each other, "Let's go and see what these people have up their sleeves and give ourselves a good laugh." A large group gathered together and started toward the boy's house.

They caught sight of the house while they were still far off, and they were amazed. Some became ashamed and turned to go back home. Others stood at the front of the house unable to move. Then the old  woman of the house came out and took the hands of all those who had gathered, and she led them inside. Though they entered and sat at her bidding, they could not raise their heads to look their host in the eye. The old man sat tall and straight, and in a voice as clear and pretty as the cuckoo, he began to speak, explaining everything that had happened.

"Because of my poverty, I was unable to mingle

freely with you, but the Great Owl god, the Guardian of the Village, took pity on me. And because there was no evil in our actions or in our hearts, he gave us this great blessing. It is my earnest wish that we be united, and that we enjoy one another's company no matter what our circumstances."

When the old man had finished speaking, the villagers showed their remorse by rubbing their hands together over and over, and they apologized profusely to him. They promised to try to get along with each other, and they all came before me to thank me and worship me.

When the rituals were taken care of, the villagers' hearts were softened and they started the party. I chatted with the fire goddess, the god of the house, and the god of the *inau* poles. As we talked, the humans entertained us with their singing and dancing.

After two or three days, the festivities came to an end. I was both pleased and relieved to see the humans getting along so well. I said my farewells to the fire goddess, the house god, and the god of the *inau* poles, and departed for my own land, the land where the gods dwell.

Before I had even reached my house, offerings of beautiful *inau* poles and barrels of delicious *sake* had arrived there. So I sent a message to gods both near and far, to invite them to a banquet. At the banquet, I related in great detail everything that had occurred while I was visiting the human village. Hearing my story, the other gods praised me with enthusiasm. I sent two or three of the beautiful *inau* poles home with each of them.

When I look toward the now peaceful Ainu village, I see that the humans are getting along with one another and that the distinguished old man has become their chief. The boy is now fully grown, with a wife and children of his own. He takes good care of the old man and old woman, as a filial son should. And every time they make *sake*, at the start of every ceremonial banquet, they remember to send me offerings of *inau* poles and *sake*. I stay in the background, watching over the village and keeping the humans safe from harm.

Translator's note: p. 172: "the place between the two ears of my head." The god is said to "sit between the ears" of the body he has been inhabiting, after the body has died but while the god's spirit still lingers in the land of the humans. Readers are to understand that the owl is dead.

Powers and Feats

Yamada-san's Toaster

by Kelly Luce

At the time of the toaster incident, my uncle owned the liquor store and I delivered bottles for him on Mondays, then went back on Fridays and picked up the empties. In this way I got to know the whole town. Pretty much everyone did business with my uncle at one point or another.

Even though I was only thirteen he let me drive his delivery truck. The hills in town were too steep for a bike; plus, I had to carry around all those bottles.

Oi-san lived behind the temple and was brown and furrowed like an old piece of fruit. We kids called him Sumomo-san, Mr. Prune, though I never knew whether this referred to his appearance or his diet. He ate his dinner with the cats that lived near the temple. He just sat right on the ground.

It was from Oi-san that I first heard about Yamada-san's toaster and how it could predict the way a person's going to die. I was setting the bottles on his mossy concrete step when he appeared in the doorway and said in a voice as wrinkled as his face, "Son, today I learned how I'm gonna go."

I had finished with the bottles and stood there, unsure what to say. I looked up at him, because even though it's rude to look your elders right in the eye like that, it seemed to be what he wanted.

He told me Yamada-san, a widow who lived at the edge of town, had a toaster that after you put in a piece of bread, it came out with a Chinese character toasted on it. That character indicated how you'd die.

"What was your word, sir?"

"Sleep. Isn't that a hoot? Now I can finally live in peace." He waved as he shuffled back inside, a bottle of *sake* clutched in his left hand.

⤺

I didn't tell anyone at home what Oi-san had said. My parents were too busy—that was the year they opened the *udon* restaurant—and my sister had just got a boyfriend and never hung around after school anymore. Plus, I had a feeling no one would care. Mine was a family of skeptics. We didn't observe any superstitious holidays, bean-throwing day or Tanabata or anything like that; all we celebrated was New Year's, and that's because you get to feast for three days straight.

I picked up Oi-san's empties on Friday and brought him an extra two bottles of *sake*, which he'd special ordered that week. On Monday he was dead. Died in his sleep of natural causes.

Apparently Oi-san had told a lot of people about Yamada-san's toaster and its prediction for him, though, because once he died, everyone in town was talking about it. Yamada-san had always been a little weird. She confirmed everything: the toaster had predicted her husband's death last year when it popped out a piece of bread that read "heart" three days before he had a coronary, and after that it had foretold her mother-in-law's fatal pneumonia. A gift from God, she told the crowd gathered around her at the market. She held the toaster under one arm, its plug swinging beneath it like a tail. When asked if she'd gotten a death-predicting piece of toast herself, she said she had.

"Well?"

Hers had read "Cancer." It was quiet for a while after that.

꙳

Yamada-san was just like any other lady you'd see around town except for one thing—she was a real religious nut. Years before the toaster, she'd knocked on our door a couple times, offering her "help." I remember thinking it was kind of nice—weird, but nice—but after she'd gone my mom would roll her eyes and go back to her TV drama. Anyway, that was back when I was little. By the time the toaster came around, Yamada-san didn't knock on doors in our neighborhood anymore.

Her house was at the edge of town, partway up a huge, terraced hill with bamboo at the top. For a widow living alone she had a pretty big standing order at my uncle's store—eight tall one-liter bottles of beer. That was more than a liter a day! She who smelled so sweet it hurt your nose, like overripe peaches, and spoke very properly and always wore something with lace on the collar; how could *she* go through that much beer?

I thought of her at her impeccable kitchen table pouring the beer into a glass and waiting patiently for it to settle, then taking the tiniest sip. I pictured her melting at the first drop of bitter liquid in her throat, her creamy makeup running down her neck and the starch on her collar drooping until her whole body oozed into a peach-scented puddle of foam.

The toaster became a sensation. Some people thought it was a trick she was using to try and convert people, while others believed in the toaster's power but disagreed about what ought to be done with it. Some wanted to enshrine the toaster and worship it like a Shinto deity. Others thought she should sell it to the government.

But the thing people argued about most was whether or not it was right to use the toaster's powers, to become One Who Knew. Soon the town divided itself between Knows and Don't-Want-To-Knows. Each group, of course, claimed the moral high ground—there was no room for compromise. Conflicting opinions on the topic spoiled countless friendships and were even named in the Satos' divorce proceedings as evidence of irreconcilable differences.

Yamada-san didn't get involved in the politics of it. She let anyone use the toaster. She believed it was a gift from God that should not go to waste. Every day there was a line out her door of people, soft pieces of bread in hand, hoping to find out in what fashion they would meet Death.

But some of the Don't-Want-To-Knows were upset. One man, a retired professor from Keio University who everyone just called "Mr. Doc" went so far as to stand at Yamada-san's open door and protest. He was there talking quietly and intently to a young mother and her toddler on the front steps when I came the next Friday to drop off Yamada-san's beer. They paid no attention to me as I stepped past and set the bottles in the entranceway. I could hear someone crying in the kitchen.

On the way out I passed the mother and child, who were walking toward the road with Mr. Doc. I guess he'd convinced her not to go in. I kept my head down but as I passed he called to me.

"Keisuke."

I turned, stunned he knew my name.

"Are you planning to find out?"

I shrugged, then shook my head. It seemed like an awfully big thing to know. Plus I kind of liked thinking that maybe I'd never die, like by the time I got old they'd have invented a cure for everything.

"I'm fighting a losing battle," he said. "You just can't protect people from themselves."

I nodded, then bowed slightly and walked quickly back to the truck. On the drive down I passed four groups of people climbing the hill to Yamada-san's house. I wondered if Mr. Doc would be able to stop all of them.

❧

By Monday every house I visited buzzed with talk of the toaster. Mrs. Kawabata was predicted to die by fire—the same as Mrs. Shinjo. Both were librarians. Extra fire extinguishers were purchased for the older wooden library building, and a state-of-the-art sprinkler system was installed.

A newlywed couple canceled their honeymoon flight to Hawaii because both of their pieces of toast had popped up bearing the character "air."

At dinnertime my parents and sister talked about how nuts everyone was, but I kept quiet. I didn't necessarily believe in the toaster, but I was at least willing to be convinced, maybe.

The news reached all over the prefecture. The line spilled out Yamada-san's door and down the steps. News vans crowded the narrow street so that I had to drive fifty meters away to park.

Mr. Doc held forth on the front stoop. "Don't let curiosity pollute your mind!" he bellowed at the line, which was full of unfamiliar faces. A few college-age kids stood with him, holding signs and chanting, "Knowledge of death sullies the will to live!" The crowd ignored them and was silent, as if in line to receive a blessing. I stepped through the mob with the beer, excusing myself and sneaking peeks at the faces. Some people seemed lost in thought, staring up at the bamboo grove beyond the house, while others whispered nervously to one another.

"Hey, no cuts, buddy," someone said as I passed. I held up the crate of beer and almost said, "Delivery," but then I thought that maybe Yamada-san didn't want these people to know she'd ordered all this beer, so I turned back.

I lingered near my truck and watched people come down the stairs, each clutching a piece of toast. So many People Who Knew. Some looked confused and some relieved. One woman was bawling so hard she dropped her toast, and when she did I saw what it said: *suicide*.

That was eerie, but even eerier were the ones whose faces were blank and empty and lost. Like maybe they were already dead.

A cry rose from the front of the crowd and suddenly everyone got very noisy. People gestured and talked amongst themselves, and some turned away and started heading back toward the road.

"Broken? Right! I *knew* it was a fraud."

"Just my bad luck . . . should've come earlier."

"Not really sure I wanted to know, to be honest. . . ."

I waited until everyone left, then approached the door with my crate.

"Yamada-san?"

She stepped into the hall, prim as ever.

"Keisuke! How good of you to come amid that throng. I noticed the truck outside earlier and thought you'd given up."

"No, ma'am." I held the crate out and she took it without a word. I shifted around, trying to sneak a peek into the kitchen.

"Come on in and have a drink," she said.

There it was, unplugged, sitting right smack in the middle of the round yellow table; a silver single-slice toaster trimmed in black with rust lining the opening. The table was littered with crumbs. I wondered if you had to eat the toast in order for the prediction to come true, or if just toasting it was enough.

"Well, there it is."

"Is it . . . broken?" I asked.

"Seems to be." She frowned.

"Did it really work, though?"

Her smile returned, serene beneath her lace collar. "Oh, yes! God's methods sure are beyond our comprehension. Who are we to judge His ways?"

"But . . . maybe you can get it fixed."

"Maybe. But perhaps this is simply the appliance's fate."

She took a bottle from the crate and gestured with it toward the back door. "Please, come."

⟿

I followed her out the back door. The yard had been completely overtaken by a jungle-like garden that seemed out of step with Yamada-san's tidy appearance and manners. We picked through vines until we reached the back of the yard, where a stone shrine stood against the first tall mud terrace. The family grave.

"This is where my ancestors rest, and most recently my husband," she said, picking up the bottle opener lying at the base of the shrine.

"He loved beer. His favorite thing in life was a cold beer in the garden at sunset. Ah, Shuji," she said.

She opened the beer deftly and poured it all over the shrine, slowly dousing the statuary in caramel foam. She shook the bottle wildly at the end, spraying us both with drops of beer. She looked like my sister dancing to a Morning Musume song when she did that.

When the bottle was empty she set it on the ledge where offerings are left. The family name, Yamada—heavenly mountain and earthly rice field—was carved in fancy calligraphy above the shelf, and beer meandered down the grooves in the stone like a lazy river in summer.

She sighed. "I do that every day. That is my offering to him."

After what I'd just witnessed, I felt comfortable enough to ask, "Yamada-san, what about the eighth bottle?"

She laughed. "You are an astute fellow."

⟿

She went in the house and returned with the toaster and another bottle.

"Do you know what baptism is?"

I shook my head.

"Baptism is a ritual that washes away original sin, she said, setting the toaster on the offering ledge." She reached again for the opener. "It makes you pure."

Then she held the bottle over her head, closed her eyes, and turned it upside-down.

I reached out automatically to help her, to save her from herself, but she raised her palm. The beer gushed over her hair, her face, onto her white starched shirt and long beige skirt. Her hair flattened out. Here and there her cheek makeup ran and revealed darker skin underneath.

About three-quarters through she stopped, opened her eyes, and held the bottle out to me.

I didn't move. All I could hear was the drip-drip-drip of beer hitting the dirt around Yamada-san's feet. I know what my uncle would've said: what a waste of alcohol. He always said it was a sin to waste liquor.

My impulse was to take the bottle—maybe she wanted me to hold it for her—but then she raised it to the sky and said, "For once, they came to me. I did the best I could, I explained what God truly is and how to be saved, but no one listened."

The remaining beer sloshed around inside the bottle. Her eyes were closed. It seemed she'd forgotten I was standing there.

"They just wanted the piece of information," she said. "Like I was some kind of palm reader! When the show was over they left as quickly as they came."

She opened her eyes and looked around, teetering as if she'd drunk all that beer instead of showering in it. When she noticed I was still there, she held the bottle out to me once again. Strands of wet hair clung to her cheeks. She smiled a smile I've never forgotten, a smile like a girl playing in a puddle.

I stepped close to her, close enough so that I could see the pink brassiere through her damp blouse. I tried to follow her cues, and together we emptied the bottle into the toaster's vacant slot.

She looked toward the sky. I wondered if she was thinking of her own death. I guess we both knew how she was going to go, I thought.

I followed her gaze. I could see the hilltop behind us and the bamboo growing way up there. The stalks moved slightly in a breeze I couldn't feel, revealing and concealing slivers of blue that seemed to form words faster than I could read them. *Well? Why not?* I thought. Maybe that, too, was a marvel for anyone who cared to see it that way.

Jet Black and the Ninja Wind

by Leza Lowitz and Shogo Oketani

The full moon party had just started, and Jet stood in Amy Williams' kitchen, wearing the two-dollar black dress she'd bought at the thrift store.

"That's such a cool dress," Amy told her, pushing a drink into her hand. The girls gathered, staring as if trying to remember whether they'd seen the dress in a catalog or a store window. Still, Jet knew it would have been cooler to have a date or to buy clothing that hadn't belonged to someone living in an old folks' home.

"Yeah, she said, "just put a hood on this thing, and I'd look like the grim reaper."

The girls in their sleek new outfits laughed. Jet could hardly believe it. She knew she'd changed, that people looked at her differently, and even her mother, staring at her one morning, had said, "The tomboy's gone. You've become a woman." And now Jet wanted nothing more than to spend the evening with the girls who'd always ignored her. But she couldn't. She had ten minutes before she had to leave. *The game.* Tonight was the night of the game. Saturday night had been ever since Jet could remember. She hated the game like she hated nothing else.

She took the drink anyway, not sure what it was—orange juice and something that smelled like rubbing alcohol. Amy Williams cranked the music. Boys were arriving. The girls began dancing in the living room just as the star quarterback threw open the door, a cooler on his shoulder. Jet tried to dance. How did they make it look so easy, swaying and turning gracefully? She'd have been more comfortable doing a spinning kick or a backflip. Now she had to make up her mind. Was it better to awkwardly explain she had to leave soon, or just slip out and later invent a story?

Her senses stilled. she took in the music blaring, the thudding baseline, the hollering boys, but behind all that, if she focused, there was the battering, off-rhythm engine of the truck turning onto Amy Williams' street. Kids were crowded around the door, so she went upstairs and into the bathroom. She took off her sandals, lifted the window screen and slipped out onto the roof's overhang, then jumped down to the ground. She caught the top of the fence and swung herself over it. The truck was still moving, nearly to the house, when Jet reached the door and let herself in.

"Don't stop," she whispered to her mother, sliding down in her seat. A duffle with clothes for the game was on the floor, and as soon as they turned the corner, she began to change.

"Have fun?" her mother whispered, slumped at the wheel, more gaunt than ever.

"Best time of my life," Jet replied, "all ten minutes of it."

Satoko drove them out of the suburbs and into the mountains, over roads muddy and rutted from a week of heavy rains, though now the sky was clear, and the full moon hung in it as if Amy Williams herself had put it there.

The narrow road skirted the steep drop, hugging the edge of the mountain peaks that glowed in the moonlight. As they went around a bend, the back wheels fishtailed. Jet gasped and clutched the seat. The truck almost turned sideways, skidding toward the cliff. Her mother jerked the wheel and hit the gas, and the truck slid back toward the mountain. She brought it under control and pulled it to a stop. She pressed her foot on the emergency brake, locking it in place. Her breathing sounded labored. She'd appeared unwell for months now.

"This is the last time," she told Jet.

"I've heard that before," Jet said, but the sound of her own voice wasn't convincing. The words came out whispery with fear.

"Have I ever said this before?" her mother asked. "Have I ever told you it was the last time?"

"No . . ."

"Well, it is. You'll never have to come up here again."

"No more game?"

"No. The game will be over."

Jet stared out over the hood of the truck at the muddy road. Her mother seemed to have calmed. Jet could sense her exhaustion, the slowness of her breathing, even the tired beating of her heart. Her mother had said she had bronchitis, but her cough only got worse and worse, and Jet wondered for the first time whether her mother's problem might be more serious. All week she would look exhausted and stay in bed, or meditate, and then, on the night of the game, she would pull herself together and become the woman Jet had always known her to be. She would concentrate her energy, focusing herself, slowing her breath, her eyes becoming still. Even now Jet could feel the slow expansion of calm around her, could see the precision in her movements. On the nights of the game, her mother would even cease to cough.

"I promise you," she told Jet, "this is the last time."

"Okay, Mom. I'm thrilled." But Jet knew this wasn't true. The intensity of her mother's concentration distracted her.

"You take the truck up to the parking spot," her mother told her.

"What?"

"Take it up. I'll get out here. You can find me."

"You mean like—"

"The same rules as always," her mother said.

She got out and stepped down into the mud. She slammed the door, and Jet slid over across the old vinyl seat whose split seams trailed bits of stuffing. When she looked out the window, there was only the cliff alongside them, no sight of her mother. But this didn't surprise her. She released the parking brake and steered the truck up along the mountain. *What if it really was the last time?* she asked herself and tried to stop being angry about the party. *If the game is over, what's next?*

The parking spot was no more than a widening in the road where the limbless trunk of a dead tree stood at the foot of a jumble of immense boulders. Hundreds of times Jet had climbed the mountain, crouched, pausing to watch for movement. She wrapped her body in black cloth and hid her face, leaving only a slit for her eyes. *One more time,* she told herself, but as soon as she was out of the truck, she stopped and stared up at the moon.

Like a sign written across the sky, it seemed to be saying, "Loser, you couldn't even get a date to the prom. Now you're missing the coolest party ever, and you're going to graduate from high school without ever being kissed."

She tried to think of a witty comeback. She stared at its face, at the craters like acne, and thought of the unpopular kids, the ones who didn't get invited to parties either. She'd never even had acne. She was just different from everyone else. That was her curse: forced to be weird, to hide everything.

There was a faint buzzing sound, and something, like a bird or a bat, flew close to her face. It brushed alongside her cheek, the sound clearer, a thin hiss of displaced air. A long knife struck the dead wood of the tree and embedded itself, quivering.

Jet dropped to a crouch, looking up and around, then scuttled alongside the truck. Her mother couldn't have thrown it, could she? This wasn't part of the game. They didn't use real weapons, only sticks, rocks sometimes.

She was kneeling in the mud, her heart beating fast, moisture seeping through her pants, making them heavy, she realized. She shifted onto the balls of her feet.

Stay light, she told herself. Nothing moved on the mountainside. She didn't sense anything: not a single living creature, nothing.

"Mom?" she tried to call but the word got stuck in her throat. How stupid could she be? Whoever had thrown the knife wouldn't miss next time. She knew that she should stay on the move, but she couldn't stop trying to figure out what had happened, whether her mother had changed the game because it was the last time, or whether something had gone wrong and someone else was out here. She'd said "same rules as always," hadn't she?

Staying in one place is dangerous! Jet told herself.

She sprinted and jumped, catching the handle of the knife and pulling it from the wood. She landed among the boulders and moved quickly, with small, darting steps against the stone, until she was on a perch in the middle of the jumble, hidden from sight.

She turned the blade over. It was an army knife of some sort, long, its handle heavy. It would be easy for her to use, but then she almost dropped it, realizing that someone had meant to kill her. Why? What had she done?

No, it had to be her mother who was trying to scare her. But how could Jet play this game if they were using real weapons? Maybe her mother wanted to teach her to take her training more seriously? Jet had once heard a story about a crazy war vet living up in these mountains, a man who had deserted, who'd gone AWOL on a visit home, and who hunted anyone who came onto his land. Maybe that's what was happening. And if so, then her mother might be in danger, too.

"Mom?" she shouted this time and moved quickly, changing her hiding spot. "Be careful!"

She placed her steps to leave the fewest traces. She ran along the side of a long flat boulder as big as a house, then crouched in a new hiding spot. There was no sound. Nothing. Who was out here with her?

"Mom," she shouted again, "if it's you, I don't want to play. Stop trying to scare me."

She changed places again and listened. There was no response, not a sound anywhere.

She knew every way up the mountain. The wind was picking up. Small clouds shuttled quickly across the sky, beneath the moon, their shadows gliding over the earth.

She concentrated her mind, listening, moving her senses out, watching the shape and hues of the landscape for traces of another person, for even the faintest pattern of footprints. But she sensed no one. Her mother had taught her to sit and feel everything for almost a mile around—birds, rabbits, people walking. The desert seemed empty, as if someone had cut Jet off from the world—or as if nothing was alive, or she wasn't.

She had two choices, to be slow and cautious or to find her mother before someone else did. As a cloud passed beneath the moon, she sprinted, running into its shadow. She was fast. No one could beat her in a race, and she would be a hard target, weaving and leaping.

Her ankle twisted and her foot was pulled from beneath her before she could even feel the pain. She struck the mud face-first and rolled. It had been a sharp trip wire, she instantly knew. She could feel the swelling in her ankle, the blood filling the soft leather of her moccasin boot. She wanted to cry, to scream her mother's name, but stopping now could get her killed. She leapt behind another long rock and lay still, trying to become invisible. The mountainside was irregular, an obstacle course of stone and fallen trees, of mud and sheer cliffs. Her mother had chosen it for this, to teach Jet all of the skills that her mother claimed she would someday need, though Jet never had.

Maybe that was why she didn't cry now. The training. The lessons.

The constant expectation that things would be more dangerous than they really were. But though she tried to sense what was around her, she couldn't focus. Her thoughts collapsed to fear. There was only her heart hammering in her chest, her body, her muddied arms and legs, her throbbing ankle, her cold fingers still gripping the handle of the knife.

The wind was getting stronger. She took a few deep, slow breaths, as if pulling it into her body. It would help her. She had always been good in the wind. Her mother had taught her to move with it. She'd said it was Jet's gift.

Ignoring the pain in her ankle, she ran again, this time moving with the wind, fitting her body to its contours so that she brushed past stones, through trees, not traveling directly toward the peak where she normally found her mother during the game, but letting the wind carry her along an indirect route that no one could know unless they too were running in the wind.

Her feet danced from rock to rock. She avoided the moonlight, threading her body along shadows. The texture of the wind pleased her, and though she almost forgot her pain, she didn't stop looking for the person who had thrown the knife and set the tripwire. She still couldn't sense them or see any trace.

The low, flat peak of the mountain came into sight past trees and boulders, and moments later, something brushed against her thigh, catching in the cloth of her pants. She didn't stop running, and even as her fingers touched it, she knew what it was. A dart, its metal tip barbed, maybe poisonous. In her mother's stories, they always were. She felt a sob building in her chest and tried to calm herself. Another one shot past and pinged off a rock. Where was her enemy? Above her, on the peak— that's where he had to be.

Move with the wind. Feel the elements. The deep hum of the earth reached up through the mud. There were the fluctuations of the wind. The heat in her chest, the air in her lungs, the solidity of her body. All this she could blend. But whoever was up there had incredible vision and aim. Another dart flickered past her face. *Focus!*

And then her mind calmed and opened outward, and she could sense the world again, the life out there, across the desert's Martian landscape that descended behind her. She knew each thing in its place. Lizards and snakes sleeping beneath rocks. Animals in burrows. A distant coyote sniffing the night air, sensing her. She had never felt this alive. Someone was on the peak, the presence faint, cloaked as if by an incredible act of focus, but still discernible. She directed her attention, searching into whoever this was.

Her enemy's energy hummed with anger, with hostility. In the body standing on the peak she sensed an intention to hunt and kill her, and just feeling it, she was terrified.

What choice do I have? she asked herself. *I can't just run away. Mom is out here somewhere. I have to do this. Stay calm!*

She began to move again. Keeping close to shelter, she sprinted, twisting and leaping with the wind. She knew every ravine, every mound in the earth. She also knew how to dim her presence, to slow her heart and breath even as she ran, to let her entire existence blur into the wind. It gusted hard, and she commanded her own life force to become faint, like a drop of water wiped along the surface of a dark window.

She didn't head directly for the peak but around the mountain, to a cleft she knew, just at the back, at the base of a stand of gnarled trees, their branches misshapen from the wind. It was the only way she could think of to invade the higher ground. She timed it perfectly with a strong gust, with the brief passing of a small cloud over the moon, with the distant cry of the coyote that she sensed was ready to howl, and then she was twisting through the air, taking shape, her foot reaching for the earth as she swung the knife. The figure stood on the flat surface of the peak and spun toward her.

Sparks flashed as her enemy lifted a blade and deflected the knife. The figure was wrapped in black, just as Jet was. This was no crazy war veteran, but someone far more dangerous.

The moon appeared from behind the cloud, and the enemy kept its back to it, silhouetted, the bright pallor shining into Jet's eyes as wind poured against the mountain with incredible force. Jet tried to use it, circling, feeling the pulse of the stone beneath her feet. But even as she twisted and leapt, the figure hardly seemed to move and yet avoided every strike, simply shifting slightly or again deflecting Jet's knife.

Jet never stopped, attacking repeatedly as she swirled close to the silhouetted figure. She timed her kicks and circled, trying to get the moonlight out of her eyes. She focused her strength and energy, but her fists and feet and knife passed, with each of her attacks, as if through the wind.

All the while Jet was trying to sense this fighter's energy, at once masked and hostile, burning with a deep core of anger. But her enemy didn't act on this rage, didn't give in to impatience. It easily avoided every strike. All of the tricks Jet's mother had taught her, to dodge and fall back and attack, to follow the wind, letting herself retreat or stumble even as she struck—nothing worked.

Another small cloud passed between the moon and the mountain, and even as Jet began to formulate a plan, she realized her mistake. She should have planned already for the split second when the moonlight would vanish. Her enemy had done this.

As Jet was leaping to the side, trying to stay with the wind, a foot struck her stomach, suspending her in the air as if she'd been pinned there. And then she was falling, trying to find the earth with her feet even as she couldn't breathe.

A hand caught the back of her head, gripping her hair through the black cloth. Her enemy jerked her head back and put the knife to her throat.

The wind suddenly died. The cloud passed from before the moon. The desolate landscape of the desert mountains stretched out like a vision of another world. Was this the last thing Jet would see?

"You've been lazy," the fighter hissed. "You've never wanted to learn."

Jet tried to pull away, but the blade stayed at her throat. The fist held her hair.

"What good are you to me? Tell me that!"

This time she heard clearly: it was her mother's voice.

"Mom," Jet cried out. "What are you doing? Are you crazy?"

Her mother's lips were close to Jet's ear. There was a long silence before she said, "I've trained you since you could walk, and all you think about is parties and clothes. Millions of kids go to parties and wear cool clothes. But only one or two people in the world get to learn what I've taught you. You still don't understand, do you?" She sheathed the knife and unwrapped her face.

Jet had begun to cry, shaking not just with fear and hurt, but with anger.

"What?!" she shouted. "You almost killed me! You could have—"

"Jet," her mother whispered. She took a step closer and her knees buckled. Jet caught her mother's arm and held her up.

"Jet," her mother said. "This was the last time. I had to make you see. I didn't have the energy left, but I had to. I had to try to make you see."

"What's wrong, Mom?"

"Help me, Jet. Help me to the truck."

Jet held her mother's arm as they walked toward the edge of the slope. Her mother leaned against her, gasping now, heavier than anything Jet had ever felt.

"But how . . . ?" Jet began to ask, recalling the warrior she had just fought, the figure shifting almost imperceptibly in the wind.

Her mother didn't answer. The walk down the mountain took an hour, her mother leaning heavily against her, her breathing labored, her body exhausted in the night from which the wind had fled.

⌒

Back at the trailer where they lived, Jet helped her mother to bed, then bound her own cut ankle. When she returned to her mother's bedroom, she was surprised to see her still awake.

"Do you remember the story I used to tell you?" her mother asked.

"Which one?" Jet said. She sat in the chair next to the bed.

"The one about our ancestors, in the country called Hinomoto. You loved it when you were a girl. It was your favorite."

"Yes," Jet told her. "I remember."

And then her mother began telling it, as if Jet had asked again, the way she used to, needing to hear it almost every day. When had that been? When had Jet stopped asking?

"Hinomoto means 'land of the rising sun,'" her mother said. "It was a great land, once ruled by the Emishi, a native tribe. Their mountains and forests gave them nuts and fruit, and their oceans and rivers held great schools of fish. Nature offered them such wealth, they didn't have to fight their neighbors."

Jet nodded, exhausted but totally present, sensing how much was changing, the difference in her mother. The words that she must have heard a thousand times sent goose bumps along her arms, and she rubbed them away as if she were cold. When she was little, each word of the story had meant another night in their home, another moment of peace—not moving, not running, not looking for a new place to live, not scared.

"But one day," her mother said, "a tribe called the Wa arrived from the mainland. They came with many soldiers. Their king, who called himself the Mikado, said to the Emishi leader: 'You must give your country to me. We will change the forests into rice fields and build beautiful shrines. I promise you a much richer life than now.'

"Of course, the king of the Emishi wasn't interested. 'We don't need more wealth, and for us there is no greater shrine than nature. If you want to live in this land, we'll welcome you. But you have to keep our laws. If you don't, you must leave,' he said proudly."

Though her mother's chest heaved with a deep, tired breath, she seemed to smile.

"No one had ever talked to the Mikado like that. Everyone surrendered to him, either for the promise of power and wealth or because they were too scared to fight back. But not the Emishi. Enraged, the Mikado attacked with his armies. The Emishi were quickly outnumbered and defeated."

Her mother spoke in such a sweet, soft voice, so unlike the commands she bellowed when training Jet to fight, or the way she had spoken to her harshly on the mountain only hours ago.

"The Emishi abandoned their capital and fled to the north, where they built new homes surrounded by mountains and forests. But the Wa were not satisfied. They invaded there, too. This time, the Emishi decided to fight back. It was a long, long battle. Many Emishi died—not just the men, but also women, children, and even babies. Finally, the Emishi surrendered. And here is the saddest part—they were sold as slaves to the Wa. Their only hope was the dream of returning to their homeland someday."

Her mother began to cry. Jet had never seen her do this before. She didn't know what to say, how to react, and she bit back her own urge to cry.

Her mother didn't wipe her face. She didn't try to hide what she was feeling.

"Eventually," she said, "the age of the Mikado ended, and the samurai lords attained power. There were various classes of samurai—the lowest were mountain bandits—and among them were different classes too. The Emishi were the slaves of these bandits, and their job was to get secrets from samurai lords and sell them to their rivals. They were skilled at moving in the darkness, spying and using weapons to defend themselves. They hid in the night. This was the time before electricity. The whole night world was dark."

She closed her eyes, but spoke with the same steady voice she'd used when telling this story to Jet years before.

"One day, a girl was born to one of the slaves within the bandit society. She grew up to be beautiful, strong, and smart. Her father sent her to a samurai castle disguised as a servant so she could learn of the lord's military strength and discover when he would attack his rival. . . . She accomplished her mission only by using the power of the elements. You see, the women in this family always had the greatest control over the elements. This girl knew how to become invisible in rain, to stand as still as stone, but it was the wind that she most loved, and it carried her through the chambers of the castle to the door, and it carried the lord's words to her ear."

Her voice trailed off faintly.

"Go on," Jet urged.

Her mother opened her eyes and looked at her.

"Even though the girl had a mission, she saw only an opportunity to be released from slavery. She was independent, you know. . . ."

Saying this, she smiled again.

"She became close to the lord and confided in him, 'My master has joined forces with your rival and is planning to attack you. He and other warrior families are preparing for battle. Now is a good chance to attack them first.'

"Furious, the lord attacked his rival and the warrior families in the mountains, and defeated them. But the clever girl had already told her plan to her enslaved tribe, who escaped into the forest just before the attack. This is how the enslaved warriors were able to free themselves and return to their homeland. They rebuilt their villages and lived peacefully in nature ever after."

Years ago, Jet had believed in ever after. But she no longer knew what that meant. When she was little, she would interrupt her mother at this part of the story and ask if the Emishi were still there, and her mother would tell her about how they still existed peacefully within nature, how each new generation learned about the brave girl who helped their ancestors escape. But the generations were getting smaller and smaller, moving to the cities, forgetting.

"Jet," her mother said, interrupting her reverie.

"What, Mom?"

"I won't be here much longer. You're going to have to go back."

"What? Where?" Jet asked, completely bewildered.

"To Hinamoto. To Japan . . . You see, all those times I made you go up to the mountains," Satoko said, struggling to draw enough breath to speak, "all that hard training, I hope you will soon understand why I made you do it."

"Of course, Mom," Jet replied, though she didn't really understand at all. Almost every night since she could remember she'd had to train, in the forest behind their trailer or in dusty fields along the highway, and always on Saturdays, more seriously, in the mountains after dark, so that she could be tested. She'd often shown up at school with her clothes mud-caked and torn, and had told her teachers that it was from soccer practice. Then there were the bruises, scratches, and scars. Other kids called her crazy, but she wasn't allowed to explain. When the school bully started picking on her, she couldn't even use her secret training to fight back.

There had to be a middle ground, she reasoned, but she had yet to find it. Though she'd always wanted to be an all-American kid, she'd had a Japanese mother with strange ideas about child rearing and an American father who'd left when she was a baby. Not to mention the fact that she was an Asian girl living on a Navaho Reservation in the desert. You couldn't get much stranger than that.

Or could you?

Whenever she asked her mom to explain why she'd fled Japan, Satoko's answer was always "Later. We'll talk about it later."

But "later" came too late.

"You see," her mother confided, "our family has a treasure. People all over Japan want it, and we've been fighting them off for centuries."

"Treasure? What kind of treasure?" Jet asked, picturing pearls, jade, and gold.

Satoko didn't tell her. "Your grandfather and I have been protecting it for years. But now that's up to you. Without you, it will be lost forever.

That's why you must go back to Japan. You must find the treasure and save the magic mountain. It's your mission. It's what I trained you to do."

"Me?" Jet asked. "And what is the treasure?" How could a mountain be magic? Carpets, sure, and markers, too. But a mountain?

Satoko closed her eyes and nodded, smiling gently through her pain. "Many people will try to find you to get at it. Some of them may even want to hurt you."

"Hurt me?" Jet asked, disbelieving.

"You must protect yourself. You must finally use the skills I taught you. You'll have to dig deep down. Can you do that? For me?"

"Of course," Jet answered. But there were so many questions. "How will I . . . ?"

"Be patient," Satoko said. "And don't let yourself be weak like I was. Trust me. Just go with the wind, become the wind, don't try to resist."

"Become the wind?" Jet had no idea what her mother was talking about. She was scared, and her mother's words confused her. All of these years of training and her mother had never mentioned any of this—how was that possible?

Satoko drew her close. "Soon you will meet your grandfather. He will welcome you, and all will become clear. Ask him to teach you more about the wind. He will help you understand its secrets. You aren't ready yet, but you have the gift. I hope that one day you will use it."

Satoko closed her eyes and breathed steadily, then less steadily, and finally roughly, until she couldn't breathe anymore.

"I'll find Grandfather," Jet told her, holding her mother close. "I promise. And I'll bring you back home and become the wind."

Hachiro

by Ryusuke Saito
translated by Sako Ikegami

Long ago, in the land of Akita, there lived a mountain youth named Hachiro. Like all products of the mountains, Hachiro was rugged and large. So large in fact, he was as tall as that oak tree over there. And like an oak tree, he grew straight and true. The muscles in his arms, shoulders, and chest were as hard as carved oak. His height, size, and strength were so marvelous that the mere sight of him caused people to shout in surprise and laugh with delight.

But Hachiro was such a simple youth that no matter how large he got, he wanted to grow even bigger. Every day, he would dash down from his home in the mountains all the way to the shore, and roar at the sea.

Just imagine. With each roar, Hachiro's chest would creak and groan and grow a little bit larger and wider, swelling like the bellows of the blacksmith, growing bigger than the baskets of the bamboo weaver, larger than the great creels used by fishermen along the shore, and finally so enormous that an entire house could have fit inside.

As his chest broadened, he grew taller, and birds of all sorts—siskins, starlings, and titmice—began to build nests in his hair. Even birds like the cuckoo that don't ordinarily build nests of their own, flew around his head and sang along with the others, "Peep peep, chirp chirp, tweet tweet, cuckoo!"

Hachiro woke up early every morning because the birds in his hair would begin chirping at the break of dawn, peeping, chirupping, tweeting, and cuckooing. Their songs were so loud that Hachiro simply couldn't sleep late. He didn't want to frighten the birds, so he'd try hard to stay still, even after he awoke.

Soon, though, he would feel the need to grow bigger, to rush down to the shore, yet he struggled against the urge because he loved the little birds so.

But it was no use. From deep in his now cavernous chest would come the burning desire to grow bigger, rising from within like billowing clouds on a summer's day. And with a great shout he would leap to his feet and race to the shore. At times like these, Hachiro was magnificent. The birds scattered through his hair would instantly take to the air. Their nests remained, so they never flew far, but circled Hachiro's head like mists surrounding a mountaintop, singing their bird songs: "Cheep cheep, chirp chirp, tweet tweet, cuckoo!" It was a beautiful sight to behold.

When Hachiro reached the shore, he'd plant his feet, each as huge as a cow, deep in the sand. He'd place his gigantic hands, each the size of a camphor tree, upon his hips. Pursing his lips, he'd blow away the clouds hovering around his chest. Then he would yell out toward the sea, "*Hoihoi!*"—Hey!

But the sea was so much bigger than Hachiro, it would pretend to ignore him, letting its waves pound the shore. Hachiro would have to say, "There's no helping it. That's how it is. That's just how it is," as he headed back up into the mountains.

⌒

One day, when Hachiro arrived at the seashore, he saw a cute little *warashi*, a tiny boy, crying his eyes out. The little boy would look at the sea and wail, look back at the sea, and just sob away.

Hachiro picked the small child up by his collar and laid him gently on his palm, which was the size of an eight-tatami room, and asked the boy why he was crying. Still heaving with sobs, the little boy explained. Every year, every single year, the sea would rise up and grow mean and rough. It would flood the farmlands of the boy's father and ruin them. It looked as if this year's flood was coming soon, perhaps today, and his mother and his father and all the people from the village had gone to try and ward off the waves, leaving him all alone.

Hachiro was a kindly mountain youth and felt sorry for the little boy. He did his best to try and comfort him.

"Don't cry, little guy. It's okay. I'll play with you."

But the tiny, pea-size boy just looked over to where his parents and the villagers were struggling to dam up the shore against the waves and sobbed loudly. He looked at the dark sea, which laughed nastily and bared its cruel white teeth, and it seemed he might cry his eyes out. He sobbed so sadly that Hachiro, who for all that he was a giant mountain youth, began to feel quite wretched too, and finally shed an enormous tear, huge as a millstone.

"All right, I get it. Hang on, okay?" Hachiro said as he headed out toward the pathetic little embankment where the villagers were shouting and arguing as they tried to bolster it.

"Hey! Hold on there. I'll take care of that for you," he said to the farmers, and he peered out at the sea.

By this time, far offshore, the sea had grown dark and ominous. Capped with ragged gray clouds, the sea sent white water splashing and spraying high above like a gigantic fountain.

Hachiro kicked away the menacing waves that snapped at his feet as the water poured over him. Carefully, he placed the little boy in his hand somewhere safe and dry, and then sped back to the foot of the mountains.

"Umph!" he groaned as he tried to lift up a mountain. But a mountain is still a mountain. It may have creaked and shifted a bit, but it remained firmly rooted to the ground.

Hachiro began to wonder if this wasn't going to work after all. But then, he remembered the little boy crying so hard that his tears flew all around.

"You darned old mountain!" he bellowed.

Hachiro grabbed the mountain with one hand on the peak and one on its foot. It wobbled and made squeaks, groans, cracks, and all sorts of odd noises, but finally, he managed to get it up off the ground. With his face flushed bright red from the great effort, he staggered right and left as he carried his heavy burden, down toward the shoreline. As he neared the beach, the villagers were awed to see an entire mountain in his arms. But the old sea grew angry and blew a cold, cold wind whistling toward the shore. The mountain on Hachiro's shoulders began to shudder and tremble as it cried, "Hey Hachiro, it's cold! I'm freezing!"

Hachiro scolded the mountain, saying, "Cut the noise! Don't you feel sorry for the poor little boy?" Then he tossed the mountain deep into the sea. "Yah!"

Do you know what the sea did? It broke into two, yes, right into two seas, and the splash from the mountain flew up high enough to blacken the sun. Then, seawater came pouring down from the skies like an afternoon cloudburst, rumbling as it escaped out into the depths, away from the shoreline.

The farmers who had been watching were overjoyed, exclaiming, "We're so grateful! You've stopped the sea from flooding us. Now our fields will be safe. You're a wonderful mountain lad, Hachiro!" Though the little boy had been crying just moments before, now he clapped his hands, cute as tiny Japanese maple leaves.

Hachiro's widening grin was just revealing his bright white teeth when the little boy looked toward the sea again and began to wail.

⮌

Hachiro turned and saw that the sea was furious. The waters of the ocean had conferred offshore, and gathered in determination to swallow up the farmers' fields. It surged closer, roiling and whirling. The villagers fell into a frenzied panic, and the little boy was flinging teardrops right and left as he sobbed.

"Don't cry, little one," said Hachiro. "You'll make me want to weep, too. But don't worry. Watch!" Then he turned and called to the mountain that he'd thrown into the sea, its peak still visible above the waterline. "Hey mountain. Yes, you there complaining of the cold. I'm coming out to join you."

By now the sea was already sweeping toward the shore with a thunderous roar that threatened to swallow all the fields at once. Hachiro patted the crying little boy on the head before turning toward the sea. He grinned back over his shoulder, said "I'm off!" and charged into the oncoming surf, shouting at the top of his lungs with his arms spread wide, pushing the waves back with his chest as he plunged into the depths of the sea.

The sea shoved Hachiro. Hachiro shoved back. The sea shoved again. The waters reached his belly, then his chest, and then his shoulders. They finally rose to his neck and all the way up to his nose. Hachiro yelled loud enough to topple everything in sight, "Now I know! This is why I always wanted to grow bigger! To be big enough to be of use someday! Right, little *warashi*?"

The farmers who had gathered at the shore shouted out, "That's exactly why you grew. You're absolutely right, and you've helped us so much."

They were crying.

But the little boy, well, he was still very young and didn't quite understand what was going on. When the waves had covered Hachiro's head, those birds who nested in his hair flew up all at once, singing, "Cheep cheep, chirp chirp, tweet tweet, cuckoo!" and the boy was so delighted that he began to clap his tiny hands in joy.

After Hachiro had disappeared under the waves, little bubbles twirled and burst above the water where his head had been. It seemed almost as if Hachiro was laughing along with the little boy.

Now that Hachiro had planted himself in its belly and was keeping it firmly at bay, the sea had no choice but to give up and go out deep where it raged to itself, tossing up waves in a temper. That is why even today, the sea throws its tantrums far off shore.

So this is how Hachiro Lake was formed, and Hachiro still protects us from the sea. A mere whistle from Hachiro will have whitecaps speeding away from Kado village out to the Wakimoto coast.

The mountain that Hachiro sank halfway up its belly in the sea, well, it's still as full of complaints as ever and continues to cry, "It's so cold! I'm freezing," as it shivers in the icy Tohoku winds. The villagers tease it with the name Samukaze-yama—Cold Wind Mountain—and when the bitter breeze blows in from the sea, the mountain cowers and whimpers shamelessly.

Of course you're wondering what became of that little *warashi*, right? Well, that boy grew bigger and bigger every day, wanting to be just like Hachiro, to be of use to those in need, and he's out there now, doing just that, somewhere in the great wide world.

The Lost Property Office

by Marji Napper

"I think this is a waste of time, Mitzi," said my friend, Maki.

"If you don't look, you can't find it," I said.

"I don't think I'll find it even if I do look."

We had been having this conversation for nearly a week now. I was beginning to get tired of it. But it's true that you can't find something if you don't look. If I'd been Maki I would have tried the lost property office the very next day, in the hope that someone might have handed in my lost homework and books. She had to give her project in by the end of the week, and she'd done so much work on it that she was bound to get an A. I couldn't understand how she could work so hard on something and then just let it go.

Maki and I had been friends since we had started at the international school a few months earlier. Her family had just returned to Japan after two years in America, and she spoke good English. My father had just finished his posting in Spain and had been transferred to Tokyo, and my mother and I had come too. It wasn't the constant changing of schools and friends that got to me so much, but the constant change of languages. It was okay at school, because the lessons were in English. It was all the rest that frustrated me. It's hard to be living in a new country where you are unable to read or even have a proper conversation with the people you meet. And Japanese is so different from English—you can't even guess at words and their meanings like you can when you are learning Spanish.

We seemed to have been walking through tunnels forever. That's what the underground railway system is like. You can practically walk from one end of the city to the other through the wide, high-ceilinged tunnels that connect the stations and their exits. Tokyo Station is almost a city itself.

The lost property office was supposed to be near exit C20. We had been looking for ages, and we'd asked at least ten people, none of whom knew. Maki was getting nervous and crabby. I could tell she just wanted to give up and go home, but I didn't.

Finally we found it. The door was in the middle of a long, blank, white wall. I had spotted the words *Lost Property* in blocky roman letters beneath the Japanese writing. I began to push open the door.

With a sigh of resignation, Maki followed me in.

Inside the office was a long, white counter with some boxes of pens and two or three piles of forms. Everything was white, and it looked almost like a clinic. There was no one behind the counter though.

"Let's go," said Maki.

"I can't believe you'd come all this way and then go home without even asking!" I said.

"I can't believe I came all this way," said Maki.

She turned round and was making for the door when I spotted the bell.

"OK," I said, "You go if you want to. I'm going to stay and ask."

"I don't like it here," said Maki in a small voice. She looked at me pleadingly.

"Well, you go home and I'll ask," I said, in a more kindly voice. I wasn't quite sure how I was going to ask, because my Japanese still hadn't progressed beyond the basics.

She said, "Thanks," in a whisper and shot out the door. I rang the bell.

Immediately a man came in from a door behind the counter. He wasn't young and he walked with a stick, but his hair was still black, not white—more parent material than grandparent. He had eyes the dark brown of burnt sienna. I liked him instantly.

"Can I help you?" he asked in a helpful voice.

"I hope so," I replied. "My friend left her homework on the train last Thursday. I was hoping someone had handed it in."

"Why didn't your friend come?"

"Well, she did. But she's shy."

"I see," said the man.

He didn't sound very encouraging, and suddenly I wondered if I had been stupid to come here after all.

"Her homework and some books," I said. "She left them on the train."

"I see," he repeated. "A project on the Aztec civilization? Written by Maki Takeyama?"

"Yes. Yes . . . that's it!" I agreed excitedly. "Have you got it?"

"We've got everything that has been lost," he said, so solemnly that it made me want to giggle.

"Everything?" I asked, stifling my laughter.

"Yes."

"The ring of power from 'The Lord of the Rings'?" I suggested.

"That was destroyed, not lost. Anyway, it was fiction."

"The Gordian Knot?"

"Cut, not lost," he pointed out.

"The lost city of Atlantis? The philosophers' stone?"

"Yes and yes," he said.

"Uh-huh? How about the kitten I lost when I was eight?" I asked.

He seemed to be as amused as I was.

"The tabby kitten you had for your birthday? It disappeared the next morning. You searched for it everywhere. You cried for weeks because you didn't know if it was okay."

"Yes, that one," I said, my voice just a whisper threaded with fright, because this was personal, and how could he know?

He bent down then and rummaged behind the counter. When he straightened up he had a tabby kitten with white paws, which he placed carefully on the countertop. The kitten opened its mouth in a small pink mew, just as it had on my birthday five years ago. And I felt exactly the same rush of excitement and delight I'd felt five years ago. All my *oh-yeah*-ness dribbled away. I had absolutely no doubt that it was the same kitten. It even had the red-and-green bow that my father had bought for it in the market in Seville and had tied around its neck. I picked it up. It was small and soft and solid. It moved uneasily and I could feel its heart beating against my palms.

"Can I keep it?" I asked in a small voice.

"Technically, yes. It was given to you."

"But?" I asked.

"But a small boy, who has loved this cat for five years, will wake up tomorrow morning and find that his pet has died."

"Cats have nine lives," I protested.

"Yes, but they have to stay with the animal. They're not that divisible."

I remembered all the misery and anxiety I had felt when it got lost. I almost felt it all over again. Then I thought that was exactly how that little boy would feel if I took my kitten back. I stroked its stripy head, and reluctantly, I handed it back to the lost property man. He held it cupped in his hands for a moment, and then suddenly the kitten disappeared.

"What happened?" I asked.

"It isn't lost property anymore," he said. "You've found it."

"So now it's the little boy's cat?"

"Exactly. Case closed. That's how it works."

He rummaged behind the counter again and brought out a red folder with a map of Peru on the front and three new, expensive-looking books.

I was about to take them when another man came in. He nodded to the lost property man and then to me. He pulled out a large bag from his pocket. It only occurred to me much later that the bag was far too big to fit into his pocket. From the bag he withdrew a necklace that seemed to be made of diamonds, but perhaps it was only imitation. There were also two rings. He then produced a notebook computer, two briefcases, and a bag of peaches. "The computer and briefcases won't be a problem," he said. "But we can't do much about the jewelry unless people come in to claim it. Is that your homework?" he added, turning to me. "I hope you don't mind, but I read it. I really liked it."

"Um, it's my friend's. But I don't think she'd mind."

"Oh good." Then he turned back to the older man and said, "We're going to have to get some more Finders, uncle. We can't keep up, you know."

And looking at the two of them, one on each side of the counter, I suddenly realized that of course they were related. The younger man was taller, but he was more or less the same build and they had the same beautiful eyes. The younger man looked like a less time-battered version of the older.

"I'm good at finding things," I said.

The older man bent over the counter to look more closely at me. Then he gave me a tremendously friendly smile.

"I rather think you are," he said. "Would you like a job for summer break?"

"Yes!" I said, without even pausing to consider it.

My father was on a business trip and my mother had gone with him. I was staying with my Aunt Jane, who had been living in Tokyo for as long as I could remember and who was so engrossed in her job that she didn't notice what I did. The summer break was starting in a week and Maki was going away with her parents. Until this moment I hadn't been looking forward to the summer, but if I had a job . . .

"Take this home and ask your mother to sign it," he said. "If she has any questions, she can phone me on the number at the top of the form. My name is Motomeru and this is Yuki, my assistant and also my nephew."

On the train going home I was really excited. I'd found Maki's homework and I had something interesting to do for summer break. I didn't think then how strange it was that I, who could only speak the most basic Japanese, had had such a long conversation and hadn't missed a word.

When I got home there was a note from my Aunt Jane. It said that she was at a meeting but that she would be home in time to cook dinner. A likely story! I clipped Marmaduke's leash to his collar and then we walked round to Maki's house, which is only a few streets away from Aunt Jane's.

Mrs. Takeyama answered the door. I like Mrs. Takeyama. She has always been kind to me, ever since Maki and I met on our first day at the international school. She doesn't seem to mind Marmaduke, though I don't think she really likes dogs in general. Mr. Takeyama thinks Marmaduke is brilliant and always asks after him if I turn up at their house without him.

"You found Maki's homework!" were Mrs. Takeyama's first words on seeing me. "You are an angel, Mitzi," she told me, smiling.

"You found it!" Maki squeaked.

"Well, the Lost Property people found it. I just collected it."

She jumped up and hugged me. That was very unlike Maki, which just showed how miserable she had been.

I spent the evening with the Takeyama's. We played games and ate hugely. Mrs. Takeyama thinks I need large amounts of Western food to sustain me, so she made a brilliant chicken and pasta dish that she'd learned to cook in America. Later we watched a DVD (in English, for my benefit), as we ate Japanese cakes, sweet peaches, and tiny aromatic grapes and laughed at Marmaduke, who had eaten so many snacks that he looked like he'd swallowed a soccer ball.

I got home just a few minutes before Aunt Jane. Things that would have left a normal adult crushed with guilt (leaving a thirteen-year-old on her own all evening, except for the dog, and without dinner) affected her as much as an ice cube hitting the *Titanic*. This had hidden advantages, of course. When I asked her to sign a form—"Summer project!" I explained, airily—Aunt Jane assumed it was something to do with school and signed it without reading it.

When I went to the Lost Property office the next day after school, I was sure I'd never be able to find it again, but I headed for exit C20 and to my astonishment I found it—the plain door in the white wall, with the sign saying *Lost* and *Property*. Mr. Motomeru took the form and looked at it. There seemed to be something suspicious in that look, as if he knew I had got it signed without being entirely honest.

"You can start next Saturday morning," he said.

🙢

Tokyo Station, in spite of its vast size, is almost litter free. So, on my way to work on Saturday, I easily spotted a lost toy. It was in a corridor broad enough to take eight people walking abreast. The toy was lying on the floor, next to the wall. It looked like one of Marmaduke's toys, chewed and discolored. It might once have been a rabbit and it was filthy.

I opened the door of the lost property office to be met by a blast of bawling infant. I almost backed out again. A woman was standing at the counter trying to talk to Mr. Motomeru, and her child, slung over her shoulder, was screaming so loudly that they could probably hear her all the way to exit A1. As I pushed through the door, the screaming stopped. The silence was so loud that everybody froze. The child gave a hiccup and held out her hand toward me.

After a confused moment, I realized that the little girl wasn't holding out her hand to me but to the disgusting, dirty toy I had. I walked over to her and gave it to her. The mother was instantly all apologies and gratitude. She spoke so fast that I wouldn't normally have understood a word. But that morning I did.

Mr. Motomeru smiled at me.

"I can see you're going to be a good Finder," he said.

Yuki and I spent the morning on the trains. We didn't really go anywhere, we just kind of train hopped, looking for things that people had left behind. Occasionally we managed to return an item to someone before it was really lost. An elderly gentleman dropped a book as he shuffled off the train, and Yuki pulled me out just before the train doors closed and gave him the book back.

"Time for a break," Yuki announced. He flopped down on one of those fearfully uncomfortable plastic seats with no backs, gave me a bottle of green tea, and opened another for himself.

"How long have you been doing this?" I asked.

"Since I left school," Yuki replied, and downed the drink. He didn't say how long ago that was. But it seemed an odd way to spend your time—train hopping your way around the metro and the Japan Railway lines picking up lost cases, jewelry, and children's toys.

"Are you ready for something a little more demanding?" he asked.

"I'm ready for anything!"

That made him howl with laughter. He clapped me on the shoulder and took my now empty PET bottle, sending it zinging into a recycling bin with deadly aim.

"Mrs. Hashimoto is coming into the office this afternoon. We need to find her photo," Yuki added.

Before I could ask who Mrs. Hashimoto was, Yuki took hold of my arm and the ground started to shake. I thought it was an earthquake at first. Then the world shifted and changed. It wasn't painful or difficult but it made me feel confused for a few moments.

"Where are we?" I whispered.

"Tokyo Station," said Yuki.

I gaped. It was Tokyo Station, but not the one I knew. It was the original building, the one you see in those historic photos of Tokyo—all quiet and deserted looking, though it was busy enough this morning. The red brick façade was the same, but the tall buildings and signs in English and the modern cars and tarmac roads had gone.

Yuki said, "There she is."

I saw a young woman in a kimono, and with her a young man in a Western business suit. They looked distracted and were hurrying into the station with a couple of suitcases and some bags stuffed with belongings. One of the bags was so badly packed that you could see things were going to fall out of it, and sure enough, they did. A shoe fell out first, then a paper fan, and finally a photo in a small wood frame.

Saying: "Don't move!" Yuki dove for the photo, scooped it off the station floor, and dashed after the couple, running like a greyhound. He nearly made it, but they unexpectedly turned left and disappeared into a wave of people, and we couldn't see them any longer. He came back with the photo in his hand.

"Oh, well," he said, grinning. "It was worth trying."

And he held my arm again and the old world shimmered away and we were back where and when we had been only a few minutes before.

When we got back to the office, Mr. Motomeru was sitting on the padded bench talking to a very small old woman. She was dressed in a kimono, and she was so bent over that her back seemed to be one large hump. Her hands and head trembled.

In a frail, quavering voice, she was saying, "It was my husband, in his graduation gown. The frame was wooden, quite cheap. You think I'm silly, don't you?" she added, sadly. "I think I'm silly—coming to a lost property office that wasn't even here when I lost his photo." She paused a moment. "I can't think why I came, really. But it's the only photo I ever had of him, and some days I can hardly remember his face. I can't bear to die not being able to remember his face." And her voice quivered away into nothing, and a tear dropped onto her lap.

Yuki crossed the room and put the photo into her hands.

She sat for a moment motionless, silent. Another tear dropped onto her lap. She didn't ask how. I suppose *how* wasn't important to her. She just stared and stared at the photo and then hugged it to her chest. I suddenly understood how Yuki could do this job day after day without getting bored. He did it for the Mrs. Hashimotos, who came for things lost in hurry or confusion, things that money couldn't replace and that they were too desperate to do without; he did it for people who came in spite of the apparent craziness of asking for something so long lost that it was beyond belief that it might have turned up. Beyond belief, but not beyond hope.

"How?" I asked, when Mrs. Hashimoto had left. "How did you know when she was going to come in here? How did you go back to the right time and place to find it? How did you have my kitten ready for me? How can I understand everything that's said in this office when I can barely manage a simple conversation in Japanese outside it?"

"Slow down!" protested Yuki. "Life is more complicated and simple than you think."

I looked at him to see if he was teasing. He smiled a smile that held a promise.

"Did you learn to speak English on the day you were born?" he asked, and when I shook my head, "Or Spanish on your first day in Seville or Japanese on your first day in Tokyo? You have a million questions, but you don't have to ask them all on the first day. And we probably couldn't explain the answers so that you'd understand them today. Experience and time will help you learn what you want to know."

It was on the tip of my tongue to reply that experience and time would teach us everything, but then, suddenly, I knew what he would say to that. *Only if you want to know.* Well, I did want to know. The promise in Yuki's smile was, I thought, a promise of adventure and answers.

They sent me home after lunch. Hopping trains and hopping time, they assured me, took it out of you.

On the way home, tired and happy, thinking about the things I had learned and wondering about the things I was going to learn, I missed my station. As I got off the train to find another to take me back, I realized that there was no need ever to worry about being lost again. Yuki, I thought, would always know where to find me.

Anton and Kiyohime

by Fumio Takano
translated by Hart Larrabee

Anyone who has been to the Kremlin knows the great bell—the Tsar of Bells—near Moscow's Cathedral Square. It stands more than six meters tall and weighs two hundred tons, but no one has ever heard it ring. The bell is cracked and broken, and has lost a chunk two meters wide. Even in Russia, where everything is grandiose, the scale of the bell is unrivaled.

There is a story about how the Tsar of Bells came to be broken. Long, long ago, in the days of that half-legendary old country the Soviet Union, there was a scientist named Anton who lived in Tokyo. With his record of scientific achievements and an impressive title bestowed upon him by the Soviet state, he enjoyed special treatment by the Japanese authorities. In the course of his work Anton called annually at the home of a dignitary named Managono Shoji, and there came to know the man's daughter, Kiyohime. A romance seems to have blossomed, yet when Anton was summoned back to his homeland he left without saying good-bye. Enraged, Kiyohime transformed into a flaming serpent and pursued him to Moscow. Anton fled to the Kremlin and hid inside the Tsar of Bells, but she coiled herself around it, scorching him to death and breaking the bell. Then, her passions spent, the serpent cast herself into the Moscow River and met her end. Such is the tale of Anton and Kiyohime.

Although the current government of Russia has never acknowledged it, Anton is said to have been a Soviet spy. Did he make some commitment to Kiyohime about their future? Or was hers a love unrequited? It is impossible to know today.

⌐

Listening to the tolling of the "Bell of Time" in Ueno Park, Olegs was thinking about the legend of Anton and Kiyohime. The cherry blossoms were nearly in full bloom. In their banter that morning the weather forecasters had said that, barring evening showers, Saturday would be perfect for blossom viewing. Each of the identical blue tarps already spread throughout the park was a claim staked in the battle for the best locations—now one of Japan's rites of spring. Some groups were even getting a head start on their carousing.

Olegs passed through the Ameyoko open-air market on his way to the station and then took the train to Akihabara to browse the *otaku* shops and electronics stores before returning to his lodgings in Ikenohata. It was actually his uncle's place; Olegs was just passing through. Uncle Peteris was a physicist, and from Ikenohata he could both walk to the university where he worked and reach the particle accelerator at the research center in Tsukuba without changing trains. The boardinghouse itself was an eclectic prewar mix of Japanese and Western styles, and would have been an appealing place to live even if the location had been less convenient.

Olegs had just finished a short-term exchange program at a university in western Japan and planned to spend a few days in Tokyo before returning to Latvia. Most in the program had been college students but Olegs was among a select few still in high school. Latvia had a special Japanese-language school—a well-kept secret—that students could attend even from a young age. Studying there had enabled Olegs to arrive in Japan with a better command of the language than most who majored in the subject at university.

Olegs returned to Ikenohata in the evening just as Peteris was leaving.

"Olegs, I'll be staying at the lab tonight and heading straight to Tsukuba in the morning. I think I mentioned this before, but our team finally has some time on the accelerator."

"Sorry to have come when you're so busy, but I'll be okay." Olegs flashed a confident grin. "Everyone here's real nice, and my Japanese is loads better than yours."

"I'm not worried. I'll be back by noon Sunday."

"Does this mean you're going to shoot the time cannon?"

"That's right. If all goes as planned we'll launch at six tomorrow night."

"But Uncle, your experiment will change the past, right? You're try-ing to keep Anton and Kiyohime from meeting—to save Anton. If you succeed, won't that also change the present?"

"There's nothing to worry about. Our calculations take everything into account. We won't be creating any 'grandfather paradoxes.' Don't look so concerned." Peteris patted Olegs on the shoulder. "We'll just ex-ecute a minor phase shift at the moment when Anton and Kiyohime meet. I know exactly when that was. There's a plasticity to time-space like that of a nervous system. Information moves back and forth across the gaps between past, present, and future to ensure balance is maintained. Our molecular-level experiments irradiating tachyon particles ended ages ago. We've proved the theory is sound."

"Well, the physics is way over my head. But what's really been bug-ging me—I've been kind of afraid to ask—is, was Anton really a Soviet spy? And if he was, why do you want to help him when you hate Russia and the Soviet Union so much? I don't get it."

The immolation of a Soviet spy is something that an Eastern European who loathed the USSR might be expected to welcome. Indeed, it would not have surprised Olegs in the least to hear Peteris bemoan the fact that Kiyohime hadn't torched the entire Kremlin while she was at it.

"Yes, Anton was a Soviet spy. But I want to help him anyway." Peteris's candid admission caught Olegs off guard. "As a scientist he was my friend. That's all. Wish me luck." He raised a hand as if to ward off any further questions from his bewildered nephew, picked up the bag of fresh *taiyaki* the landlady had provided as a snack, and stepped out the front door into the darkening street.

⌒

Olegs awoke the next morning, a bit later that usual, to find that the fam-ily Peteris boarded with was already getting ready for cherry-blossom viewing. The landlord had left bright and early to help the local neigh-borhood association set things up.

Knowing he would be of little help in preparing the boxes of tradi-tional picnic fare, Olegs headed out for a walk. The trees were sure to be in bloom everywhere, not just at the famous sites, so he decided to head toward Yanaka. His map showed dozens of temples there. According to his guidebook, the Nezu, Sendagi, and Yanaka areas were all considered one continuous neighborhood. A residential area, it was also a tourist destination popular for its old-fashioned workshops and cafés.

Wandering through the narrow one-way lanes, Olegs noted the small temple gates scattered among the old-style row houses. Most of the temples to which they led consisted of just a main worship hall, a priest's residence, and a modest graveyard, but all were meticulously maintained. Everywhere the cherry trees were in full bloom.

As he ambled along enjoying the scenery, Olegs soon realized he had lost his way.

Early April in Tokyo was quite warm, comparable to early summer in Riga. But when a gust of wind carrying a scattering of cherry petals blew across the back of Olegs's neck he tugged his jacket closer against a sudden chill. Sensing a flicker of motion just out of sight he looked up and saw a small, weathered temple gate at the end of the alley.

Although it looked similar to the other small temples he had already passed, Olegs found himself drawn to this one and stepped hesitantly through the gate. The approach led directly to the main hall, passing a narrow graveyard on the right. A cluster of stone monuments with moss-covered bases stood between the graveyard and the path.

Something white had been set at the base of the large monument at the rear. Drawing closer, Olegs saw it was a bottle of *sake* wrapped in white paper. He was astonished to see Peteris's full name written on it in Japanese.

The inscription in the stone was weatherworn and the old-fashioned calligraphy would have been hard to make out even for a Japanese, but Olegs felt reluctant to give up without trying to decipher a character or two. Running his fingers over the rough stone, he suddenly brought them to a halt.

"Kiyohime . . . ?"

He was certain he had read it correctly. Absorbed in the inscription, Olegs was startled by the unexpected crunch of footsteps on the gravel path behind him and whirled around.

A young priest stood before the main hall, having appeared as if from nowhere. Olegs often found it difficult to gauge how old Japanese people were, but he knew the man had to be somewhat older than he was. His well-shaped head was cleanly shaven, his facial features composed, and he wore stylish black-rimmed glasses. As the priest stepped closer, a single cherry petal slipped from the shoulder of his black robes and fluttered to the ground.

"Hi. You must be the physicist's son," said the priest in unaccented English.

"No," Olegs replied in Japanese. "I'm his nephew."

"Well," the priest switched to Japanese without missing a beat. "You look just like him. Peteris brought that by this morning before heading to Tsukuba, as an offering for the experiment's success. I must admit I never thought tachyon particles even existed except in vintage science fiction. Peteris is quite a scholar, isn't he?"

"Thanks. It isn't easy, though. Always being compared to somebody so distinguished."

With an easygoing smile, the priest invited Olegs to join him for a cup of tea.

Sitting on cushions on the open veranda of the main hall, they introduced themselves. The priest gave his name as Kyuan. He seemed accustomed to dealing with foreigners and didn't make a fuss over either Olegs's unexpectedly good Japanese or his interest in visiting temples and shrines.

Olegs made up his mind to ask about the stone monument. "Is that Kiyohime's grave?"

"It's a memorial. But you're welcome to think of it as if it were her real grave."

"What's the connection between your temple and Kiyohime?"

"There are stories that have been passed down, but no credible historical evidence. Isn't it enough, though, that there *is* a connection? After all, the people of Edo love the Kiyohime story. They couldn't get enough of the classic Noh version, so they adapted it to Kabuki, and now look how many variations have been produced. This year's Kabuki calendar even began with a performance in which the great Ichikawa Danjuro himself was the one to stamp out Kiyohime's rage. Being a fan of the *aragoto* style, I was excited to see the alternate ending with the demon driven back to the stage along the *hanamichi* walkway."

"'Demon . . . ?' You make it sound like Kiyohime's the villain."

"That's just how the people of Edo show their love. Like the way fan fiction reworks famous stories."

Kyuan refilled their cups and plucked a dry sweet from a dish. A scattering of petals fluttered onto the veranda. "The way to console the spirits of the dead is by keeping them alive in memory—by thinking about them from time to time—not by erecting splendid gravestones inscribed with generous eulogies. Year after year the people of Edo flock to see new variations on the Kiyohime story performed and experience her passion and pain as if it were their own. She knows that even being cast as a demon to be subdued is, in its own way, a form of love."

"Well, maybe Kiyohime's fine with that, but it has to be rough on Anton. He ends up looking like a total creep."

Kyuan laughed. "Well, you're a handsome young man. And I see you know how it feels to be pursued by a woman." Olegs felt taken aback, as if the priest had seen right through him and uncovered his hidden conceit.

"But . . . Well, I was just wondering how my uncle's experiment would go." Olegs's attempt to change the subject was forced but Kyuan let it go. "If they succeed, Anton will be saved. And Kiyohime will no longer be a monster that cursed a man with a hideous end, will she? Even the Tsar of Bells at the Kremlin won't have to be broken."

"You do not, I see, despise Russia as your uncle does."

"No, not as much as my uncle. I mean, I feel—how should I put it—more lukewarm than most Latvians. I'm definitely not part of the pro-Russian crowd. Russia's a difficult neighbor, but I feel no hatred."

"Someday the Russians will find in you a very formidable opponent."

"Why? I just told you I don't hate Russia."

"Exactly." Kyuan paused for a moment and looked at Olegs as if to make sure his meaning had gotten through. "Hate is the same as love. You must have heard the saying, 'The greatest hate springs from the greatest love.' Well, hate also morphs into love before you know it. The powerful emotions, the obsession with the other—it's just like being in love. Your heart is under the control of the other. The more you hate them the more you are captive to them. Those who hate Russia, and revel in their loathing, have lost their hearts to Russia as surely as someone consumed by love. But you're different. Could the Russians ask for a more formidable adversary? After all, yours is a heart they cannot steal."

Like a flash of light Olegs grasped what Kyuan meant. The priest stood up and held out his left hand. A single cherry petal settled into his palm as if beckoned there.

"But be careful during your stay in Tokyo. This is a city that worships many deities and monsters, in a location said to be ideal for containing their power—or for drawing on their strength. They say Tokyo sits on a 'dragon vein'—a path traveled by dragons. You know Shinobazu Pond, that artificial lake in Ueno Park? It was built as a watering hole for dragons. That area is a 'power spot,' the sort of place where you can easily become disoriented and fall prey to unseen forces. Be careful, particularly tonight." The cherry petal, rather than falling from Kyuan's hand, seemed to have vanished within it.

Before Olegs had a chance to ask what Kyuan meant, the priest resumed speaking.

"Tonight at the Kremlin there will be a memorial service for the Tsar of Bells. Or so we describe it here in Japan. It's actually a Russian Orthodox ceremony, a *panikhida*, paying tribute to Anton's memory."

"I've never heard of that before."

"Today is the anniversary of Anton's death. The ceremony will be broadcast live and streamed on the web. It starts just after five o'clock here. People will probably be watching on their cell phones during their blossom parties, and there are public viewing sites all around the city. But I really have to be going. I must be in Ueno tonight, too. You should be getting home. When you get out to the street, take a left and you'll come to a busy road that's well marked. From there you'll be able to find your way."

Figuring that Kyuan must have his reasons, Olegs didn't give much thought to being rushed from the temple. Then, just as Kyuan had said, he immediately found his bearings. Still, how had Kyuan known he was lost? Olegs only realized how peculiar that was as he ate a late lunch of fried-rice omelet at a greasy spoon in Yanaka's Yomise shopping arcade.

↬

No, he had sensed that things were strange even before lunch. There had been puzzling signs, both seen and unseen. In fact, there was something odd about the entire Yanaka area.

The Yanaka Ginza shopping street, which he had expected to find swarming with weekend tourists, was surprisingly quiet. Indeed, by midday a number of stores were already closed. Along the side streets, colorful long-sleeved *furisode* kimono had been hung out to air. As a man loaded beer crates into a car, a middle-aged woman in *furisode* walked by with a cloth-wrapped bundle in one hand and a cell phone pressed to her ear. People seemed to be closing up shop early to enjoy the cherry blossoms.

As Olegs watched he had a sudden revelation. If a dragon vein ran through Tokyo, could there be a "serpent vein," too? What if the wrath of Kiyohime, taking the form of a serpent, followed such a route from Moscow back to Japan and cursed Peteris's experiment?

Finding himself near Nippori Station, Olegs boarded the Yamanote Line. The train was crowded with men carrying bulky parcels and women dressed up in *furisode*. Ueno Station was packed, even more congested than during the morning rush hour. His guidebook said more than three hundred thousand people visited Ueno Park daily during cherry-blossom season. Three hundred thousand people! That was almost one-seventh the population of Latvia! How in the world was he ever going to find Kyuan?

Afternoon yielded slowly to evening. Great LCD screens had been set up before the museum and at the baseball field. Olegs navigated the sea of people carefully to avoid getting tangled in the trailing sleeves of the women's kimono. Overhead, the cherry blossoms were more splendid than before, having grown an even deeper shade of pink since the previous day.

Swept along by the crowd, Olegs headed toward the fountain. In the plaza a panoramic view opened up around the distinctive façade of the Tokyo National Museum. The illuminated fountain sparkled, and large-screen displays glimmered brightly all around. No sooner had the test image faded than a cheer rose from the crowd. The memorial service for the Tsar of Bells, broadcast live from Russia, had begun.

Dressed in ceremonial vestments glittering with brocade and jewels, the priests had just arrived at the square before the Tsar of Bells. Government officials and military leaders stood in orderly rows. The President and Prime Minister observed the proceedings with their wives from the stand of honor as the censers were swung.

Uncertain what would come next, everyone watched closely as the ceremony got under way. Many were also tapping at their cell phones and laptops.

Olegs looked around carefully. Would Kyuan be wearing his black robes or street clothes? What if instead of jeans and a sweatshirt he wore hip-hop fashion with a cap pulled over his shaved head?

"Olegs! Over here!"

Olegs stopped dead in his tracks, stunned to hear someone calling his name. But it was just the landlord's family and the folks from the neighborhood association. They had managed to secure a choice spot near the fountain.

No sooner had Olegs sat down with them on their blue plastic tarp than he was handed a plate of sushi rolls and grilled chicken skewers. The landlady and her elderly mother-in-law both wore *furisode* that smelled of old-fashioned camphor mothballs. Olegs was sure he had been taught that only unmarried girls wore *furisode*, and then only on special occasions. Was this really how people enjoyed the cherry blossoms?

Suddenly the crowd let out a roar. Something was happening at the Kremlin. Peering up at the display Olegs saw that a beautiful young woman with black hair, wearing *furisode* with a cherry-blossom design, was now addressing the priests and the President. In Ueno Park, the women in *furisode* all stood up from their picnics and moved toward the plaza together with those who had been walking through the park. A number of people pulled out *shamisen*.

From somewhere came the sound of singing in the *nagauta* style of the Kabuki theater, and at the Kremlin the woman in *furisode* began to dance before the bell.

> *Apart from the flowers there are only pines*
> *Fleeting blossoms give way to endless yearning*
> *And darkness brings the ringing of the temple bell*

Unraveling the meaning of *nagauta*, with its archaic language and peculiar vocalizations, can be a challenge. Olegs, however, found everything coming together so clearly that he took no notice of his own uncanny ability to make sense of the lyrics and the situation.

The woman at the Kremlin—a *shirabyoshi* dancer—turned to face the bell. The intensity of her gaze made Olegs shudder. She wore a tall, gold-colored court cap, and as she began to dance the women in Ueno fell into step.

There is much to resent in the tolling of the bell
Struck as night falls, it evokes the impermanence of all things

The *nagauta* continued, comparing the ringing of bells at certain hours with Buddhist teachings. The paper lanterns hung among the cherry blossoms were now lit, enveloping the dancing women and their colorful *furisode* in a dreamy pink glow. Olegs had been watching, entranced, when he was abruptly brought back to his senses by a glimpse of black clothing.

Saying that he needed to find a friend, Olegs excused himself from the landlord's party. The dancing now under way made the search for Kyuan even more of a challenge than before. The tone of the *nagauta* changed, shifting to a lively cataloging of famous pleasure quarters throughout Japan. Jostled by the crowd, Olegs glanced up at the monitors. At the Kremlin the *shirabyoshi* dancer had removed her hat, and her pale blue *furisode* seemed different. Her kimono sash, its ends dangling loosely, was decorated with circular designs. He was certain her *furisode* had been red before.

Beyond the dancing women Olegs saw a man in black robes. It had to be Kyuan. Then he noticed other men wearing black throughout the plaza. Restless and seemingly unable to contain themselves, they, too, began to dance. But one priest did not join the others. That was Kyuan.

Iris and blue flag are sisters
And so similar the color of their flowers
Who can say which is the older and which the younger?
From east and west all come to see the flower-like face
And gazing upon it fall more deeply in love
With the winsome maiden

Fireworks were being launched into the sky. As he struggled to make his way through the crowd, Olegs heard people saying Twitter and Facebook were down. Catching sight of Olegs as he approached, Kyuan smiled as if to say he'd been waiting for him.

Neglecting preliminaries, Olegs abruptly demanded, "You said there's a dragon vein in Tokyo. Is there a serpent vein, too?"

"A serpent vein? Hmm. Well, if you think so, there may be. And if you don't, then I suppose not."

"Stop fooling around and tell me! I'm serious. If the accelerator shoots an elementary particle across time, couldn't that rouse a serpent in Tokyo?

"Calm down. Don't give in to your emotions. Outsiders like you are especially vulnerable to being possessed." Kyuan turned to face Olegs directly, paused for a moment, then spoke quietly and firmly. "Regardless of what happens from here on out, you must accept that what happens will happen, and what doesn't won't. If you can't, you'll never make it back."

More and more people joined in with the music. Performers in Ueno played everything from electric guitars to baroque flutes and beat boxes. At the Kremlin a balalaika ensemble played the *shamisen* parts as if it were the most natural thing in the world. The music grew calmer and the *shirabyoshi*, a long strip of cloth in hand, began a graceful dance. Her costume, once again transformed, was now a lavender *furisode* decorated with boughs of weeping cherry.

> *I first learned of love and then experienced it*
> *For whom did I redden my lips and blacken my teeth?*
> *It was all to show my devotion to you*

The sun went down. The sleeves of the *shirabyoshi's furisode* now depicted ceremonial drums decorated with flames against a saffron ground. A small drum hung around her neck. She tapped it daintily with little drumsticks as the *nagauta* conveyed the passion of a woman tormented by love. In Ueno, lasers concealed on the roofs of the museum and temple buildings billowed across the sky like the northern lights.

As the *shirabyoshi* knelt and leaned backward, Olegs was struck by a sudden realization: she was no ordinary dancing girl; she was the spirit of Kiyohime. He turned toward Kyuan for confirmation, but the priest simply knelt and took up his prayer beads.

What had happened with the time cannon? It was just turning six o'clock. If all had gone as scheduled, it was being fired at that very moment.

The air began to resonate with the sound of bells from all directions. The Bell of Time in Ueno Park, normally rung softly, had been struck so hard it could be heard clearly over the clamor of the crowd. But a sixth sense told Olegs that this was not the only bell ringing. At Ueno's Kan'ei-ji, Senso-ji, and Zojo-ji temples, at the Kremlin's Bell Tower of Ivan the Great, at the Cathedral of Christ the Savior, at Gohyakurakan-ji, the Danilovsky Monastery, Ikegami Honmon-ji, Tsukiji Hongan-ji, Shibamata Taishakuten, Novodevichy Convent, Kazan Cathedral, Donskoy Monastery, and the Church of Simeon Stopnik—indeed, everywhere there were bells to be found in Tokyo or Moscow, every last one of them was ringing.

The strumming of the *shamisen* and balalaika intensified. Constellations were now visible in the night sky, and cherry petals danced in the lantern light like myriad twinkling stars. Countless glistening strands began rising from the ground, silver filaments that Olegs soon saw were tiny translucent snakes.

In a deep, operatic voice that rose from the depths of his belly, Kyuan slowly began chanting a sutra.

The tiny snakes, spurred by the swaying of the women's *furisode*, stirred fallen cherry petals as they rose into the heavens and formed a band of light like the Milky Way. The *shirabyoshi*, holding tambourines in each hand and wearing a white *furisode*, began dancing more vigorously.

Kyuan continued chanting.

Olegs felt sure Kyuan would not respond, but he could no longer contain himself. "You can't . . . ," he said. "You're not trying to stamp out Kiyohime, are you?"

"Of course not," said Kyuan, unexpectedly interrupting his chanting. "There's not a thing in the world that deserves to be stamped out. All is one under Buddha."

Olegs no longer knew where he was, or even who he was.

Something enormous rose into the sky over Tokyo as if drawn from the earth. The Milky Way of little snakes morphed into one giant serpent, emitting silvery plasma as it ascended into the heavens.

The *shirabyoshi* looked toward the Tsar of Bells with an unearthly air as the *nagauta* approached its climax. Clouds gathered in the Moscow sky, and the square grew suddenly dark. The giant serpent that had risen over Tokyo crossed Siberia in an instant, tracing an arc of fire as it plunged toward the Kremlin.

The flowerlike figure, her hair in disarray
Recalling again that accursed bell
Takes it by its dragonhead and, seeming to fly
Carries it away and disappears

The serpent set upon the Tsar of Bells, coiling around it in a burst of silver flame, drawing it in, wrapping around it again and again. Beloved, despised, unforgettable bell! Wellspring of inexhaustible emotion! Helicopters from the Russian Ministry of Emergency Situations arrived one after the other and vainly doused the serpent with chemical fire suppressant before being driven away by the violent updraft.

The serpent clasped the bell in a prolonged embrace. Finally relaxing its grip, the serpent drew away and took again to the sky. Olegs could feel something pulling away from his own body. He looked up and saw the serpent, fluttering in the wind like a celestial robe of feathers, descend slowly into the Moscow River. The spent body of the serpent struck the surface of the river with a great crack, raining spray over the Kremlin and even onto Red Square and the roof of the Bolshoi Theater.

Olegs regained consciousness in Ueno with a woman's sigh echoing in his ears, followed by a man's slightly nasal murmuring in Russian, "Ну, ладно . . . Это меня освободило . . . (It's all right. I am released.)."

⤿

Peteris returned home the next morning looking utterly exhausted. Despite his confidence, the experiment had failed, and he couldn't for the life of him understand why. Peteris said he now had to stand by for time on the university supercomputer and would be unable to take Olegs to the airport the next day. That was fine with Olegs, but he hated to see his normally genial uncle so irate and unapproachable.

Olegs knew the time cannon had been unable to separate Anton and Kiyohime. But it wasn't so much that the experiment had failed as that they had rejected the intervention. Anton had been set free—from country, from science, and from time.

The landlord was in bed with a hangover. His wife and mother sat at the low table in the living room watching television. Outside, the cherry blossoms scattered in a storm of falling petals.

Carrying a detailed map, Olegs spent his last day in Tokyo searching for Kyuan's temple, taking careful notes as he went, but was never able to find it. Yanaka was bustling as if nothing had happened.

⤳

The great bell at the Kremlin remains broken. But this, too, is all right.

Talents and Curses

Love Right on the Yesterday

by Wendy Nelson Tokunaga

I learned my destiny the day I first laid eyes on Rie Ando. It was her television debut, her appearance as the week's "Bursting Young Star" on my favorite TV show, *The Best Ten*. Her song, "Love Right on the Yesterday," had been released only that day, so there was no way she could have been in the top ten yet, and at that moment it was impossible to know she would be number one the following week, the fastest number-one debut ever. But clearly she was someone special, the type of idol singer who arrived out of nowhere, yet the next day you couldn't remember a time when you didn't know her, as if she'd been a part of your life forever.

Rie wore a lacy pink camisole top over a white, cap-sleeved blouse—the layered look that had been on the cover of the latest issue of *PopSister*. Her ecru, tiered petticoat skirt reminded me of an outfit I'd seen the previous Sunday in the window of Ciao Panic in Harajuku. Her hair hung shoulder length and perfect, shimmering like a waterfall.

But it was when she sang that I knew for sure.

I need you! Love right—on the yesterday!

Bright, open, sparkling, her voice boasted a confidence, an unexpected sophistication from a singer who was fifteen but still managed to come off as a cute young girl. The melody rang out as new but familiar, catchy but unrecognizable, and I realized immediately that I was witnessing a historic, monumental event.

After that I bought every CD, tribute book, calendar, DVD, pencil case, pair of house slippers, and T-shirt. I switched to drinking Pocari Sweat from Calpico because Rie Ando was the Pocari Sweat mascot. A life-size cardboard cutout of her graced every 7-Eleven in Japan.

I learned that her birthday was July 21, that she was born in Kumamoto City, that her real name was Noriko Yoshikawa, that purple was her favorite color, that her blood type was O, and that her measurements were 84-59-84.

I committed every Rie Ando song to memory, performing them hundreds of times at Sing-Sing Karaoke Box, and hundreds more times in front of the mirror on my bedroom closet door.

But it was when I made the pilgrimage to Tokyo Dome to see her live and in concert on the first stop of her Shiseido Cosmetics Super Pink Peachy tour that I allowed myself to believe that my secret dream could come true; that I would become the next Rie Ando.

～

"This is something I *really* want to do," I said to my mother.

She sighed, her forehead wrinkled as a prune. "You're too young."

"But Rie Ando debuted when *she* was fifteen."

"Well, you're not Rie Ando."

It didn't impress my mother that I'd won seven singing competitions with my version of "Love Right on the Yesterday," including the grand prize in the Cup Noodle New Voice Karaoke Contest, beating out singers from all over Chiba Prefecture. I'd taken this as a sign that I should get started on my musical career. I was determined to go to the open auditions in Tokyo put on by the big music production companies. But there was a catch: you had to get a form signed by your parents. My mother wouldn't budge.

By now Rie Ando had become the biggest idol singer Japan had ever seen. Her nickname was Rie-*Himesama*—Princess Rie—because she looked so elegant, as if she should live in a big castle, or at least a fancy condo in Roppongi Hills. Yet somehow she never came off as stuck-up. She seemed a regular, down-to-earth girl—the classmate who would let you copy her algebra homework, borrow her favorite Hysteric Glamour muffler, or tell you the shocking secret about the unmarried assistant principal at your high school.

"Do you know what it's really like being in the entertainment industry?" my mother went on, the emotion rising in her voice. "Only one in thousands will be as big as Rie Ando. And so many girls don't make it."

"But I think I have a chance."

"And the ones that do make it don't get very far," she said, as if she didn't hear me. "Their fame lasts only five minutes. Then it's over. What kind of a life is that?"

It was pointless to talk to her. "What if I ask Dad?"

She frowned and shook her head. "You'll be wasting your time."

Dad worked at a big insurance company in Tokyo and rarely got home before ten o'clock. Mom would leave his dinner out for him and then go help my younger brother Yoshi with his homework. That night I waited until my father was just about done, finishing his miso soup. As I refilled his rice bowl I pled my case.

"Yumi," he said. "You need to listen to your mother. Being in show business is tough."

"But I know this is my destiny."

He smiled. "It's good to have a passion and you have a nice voice. But it's not as glamorous as it looks. It's best to enjoy singing as a hobby."

His patronizing tone made my face flush. "Please, Dad. *Please.*"

He paused, thinking of something to appease me. "If you still feel this way when you graduate high school, we can think about it."

I would have laughed if I hadn't been so heartbroken. Didn't he know that the idea of an idol debuting at eighteen was as ludicrous as starting kindergarten at the age of eight?

ᔐ

"My parents won't let me go," I wailed to my friends Chisato and Naoko at school the next day.

"That's so unfair," Chisato said. "You sing better than Rie Ando. You deserve a chance."

"You can't give up your dream, Yu-chan" Naoko said.

"I won't give it up—I won't," I said.

My parents were ruining everything and I didn't know how I could change the situation.

Rie Ando's songs always blared from the cafés, boutiques and clothing stands jammed into Takeshita-dori in Harajuku, where Naoko, Chisato, and I spent every Sunday afternoon. All the kids dressed in the trendiest clothes, and everyone crowded into the long, narrow street or spilled over into the side alleys. It was so packed that you couldn't move much faster than a caterpillar, but all the noise and excitement and the sweet smell of strawberries and whipped cream from the crepe stands always made me feel that Harajuku must be the best place on earth.

Another thing you could always count on at Takeshita-dori was the photographers. They reminded me of bats, the way they perched upon the stairways and side streets and then would swoop out, aiming their long-lens cameras like rifles, taking pictures of the girls who looked the most fashionable. They'd sell the photos to magazines for spreads on street fashion, and if you looked good enough, they'd publish your photo with your name, age, and occupation. No photographer ever paid any attention to Chisato, Naoko, or me, and we never expected that they would.

But on one Sunday I was wearing a new outfit that I'd just bought with my prize money from the Cup Noodle contest, and to my surprise, several photographers took my picture.

Then a bunch of them started taking photos of me every Sunday, and soon after I noticed the pictures showing up in magazines like *Zipper*, *Young Street*, and *Up!Venus*. The caption always said: *Yumi Kitazawa, 15, high school student*—there wasn't much else to say.

I clearly remember my ensemble on the Sunday my life changed. It was four months to the day that I'd won the Cup Noodle contest. I wore a white, tight-fitting T-shirt dress a few inches above the knee and a black-and-white polka-dot jacket with a Peter Pan collar. I paired this with short black leggings and bright green platform high-tops with white laces, and finished it off with a black scarf made from fabric that looked like shredded rubber, and an oversize gray, slouchy shoulder bag dotted with silver studs.

My friends and I were walking along the street as usual when a guy approached me who seemed different. He wasn't scruffy-looking like the typical photographer; in fact, he didn't even have a camera. He wore a suit and looked more like a *salariman* or an actor on a home drama.

"Excuse me," he said, bowing. "Are you Yumi Kitazawa-san?"

He already knew my name! Naoko and Chisato began to giggle. I stood there, silent.

"I'm sorry to be so rude and stop you like this," he said.

He spoke in formal Japanese like an NHK news anchor. He was old—at least thirty.

"I recognized you from your pictures in these magazines." He opened a black leather case that resembled a fancier version of my schoolbook bag, and pulled out a thick binder. Inside were photos of me from every magazine I'd been in. "You *are* Yumi Kitazawa-san, correct?"

My first reaction was what is he? Some kind of pervert? Should I just run away or deny that I'm this Kitazawa girl? My mouth went dry, as if I'd swallowed a spoonful of sand. But in the end I cleared my throat and said, "Yes, that's me."

"I represent Morita Pro Music."

Naoko gasped much too loudly. Chisato went, *"Heyyyyyy!"* My knees seemed to turn inside out. I concluded that I must have been dreaming. He went on talking, but somehow I could only comprehend every other word. He handed me a business card.

"If you're interested in possibly working with Morita Pro Music, have your parents contact us," he continued. "Again, I'm sorry if I've caused you any inconvenience. We look forward to hearing from you."

I held the card as if it were a delicate piece of china. If you'd told me while I was getting dressed that morning that I'd be scouted that afternoon by Morita Pro Music, the very production company that had discovered Rie Ando and dozens of other idol singers, I'd have thought you'd had a couple of shots of whiskey with your breakfast coffee.

All I could do was bow as low as I could and thank him. He bowed back, then turned around, disappearing into the crowds.

Chisato was practically sobbing and couldn't speak.

"Yu-chan," Naoko said. "It's your dream, but . . ."

She didn't have to say another word. Yes, it was my dream, and something meant to be, and yes, my parents would be against it. But what she didn't know was what I was saying in my head, that nothing would stop me from getting what I wanted.

☙

"It's fate," I told my mother. "To have this guy come up to me. You have to let me go."

"I don't have to let you do anything," was her reply.

"But this is a chance in a lifetime."

"We've already had this discussion."

"But—"

"I've heard enough, Yumi. That's enough."

I was relentless, pleading for weeks, fearing that if we waited too long to contact Morita Pro Music they would forget all about me. I must have worn my mother down, because finally, after hashing it out with my father, she reluctantly agreed to accompany me to an audition at their office in the Shinjuku district of Tokyo.

"Yu-chan, I want to make one thing clear," she said in a stern voice the rainy Saturday when we rode the train in to Tokyo. "This is just to check it out. It doesn't mean that I'm giving you permission to pursue this."

I nodded, but felt my frustration once more approaching the boiling point. Couldn't she possibly understand what this meant to me? I asked her something I'd never asked her before. "Didn't you have an idol when you were young?"

"Yes, of course. There were idols in the 'olden days.'" She smiled. "Akiko Takeda. She debuted when I was fourteen."

The name sounded familiar, but that would have been about twenty-five years ago; I knew nothing about her.

My mother stared out the window, her face becoming smooth and relaxed, and began to sing softly to herself. I couldn't hear every word, but the song seemed to be about a spring day with the cherry blossoms blooming and a girl being newly in love.

She stopped and gave a laugh, as if she were embarrassed to be caught singing on the train. "We all went crazy for Akko-chan—bought all her records, watched her on TV, went to her concerts. She was everywhere." She looked at me. "Akiko Takeda was just as famous as Rie Ando, even more so."

I found it difficult to picture my mother as a teenager and even more difficult to believe that anyone could have been as big as Rie Ando. My mother's smile faded, and she turned toward the window. She seemed to be thinking hard about something. I didn't want to risk souring her even further about the audition, so I just nodded and kept quiet. We rode in silence until we reached Shinjuku Station.

Although it was the biggest and most famous production company in Japan, Morita Pro Music was housed in a plain and rather dismal seven-story office building not too far from the west exit of the station. We rode the elevator to the fourth floor and met Fujita-san, the man who'd spoken to me in Harajuku, and some other people whose names I forgot the moment after they introduced themselves.

On the phone they'd told me to have a song ready, so I was prepared to sing Rie Ando's "Love Right on the Yesterday." Not only was it my favorite, it was also a lucky song, the one I always sang in the karaoke contests. I knew Morita Pro Music thought I must have the right look for an idol singer, since they scouted me from my pictures. And to be an idol it didn't matter if you couldn't sing too well. But I was determined to show them I was good at that too—maybe even better than Rie Ando.

Fujita-san took us to a room lined with huge mirrors. It wasn't what I expected, not fancy or glamorous at all. A long strip of black adhesive tape on one of the mirrors seemed to cover a thick crack. There was only a small table and some fold-up chairs where Fujita-san's assistants took their places, and a wooden stool in the middle of the room, where he told me to sit.

"We'll be videotaping you and just want to ask you a couple of questions," Fujita-san said. "Are you ready?"

"Yes."

"Yumi-san, what are your hobbies?"

Trying hard not to be consumed by nerves, I willed myself to be poised and enthusiastic like Rie Ando. But Fujita-san's question stumped me. Hobbies? My mind went blank.

"I love to go to the karaoke box and sing," I finally said. There was silence, as if he were expecting more. I combed my brain for ideas. "And I go to Harajuku every Sunday, and I also collect stuffed animals." It was lame, but it was the best I could do.

"How many stuffed animals do you have in your collection?"

What a relief that he seemed to find enough legitimacy in one of these pathetic responses to continue the conversation. And I knew the answer without even thinking. "One hundred and nine."

Thankfully Fujita-san asked no more questions, and said that now it was time for me to sing.

I stood in the middle of all the mirrors, feeling not much bigger than an ant. I was glad to have the interview end, but now I turned fidgety and nervous. A young woman dressed in a dark blue office-lady uniform handed me a microphone. I jumped when the introduction to

"Love Right on the Yesterday" blasted out of speakers that seemed to surround the room.

Luckily, my voice rang out loud and clear, though I couldn't stop bending my knees. I was convinced that everyone was staring at them flexing up and down like a chicken's. I concentrated hard to hold them in place, to stop the wobbling, while at the same time trying to make sure I wouldn't forget the lyrics, which I somehow was struggling to remember. Out of the corner of my eye I could see my mother pulling at her hand as if she were peeling an orange and looking like she had a headache. I tried to put her disapproval out of my mind.

I made sure to smile in the same way as Rie Ando, and point with my index finger toward the audience, which consisted of only seven people, including my mother, and all sporting uninterested looks. I also made a point of holding the note longer on the word "yesterday" than on Rie's version, hoping to show off my stronger voice.

"We can't believe how great you are! You've passed the audition!" That's what I wanted someone to say once I finished and the music faded. But instead no one even clapped, and Fujita-san looked bored when he stood up and said, "Thank you Yumi-san. We'll be in touch."

Afterward my mother took me to the Spick and Span coffee shop in Shinjuku Station. I hadn't eaten a thing all day, feeling much too jittery to think about food. But once the audition ended I was starving. In spite of Mom's dubious expression, I ordered the *Dokkiri* deluxe sundae—three scoops of vanilla ice cream doused in chocolate sauce, a cherry topping each mound—and began wolfing it down immediately.

"Don't eat so fast, Yu-chan. You'll get a stomachache," my mother said.

"Do you think I did okay?"

She sipped her milk tea. "It doesn't matter what I think. It's what *they* think. They must be seeing hundreds of girls."

I put down my spoon. That was true, and I felt like an idiot not to realize it. Just because there hadn't been some big group of girls waiting to audition didn't mean I had no competition.

"You may have some talent, but there are many girls who can sing just as well or who are just as cute. And they may even prefer someone who doesn't sing too well. You know, someone who's charming but isn't so talented that she makes her fans feel bad."

I sighed.

"And you need to remember that if you did pass, and *if* we did decide this was something we'd let you do, you'd have to move to Tokyo, go to the Morita Pro school, and live on your own. They wouldn't let you commute from home."

We'd talked about this before after she'd first spoken to the people at Morita Pro Music, but she always made sure to bring it up, as if these facts would cause me to change my mind.

"You'd be a company worker like your father—an employee of Morita Pro Music. It's a job, you know. And you wouldn't have time to see Chisato and Naoko. You'd be very busy, working all the time."

I nodded.

"And your mom would miss you, you know?"

She always made sure to say this, too. Yes, I knew she would miss me. The lump in my throat grew bigger by the minute. My eyes fixated on the runny ice cream in front of me, turning to soup in the glass boat.

My mother stared at my face. "Are you absolutely sure you'd want to do this?"

Yes! I've never been so sure about anything in my whole life! I wanted to scream, but instead I only nodded. I was too exhausted to utter a word, and what did it matter? I'd said it to her many times before.

She knew the answer.

On the train ride home my mother read her home décor magazine and I sent messages to Chisato and Naoko on my cell phone, telling them about the audition and that I really wasn't sure if I had a chance. Immediately they wrote back, saying they knew I would pass, but I wasn't so confident.

With another thirty minutes to go before we'd arrive home, I fiddled with my phone. What was the name of my mother's idol again, I wondered. Akiko Takeda? What did she look like? I typed her name and found her picture immediately. Of course she looked hopelessly out of date. Dressed in a sailor suit, she had short, feathered hair, and her teeth looked a little too big for her mouth. But she was cute and sparkly with bright brown eyes, a dimple on her left cheek, and a sweet smile. Underneath her picture it said:

Akiko Takeda, nicknamed "Akko" and winner of the pres-

*tigious "Newcomer of the Year" award, was one of the big-
gest idols in the 1980s, with hits that included "Spring Song,"
"Heart Kimagure" and "Kuchibiru Wonderful." But her life
was tragically cut short at the age of seventeen when she leapt
to her death from the seventh floor of the Morita Pro Music
building in Shinjuku. She left no note, but it was widely believed that she was despondent over her career, although at
the time of her death "Kuchibiru Wonderful" was number
one on the charts. Thousands of fans kept vigil for days at
her death site and the subsequent copycat suicides that swept
the nation over the ensuing weeks and months were dubbed
"Akko Syndrome."*

I gazed at my mother's face, then took her hand and patted it. "Don't
worry," I said. "I'll be okay."

⤳

During the following weeks, each day when I arrived home from school,
I hoped to hear the good news that I'd passed the audition. But no phone
call came. What a relief, though, to find that a letter hadn't arrived either,
saying how awful I'd been and how Fujita-san must have been having a
poor judgment day when he tracked me down in Harajuku.

Only Chisato and Naoko knew about my audition.

"What are you going to do if you don't pass, Yu-chan?" Naoko
asked. "I mean, I'm sure you will, but . . ."

I didn't know how to answer her question.

It was a Friday afternoon when I came home to see my mother sitting at the kitchen table. She wasn't chopping carrots or beating eggs or
drinking coffee. She wasn't watching *Longing to Hug* on television. She
wasn't even wearing her favorite apron—the one with the fat penguin
that said *Let's Housewife!* She wasn't doing anything. It was quiet. I could
only hear the ticking of the orange wall clock, the one in the shape of a
watering can, and the humming of the refrigerator.

My mother's face looked drained of color. It must be something
bad, I thought. Someone must have died.

I sat down across from her. "What happened?"

She didn't answer.

"Mom?"

She looked me in the eye. "Yu-chan, are you absolutely sure you want to do this?"

It took me a moment to understand her question. "Did they *call?*"

She nodded, but she wasn't smiling.

"So can I? Can I?" I'd never felt more desperate in my entire life.

She clasped her hands, and I could hear the cracking of her knuckles. "I talked to your father," she said with a small, resigned sigh. "He said it's okay."

The rush ricocheting through my body lifted me up from my chair. I threw my arms around her shoulders and pressed my cheek to her neck, holding on as tightly as I could. I was determined to make sure that she would never regret letting me go.

The Dragon and the Poet

by Kenji Miyazawa
translated by Misa Dikengil Lindberg

At high tide Chanata the dragon lifted himself up out of the water flowing into his cave. The morning sun glittered as it streamed through the cave's sliver of an opening, illuminating the contours of the rough sea floor and the red and white sea creatures suctioned to the rocks.

Chanata gazed for a moment, mesmerized, at the misty blue water. Then he raised his eyes to the narrow mouth of his cave. He looked out over the ocean, which danced and sparkled in the sunlight, to the pale, blue-green line of the horizon.

"Oh, if I were free," Chanata sighed, "I would swim out into the endless ocean. With a gust of smoky, black breath, I would soar up into the clear sky. But, alas, I am imprisoned here. The mouth of this cave is barely large enough to afford a glimpse of the outside world. Oh, Dragon King, Your Highness. Forgive me for my crime and release me from this curse!"

Chanata turned and looked sadly back into his cave. Thick beams of sunlight streamed in, reflecting off the shimmering blue and white scales of his tail. Suddenly Chanata heard a young voice calling from outside. He turned to see who it could be.

"Most honorable Chanata. Emboldened by this morning's sun, I have come to ask for your forgiveness." A wealthy-looking young man, decorated with golden charms and bearing a long golden sword, sat on the flat, moss-covered stones outside the cave.

"What have I to forgive you for?" Chanata asked.

"Oh, dear dragon. Yesterday I took part in a poetry recital competition. The people there could not stop praising me and my poem. Even Alta, the most esteemed poet in the land, rose to offer me his seat of honor. He crowned me with a wreath made of vines and sang a sweet hymn in my honor. Then he left. With no place for him here any longer as a poet, he took off for the distant, snowy mountains of the east. The other people at the competition soon set me on a rickshaw, and I—oh, I became intoxicated by the beauty of the poem I had just sung. My heart fluttered with excitement, and I felt as if I would drown in the shower of praise and flowers thrown upon me.

"But later that night, after I left the house of Rudas, the wealthy host of the celebration, something very strange happened. I was returning to my poor mother's house, walking through glistening, dewy grass, when suddenly the moon disappeared behind a milky, reddish cloud, and the sky grew dark. As I looked up to see what had happened, I heard a voice whisper from the Miruda Forest:

"'Young Surudatta. You stole your poem from Chanata, the old dragon trapped in the cave. You used the poem to win today's competition and drive the old poet Alta to the east.'

"Suddenly my legs began to shake uncontrollably and I could not walk any farther. I spent the rest of last night there on the grass, anguished and confused. Slowly, I began to remember that I went to the cliff above your cave every day, never knowing you were there, of course. Exhausted from composing and reciting poems, I would sit and doze off. It was on one dark, windy day that I thought I heard a poem in a dream. But Chanata, now I realize that it was *you* who composed that beautiful poem! You are the one who should be honored by everyone, not me. Oh, dear dragon, our true poet, tomorrow I will throw ashes on my head in repentance. In the town square, I will apologize to you and everyone else. Can you ever forgive me?"

But Chanata only asked, "What was the poet Alta's hymn like, the one he sang in your honor?"

"Well, my head is a little muddled from everything that has happened, so I don't know if I can remember his glorious words and melody exactly. But I think it went something like this:

> *No sooner do winds sing,*
> *Clouds billow,*
> *And waves resound,*
> *Than you sing their song, Surudatta.*

The stars follow your words,
The land forms to your vision.

You create the model of beauty and truth
For the future.

In time you will become this world's prophet,
For you are an architect, Surudatta.

"May the great poet Alta find happiness," Chanata said.

"Surudatta, the poem you recited last night is every bit as much yours as it is mine. Do you really believe I recited that poem in my cave? Or was I just thinking it? Did you, up on the cliff, actually hear that poem? Or did you compose it?

"You see, Surudatta, when you heard the poem, I was the clouds and the winds, but so were you. Had Alta been meditating at that same time, he probably would have sung the same poem too.

"But Surudatta, Alta's words and your words would not have been the same. Nor would mine and yours have been the same. The rhythm would probably also have been different. So you see, that poem belongs to you, just as it also belongs to the spirits of the clouds and the wind."

"Dear dragon, does that mean you have forgiven me?" Surudatta asked.

"Who is forgiving whom? We are all the winds, the clouds, and the water—each and every one of us equally so. Oh, Surudatta, if I were free and you were not afraid of me, I would comfort you in my arms right now. But since that is impossible, I would like to give you a small gift. Hold out your hands." Chanata produced a tiny red pearl and offered it to the young man. The pearl was bright, flaming red as if a million fires burned within it.

"Take this pearl as an offering when you go to the ocean in search of the sunken sutras," Chanata instructed.

Surudatta fell to his knees before the dragon. "Oh, Chanata. You have no idea how long I have yearned for this moment—to meet one with your wisdom and receive the gift that will help me on my journey toward truth. How can I ever begin to thank you? I have one question, though, if you will permit. How is it that a mighty dragon like you is trapped here in this cave?"

"A thousand years ago I reigned over all the winds and clouds," Chanata began. "One day I wanted to test my strength, and in doing so I caused terrible misfortune to humankind. The Dragon King banished me to this cave for a hundred thousand years and ordered me to watch over the border between land and sea. I spend every day here regretting my crime and offering apologies to the king."

"Oh, Chanata. I still have my mother to look after. But when she is happily reborn in heaven, I will immediately go to the ocean and begin searching for those great lost sutras. Will you wait for me here until that day comes?" Surudatta asked.

"A thousand human years is not even ten days to a dragon," Chanata answered.

"One more thing," said Surudatta. "Will you hold onto this pearl until then? In the meantime, every day possible I will return here to observe the sky and water and gaze up at the clouds. And together, you and I will discuss plans to create a new world."

"You do not know how happy that would make this old dragon."

"Farewell, Chanata."

"Farewell."

With a glad heart, Surudatta walked off along the rocks, while Chanata the dragon eased himself into the deep water near the back of the cave and quietly began repeating his prayers of repentance.

Just Wan-derful

By Louise George Kittaka

The good news: Eighth grader Takeshi "Tak" Matsumoto had just landed a leading role in a series on national Japanese TV. The bad news: His co-stars were a guy who modeled for romance novel covers in his spare time, a woman who sounded like Minnie Mouse on helium, and a purple dog.

Note to self: *Find out if that contract Mum signed with the TV studio is binding.*

⤙

It was originally his mother's idea to sign up Tak and his younger sister, Keina, with a talent agency. Keina got some modeling jobs right away, but Tak was already bigger than the standard sample sizes for kids' clothing, so he got nothing. Occasionally the agency called about auditions for this or that, but Tak usually wasn't Japanese-looking enough when they wanted a Japanese kid, and he wasn't *gaijin*-looking enough when they wanted a *gaijin* kid. His mother was from New Zealand and his father was Japanese. Being labeled "half" didn't bother him, but it bothered his mother. She spent a lot of time explaining to Japanese people that "bicultural" was a better description for kids like Tak and Keina.

⤙

When someone from the agency called in February about the audition, Tak hadn't been too excited. They told his mother it was a voice-over job for a new kids' TV show. But he was trying to save money to get a DJ set, so he agreed to give it a go.

The auditions were being done in boy-girl pairs. Tak got called with a half girl who said she was in the eighth grade at an international school. He was just wearing a T-shirt and baggy shorts, but she was dressed up like something from one of those lame teen fashion magazines that Keina liked to drool over. He immediately sized her up as a "*chanto shita* girl"— his name for those really annoying girls who try to act so perfect. She had a toothy grin on her face the whole time, which she probably thought made her look cute. It actually made her look constipated, thought Tak.

The man and woman leading the audition asked them to sing "Twinkle Twinkle Little Star," then read a dialogue in English. Naturally, Chanto Shita Girl did all this perfectly. Tak decided just to have fun with it. The music for the song was way too high, so he did it in a falsetto voice. And while he could *speak* English like an eighth grader, Tak went to regular Japanese school, so he certainly couldn't *read* it that well. He put on a fake accent to help cover up the words he couldn't pronounce. By this time, the two interviewers were in fits of laughter, but Chanto Shita Girl's smile was strained—she definitely didn't approve of his antics. Not that Tak cared.

Note to self: *Never, ever date a* chanto shita *girl.*

↜

Tak figured that he had well and truly screwed up the audition, so the first surprise was when the agency called three days later to say he had got the job. The second was that he wasn't doing a voice role—he was being offered one of the leads in a regular English educational show. His mother immediately got very excited and started talking about "my son, the star!" while his father gave his usual speech about how it couldn't interfere with school. Keina was just plain jealous.

One of the talent agency's staff accompanied Tak and his mother to a meeting at the TV studio. The show was being filmed at the AJE-TV (All Japan Education Television) headquarters in downtown Shibuya. The producer told them the show was called *Wan-derful English* and would be aimed at Japanese elementary school kids. Then he explained the "concept": An American family moves to Tokyo and adopts a robot dog, then they have to "teach" it English.

Note to self: Wan-derful English? *Someone got paid to come up with that title?*

⌒

Tak was asked about his schedule and he told them Sundays weren't good, since that was when his American football team practiced. He was fine with missing school, though. Then his mother had to jump in and ask how filming the show would affect summer vacation, since the family always visited Tak and Keina's grandparents in New Zealand. The producer said filming for the entire series would wrap up by mid-July, and they understood that summer vacation was important to "*gaijin* families." Tak's mother didn't look too pleased, and started to explain that the correct term was "bicultural Japanese–New Zealand family," but thankfully, the producer had another meeting to attend and so Tak managed to escape with minimal embarrassment.

Note to self: *Don't bring Mum to the studio again.*

⌒

The following week, his mother had to meet at the talent agent's office to sign Tak's contract for the show, and Tak got called back to the studio yet again to meet the other actors. He had given his mother strict instructions just to drop him off and then wait until he phoned her at the end.

Tak's TV "Dad" was Trent from LA, who taught hot yoga when he wasn't modeling or acting. He gave Tak his card, saying he was a finalist in an online contest to choose a cover model for some romance novel. "Mom" was Narelle from Sydney, and she spoke in the very high voice used by women who teach English to little kids. At first Tak wondered if she was being smart by staying in character, but he soon realized this was her normal voice. It was making his ears bleed. Neither "Dad" nor "Mom" looked a day over thirty. The other regular cast member was a young woman called Shana, another "half" like Tak. He had seen her on TV before. She seemed nice enough, if only he could get his head round the fact that she was doing the voice for a robot dog.

Tak's character was "Jimmy Johnson." Someone sure spent a lot of time thinking up *that* name, Tak thought. As for the robot dog, he was Wan-chan, or "Doggy" in Japanese. At least now Tak understood the play on words for "Wan-derful English"—it made sense, kind of. Wan-chan had been designed by a famous robotics expert from Tokyo University,

Professor Handa. The dog itself was still a secret to the cast and most of the crew and would be "revealed" on the first day of rehearsal.

"I wrote the website for that cover model contest on the card I gave you!" Trent called as Tak left the studio. "Be sure to go online and vote for me!"

Note to self: *Be sure to lose his card on the way home.*

~

The agency faxed the rehearsal and filming schedule for the first month. The basic pattern would be rehearsal on Thursday evenings from 5:00 to 9:00 p.m., and then filming on Saturdays from 10:00 a.m. for "as long as needed." Tak was pleased that he had Sundays free for football, and his father was pleased that Tak wouldn't be missing any school.

In mid-February the scripts for the first two episodes arrived, since they would be filming two at a time, starting that weekend. The first episode centered on a friend presenting the Johnson family with the robot dog as a "welcome to Japan" gift. There was also some extra dialogue at the end for the show's interactive website.

Tak had only just received the script three days before the first Thursday rehearsal. Although he had snickered at the very simplistic English at first, by Thursday he was rather grateful that most of the first two episodes consisted of lines like, "Hi, my name is Jimmy! Nice to meet you!" and "I'm fine, thanks! How are you?"

Thursday's rehearsal took place in a meeting room. As Tak entered, he saw the star of the show sitting on the table, Wan-chan himself. The robot was about the size of a miniature poodle, but had long ears like a spaniel and a corkscrew tail. The oddest thing of all was his color—bright purple. On seeing Tak arrive, Professor Handa pushed a remote control and Wan-chan suddenly stood up and came walking across the table. He stopped in front of Tak and raised his right paw.

Tak jumped back when the robot said, "Hello, Tak!" Then he realized it was just Shana talking.

"*Yoroshiku.* Nice to meet you. But I'm not Tak, I'm Jimmy." Everybody laughed and clapped.

Note to self: *Make sure that nobody at school finds out I'm on this seriously weird show.*

✎

The first week went by in a blur for Tak. After the first rehearsal, the producer wanted a lot of changes made, and a new version of the script was faxed on Friday afternoon. On Saturday he spent the whole day in the studio, and Tak couldn't believe how long it took to make two fifteen-minute TV shows. He ate lunch and dinner with the *Wan-derful English* cast at the studio, and when he finally got home at ten on Saturday night, he rolled into bed exhausted. It was hard to get up the next day for his American football. He was glad spring break was just around the corner.

✎

Tak noticed a new character was joining the cast for the third show. The script said, "Jo, Tak's 13-year-old cousin from the USA, who comes to stay with him in Tokyo." This was potentially good news—having some-one else his age on the show might help to dilute some of the "weird" factor for him.

When he arrived at the next rehearsal, out of breath and sweaty since he had run all the way from the subway station, he didn't see any sign of the boy playing Jo. He took a seat at the table next to Narelle and rummaged through his bag for his script. He found it crumpled and damp at the bottom of the bag, after realizing his sports drink had leaked.

A girl's voice called out, "*Ohayo gozaimasu!*" Tak knew that the TV people greeted each other with "Good morning!" as they entered the studio, even in the evening, but he kept forgetting to do it. Looking up to see who owned the voice, he groaned out loud. "Jo" was a girl? Chanto Shita Girl!

One of the producers introduced the newcomer. "Everybody, this is Rena. She will play the role of Jimmy's cousin, 'Joanna,' or 'Jo.'"

Rena bowed politely to everyone and introduced herself in Japanese and English. Trent winked suggestively from across the table, while Narelle dug Tak in the ribs with her elbow. "She's cute!"

Rena was directed to the vacant seat on the other side of Tak. As she sat down, she wrinkled her nose and frowned slightly. Tak guessed he still smelled sweaty.

"Didn't expect to see you here," he commented.

"I didn't expect to see *you*," Rena retorted, taking out a pink plastic folder with her script nestled neatly inside. Tak snatched up his own tattered script and turned away.

Note to self: *Bring a plastic bag next time. This girl makes me want to vomit.*

~

After spring break, the new Japanese school year began in early April. Tak moved up to ninth grade, his last year of junior high school. All his teachers suddenly started talking about the high school entrance exams that Tak and his classmates would be facing in less than a year's time. Between rehearsals and filming for the show, American football, and his homework, the days were flying by.

AJE-TV began airing the show on Tuesday afternoons in mid-April, as part of the lineup for the new school year. Tak's mother recorded the first episode on their DVD player, and the whole family sat round to watch it after dinner that night. The show was surprisingly entertaining in a quirky way, and even Tak's father laughed out loud in some places.

Since Tak's friends were all busy after school with their club activities or studying at cram school, he was reasonably confident that none of them would see the show. His mother and Keina were dying to tell their friends, but he had sworn them to secrecy.

~

As he grew better acquainted with the other cast members, he began to enjoy hanging out with them. Trent shared his interest in hip-hop music and was friends with one of Tokyo's leading DJs. He promised to take Tak to a show sometime. Narelle, once Tak got used to that squeaky voice, was surprisingly funny and knew a lot of good jokes. Shana had another regular role as a host on a music show and entertained Tak with stories of the singers and groups she had met.

He was even getting fond of Wan-chan. Working with a robot co-star didn't always go as planned. Filming stopped when something malfunctioned, and Professor Handa would run on to the set and tinker with his creation until the problem was fixed.

In one scene Wan-chan was walking along the Johnson family's dining table, but Professor Handa's timing with the remote control was off and he didn't stop the robot quickly enough. Wan-chan walked off the end of the table and crash-landed on the studio floor. The cast and crew watched in horrified fascination as the little robot split in half right down the middle.

Professor Handa rushed over to his creation and sadly cradled the two halves in his arms. "I don't think I can fix this today," he muttered, shaking his head.

"*Itai!* It hurts!" Shana ad-libbed in Wan-chan's voice, and a wave of laughter eased the tension.

The producer and writer went into a huddle with Professor Handa and then declared that the schedule was too tight for delays. All of Wan-chan's scenes would be filmed from his right side, which had sustained less damage. There would be no close-ups of the robot, and the scenes where he was supposed to move were quickly rewritten.

Note to self: *I guess the show must always go on—even if the star is broken into two pieces.*

↩

The only real problem was Rena. Tak just couldn't get along with her. She always knew her lines perfectly and rarely messed up, unlike Tak. The rest of the cast and crew knew it was his first TV show, and they were patient with him. Everyone else seemed to think his jokes and antics were hilarious but Rena usually just put on that strained, fake smile she used when she didn't approve of something. Unfortunately for Tak, Jimmy and Jo had a lot of scenes together. In the breaks, he made a point of talking to the other cast members and ignored Rena as much as possible. On the few occasions when she tried to make conversation with him, Tak responded with one-word answers.

↩

One Monday in early May, Tak realized that his cover was blown. He had scores of text messages from his football teammates in both Japanese and English. "*Wan-derful!*" "*Woof, woof!*" "*Hi, Jimmy!*" When he checked his email, it was the same thing. It didn't take him long to work out what had happened.

One of his football friends attended the same international school as Rena and was friends with her on Facebook. She had just posted a link to the brand-new *Wan-derful English* home page on AJE-TV's website: "*My new TV show! Please check it out!*" If you clicked on the link, it led to a big photo of the cast with Tak smack-bang in the middle, hugging Wan-chan and grinning like an idiot. Tak's teammate had reposted this on his wall and tagged Tak.

A boy at his school used to be in the football team, and by Wednesday it was all over Tak's school, too. Even the seventh graders were coming up to him and addressing him as "Jimmy."

In a way, he was relieved that it was all out in the open now, and he was enjoying all the attention. He was, however, furious with Rena for starting it all. *My new TV show!* To top it all, he got a friend request from her on Facebook that evening.
Note to self: *No WAY.*

⤶

The next day was the weekly rehearsal for the show. The first episode they were filming that week only involved Tak, Rena and the robot. Trent and Narelle were coming in later, as was Shana, since she only had to do voice-overs.

Tak didn't say anything to Rena until they were taking a break while the producer and writers discussed some last-minute changes.

"I saw your Facebook post! '*My new TV show! Please check it out! Oh, I'm such a big star!*'" Tak said, mimicking Rena's voice.

Rena put down her can of juice. "I didn't say I was the star," she pointed out.

"You sure act like you think you are," Tak retorted. All the frustration he had felt since day one came tumbling out. "You always have to be so . . . *chanto shita* about everything! You're just Ms. Perfect, aren't you!"

Rena's face suddenly crumpled up and her eyes became shiny.

Oh, geez, thought Tak. Now I've made her cry.

But Rena didn't cry. She just sniffed a couple of times, as if to compose herself, and took a sip of juice. "Is that what you think of me?"

"Well, you never make mistakes. Just because you've had more experience! This is my first TV show."

"It's mine, too!" said Rena.

"*Maji de?* Really?" Tak was astonished. "You're so . . . good!"

"Thanks—I think," answered Rena with a slight smile. "I practice a lot. I'm always so afraid of messing up in front of all the other actors and the crew," she admitted.

"Me, too," agreed Tak. He still couldn't believe that Chanto Shita Girl was a newcomer to TV, just like him.

"So, um, like I said, I practice a lot," said Rena, taking another drink of juice. "If you want, I could . . ." She trailed off, unsure of Tak's interest in what she was going to say.

"You could what?" Tak prompted.

"Well, I could, um, practice with you." She glanced at Tak so he nodded. "I was so nervous before shooting my first episode that my Mom asked my agent for some help. She got the producer to let me talk to Narelle, and she Skyped with me and we went through my lines. It helped a lot. Maybe we could Skype or something . . . on a Friday after school?" she said tentatively. "Um, do you have Skype?"

Tak nodded. Rena's idea wasn't half bad. "Fridays evenings are usually good. Do you want to try for next week?"

"OK." Rena looked a lot happier now. "That would be . . . *wan*-derful!"

"Sure," Tak grinned. "But leave the jokes to me."

Note to self: *Look her up on Facebook. She's not bad for a* chanto shita *girl.*

Ichinichi on the Yamanote
by Claire Dawn

train jerks suddenly
I fall forward, into Kou

whose letter won my
Sunday with a Star contest

this day could be fun
but every second is planned

museum morning
pasta at Keio Plaza

after, Ueno Zoo
where the press can take pictures

a day more scripted
than the last movie I made

Kou holds out his hand
"you want to escape with me?"

I know I shouldn't
I don't know him from Goku

⌣

we step from the train
a split-second decision

security sees
they step onto the platform

quick musical notes
tell us the doors are closing

we slip back onto
the train, watch faces change

as the doors slide shut
the recognition dawning

they have lost their charge
in busy Harajuku

with *salarimen*
packed on the Yamanote

no one notices
two teenagers, grinning wide

a Japanese boy
holding hands with a black girl

&

north to Shinjuku
then Kabuki-cho exit

the red light district—
now I wonder about Kou

suddenly, I'm scared
though I'm sure he was vetted

but it's daytime, right?
what harm can happen here now?

I let out my breath
when he pulls from his pocket

cinema tickets
for the new Ghibli movie

I use my cell phone
to text my mother—"I'm safe"

then power it off
for one whole day of freedom

～

there is time to kill
we find a Baskin Robbins

sakura ice cream
for me; Kou—melon soda

"why'd you come with me?"
I shrug my shoulders, don't know

"*kankei nai*" he says
it really doesn't matter

～

at the cinema
he buys popcorn and soft drinks

we show our tickets
elevator up four floors

poster in the hall
of my latest film, out soon

my face stares at me
can run, but not hide, from self

"you're cute when you're mad"
can't help smiling, how'd he know?

we sit in silence
animations on the screen

concentration's tough
as Kou's knee keeps brushing mine

afterward, I ask
"what's your favorite Ghibli?"

"Whisper of the Heart—
Mimi o sumaseba"

I laugh, he asks why
"you're a romantic! that's why"

⌒

Sri Lankan café
where he insists he's treating

"why did you do this?"
I think he means escaping

he shakes his head, no
he's talking about today

Sunday with a Star
spending the day with a fan

"talent agency
  says it's a good thing for me

"interact with fans
they will love me even more

"when I'm just a girl
when I breathe, eat, watch movies"

but what I don't say
is that I enjoy it too

today I'm no star
I'm no idol, I'm not rich

I am just a girl
nervous, eating with a boy

his first laugh escapes
and the hairs on my arm stand

he has a great smile
teeth perfect, straight and even

a regular boy
while my face is on billboards

I stiffen, mid-thought
remember my place, and his

I'm sure he sees it
but he doesn't say a thing

‿

"your favorite Ghibli?"
Kou asks me my own question

Howl's Moving Castle—
Hauru no ugoku shiro

he says, "I wonder
why foreigners love that one"

I'm stung, since to him
I'm *gaijin*, not *nihonjin*

despite the money
despite my face everywhere

despite the fact that
I've only ever lived here

I am still *gaijin*
never really Japanese

〜

again, he feels it
the chill radiates from me

a change of subject
"what's a typical day like?"

Kou settles the bill
"so busy" I say

"TV looks easy
but the days are eternal

"there's always something
to be done, somewhere to be"

I ask about him
he says little of his mom

dad is a farmer
three big sisters, he's youngest

the only boy, he
shoulders his family's dreams

⤶

back to the station
lost in thought, with fingers linked

we take another
train back to Harajuku

scene of our jail-break
home to Gwen Stefani's girls

sign says: hugs for free
I get one from a tall man

Kou looks on—jealous?
must wish he had a sign too

at Yoyogi Park
the costumes are amusing

'50s swing dancers,
Japanese Elvis Presleys

"like America?"
he points to the spectacle

"I wouldn't know, I'm
Barbadian—I live here"

we sit on the grass
I describe my family

mom and dad met here
came to Japan as teachers

left the same island
a fifth the size of Tokyo

to fall in love while
fifteen hundred miles apart

dad, Okinawa
mom was in Iwate town

"*honto ni?*"—really?
Kou is from Iwate, too

from the prefecture
his town is Ichinohe

where I've never been
he says, "you should come visit"

then averts his eyes . . .
he stands, takes my hand, leads me

to the Meiji Shrine
through a giant *torii* gate

~

at the prayer box
he drops in his offering

bows his head, claps twice
to get the god's attention

makes his brief prayer
bows once more before he turns

I ask him his wish
"if I tell, it won't come true"

that idea's Western
I know we don't think that here

let him off the hook
but hope it was about me

⤻

a final train ride
to Ueno this time where

he has a ticket
for the Hayabusa Line

ritzy bullet train
back to his Iwate town

today was so fun
I felt like a normal girl

"thanks for today, Kou"
eyes down, he tells his secret

his family does
not know where he went today

his mom thinks *gaijin*
should stay in America,

Japan doesn't need
our warring, arrogant ways

fighting back tears, I
pause before I can respond

"America? but I'm
Barbadian, different"

to her it's the same
she won't try to understand

he's shaking his head
ignoring his mother's will

"today is happy"
he pulls me into a hug

I wish for a kiss
I should have prayed at the shrine

too soon, I'm released
his ticket slides through the gate

and then so does he . . .
disappearing from my sight

fleeting, like a dream
leaving no proof he was real

へ

he must feel the same
he returns, pulls out his phone

presses some buttons
"shall I send?" he asks softly

I take out my own
turn it on, many missed calls

my mother, father
security, agency

later I will care
now I turn on infrared

receive his details
wonder if he sends them all

if I will receive
Kou's blood type and his birthday

so I can work out
our compatibility

I offer to send
he stops me, says it's not safe

"but you're my friend now!"
shakes his head, "maybe in time . . ."

breathes, "*sayonara!*"
I say, "*mata ne*"—later!
my promise to meet again

A Song for Benzaiten
by Catherine Rose Torres

The cherry-blossom season was even more fleeting than usual the spring I arrived in Tokyo, so my foster brother, Hiro, said. He added that I was to blame for it. "Rain is the worst thing that could happen this time of year," he said, shaking his head at me. "We should think of a sunnier name for you." So I became "Aya," which means "bright" in Japanese. Mr. and Mrs. Nojima, my foster parents, must have been relieved to have something less troublesome to call me than "Rain."

Three days after I arrived, Hiro flew back to California, where he was studying architecture at UCLA. It was as though he had stayed on just to baptize me with my Japanese nickname. "Don't be too nice, all right?" he said as he got into the car with his father, who was driving him to Narita Airport. "My parents might decide to adopt you and boot me out."

He shouldn't have worried. I did my best to be polite and pleasant to the Nojimas, but something held me back from warming up to them. I couldn't even bring myself to call them *Otosan* and *Okaasan* even though they immediately took to calling me with the familiar Aya-chan. I've seen what happens when people claim what isn't theirs.

My life in Tokyo was an unbroken stretch of schoolwork once classes started. Though the school I went to was a SELHi and most of our classes were in English, I had to take pretty intensive lessons in Japanese with the other exchange students. Not that I minded—on the contrary, it was a nice way to keep my mind from wandering back into the past.

Sometimes, they took us on field trips to learn more about the local culture. The first place they took us to was this temple in Asakusa with a huge red lantern suspended in its gateway. But what I remembered most from the visit wasn't the lantern but a bronze figure frozen in meditation in the courtyard, a lotus-shaped halo emanating from its head. I was so entranced by its serene expression that I didn't notice one of the teachers come up behind me and was startled when she spoke.

"Kannon is the bodhisattva of mercy and compassion," she said. She pointed to something bulb-shaped in its hand. "She's holding the wish-fulfilling jewel." I nodded politely, then squinted into my guidebook until she left to snap a photo for another student. Then I brushed my hand against the jewel and whispered a wish for my brother.

We couldn't have been more different, my brother and me—I mean Rigel, my real blood brother back home in the Philippines. I could play nursery rhymes on the piano by the time I was three, when my mother bore him. I remember Mom sitting beside me on the piano bench, her round belly squashed against the keyboard, as I played "Mary Had a Little Lamb" or "Twinkle, Twinkle Little Star" for my yet unborn sibling. By the time I was twelve, I could play the piano plus the violin well enough for a local newspaper to feature me in its pages, calling me a prodigy.

But even as my "gift" flourished—that was how my parents and teachers called it—Rigel seemed to be caught in some sort of developmental time warp. He'd been slow to start walking and speaking as a kid, but my parents dismissed his condition as a natural outcome of being born and growing up in the shadow of a hyper-talented sibling. We became known in the school we both attended as Little-Miss-Mozart-and-her-moron-kid-brother. Poor boy, people would say, he got the short end of the stick—his big sister must have used up his share of IQ.

He was eight when my parents finally decided to take him to a specialist and he was diagnosed as intellectually disabled. I was in the waiting room with him when the psychologist spoke to our parents, and I overheard him ask them why they hadn't had him checked sooner. I remember Mom bursting into tears as he continued. "I don't mean to suggest that you've been anything but good parents, but perhaps your daughter's gift, shall we say, drew away some of the attention that your son badly needed."

I couldn't believe my ears. I didn't know why I was being blamed for my brother's condition, when I adored him and never ever dreamed of hurting him. But though I could ignore the neighbors' dumb talk about us being "the Lone Ranger and Tonto," playing on the Spanish word for stupid, it was harder to dismiss the doctor's words. I resented what they seemed to hint at—that I had robbed my brother of my parents' affection.

From then on, I kept my distance from Rigel. I used to play the piano and violin for him, even trying to teach him how it was done, guiding his hands, his fingers, though he seemed to like it best just listening to me play. The music did something for him. He'd sit there on my bed or beside me on the piano bench and watch my hands, open-mouthed, and as I finished each piece, he would look up at me, blinking, then slowly break into a smile, as though he'd returned from some wonderful secret place. But I stopped doing that after he was diagnosed. Those first few weeks, he would sidle up to me as I practiced, waiting for me to play for him. But I steeled myself. Deep inside, I felt like the victim. This is what I get for being a good sister to you, I thought. After a while, he would leave, his eyes round and glistening.

⮌

Hiro came back at the end of June to spend his summer break in Tokyo. When our school was let out in mid-July, he decided to act as my tour guide for the month and a half still left before he had to go back to the States. He took me everywhere: To grab a bowl of ramen or a plate of curry rice at his favorite shops. To Harajuku, where he pointed out some of the most outlandishly dressed specimens, joking that I could get some fashion tips from them. Once, he even took me hiking to Mt. Takao on the outskirts of Tokyo, to get away from the muggy city.

Sometimes as we roamed about, just the two of us, I felt a vague warmth stir inside me—when he held my hand to show me how to use the chopsticks properly, or when we huddled beneath a single umbrella after being caught in an unexpected shower. The feeling never stayed long, though, always chased away by the thought of my brother. What was he doing back home, I'd wonder. Sometimes, I would resolve to make an excuse to stop going on those outings with Hiro, but I couldn't bring myself to do it. What's the danger, I asked myself—he would be leaving by summer's end anyway.

⮌

As the date for Hiro's departure drew nearer, I racked my brain about how to return his kindness. I didn't have enough money to buy him a meal at a family restaurant or even Mos Burger. So one afternoon, I bought some *onigiri* and his favorite Mt. Rainier cold coffee from Family Mart and put them all in lovely ceramic dishes and cups on a lacquer tray, every one of them borrowed from his mother's kitchen. We ate on the tatami floor of his room, which had been given over to me when I arrived in April. He said it was nicer than eating out.

He scanned his room, as if trying to reacquaint himself with it, and his eyes fell on my *hegalong* propped up against the wall at the foot of the bed. I had bought the native two-string lyre from a T'boli craftsman on the banks of Lake Sebu when I'd visited with my family back in happier days. It was my sole link to a past self I could barely remember, and wasn't really sure I wanted to.

"What in the world is that?" Hiro asked, spotting the instrument leaning on the wall at the foot of the bed. He looked as perplexed as his parents had been when they saw the thing slung over my shoulder the day they met me at the airport.

I reached for the *hegalong* and handed it to him. "Go ahead, try it."

He took it, cradled it on his lap like a guitar, then shook his head. "How do you play this thing anyway? It's got only two strings?"

I gently relieved him of it, adjusted the strings, and started plucking a melody.

I stopped halfway through the song, suddenly remembering the promise I'd made myself before leaving Manila. How could I have forgotten?

He was staring at me, mouth half open, when I opened my eyes. He, too, seemed to have snapped back from a distant place only he knew about.

"*Sugoi*, Aya-chan! That was brilliant."

His words made me flinch.

"What else can you play?"

"I used to play the piano and violin," I said, biting my lip. Hoping to change the topic, I added, "Now the only keyboard I play is the computer's."

Thankfully, he didn't probe. In fact, he seemed just as relieved as I was to change the topic. We'd moved on to talking about his life at UCLA when his cell phone rang. It was a friend of his—they were throwing an impromptu send-off dinner for him somewhere in Shinjuku.

"*Ja, mata ne*,"—see you later—he said, after thanking me for tea. He slipped out the door with the tray of used crockery, ignoring me when I said that I was the host so I should clear them. On the top step of the stairs, he paused and turned back to me. "Hey, why don't you come along?"

I looked at his expectant face. I was about to say yes when the memory of my brother's face floated up in my mind. What was I thinking? I hadn't come here looking for fun or affection, but to suffer like an exile for what I'd done to him. "I have an essay to hand in on Monday," I said, gently closing the door and leaning my head against it. For a moment, there was only silence, then the sound of footsteps, fading back to silence.

⌒

The following afternoon, he came knocking on my door. When I opened it, he strutted in, took the *hegalong* and slung it over his shoulder.

I watched him openmouthed, and he returned my gaze, brows raised. "What? We're going for a ride." He refused to say where, so I hopped on my bicycle and rode after him, my curiosity getting the better of me. We chained our bicycles at the edge of a park near Kichijoji Station. "Inokashira Koen," a sign read. I followed Hiro as he trudged down the grassy path shaded by trees, my *hegalong* thumping behind him next to his backpack. I caught my breath when we emerged into a clearing, a beautiful lake teeming with boats in its midst.

My amazement grew as I looked around. Around the lake, young people in dreadlocks and Afros and all sorts of hats and hairdos had laid tie-dyed sarongs and woven blankets on the bare ground to display their artworks: postcard-size photographs and sketches, painted matchboxes, twisted-wire ornaments, beaded jewelry, dream catchers, and whatnot. Those who had nothing to peddle showed off their talents. There was someone juggling empty wine bottles, another blowing on a didgeridoo, someone else thumping a tabla, and another doing pantomime. I felt my heart seize up, looking at them.

Hiro seemed to read my mind. "They're only here from late spring until early autumn, then they hibernate. When I heard you play your . . . that two-stringed thing, I told myself I should take you here. But first we must pay our respects to the guardian of this place."

He took my hand and led me to the other side of the lake, where a temple, much smaller than the one in Asakusa, stood nestled among the trees. We stood in front of the one-floor wood building, painted a bright red. Hiro rang the bell that hung from its eaves and pressed his hands together, bowing low. I did the same, saying as I straightened up, "Kannon."

"Close enough." Hiro nodded. "It's Benzaiten, the goddess of music, learning, and love."

I peered through the doorway of the temple, and sure enough, the deity inside, whom I could barely make out in the shadows, held what looked like a lute instead of the bulb-shaped jewel.

"Come, we have her blessing now. I've picked the perfect spot for you." He took my hand and, half running, pulled me toward a spot by the lake where the traffic of pedestrians seemed thickest. Beneath a gnarled old tree, in a gap between two rugs covered by trinkets for sale, was a cardboard sign with the word "Reserved" scrawled on it. Hiro took it, folded it in half, and crammed it into his backpack.

"Go on, sit down," he said, waving me toward the railing that bordered the lake, which the other performers used as a perch. He eased the *hegalong* from his shoulder and held it out to me like a bouquet. "It's time the world gets to know your music."

I stood stock-still beside him, the blood draining from my face. "No, wait, Hiro. I can't do it, I'm sorry." I looked around me, casting about for an excuse. "The lake looks so pretty—why don't we go for a boat ride?" I turned on my heels and headed for the pier. Glancing over my shoulder, I saw him standing on the spot he'd saved for me, frowning. I waved at him and made a rowing gesture, but he merely shook his head and backed away until he was leaning against the railing. I suddenly felt angry. How dare he put me on the spot? I never asked him to bring me to this place. But I felt sad, too, knowing that something in our friendship had splintered that afternoon. I tried to catch his eye one more time, but he was gazing down at his hands. I veered away from the lake toward the spot where we had left our bicycles and pedaled away as my tears began falling.

I didn't hear him come back that night. When I came down in my school uniform the next morning, he was waiting on the landing, holding the *hegalong*. "Sorry about yesterday. It was stupid of me to take you there and expect you to play just like that." He was gone before I could muster an answer, leaving the instrument leaning against the banister. All day at school I worried over what to say to him when I saw him that evening. But he wasn't there when I got home. He had gone with his mother to say good-bye to his grandmother in Chiba. I stayed up for as long as possible, but I must have fallen asleep, because when I woke up, the sun was up and I knew from the silence that he was gone. I ran downstairs and sure enough Mrs. Nojima was alone in the kitchen. "Ah, *ohayo gozaimasu*," she said. "Hiro left for the airport with his dad. He didn't want to wake you up to say good-bye."

〜

For the first time since I arrived, I lied to Mrs. Nojima and told her that I wasn't feeling well. My swollen red eyes convinced her. It was true though—I felt terrible. That was the end of it, I thought. But weeks later, he sent me a rambling e-mail. *I didn't mean to be rude that afternoon at the lake*, it started. *It has a story, that lake. They say Benzaiten placed a curse on it so that happy couples who go boating on it would end up parting.* He confided then that his ex-girlfriend used to play the *shamisen* in that park every Sunday. He would always go with her, swelling with pride as people gathered around and applauded her, some of them even asking if she was a celebrity. Once, when she finished playing, she told him she wanted to go for a ride on the lake. It was there, on a swan-shaped boat that she broke up with him. *When I first heard you play, I felt as if she'd returned. That afternoon at the park, I wanted you to be her.*

I sat in front of the computer, reading his words over and over. I felt a pang, wondering if he'd been so nice to me only because I reminded him of his ex. But hadn't he gone out of his way to spend time with me even before he heard me play? I didn't know what to say in reply to his e-mail. I knew only that the least I could do in return for his trusting me enough to tell me what he had told me, was to explain why I had refused to play that day, even though it was possible that he would end up hating me after he heard what I had to say. I wrote him a long e-mail, telling him everything about my brother and what I had done to him. There was no answer from him for some time, and I thought that my worst fear—that he wouldn't want anything more to do with me after hearing my confession—had been confirmed. But just when I was ready to give up waiting for his e-mail, his reply came: *It's not only the lake that's cursed. You and I, we too, are under curses—the kind that are hardest to break, because we placed them on ourselves. Perhaps, life threw us together to help each other break them.*

A curse. I had never thought of it as such, but I suppose he's right that I had let that episode of my past take hold of me like a curse.

When it happened I was a freshman in the arts high school I went to on the slopes of Mt. Makiling. Every year, we were supposed to put up a concert for the school's patrons and our parents. Determined to make an impression, I decided to play Paganini's "Caprice No. 24" on the violin, a difficult piece. I had overheard from my teachers that the heads of the two conservatories of music in the country would be in the audience and that the media would be covering the event.

A week before the concert, Mom came up to my room and sat on the edge of my bed as I polished my violin. "Listen, Rain. You know your dad and I both want to be there next Sunday, but since you don't want your brother to come along—"

I didn't even let her finish. "How often does this happen, Mom, once a year? I don't even get to see you and Dad anymore except on weekends. And you know what it's like when people see Rigel—they say hurtful things and it would just spoil the whole evening for us all."

She was silent. I kept on buffing the surface of my violin, refusing to even turn around and look at her. Finally, she got up and padded away. I sulked all that weekend, refusing to come down for meals, saying I had to practice. I didn't even bother to give Dad the usual peck on the cheek when he dropped me off at school on Monday.

When he came to pick me up the following Friday, he greeted me by saying that he and Mom would both be there to see me perform at the concert. "We wouldn't miss it for the world," he said, tousling my hair. "We've asked Aling Cora to look after Rigel for the evening." Aling Cora was our neighbor, an old widow.

I don't remember ever having played so well as I did that Sunday evening, when my violin solo was met with thunderous applause. Perhaps, a part of me knew that, thereafter, music would be for me something tainted with guilt, like a curse. Because that night, my brother, wanting to go and watch me play, tried to climb out the window of the room where Aling Cora, unable to pacify him, had locked him up—he fell, broke both legs, and injured his spine, and after that he never regained the full use of his body. As if it weren't enough that he had never had the full use of his mind.

That night, as I stood outside the hospital's operating room with my parents, the psychologist's words rang in my ears. I knew then what I had to do. I would take myself someplace where I couldn't usurp what belonged to my little brother—where I didn't have to tower above him, soaking up all the air and sunshine and leaving him to wither in my shade.

The following month, I applied to join an exchange program for my sophomore year. Anywhere would have been fine, and they matched me with a school in Japan. Before I left, I promised myself something else: that I wouldn't play—not the piano, not the violin, not any instrument— except for myself. I knew it was my music that had warped me, making me willing to risk everything, even Rigel, to be praised and applauded.

"Aren't you bringing your violin?" Dad asked me as he picked up my luggage to take it to the car on our way to the airport. I didn't know what to say, so I grabbed the *hegalong*, which was leaning against the wall, and said, "I'm bringing this—I want to learn a new instrument."

I thought I was giving up everything then: my brother, my parents, my music. . . . It hadn't occurred to me that perhaps leaving was my way of finding them again so that we could start over.

～

The cherry blossoms returned just before I was due to leave for Manila. So did Hiro. I came home on the last day of school to find him snoring on the couch. I stood there, staring at him as if he were an apparition. Until then, I hadn't allowed myself to believe that he would bother to come back before I left. He had told me earlier that he only had a few days before the spring term started. I was still gaping down at him when his eyes fluttered open.

"Hey." A grin spread slowly across his jet-lagged face. He held out a hand and squeezed mine when I gave it to him.

"You came back."

"We've got something left to do, haven't we?" He stifled a yawn. "We'll go back there tomorrow morning, and we'll do it right this time."

I looked down at my palms. What about the curse on the lake, I thought, though I didn't dare ask him. But he seemed to read my mind.

"Don't be afraid of the lake. We'll break the spell."

"How?"

"You remember who placed it?"

"Benzaiten."

"The goddess of music."

I let his words sink in, then nodded, understanding.

The sky was streaked with dawn as we hopped on our bicycles the next day, the *hegalong* slung across my back. We pedaled down the still-deserted roads to Inokashira Koen, leaving our bicycles on the otherwise empty lot, without even bothering to chain them. We headed toward the lake and crossed the bridge to the other side. We righted one of the upended boats and, taking an oar each, paddled to the deepest part of the lake. Gently, I swung the *hegalong* over my shoulder and cradled it in my arms.

As he watched, my audience of one, I strummed a melody, and another, and another. In my mind, I was playing for Rigel in his wheelchair, and I decided, at that moment, that the first thing I would do when I got home would be to play for him what I had performed that fateful evening. I didn't stop playing until the sun had burned the mist off the lake and my fingers were raw and red. Afterward, I felt strangely cleansed. Hiro took my hands in his and said in a whisper, "See? It's broken." I looked at him and I wondered which he meant. Deep inside, I hoped he didn't just mean the baggage I brought with me from my past, but the spell on the lake. I wasn't about to ask him.

⤳

Hiro was right when he said that the curses that are hardest to break are those that we place on ourselves: guilt, anger, grief. . . . Yesterday morning at the lake, he helped me free myself from a self-inflicted curse at the risk of bringing another one down on our heads. Whether or not that, too, was broken, only time will be able to tell. In three days, I will leave Japan to return to my brother, my parents, and yes, my music. We will say good-bye, possibly forever. But I hope that we shall see each other again—that my playing has pleased Benzaiten. I guess only time will tell.

Insiders and Outsiders

Fleecy Clouds

by Arie Nashiya
translated by Juliet Winters Carpenter

It was raining.

I hate rainy days. Putting up umbrellas creates distance between her and me.

I hate the way the umbrellas get in the way so I can't see her profile, the way it's harder to catch what she's saying over the sound of the rain. And I hate it too when we're walking side by side with our umbrellas up and somebody comes along from the opposite direction and there isn't enough room on the sidewalk for all the umbrellas and our conversation gets interrupted, even for two or three seconds.

Her umbrella was cherry-blossom pink.

Was mine the green of new leaves? Softer than turquoise, brighter than chartreuse, an umbrella the fresh green of young cherry-tree leaves . . . Actually I think the one I was carrying that day might have been hyacinth blue, the same as now. Hyacinth blue has a kind of muddy tint like an overcast sky that strikes me as a more real, more genuine color than clear pale blue, which is why I tend to like it more. Maybe her new cherry-blossom pink umbrella made such a strong impression on me that in my mind my umbrella changed color to harmonize with hers.

Her umbrella was definitely cherry-blossom pink. Not peach pink, not salmon pink, but the delicate pink of cherry-blossom petals. I remember I was happy because the color was so elegant and it suited her so well. When she had on something that suited her perfectly, I felt as excited as I did when I found a hat that looked perfect on me, as proud as if I'd looked in a magic mirror and glimpsed my own shining future.

"Saki, you have such terrific taste!" I blurted, feeling as awkward as if I were bragging about myself.

"What's got into you?" She looked embarrassed, a little taken aback.

From the time we were in nursery school together till we went to the same cram school to get ready for junior high entrance exams, and even now, in high school, it's always been the same.

"You like the rain, Saki, don't you?"

"It all depends. On a day like today with exams coming up, it makes me feel like, Oh well, might as well go straight home and hit the books, so it's a good rain, know what I mean? Keeps me from wanting to go somewhere and goof off."

To me the rain was a disappointment. During the week before exams, as well as during exam week itself, club activities were called off. I'd been waiting and waiting for this chance to go home from school with her—and then it had to go and rain. The rain was irritating, with its bothersome umbrellas.

In junior high Saki and I had been in the same club. In high school she picked something different, which meant we had after-school activities on different days, or finished up at different times, so we couldn't go home together every day the way we used to. I was secretly glad when exam time rolled around, since it meant I could be with her after school.

"Well, I hate having my shoes and my schoolbag get all wet," I said.

"Nobody likes that."

"And lately when it rains, I sneeze. Must be the humidity . . ." Even as I said it, I let out a big sneeze like a comedian, and she laughed. Whenever I can tell she's having fun, I feel satisfied, like I'd just finished eating a piece of sweet fruit.

"Here comes the bus," she said and got in line, taking out her pass and starting to fold up her umbrella.

When we get on the bus I always let her go first, especially on rainy days. That's because I hate it when the bus stops and I try to fold up my umbrella with perfect timing but end up getting my shoulders all wet. To keep that from happening to her, I hold my umbrella over her furtively while she climbs into the bus. I would get wet anyway, I'm such a klutz, so the extra drops that fall on me while I'm holding my umbrella over her don't mean a thing.

I hate how the floor of the bus gets all slick and wet on rainy days, and how you have to scrunch into a damp seat clutching your wet umbrella. But sitting next to her takes away the pain. Sitting next to her is as natural as custard cream in a cream puff, and even more reassuring than a bowling lane with bumpers in the gutters.

From elementary school through junior high, whenever the class had to form pairs she and I would always pick each other as a matter of course, until everybody came to expect it. We never paired off with anybody else. In gym class and group activities we were always together.

She and I were always best friends, special friends.

Her favorite place to sit on the bus was a double seat toward the back, behind the exit door, on the side closer to the sidewalk. The best seat was the one in front of the protruding wheel well, but the odds of getting that were low. When it wasn't available she would sit behind the wheel well, but on that day, that seat was taken, too.

She got on before me and I found her squeezed into the narrow seat on top of the wheel well, her knees folded up by her chest. The seat across the aisle one row back was free, but she said no. "The view's better here," she explained, wiping the steamy window with her hand.

I couldn't see any real difference in the scenery whichever side we were on, but she always preferred the side closer to the sidewalk. In the morning the bus was so jammed that we got shoved every which way, so she never cared which side she was on, but on the way home she made sure to pick a window seat facing the sidewalk.

When the bus started up, she and I talked about exams and what would be covered, what we were nervous about and what we thought we could pull off okay. After the first stop, I pulled out my electronic dictionary and started testing her on English vocabulary. She tossed off the answers, then interrupted: "Got any tissues?" I handed her a packet, and she pulled one out and used it to give the window a thorough wiping.

"What is it?" I asked.

"I couldn't see outside."

So what, I thought. The bus took the same familiar route every day. I craned my neck and looked out the window, but all I could see was an ordinary shopping street in the rain. My interest flagged, and I turned my attention back to the dictionary.

After answering a few more questions, she said, "'Fleecy clouds' means cottony clouds, right?"

"What's 'fleecy' again?" I asked. "Doesn't it mean woolly, like the coat of a sheep?"

"That's right. A sheep's coat of wool. The funny thing is, English 'fleecy clouds' doesn't mean the same thing as 'sheep clouds' in Japanese."

"Why not? Cottony clouds, woolly clouds—same difference."

"You'd think so, wouldn't you? But I looked it up. They're totally different."

She opened her notebook and explained, referring to what she had written down. "What we call 'sheep clouds' in Japanese are clouds that look like a flock of sheep in the sky. The technical term in English is 'altocumulus clouds.' But in English 'fleecy clouds' are puffy, cotton-like clouds—the kind known as 'cumulus.' So not only the shape but the altitude is different."

"I still don't get it."

"Literally, 'fleecy clouds' means 'clouds like a sheep's coat,' and yet to our way of thinking, puffy clouds are cottony, not woolly. I mean intuitively, not the technical term."

"Complicated, man!"

"You got that right!" She giggled.

Whatever we talked about, it was always fun.

"So this is what you're saying?" I asked. "Between English speakers and Japanese speakers, how people describe puffy clouds depends on whether they've had more contact with wool or with cotton—is that it, professor?"

"Yes, my star pupil."

"Why the sudden fascination with clouds?"

"There's a shop called Fleecy Clouds, you know. Right by the bus stop we passed a minute ago."

I drew a blank.

"What kind of shop?"

"I guess you'd call it a boutique, maybe? A little clothes store. One that's actually kind of cool. You wouldn't expect to find any interesting shops on this street, would you? It's little, and all it's got in the display window is one torso mannequin, but the clothes on display change a few times a week, so I always keep an eye out from the bus window."

"Yeah? What kind of clothes are they?" I'd never noticed any such shop.

"Casual, but not our kind of casual. The kind I'd like to try wearing when I get a little older. The kind that if you wore them to an art museum or somewhere, you'd look like you stepped right out of a painting. Someday I'd love to dress that way, like a grown woman who stepped out of a painting." She laughed, looking out the window in shy embarrassment.

If she said so, I was sure it must be a shop of discriminating taste.

But really now—a *boutique*?

To me the word "casual" only meant the clothes I lounge around in on weekends, or denim jeans like the ones I used to wear to cram school. For the life of me I couldn't imagine what kind of clothes she meant, what kind she wanted to wear when she grew up. Just knowing she had her sights set on a not-so-distant time when she'd be an adult gave me an indescribable feeling, as if she'd already left me behind.

"Have you ever been in a boutique, Saki?" I asked.

"If you count name-brand specialty shops in department stores, I've peeked in, but I'm always afraid they'll think, What's a high school kid doing here? They're still kind of intimidating."

"But you do go in sometimes."

When I went to department stores, I passed right by the gorgeous salons. I only thought to myself, Wow, there are actually people in the world who go to a fancy place like this and pay ten or twenty times the normal price for their clothes. I never imagined a time when I myself might wear clothes like that, never felt like trying them on.

My current interest in fashion was pretty much limited to wondering how I could make my school uniform cuter, the way everyone does. Which one I should put in my breast pocket to jazz things up—a hair clip or a ballpoint pen with a cartoon character on top? That kind of thing.

"You're amazing, Saki. Even after I'm all grown up, I don't think I'd ever have the nerve to go in a boutique, especially a real shop like that, not just a corner in a department store. I'd have to talk to the saleslady, and there wouldn't be many items to choose from, and the prices would be out of control, you know? I'd feel like once I entered enemy territory I couldn't leave till I'd bought something. It'd be really hard to make myself go in."

"'Enemy territory'? That's a bit extreme." She'd been looking out the window, and swung her head back to look at me. Her eyes were so pretty they made me jump. Even up close, her skin was fine-textured, without pores. "It won't be long before we're adults and clothes from Fleecy Clouds will look good on us. Won't that be fun?"

Probably, if she said so. Whatever she chose was bound to be right.

"But first we have to pass our exams," I said.

"Indeed we do." She picked up my electronic dictionary, and this time she started quizzing me.

Being with Saki all the time came naturally. We lived in the same neighborhood, in condominiums with almost exactly the same floor space and layout. Our parents were in the same business, our families were just the same size. She and I shared nursery school, elementary school, after-school lessons, and cram school. We applied to and were accepted at the same number of junior high schools, and when we both started attending the same girls' combined junior and senior high, it seemed like the most natural thing in the world.

We always liked the same things. Back in lower elementary we watched all the same shows on TV, and in upper elementary we liked the same comedians. When I sang with her, I could harmonize. We took piano lessons at the same place, and after I got sick of it in fourth grade and quit, she quit in fifth grade to concentrate on entrance exams for junior high. We both liked learning English conversation until third grade, when the teacher left—but then at the end of that year we started to go to cram school together, so we always saw each other after school.

In junior high we joined the same volleyball club. When we moved on to senior high, we continued with volleyball, until she changed clubs with the excuse that she'd suffered an injury. I had to stick with volleyball.

On school tests I'd usually outscore her by a dozen points or so, but overall it worked out to a difference of just two or three points in our grade averages, so she never minded. If she'd answered a question or two differently, the results could just as easily have been reversed, so I could never lord it over her like I was smarter or something.

Our height and our hairstyles were pretty much the same, and all our lives people had been telling us we looked alike. We enjoyed acting like twins.

Other girls liked to talk about boys and romance.

When our classmates got into animated discussions about who they liked or which celebrity they wanted for a boyfriend, we would hang back a little and look on with polite smiles. They'd carry on about what present they gave some boy or what he gave them, whether they should tell a boy they liked him or how a boy had declared his love, and other silly stuff. We couldn't come right out and say "Borrrring!" or anything so uncool. We would cock our heads slightly and say "Hey, that's great!" and listen oh-so-sweetly. Later on, when she and I were alone, we'd have a good laugh and feel relieved. We weren't being critical of our friends. Our laughter meant, You and I are on top of things, isn't this cool? We felt a conspiratorial kind of satisfaction. We two always made a special combination.

In junior and senior high, especially since we went to a girls' school, people's expectations and desires concerning the opposite sex were extreme. Pick up any novel or newspaper, or turn on the TV, and everybody and his brother is in love, or at least that's how it seems. But I always figured there must be a surprising lot of people out there who never loved anybody. It's just that when everyone around you is excited about their little romances, it takes courage to come out and admit, You know, I've never actually been in love. I know, because I was like that.

↬

When we got to school that morning, the classroom was livelier than usual. They must be carrying on about the usual stuff, I thought—somebody had made a declaration of love, or kissed somebody, or gone beyond kissing—so I paid no attention and just took my seat. But so many people were dying to tell about it that without my trying to find out, the information came to me.

"The art teacher's getting married."

So that's all it was.

Well, well, congratulations.

In contrast to my outer expression, inside I was thinking spitefully, Ew, who'd want to marry that guy?

"Omigod!" Somebody gave an exaggerated scream.

Another voice said, "You're kidding, right? I had a teeny crush on him myself!"

"Who's he marrying? It isn't one of us, is it?"

Young, unattached male teachers in a girls' school get treated like pop stars. Scarcity value makes them prime targets of pseudo-love. The gossip went on.

"I heard it's someone he's been seeing since college."

"Argh! Who knew there was somebody like that in his life! Argh!"

"Oh no, Saki's crying!"

I couldn't believe my ears. I spun around, but so many people were clustered around her that I couldn't see.

"Saki, honey, I'm devastated too!"

"Don't cry. I know what—let's go find out for sure. We'll ask him in person."

A handkerchief covering her face, Saki was escorted out of the classroom by several classmates offering her their arms for support.

My total inability to share her sadness left me in shock.

To me, the art teacher was a tall man with delicate features, and that was it. I always thought the only reason she joined the art club was that she liked to draw. She alone had always been so special, giving no outward sign of any interest in casual romance or deep passion or feminine desire. I'd always liked that purity of hers, admired and respected her for it.

My agitation didn't let up even after class began.

Saki, crying. Saki, grieved at heart.

Then why wasn't I wounded and in tears?

⟿

Fleecy Clouds. Ever since she told me about the shop, I tried to keep an eye out for it on the way home, watching out the bus window, but nine times out of ten my mind would wander and I'd miss it. When the bus pulled up at the next stop I'd think, *Rats, I did it again.*

But today I didn't miss it. That's because I got on the bus alone and kept careful watch the whole time. The display window looked like a picture in a wooden frame, and in the back, lit by a spotlight, was a layered dress in soft bright colors. If you wore that dress to an art museum you'd fit right into an Impressionist painting, that's how soft the colors were.

I got off the bus at the next stop and half ran back down the sidewalk through the rain.

I hate rainy days. I'm no good at carrying an umbrella. The umbrella cuts off my view of the sky. The sight of the damp, depressing sky makes me feel like a damp, depressing human being.

I raised my umbrella high in the air and looked up at the fancy sign of the boutique she admires so much. Then I screwed up my courage and went in. Why, I don't know.

The saleslady started to welcome me, and stopped with a puzzled look.

Picking up the unspoken implication of her smile—*What's a high school kid like you doing here?*—I said huffily, "May I try on the dress in the window?"

I took off my school uniform and put my arms through the sleeves.

That other day, she'd said that soon she and I would be adults who looked good in clothes like this. But all I saw reflected in the mirror was my gawky, freaky, high school self. I looked less like someone you might accompany to the art museum than someone who might put on a one-woman comedy show. That's how pathetic my reflection looked, how different I was from the kind of person she aspired to be.

I liked Saki so much, but she lived on a higher plane than I did. Thinking it over, I couldn't stop the tears when I realized how foolish I'd been to suppose I'd never been in love.

There in the Fleecy Clouds dressing room it came to me—for the longest time, I'd felt unrequited love for my own gawky reflection in the mirror.

The Zodiac Tree

by Thersa Matsuura

Izumi stretched out her arm, held up an index finger and began drawing slow circles in the air. At her feet hundreds of electric-blue dragonflies flitted in clumsy circles above a water-filled rice field.

"Do you think she can catch one before it gets dark? I got to be home before it gets dark." Hideki was her eight-year-old brother Taka's new best friend.

"Shh," Taka said. "I had to be home an hour ago."

A single dragonfly rose, hesitated, and neared her finger. It was just about to light when Izumi caught movement out of the corner of her eye. Something hit her hard on the side of the head. She fell to her knees.

"Ow!"

There was an explosion of laughter. Muck filled her ear, coated the entire right side of her face and neck, and oozed down the inside of her T-shirt. She raked the mess to the ground, standing to get a better look at what it was: a sopping wet mud clod, a handful of rice shoots growing from its top.

"Cut it out!" Taka yelled.

More laughter.

Izumi cursed, using the side of her hand to scrape the gunk from her face and fling it to the ground. Her eye stung so badly she couldn't open it. Grit coated her tongue.

"She talks like a boy too." It was Mai.

Mai was the tallest girl in her eighth-grade class, the most beautiful too. She was thin with a long delicate stem of a neck. Stunning in both her looks and her cruelty. Just last week she'd emptied an entire bottle of calligraphy ink into Izumi's book bag.

Mai straddled her bike, her friends on either side. Another girl squatted down by the rice field holding one long sleeve of her *yukata* against her ribs. Her other hand was muddied and hovered over another tuft of rice.

"Izumi's a boy's name," the girl with the pinched fox-face taunted.

"It is not," Izumi's brother said. Hideki tugged on Taka's shirttail as if signaling that this wasn't a fight they wanted to get mixed up in.

"Listen, it's going to be dark soon," Izumi said, leading the boys to their bicycles. She rested one hand on her own bike's seat while holding the heel of her other hand up to her streaming eye. "You two go home."

"But—" Hideki rattled an empty plastic cage at her.

"We'll catch some tomorrow," she said. "I promise."

Taka stuck out his bottom lip and shook his head.

"You know mom's going to be upset," Izumi told her little brother. "I'll be fine."

The two boys hopped on their bikes and sped off, hugging the side of the road farthest from the bullies.

"That's it, run away!" The squatting girl's arm was buried almost to the elbow as she loosened another mud clod.

All four girls wore summer *yukata*—flower and goldfish prints in pastel pinks, blues, and yellows—bright-colored *obi* wrapped neatly around their waists and tied in large springy bows at their backs. Their long hair was pulled up and secured with silk flower pins and combs that dangled strings of fake pearls.

"Look at them go," Fox-face Girl said, leaning on her handlebars, one sandaled foot hiked up on a raised pedal.

The pebbly mud turned sour in Izumi's mouth. She spit twice on the ground.

"There she goes again. She thinks she's a boy," Mai said. "I bet she wants to be a boy."

The two girls flanking Mai laughed and rang their bicycle bells in agreement. Squatting Girl shook the throttled handful of rice shoots above her head, slinging drops of mud all over her baby blue outfit.

"I do not," Izumi said. It was just the way she was. It had always been easier hanging out with boys. Even before the terrible thing happened, before her mother yanked them out of school and moved them in with her grandparents, out here in the middle of nowhere.

"Hey look, she's crying!" It was the girl on Mai's left, the one with the fall-away chin and the high, perpetually shiny forehead.

"I'm not crying," Izumi dabbed at her stinging eye with the tail of her T-shirt.

"She's a boy and a crybaby," Mai declared.

"Come on, let's get her!" Squatting Girl scrambled to her feet, readying the dripping ball of gunk for a throw. "One, two—"

Izumi didn't wait; she jumped onto her bike and tore off down the dirt road toward the town. Right behind her she could hear the furious pedaling, bell ringing, and crazed shouting of the four girls. Izumi turned down the main street and immediately skidded to a halt. There were people everywhere.

The summer festival had started, and it looked as if the entire town had turned up, everyone dressed in rainbow-colored *yukata* and *jinbei*. Already Izumi heard the drums and flutes of Obon music in the distance. It almost seemed as if the festival-goers were hypnotized by the jangle of music, as if they were being led out of their homes, down the street, and to the town's only temple.

One by one the four girls' bikes squeaked to a stop immediately behind Izumi. They whispered sharply amongst themselves, probably debating whether or not to continue the fight with so many witnesses present.

"I need to wash this off," Squatting Girl whined, dropping her weapon at her feet and holding up her mud-plastered arm with a horrified look on her face.

"Hey, I think I see Hiro and Tatsumi over there," Fox-face Girl said, noticing a group of boys from the school's soccer team.

"My house," Mai said, and then addressing Izumi directly, "We're going to be back, so you'd better hope we don't see you again."

Laughter and bell ringing continued as all four turned to leave. After a couple of steps Squatting Girl looked back over her shoulder, stuck out her tongue, and used her finger to pull down the skin under one eye, leaving a gray fingerprint on her cheek.

Izumi considered going home. She imagined her mother back from work, pulling on her apron to help her grandmother with the evening meal. Taka would no doubt be stepping all over the heels of her slippers exaggerating the incident at the rice fields. He worried about Izumi too much. But despite his alarm, her mother wouldn't listen.

Izumi learned six months ago that her mother's own grief had paralyzed her. She almost never left the house anymore except for work, and she tried to keep everyone close at all times, Grandma, Grandpa, and especially Taka and Izumi.

Sometimes when she couldn't sleep at night Izumi toyed with the idea she'd lost both parents instead of one. The last place on earth she wanted to be right now was home.

There was only one choice left: the zodiac tree.

Izumi wove her bicycle through the crowd while above her the sky changed to a bruised blue-purple. Strings of red paper lanterns flickered and swung in the muggy summer breeze. Their golden glow led the mesmerized throng up the thirty-five stone steps where they would pay respects to the temple itself before descending again.

Izumi steered around a circle of people—everyone dancing with hands cupped and fans raised, spinning and clapping in unison—and made her way between the busy food stalls. The mingled smells of grilling soy-sauce-dipped corn on the cob and steamed meat buns made her wish she'd left home with at least a five hundred yen coin in her pocket. At the foot of the steps she moved away from the gathering and over to the quieter, practically unlit side of the temple.

Of all the trees that surrounded the two-hundred-year-old building, the evergreen oak stood the grandest. Its humongous trunk and scraggle of a thousand limbs was a net of protection. She placed both hands on the rough bark and asked the tree if it would be okay if she climbed. Even in the early evening the countless cicadas continued their midsummer screeching, and she took the fact that not a single one of them stopped and flew away when she invaded their territory as a sign that she was welcome here.

Izumi worked her way up the zodiac tree until she reached her usual branch. It was wide and comfortable, and from it she had a perfect view of the temple yard below, all lit up with paper lanterns. It's where she spent almost every day after school observing the monks swishing about performing late-afternoon chores in their dark layered robes. She knew their routine by heart.

There were twelve monks, and she could identify them all by their gait or their profile or the shape of their bald heads. She knew who pushed wet towels up and down the wooden floors that surrounded the structure, who plucked small pieces of trash and errant weeds from the temple grounds, and who wielded a long stick to carefully remove spiders and their webs from the rafters.

Occasionally visitors made the trek up the steps to cast offerings into the slatted wooden box, afterward clasping their hands together and praying for health or money, marriage or good grades. She liked to guess their stories. What was it they wanted so badly?

Every day at five-thirty sharp a boy appeared and swept all the steps from top to bottom. She tried to imagine his story as well, but couldn't. He was tall, probably a high school student. And his black hair reached his shoulders, so she didn't think he was a monk or a monk in training. She couldn't figure him out. All she knew is that when he shouldered his broom and disappeared around the corner it was time for her to head home.

Izumi heard a familiar squeal and looked down. No more than fifteen meters away stood Mai and her cronies. A line of four boys fidgeted across from the hysterically laughing, overly animated girls. Only Mai was calm. She was spooning shaved ice into her mouth and concentrating on the cutest boy at the end.

The sight prompted a wave of anger in Izumi. The dried muddy patch on her head and neck prickled and itched. She began picking at the flaking dirt, stripping it from her hair wishing she could get even, but knowing it was impossible.

It was at that moment she remembered the animals.

Izumi stood up carefully on the fat branch and looked around. She examined the turns and twists in the wood, she gently poked a finger into several knotholes she knew sometimes held the presents. But there was nothing.

That's okay. I'll try again tomorrow.

She stretched out one leg and dug deep into her jeans pocket, pulling out a small black bag. She tugged the drawstrings open and plucked out a random good luck charm. A dragon. Ah, she loved the dragon. It was the size of her little finger—all of the animals were—and it was carved from some fragrant wood. She inhaled the creature. Japanese cedar, she guessed. The details were astounding, she could make out the dragon's eyes and scales, its claws, and even its long flowing whiskers.

She remembered the day she'd found this one. She'd had a huge fight with her mother and left the house in tears. She'd curled up in the oak for half the day thinking, whispering her problems to the bristling leaves. She'd discovered the dragon when she returned the next day. It was nestled in the crook of a low branch.

Then came the others. They always appeared after a particularly bad day, as though the tree were trying to comfort her, to give her something to smile about, to be her friend. She had collected eleven animals in all. There was a dog, a rabbit, a mouse, but it took until the snake before she realized they were the animals from the zodiac. She replaced the dragon in its pouch and stuffed it back into her pocket. Only one more left to make twelve, she thought.

Below her the bullies and their boyfriends had spread out a mat on the ground and continued their flirting sitting down. They weren't the only ones. Quite a few couples and families were lounging around the temple grounds on mats and large plastic picnic sheets. It almost looked as if they were waiting for something to happen.

Suddenly the tree shook, and the resting cicadas screeched and took flight. Someone was climbing her tree. Izumi's heart thumped high in her chest. Who could it be?

Her answer came immediately with a huff, when two hands grasped the thick limb across from her. A foot—a black-and-white Converse high-top, actually—hooked over the branch and with a grunt there appeared a boy, pushing himself up. He was tall with mussed-up hair, wearing the *jinbei* shirt and shorts that boys typically wore to summer festivals.

"Hi," he said, smiling and finding his balance.

The boy looked familiar, but it was hard to tell in the dim glow coming from the festival below.

"Hi," Izumi answered.

The boy brought his other leg over the branch, so that they were facing each other now. Izumi's perch was a little bit higher, but because he was taller than she they were nearly face-to-face, their bare knees almost touching.

"You're way up here," he said, glancing down and then up before looking her straight in the eyes.

Izumi lost all confidence that she could remain on the branch at all. She felt wobbly and a little sick to her stomach.

"Do I know you?"

"No. I'm Hiromu. It was getting a little crowded down there and I thought I'd come up here for a while."

"Yeah, sure, okay."

"And you are?" he asked.

"Izumi."

"Izumi," he repeated.

"I've seen you before though," she said.

"School. I'm in the ninth grade. A floor up from you. You're the new girl, right? I've seen you throw a baseball with your brother. Impressive."

"Impressive for a girl?"

"Impressive," Hiromu corrected.

"Because, you know, the word is I might really be a boy."

Hiromu laughed. "And was the person who said that blind?"

Izumi didn't know what to say. It sounded like a compliment. She began to swing her legs nervously, careful not to kick this Hiromu fellow.

"I've always wanted to play baseball actually," Hiromu continued, bringing the subject back to something less embarrassing.

"Half the boys at school play, why don't you?"

He pointed over his shoulder toward the temple. "My dad's the head abbot. I'm the oldest son."

And then it hit her where she'd seen him. Not from school. He was the boy who swept the stairs everyday. She felt at once relieved and a little bit frightened.

"So no sports after school?"

"I've got chores and lessons here." He didn't seem happy about this. She wondered how much of after-school life he'd missed out on.

"Well, it sounds cool to me," Izumi said. "Being a monk. Comfortable clothes, everyone leaves you alone." Then she added, "So all this will be yours?"

"One day."

"I bet you'll miss the hair though."

Hiromu laughed so loud Izumi checked to make sure Mai and her buddies hadn't heard. He ran a hand through his longish hair. "Yeah, I'll miss the hair."

"Well, if you ever get some free time we can toss a ball around. I can teach you how not to throw like a girl."

"Hey, I can throw a ball," the boy protested.

"We'll see about that."

Izumi's gaze returned to the couples on the mats.

"Don't let them get you down. Except for that stuff on your cheek you're way prettier than they are."

Embarrassed, Izumi brought her hand up to her face and wiped. She had completely forgotten about the mud.

"Hey, here's a trick." He held up his arms. "Pick a sleeve."

"What?"

"Come on," he said.

The long pocketed sleeves of his *jinbei* swayed. It was very obvious something was in the left sleeve, the right one empty.

"Left."

"*Hora!*"

He pulled out a pink candied mini-apple wrapped in cellophane and tied with a bow.

"I bought it down there," he said. "I thought you might be hungry.

"Pink?"

"The man said it was strawberry flavored."

"A strawberry-flavored apple," Izumi repeated. "What will you country folks think up next?"

"We're clever like that," Hiromu said. "Go ahead and eat it if you want."

"Thank you," she said, untying the ribbon and peeling off the clear plastic. Hiromu took the wrapping from her, folded it, and replaced it in his sleeve.

"I didn't know anyone moved into this town," Hiromu said. "It seems when kids get old enough they just move away from it."

"Well, my father's dead and my mom decided the best thing to do was to haul us all here to live with my grandparents."

"I'm so sorry."

"It happened a while ago," Izumi said. She didn't know why she was telling the story. "I'm okay, though. My little brother too. Mom, on the other hand . . ."

Hiromu listened.

"Mom was the one driving when they got hit. It wasn't her fault, you know." Izumi realized she'd never actually told anyone the story before, never said it out loud. "An accident on the expressway. Rain. The truck in front of them slid or something. There were seven cars involved. Two deaths."

"Izumi." He leaned over and lightly touched her hand.

"It's okay," she said. She hadn't meant to say this much.

After a moment Hiromu spoke.

"It's not the same. I mean it can't compare at all, but I don't have a mom."

"Oh. I'm sorry."

"She's around somewhere. I guess the life of a monk's wife is brutal," the boy said. "She packed up and left when I was small."

"That's terrible."

"So I've been raised by a bunch of bald men who wear dresses and eat pickled vegetables for breakfast," Hiromu said.

Izumi laughed and took a bite of the strawberry-flavored apple.

"Hey, this ain't bad," she said. "So how did you know I was up here anyway?"

"Well, you're here like every day."

"You've seen me?" She suddenly felt very dizzy. "I didn't realize you were watching me."

"Not so much. It's no big deal. I thought you knew. And actually I always thought you were watching me."

"I guess we're even then." She took another bite, thinking the entire situation slightly funny now.

They sat in silence while Izumi finished her treat. Taka was probably worried about her, her mom furious. Izumi wished she didn't have to go home at all.

"What would have happened if I'd chosen the empty sleeve?"

"Not empty," he said.

The boy reached into the deep sleeve and came out with a closed fist.

"Open your hand."

He dropped something into her palm.

"What is it?" She asked, holding it up in the dim light to get a better look.

It was a carving of a monkey, long curling tail, small ears protruding from the side of its head.

"It's one of the animals from the tree," she said. "How did you get it?"

"My grandfather taught me to make them. We put them in the *omi-kuji*-fortune envelopes."

"And you also hide them in the tree?" Izumi questioned.

"Tree? This tree? I don't know anything about any tree."

Izumi squinted hard, but it was difficult to judge his face in the dark. He sounded as though he were telling the truth. Then she remembered that every time she had found one of the animals it had been the day after a really bad day. Had he seen her up here crying? Did he know she'd be back? Had he climbed up and hidden the tiny animals for her to find?

"I love it," she said, clasping it to her chest. "Can I keep it?"

"Of course."

"It'll make a set," Izumi said, retrieving the bag and dropping it in with the others. "But . . ."

"But what?" Hiromu asked.

"It's the last one." Izumi said. "They were kind of my excuse to keep coming here."

"You don't need an excuse to come here," the boy said. "I mean it gets pretty boring sweeping those steps everyday."

"Really?"

Hiromu nodded.

There was a small sound like an exhale off in the distance behind her. Hiromu's face lit up for a second and she could see him perfectly. He was staring right at her. He was beautiful. There was an explosion so loud Izumi screamed and nearly fell off the tree. The boy steadied her with both hands.

"The fireworks show," he said.

She looked down and saw her scream had given her away. Mai and her friends were all staring up in her direction. Squatting Girl was pointing and whispering into Fox-face Girl's ear.

"Hey, I've got a better view over here," Hiromu said. He was already on his feet, one hand on the trunk for balance the other reaching out to help Izumi over. She paused for a second, stood, and took his arm.

Izumi stepped over, tensing at the blasts that reverberated in the pit of her stomach. Hiromu laughed and pulled her close as ash rained down through the branches and sprinkled their hair. Izumi thought she heard the quick voices of Mai and her friends in the silence before the next burst. And for a brief second she considered looking down and sticking out her tongue the way Squatting Girl had done earlier, but she let the thought pass.

Instead she and Hiromu sat on the wide limb of the zodiac tree for another hour, not saying a word. Above them enormous sprays of green, gold, and red painted the sky, crackling as the colors faded away. And after every burst came the cheers and whistles and applause of the festival-goers below.

One

by Sarah Ogawa

He looks up from his kneeling position on the gym floor, sweat pouring down his face. His eyes bore into mine.

"You know, if you didn't wear all that stuff, you wouldn't be so hot," I chide him.

The captain of the *kendo* club grabs the towel out of his face mask and rubs his face vigorously, then his whole head. When he comes up for air he locks eyes with me again.

"It's better than body-conscious clothing that shows everything," he says.

By now this attitude is familiar, typical of most of the faculty and some students, too. We're supposed to be grateful they even allow us to have a dance club. But right now my resentment has gotten the better of me.

"If it's too hot for you, maybe you should just pack it in." There. Show him we've got attitude, too.

"I'm just getting warmed up," he snarls, and with some primitive grunts calls the whole team to attention. They don their headgear and rise as one, a troop called into battle.

In a moment they raise their swords, and cries like those of dying birds fill the air. I wonder again how they can complain, calling our music "noise" when they create this cacophony that sounds like mass slaughter in an aviary.

At the doorway I turn to bow to the gym—showing respect for the spirit of the place, not the people in it I remind myself—and see him at the far end, seeming to watch the practice but instead staring directly at me.

⤷

My whole life I had lived in Detroit. Japanese was a language of domesticity used only at home, Japan a country where relatives would ply me with ice-cold tea and sweets that looked like jewels during the languid afternoons of summertime visits.

But suddenly Dad's company decided to bring him—and our family—back to Japan. Visiting this high school in Kyoto, we happened upon the *kendo* club training in the gym. Skimming over the floor, long robes hiding their legs, they seemed to possess supernatural powers. *An enemy could never anticipate an attack*, I thought on that first visit to the school. *No one could tell the direction or strength of a strike until it hit.* I was awed.

Though my new school had no school uniforms and few rules, in those first days of classes the avalanche of Japanese language and textbooks filled with complex *kanji* closed in over my head. Everything was Japanese, even conversations with friends. I longed for even a glimmer of the life I knew in America.

A few strains of Lady Gaga echoing through a seldom-used hallway was all it took. I joined dance club the next afternoon. The kids who claimed that dead-end hallway for practice space became my new *senpai*, "the honorable ones who had gone before," eleventh and twelfth graders who had lived in New York, Nashville, Nairobi. Not everyone found them so honorable, with their low-slung pants and their pierced belly buttons, but for me they represented the hope that even I could survive here, my supposed homeland. "Overseas refugees" we call ourselves, only half joking.

༄

"The crows are gone. Let's spread out!"

With a word from a twelfth grader, everyone moves to fill up the space left by *kendo* during their water break.

"Why 'crows'?" I ask, following our team leader.

"Those dark robes. And of course those horrible cries."

She changes MD tracks and says, "This is from my studio class." She takes off, filling the open space. Her hands run down her body, across her stomach, then up and through her hair. Then her moves turn crisp, precise. She spins, then poses as the music ends.

"Awesome." I'm impressed. "Maybe we could use it for the school festival?"

"No way. For one thing it's my instructor's choreography, and a few teachers would see it as too suggestive."

"You mean sexy?"

"Yes, and then some. They think they're giving us freedom here. We don't have uniforms, right? We can drive motor scooters, right? But, truly, they are so conservative. At least from where I sit." She sinks down next to the wall and takes a sip from her water bottle. "I fought it at first, upholding freedom of expression and that kind of thing. But in the end, I caved. Maybe that's why I'm *bucho*"—captain. She smiles weakly.

"So we screen our dances to protect their sensitivities?"

She gives me a sidelong glance. "Girl," she says suddenly in English, "I screen my dances to protect the club." The *kendo* troops file back in and she gets up, somehow looking more tired than before the break.

I grab the MD player and we move. "At least we don't have to be told when to have a water break," I say, tilting my head toward the crows.

"Exactly. Thank God for small miracles."

⌒

The school outing in May is to the National Bunraku Puppet Theater in Osaka. "We're going to see a puppet show? We're in high school!" I exclaim as Mom helps me plot my train route.

"It's absolutely amazing. You'll love it." She smiles at me. "You have to dress up for the theater. It shows respect for the actors."

"But they're puppets!"

"You'll see."

And I do. Dressed in black, the puppeteers stand in full view, dwarfing their charges. Yet as they infuse life into the puppets, they seem to disappear. The dolls become real people, with delicate fingers that clutch and unfurl, eyes that blink open and shut, and eyeballs that roll and sometimes cross in consternation.

Being upstaged by an inanimate object strikes me as absurd at first. Yet as I get caught up in the story and literally stop seeing the puppeteers, I realize that their common focus and intent, their shared understanding as each takes charge of a limb or other body part of a single doll, enables them to work as one to create a being none of them could master individually.

∽

Afterward, moving across the lobby through the throng of students, I feel someone staring. Looking up, I see the *kendo* captain on the landing of the stairs above. He's outright staring at me and doesn't even look away when I see him. He's smiling with his eyes. I look around, but it's definitely me he's pinned his eyes on. I look down at the dress covered with wildflowers that I chose, then up at him with a shy smile, all I can manage. He gives me a little nod.

I wonder if he likes me. His friends pull him down the stairs and across the lobby and mine tug me in the opposite direction, saying something about photo print stickers that I don't quite hear.

∽

An early typhoon hits us. Club is canceled. I stay in. E-mail people. Update my Facebook page.

When it's over—just some high winds and a heavy rain—there's little damage, or so I think. I don't anticipate the collateral damage.

Back at school, we decide to add another dance practice day to make up for the ones we missed. I'm just signing up for it when he appears.

Looking down at where I'm filling in "Dance Club" on the gym sign-up sheet, he says, "You can't have that day."

I glance up. The playful smile I usually get is replaced by a steely set jaw.

Never one to back down, I keep writing. "Just watch."

"We have to reschedule a practice match for that day. We need the gym." He makes himself bigger the way boys do, moving his bulk so we're almost touching. I don't give an inch. The *senpai* put me in charge of reserving the gym. At least I can do this right. I sign our team name with a flourish of triumph.

"Dance already has it. But we'd be willing to share." I give him a winning smile.

"Dance isn't even a sport! You shouldn't even be allowed to use the gym!" He practically spits the words at me. The sudden fury takes me by surprise.

"Is that the issue here?" I ask in sincere innocence.

He visibly struggles to get control of himself. He focuses on a spot in the carpet, shaking slightly, breathing hard. Just when I think he'll slam a fist on the counter, he turns on his heel and leaves.

Watching his back, a sense of unease comes over me, as though I've missed some point of social decorum. I look down the sign-up list for other days. His name is there for *kendo*: Jiro Mase.

⤶

He stares daggers at me all week. I see him talking with the dance team coach, the dance team captain, but everyone defers to me on this issue, and apparently I'm the one person he's not willing to talk to about it.

Now I realize how special it felt to meet his eyes in the hallway. I try it a couple times, but it feels like a lie. I give up and just walk past him, staring into middle space.

How can it be possible to miss him so much when I didn't even know his name?

⤶

The day arrives. They use their half of the gym. It's pretty packed with the visiting *kendo* team, but they manage to get through their practice matches. Probably having never competed beside a dance club, the visiting coach keeps scowling at us.

After practice I see Jiro outside the gym. He's bowing low to the visiting team, apologizing profusely. After they've gone, the *kendo* coach lights into him. I can't catch everything, but words like "irresponsibility" and "shameful" fill the air. Jiro stands there with his head down.

I lug my bag over to where they're standing. The teacher stops and looks at me.

"I am to blame for all this. I'm terribly sorry," I say in my best Japanese, thinking that if I just take responsibility and apologize for everything, I can save Jiro.

"Just leave," Jiro says out of the side of his mouth, still looking down.

"But it really is my fault," I plead, wanting to help him.

"You have nothing to do with this," the coach says to me dismissively.

"But really! Let me explain," I begin, but before I can, Jiro speaks.

"Go. Now. Please." His words punch the air. He slides his eyes up to my face. They're red.

When I look back, Jiro is on his knees on the ground in front of the coach. Other kids walk past them like it's nothing unusual. It's surreal. The lack of compassion makes me physically ill.

I turn and go but feel like part of me has died. If I can't protect or even lend a hand to people I care about here, how can I exist? Maybe he was just posturing; maybe it was all a façade. But even if such an apology to his coach was just for appearances, I can't fake being okay with it. And I can't fake that I don't care.

⸺

Of course the gym will be empty, I think. *It's seven a.m.* But he's already there, swinging that stupid stick over his head, back and forth, back and forth, like a human metronome.

He doesn't even acknowledge me as I stand in the doorway, holding iPod speakers and my bag. I watch him. Dancing taught me to see subtlety of movement, and—here, where it's only him—I can suddenly see the precision in the movement, the sheer perfection of the repetition, as if he could go on forever, and the look of absolute concentration on his face.

It's beautiful—he is beautiful—in a precise, cold way.

I shake off the reverie. Official morning practice hasn't even started. I have as much right to be here as he does. So I set up the speakers the group always uses and crank up the sound. He moves off to kneel in the back against a side wall.

The music starts to pulse through me. I let it move my body. A bit self-conscious at first, I glance back at him in the mirror, but he's doing some kind of Zen thing, still and silent, so I concentrate on my moves. I give myself a brilliant smile in the mirror, and then there's only me and the music and the movement. I practice my looks in the mirror: intense, happy, joyous, sexy, serious. I exaggerate my movements, going as big as I can. It's safe to experiment here, where no one's watching.

And suddenly he's there behind me, the human metronome, sliding back and forth, sword slicing through the air. But he's squawking now, too, counting or something. Then I notice it's in time with the music.

He's locked eyes with himself, so I start dancing again with a vengeance. I back up the track and let the sound pour over me and fill the space between us, and it's like he's cutting the sound and I'm building the sound, and we're dancing around, over, through each other. . . .

Until suddenly we're in a heap on the floor.

I can feel the rough skirts of his robes against my bare legs. My elbow hurts like hell. His face is three inches from mine with a look between pissed off and freaked out. As I breathe in his boy smell and feel his body pressing down on mine, a slow blush creeps over his face and his pupils widen. His irises aren't black like I thought, but deep brown, like bittersweet chocolate. He just stops there for a minute. I wait. I can't figure out if he's trying to extricate himself or if he doesn't want to move. I feel his arms tightening around me, and then we both hear it. Just outside the gym, the dance girls joke with each other in their usual too-loud voices.

He rolls away from me and jumps to his feet.

"You okay?" he asks tersely.

"Yeah, I think so," I answer, slowly sitting up.

He begins to offer a hand, but seems to think better of touching me. So I sit there looking up at him.

"If I had known I was going to be attacked, I'd have brought my own sword," I quip.

He turns his back on me and retreats to the other side of the room.

⌒

We're on the same train car every morning, every evening. I don't think we were at first, but now he always seems to be there, nose in one textbook or another, earbud wires snaking into his bag. I wonder if I just didn't notice at first, or if he's changed his schedule to fit mine. We never talk, but sometimes when I get off he's watching me, gives me a little nod.

Whatever he thinks of me, he seems to be looking out for me. And while I certainly don't need anyone looking out for me, it's good to know he's there, like somebody's got my back.

⟿

Leaving the station one day, I glance back to pull my train pass out of the ticket gate, and there he is, right behind me.

I stop in surprise. "What are you doing here?" People mow into each other behind us.

"We have to move." He grips my upper arm and steers me out of the station.

"Are you a stalker or something?" I joke, feigning fear.

He looks over at me and shakes his head. "Let's walk." It's more of a command than an invitation.

I stand there looking at his receding back, annoyed at his assumption that I will follow. But in the end, I pursue him out of curiosity.

"Why are you here?" I ask.

He's silent, and when I begin to think he hasn't heard he says, "I just ... came." He doesn't break his pace.

"Then where are we going?"

He keeps walking, but when I start to repeat my question he suddenly stops dead and peers at me intensely.

"Why do you ask so many questions?" he demands.

"I just want to know what we're doing here!" I say in exasperation.

He looks at me in frustration, and then suddenly his face relaxes. "We're ... walking. Together." He says the last part so low, I'm not sure he's actually said it, and he's already moving again.

⟿

We walk a couple of blocks without saying anything. I'm about to protest when he speaks.

"I'm hungry," he says, so suddenly that I'm ahead of him before I realize he's stopped.

He holds back the *noren* curtain hanging in front of a small shop with a rickety door that slides sideways. "This is Japanese pizza. You'll like it."

I know *okonomiyaki*, know it's not Japanese pizza, know I like it. Yet I can't help wondering what would happen if my taste buds had the audacity to disagree with him.

Inside, the shop is dark, cool. A little bell on the door tinkles as he slides it shut.

"*Irasshaimase*"—welcome—someone croaks from a back room. An old woman in a flowered apron comes hobbling out, and when she sees Jiro her whole face lights up.

"*Ohisashiburi*"—it's been a while—she exclaims. "You look well. And you've brought your friend." She gives me the once-over. "Well, sit down, sit down." We choose one of the low tables with an iron griddle in the middle. She bustles around bringing us water and washcloths, turning on the griddle. We order and she asks, "Shall I bring them out cooked?" She looks at me.

I look at Jiro, questioning.

"No, I'll cook them," he says firmly, and hands her the menu.

She grins widely at us, as if his words have another meaning.

What does it mean here when a guy cooks for you? That he thinks you're too inept to do it yourself? Or is it an overture to something more? She places two stainless steel bowls on the edge of the table, refills my water, and disappears.

"I'll cook mine," I say, reaching for the bowl.

"No, you'll just mess it up." He finishes mixing one and slides the goop from the bowl onto the griddle, making a perfect circle. "Now, watch."

He starts the mixing process again with the second bowl, explaining as he goes. His words drift over me, and I watch his hands scraping, folding the batter into itself: warm, brown, strong hands, wrist twisting, fingers gripping the long-handled spoon. He slides the second portion onto the griddle, the second half of the pair of perfect circles.

"Now, we wait."

How? I think. *What can we talk about?*

We sit for a few moments. Just when I'm about to burst from the tension, he speaks.

"So, how long have you been dancing?"

I look at him and narrow my eyes. I should've seen this coming, a ploy to win me over, to get something for his own club from me, from the dance club. I could kick myself for letting my defenses down.

"Why?" I smolder.

"It's just a question!" He holds up his hands in mock defense.

"You're obviously better than a lot of the seniors. Even someone like me, who knows nothing about dance, can see that much. How did you get so good?"

Even as I curse myself for buckling under such obvious flattery, I open up to him, suspicions suspended for the moment. It's been so long since someone told me I was good at something. Praise is so rare here.

I end up telling him everything. The dread of competitive sports where I was always chosen last. The period of chubbiness. The crazy dance teacher at the world-renowned jazz studio who took me under his wing, pushing me, demanding more, until dance was all I ever did, all I ever wanted to do.

"There's this moment in dancing sometimes when—how do I describe it?—you become the music, the space, the dance itself. You're aware of everything. No, more like you're part of everything. Everything's all one. You cease to exist, but become everything at the same time."

He's looking at me raptly. "Like suddenly everything becomes really clear, your senses heightened?"

"Yes!" I exclaim, thrilled he understands.

"There are moments in *kendo* when I can see everything, even the beads of sweat dripping into my opponent's eyes behind the mask, things I shouldn't be able to see. I can feel where he's going to move, not calculate it like a strategy, but really feel it."

"Yes, that's it. The moment the music and dancers seem to fuel each other, when even the audience, the very space, seems part of the dance. When we are all one . . ."

". . . and yet we are no one."

We look at each other for a second, shocked by our mutual understanding. Of all people, Jiro gets it, he really gets it.

He shakes his head with an embarrassed chuckle. "So dance can do that to you too. I never would've imagined."

He grabs the little spatula to check the underside and pronounces the *okonomiyaki* done, continuing to call it "Japanese pizza." I tell him the only thing it has in common with American pizza is its shape: round and flat. Then I tell him about Buddy's: the oozing cheese, spicy sausage, and garlicky crust known throughout Detroit as the best. And, ironically, square.

He says he'd like to try it someday.

Without thinking, I say I'd like to take him.

Realizing what I've said, I feel my face flush. He sees my embarrassment and goes to cover it with a joke.

"All right then. Promise?" He extends his right pinky, slightly bent, toward me over the table in the traditional gesture.

"Promise!" I say laughing, shaking pinkies with him. A promise made.

And suddenly I think, *Maybe this could be something more. Maybe this guy likes me.* Because even with his superior attitude toward the dance club, there's something about this guy. Like he gets me. Like he understands something no one's understood for so long.

So before I lose courage, I ask him.

"Jiro, do you like me?"

He starts choking, and I feel like a total fool. I pull out some napkins and put them next to his plate. He takes a long drink of water.

Without even looking at me, he cuts off another big piece with his spatula and shoves the whole thing in his mouth. He's chewing away, watching the fish flakes on top of the food dance in the warm air over the hot plate. A bright blush covers his face.

"We should probably get going. I have to save room for dinner at home. You can finish mine if you want. It was really delicious," I babble, getting up. He glances up at me. "I'll just use the restroom before we go," I slip on my shoes and escape. I feel his eyes watching me as I go, but I don't look back.

When I come out, he's already at the register, paying. I grab my bag and run up, pulling out money.

"It's okay," he says, putting his body between me and the register. "I ate most of it anyway."

"It was really delicious," I say as the old woman hands Jiro his change.

"He's never brought a girlfriend here before," she says, beaming at us.

"We're just schoolmates," we say at the same time, a little too forcefully.

Her face crinkles as her smile gets bigger.

↬

"So, you hate *kendo*? And the 'crows'?" he says out of the blue. His words hang between us in the darkness as we head slowly back toward the station. Where did he hear that nickname? It suddenly sounds so malicious. The question sounds more like an accusation.

It dawns on me that our confrontations are always about clubs. But only because our clubs mean so much to each of us.

"Do you hate dance?" I ask in a low voice. "And does that mean you hate the members of the dance club?"

He has the audacity to look hurt. He turns to me for the first time since we left the restaurant. "Of course not."

"Exactly."

He stops walking then and keeps looking at me. "I don't think I understood the dance club before." He looks at me intently for a minute, and I think he might kiss me, but instead he says, "I think I get it now."

This actually gives me more of a thrill than being kissed.

We walk on a bit. I realize that for all his bravado, if something's going to happen I'm gonna have to make the first move.

So as we walk, I slip my hand into his, half expecting him to pull his away.

But he doesn't.

He gives it a little squeeze and doesn't let go.

Love Letter

by Megumi Fujino
translated by Lynne E. Riggs

You're probably surprised to get this letter. But I've been thinking about you for a long time.

Remember the first day of high school? Cherry blossoms were blooming. Your hair was still long, down to your waist. Waving in the wind, long and black . . . it was beautiful. Pink petals were dancing in the air. You smiled and called out "Good morning!"

I remember it clearly.

That was the only time you ever spoke to me. We even ended up in the same class, but you never said anything to me again. Now, just like everyone else, you just ignore me.

I know why, but it's okay. I understand. I know the truth is, you're pure at heart. You see the others saying those awful things, and you feel sorry for me. I know, because you're a gentle person.

Everybody else, they just don't understand. They don't know anything except themselves—so they get all excited about stupid little things in the class or their clubs. You shouldn't even have to be with such idiots. You're an angel . . . an angel that mistakenly fell out of heaven. That's what I always imagine when I see you with those others.

I may seem like a nerd, but since I met you, I've found an angel I want to protect, someone who could make me open up. I'd give up my life to defend you—from the messengers that might take you back to heaven and the evils of this filthy world that might taint you.

When I feel miserable and in pain, I always remember your smile. It gives me strength. I wish I could always be near you. In fact, I'd like to make that smile of yours my own and my own only. I want you to be mine alone.

But that's not why I am writing this letter. The idea of asking you to be my "girlfriend" or whatever—I really hate that kind of thing. I despise the superficial boy-girl "romance"—the idiots just copycat from stories on TV. What brings people together shouldn't be a put-on for appearances. It should be a link of the spirit—a real bond.

It's just that I heard about your parents' divorce. I noticed that you seem down, so I'm worried. I see how you answer cheerfully as before when your friends speak to you. You chatter and have fun with them as usual. But when you are quiet and by yourself, you sometimes seem on the verge of tears. . . . At times like that, of course I can't say anything to you, but I know. I know that you are struggling with something sad, all alone.

When you feel like that, it might help to listen to Kirara Kanbayashi's "Don't Cry" that was the theme of the Angel of Love: Magical Angela *drama. It might give you a little strength.*

An angel looks best with a smile, so I hope you will soon get over your sadness and be able to smile again like before. Not just the forced smile you show when you're with your friends, but your real smile from the heart.

The only ray of light for me, after all, is your smile.

See you around at school.

⌒

When I saw the letter, I practically gagged. After all, the sender was "Jellyfish." Of course, Jellyfish is a nickname. Ever since he'd written "jellyfish" when asked in career guidance what he wanted to be in the future, that's what everyone had called him. It was not because they thought he was cute or humorous. Quite the opposite—he made the ideal target for bullying.

So when I found the letter from Jellyfish in my shoe locker at the school entrance, I just thought, come on, this is no joke—don't mess up my life, too!

"What's that? A love letter?" Yukari, who always walks home with me, pounced on it, taking it out of my hand. Then, seeing the name of the sender, she grimaced.

"Yuck! Jellyfish? Creepy!"

"What's he think he's doing?" Mami snorted. "How dare he fall for Kanako! Just imagine! He just doesn't get it, does he! Incredible how rude that is to Kanako!"

And she went on, "That's what's so weird about *otaku*; they're shut up in their own world and don't think at all about other people and their feelings. Can't he even pick up the vibes?"

Mami wrapped her arms around herself and shivered with disgust.

"Yeah, people who don't think about the feelings of others are the worst," Yukari said. "No wonder nobody likes them!"

I agree with them. Jellyfish gets all involved in talking about anime, and no one else is interested. But when others are talking about TV programs or music that we all like, he's clueless.

Me, I've made an effort, listening to the popular singers I didn't really like so I'd be ready when I went to karaoke with my friends. I'd watch those boring TV dramas I couldn't care less about so I could keep up with the conversations at school. But Jellyfish wouldn't do things like that. Even though you have to go along with what everybody is doing so you'll be accepted, he wouldn't make the effort—so they'd bait and bully him and make his life miserable. What can you do about somebody who doesn't try to get along with others?

"Kanako, what're you going to do with this? Should we just throw it away?"

Yukari was waving the letter in the air, holding it disdainfully with the tips of her fingers.

"Hey, no! Don't throw it away here! Someone might find it! I'll take it home and tear it up." I took the letter back from Yukari and put it in my bag. "Never mind. Where shall we go on the way home? Me, I want a frozen yogurt."

So we stopped by the frozen yogurt place, and it wasn't until late that night that I read Jellyfish's letter. After I got home, I took a bath, and while I was watching TV and drying my hair, I remembered I needed to have a dictionary for class the next day—and found the letter again in my bag.

I just casually started reading it, but as I went on, I felt . . . I couldn't explain, but I felt kind of grabbed by the heart. How did he know? It was like . . . all those things that had been kind of churning around in my head—he'd just set them all out, clear as day, all in a row.

So true. I couldn't talk to any of my friends about my parents' divorce. What was bothering me weren't things you could really talk about with classmates, and I didn't want to wreck the fun of being with them by confiding anything very serious or heavy.

Some people want to have "best friends" who know everything about them, but to me that is just too much. I guess I did wish that there was someone who really understood how I felt and who even noticed. Still, these were girls I always hung out with, just having fun at school. When you know each other too well, it's harder to get along.

The fact that Jellyfish had been watching me made me feel kind of creepy—like he was a stalker or something—but also just a bit happy. It felt rather good that Jellyfish thought I was something special, and it was amazing that he had noticed how sad I was feeling.

The problem between my parents—it'd made me think about the things that bring people together . . . love, or whatever it is. But I wouldn't dream of telling Yukari and the girls—it'd be too embarrassing. We just don't talk about things like that.

I started thinking I might like to have a good long talk with Jellyfish. But of course I never would. After all, to have even the slightest thing to do with him would put me out *there*, in his disturbed, disconnected world. And I wouldn't be able to stay in the same world with my friends any more.

If I even spoke to him, I'd be totally alone. I might go to school, but when I saw my friends together laughing gaily over something, and went over to join them, the mood would suddenly shift. They'd go quiet, giving me cold looks like I was some kind of stranger, and then they'd just leave me there. I couldn't stand it—I'd die if I had to eat my lunch all alone at school!

So, even after I read the letter, I didn't make contact with Jellyfish. I thought there was nothing I could do to get to know him better. At school, Yukari asked me—loudly on purpose, so he would overhear what we were saying—"What did you do with that letter?" and I answered, "I threw it in the trash, without opening it, of course."

◠

Why did I ever say that?! Actually, I treasure that letter, and keep it carefully in the drawer where I store my important possessions. When Yukari asked me about it, I answered without even thinking. No matter how many times I've regretted what I said, I can't take it back. That day, if only I could have been more . . . more . . .

Now, whenever I feel like crying, I read that letter, and it always makes me feel better. When I read it, I can be with Jellyfish.

No one else ever called me an angel or thought I was good or gentle. Because I have that letter, no matter how sad or hopeless I feel, I can get my spirits back. I can try to smile again.

Even now, after Jellyfish went and killed himself, I keep going. I keep smiling.

Signs
by Kaitlin Stainbrook

I'd first seen Purikura Man just two days ago, and already I was doing what I'd told myself I wouldn't: investigating.

I ducked inside the arcade, but a group of four middle schoolers were already in the *purikura* booth. I sat on a bench outside and pretended to read e-mail on my cell phone, when really I was just staring at the screen, waiting for the girls to leave.

Over the distant roar of the trains, I could make out their squealing voices. One was arguing for the French fry background, while the others were trying to convince her it wasn't as cute as she thought.

My friends Yumi, Sango, and I had a similar debate the night we saw Purikura Man, though it had been over a lame kangaroo background instead. All day Sango had been dropping hints that she wanted to try out the new *purikura* booth in the train station. Yumi and I eventually gave up trying to convince her that *purikura* booths were all the same and went together after school.

We'd huddled around a nearby table to help Sango cut out the tiny photos and strategically place them in one of her many *purikura* albums.

I was handing a newly cut photo to Sango when I saw a man in a suit nervously look around, then slip inside the booth we'd just used.

I nudged Yumi. "A *salariman* is doing *purikura*."

She and Sango glanced back at the drawn plastic curtain across the booth's doorway. The only part of him that could be seen was a pair of scuffed dress shoes. Sango went back to arranging the new pictures in her album, thoroughly examining each one before placing it in the album. "People are allowed to take *purikura* by themselves."

"But why would a man like that want *purikura*?"

"Maybe it's his hobby," Yumi said. "Maybe he's lonely." Yumi's first instinct was always to sympathize.

"Or maybe he's involved in some kind of crime ring," I said, feeling ridiculous just saying the words. "He could be leaving secret messages about sumo gambling or something."

Yumi raised an eyebrow. "In a *purikura* booth?"

Sango sighed and snapped her album shut. "Kana, you just want to see adventure and scandal when there's only a weird guy taking pictures of himself."

"You're probably right," I admitted and watched as Purikura Man slipped out of the arcade and into the swiftly moving current of people heading for the train platforms.

⤳

But if Sango and Yumi *were* right, why was I back here again? Why couldn't I let it go? Stranger things than a *salariman* doing *purikura* happened in the world every day.

The middle school girls from before walked past, giggling as they playfully bumped into each other, phone charms jingling with every step. Finally.

I darted back inside the arcade only to walk straight into a boy about my age wearing a black peacoat.

"Excuse me," I said, flustered.

He gave me a fast bow of apology and moved to step into the booth, but I blocked him.

"Sorry." I winced at how rude I was being. "I've been waiting a really, really long time," I added, though it wasn't completely true. "And I only need it for a few minutes." Also not true.

He held my gaze, but with an indifferent expression. I nervously twisted the silver ring on my middle finger. "Please?"

He shook his head slowly and pointed at his right ear.

"Um . . ." Was he working with Purikura Man and this was some kind of criminal code? I twisted my ring harder.

He pointed at his ear again. Then, when he saw I still wasn't getting it, he started gesturing in Japanese Sign Language, forming words and sentences with his hands. He was telling me he was deaf. Or possibly that I was an idiot for not figuring it out right away.

"Oh! I'm so sorry! I didn't know," I said, my own ears burning.

He pulled out a thin, black cell phone and suddenly began pressing numbers on the keypad. When he was done, he held the phone out for me to read what he'd typed. *You were here Friday, right? Did you see him too?*

I didn't remember seeing this boy on Friday, but I knew he could only be referring to Purikura Man. I tentatively started typing a message back to him, but he snatched the phone away.

I can read your lips.

I tried not to think about him studying the way my mouth moved. "That's why I came back here."

He nodded. At least someone in all of Japan didn't think I was paranoid.

Did you see if he left anything behind? Like a clue?

"No, sorry."

He looked a little disappointed as he bowed in thanks, then ducked around me into the booth. I hesitated, but stepped in after him. He didn't look too happy as he handed me his phone.

I don't need any help.

"Two heads are better than one, right?"

He gave me a skeptical look, like he'd thought he was questioning a witness, not inviting me to play detective with him.

"I'm Kana." If I introduced myself it would be harder for him to brush me off.

Sakamoto Genki.

"Nice to meet you." We shared nods, then looked away from one another.

Apparently silences can be awkward even when you're deaf.

Genki gestured at the rest of the booth. Shall we?

We took turns examining the screen and camera, both of us trying to keep our distance from one another. Well, as much distance as two people could keep in a *purikura* booth.

I don't know what I'd expected to find. It looked like any other *purikura* booth: sparse on the inside and overwhelmingly busy on the outside.

There was a clinking of 100-yen coins falling inside the machine.

I started to ask Genki why he thought doing *purikura* would help, but realized he couldn't read my lips with his back to me. I joined him at the screen and watched as he scrolled through all the background options, picking a few at random.

The camera switched on and there we were on screen. Underneath *purikura* lights skin becomes smoother, and eyes take on a certain *purikura* sparkle. Genki didn't really need the help though.

There was a countdown on the screen and then a flash. We took all our *purikura* without changing our expressions, Genki determinedly serious and me with my usual closed-mouth smile.

The *purikura* taken, Genki methodically explored the editing options, continuing his search for clues. I doubted he'd find any hidden in glittery font colors. I stepped out of the booth and watched a group of boys gathered around a *taiko* drum game.

It was strange to think Genki couldn't hear any of the fake drum noises or the boys teasing each other. He could concentrate on figuring out the Purikura Man mystery without any extra stuff in the way.

I pressed my hands against my ears. Maybe silence would help me think too. I couldn't hear all the arcade and train station noises anymore, but somehow even the absence of sound was a sound, like a low, constant roar.

I immediately dropped my hands to my sides when Genki came out. He shook his head. Nothing.

We shrugged at each other, both of us trying not to look as disappointed as we actually felt. It wasn't just that there were no more clues; there'd never been anything there to begin with. Like Sango had said, just a weird guy doing *purikura* by himself.

Genki cut the strip of *purikura* in half and handed me one. I bit back laughter looking at the photos. The only thing that changed from picture to picture was the background. They were the strangest *purikura* I've ever taken.

Genki was suddenly fumbling to get his phone out of his pocket.

What do people never do in purikura?

"Not smile?"

They never turn away from the camera.

⤴

We did it all again, this time with our backs to the camera. Neither of us knew what we were looking for, but we didn't see anything out of the ordinary. No message or sign telling us we were on the right track.

Genki slumped against the outside of the booth and shoved our freshly printed *purikura* into his coat pocket. He might not have said it, but his body language was clear. He was beating himself up for thinking that more light would do something.

"It was a good guess," I assured him. "But what about the opposite?" I circled the booth slid my hand between the booth and the wall, trying to find the plug. "Help me?"

Genki's arms were longer than mine and after a brief glance around the arcade to make sure no one was paying attention to us, he yanked the plug out of the wall. We stepped inside the now-dark booth together and this time there was something there.

"260 up" and a key had been painted just above the camera. The writing was tiny, but cast a green glow strong enough that I could make out the small wrinkle between Genki's eyebrows as he leaned in close to get a better look.

Bang! The booth walls shuddered. Genki and I toppled into each other in our scramble to get out of the booth. "What do you think you're doing?" came a gruff voice just outside. In the arcade, Genki pulled me to my feet just in time to face the irate arcade owner in front of us.

He had a few moustache whiskers on his thin top lip that quivered as he spoke. "Find a love hotel if you want to do that kind of stuff."

He'd thought we were . . . My mind backpedaled in horror.

"It's not like that! We're doing a school project and our teacher said we should come here to conduct our experiment—our experiment for school," I said in a rush as Genki plugged the *purikura* booth back in.

"Uh huh. You and everyone else. Get out of here, perverts."

Before I could fumble my way through more assurances of our innocence, Genki grabbed me by the wrist and pulled me toward the exit.

He was completely unfazed we'd just been accused of . . . *purikura* play. I must have still looked freaked out though, because he typed out a message for me on his phone.

What's wrong? Scared?

"Only scared I'd die of embarrassment."

What's there to be embarrassed about? That was the best purikura *action I've had in a long time.*

I stared at him.

Kidding.

"Anyways, Purikura Man was leaving a message for someone. 260 up. Whatever that means. A certain time, maybe? Or 260,000,000 yen up in sumo gambling? And what was that key about?"

Genki didn't respond and instead studied the map of crisscrossing railway lines above the row of ticket machines along the wall. He rapidly signed at me, pointing to the map now and again. We were getting looks from people who walked past us as we stood in the middle of foot traffic.

"You need to write it out for me."

But Genki was on a roll and didn't want to stop in the middle of his epiphany. He led the way over to the ticket machines and pointed at the price listings, one of which was for a 260-yen ticket.

"Great, but what does 'up' have to do with it?"

He tapped the *kanji* for Yawata, as far north as 260 yen could take us. The other rail line out of the train station was the Katano Line and it only went south.

"And the key?"

He waved his hand at me. He didn't want to worry about the key yet.

"It's a wild guess," I argued. "We should wait outside the arcade and see if Purikura Man comes back." But Genki was already buying our tickets. He slapped mine into my hand—"Genki, I can't . . ."—and strode through the ticket gates, leaving me behind.

On the other side, he waved me over, but when he saw me shaking my head, he shrugged, and turned his back to me.

My phone binged then and I flipped it open to see a text from my mom reminding me I had a piano lesson at five. It was five-thirty now. I'd already missed the lesson, but I could still catch Genki.

"Wait!"

I knew yelling was useless, and as I struggled through the ticket gate, I looked up to see Genki had already disappeared into the crowds.

But when I walked in the direction of the train platforms there he was, waiting around the corner for me.

"I hate leaving mysteries unsolved," I told him, so he didn't think it had anything to do with him.

He jerked his head toward a waiting train headed north. Nods were fast becoming our secondary form of communication.

We snagged seats next to a slumbering old woman.

Usually, I liked looking out the window on train rides, but today I just wanted to talk to Genki. Where did he live? Go to school? Did he have any siblings? What did he do for fun? Had he always been deaf?

Genki was busy with his phone and I wished for what was probably the twenty-third time that day that I knew JSL. We glanced at each other at the same time and accidentally caught each other's eyes. He grinned and held out his hand, palm up. Did he want to hold hands? Right here in front of people? He hadn't exactly given me a lot of signs that he was interested. How could I say no to him without looking rude? And what if I kind of wanted to say yes? But before I could make a complete fool of myself and do something really stupid, he pointed at the cell phone-shaped bulge in my pocket. Oh.

He messed around with both phones, then gave mine back to me. Almost immediately I got a text from him.

Now I don't have to guess what you're saying all the time.

That surprised me. He'd never seemed lost when I talked to him. I texted back: *You have to guess?*

Lip reading is hard. I have to really concentrate and you talk fast when you're nervous.

Sorry. I texted him a bowing emoticon for good measure. Then, not sure what else to say, added, *Thanks for waiting.*

No thanks necessary. It's been nice having a sidekick. I glared at him and he hurriedly texted, *I mean partner.*

So who do you think Purikura Man was leaving his message for? I'm thinking yakuza *gangsters.* I was only half joking.

Genki gave me a weird look.

You don't think it could really be yakuza, *do you?* I asked, nerves already starting to squirm in my stomach at the thought, but before he could respond, our train was sliding to a stop.

⌒

We exited the train at Yawata, but standing in the slightly run-down station, it seemed as though we'd hit our final dead end.

"Now what?" "260 up" and a drawing of a key wasn't a lot to go on. "Maybe we're supposed to keep working from 260 up. Like, 260 steps north from the platform?" I turned north—the way the train had left the station—and saw we wouldn't get very far unless we could walk through walls. "Or not. Let's try starting from the front of the station."

Genki made a face.

"Unless you have a better idea?"

He mimed going to sleep.

"You want to take a nap? A break?"

Genki nodded and walked over to a nearby vending machine before I could argue that it was getting late. I couldn't stay out all night chasing Purikura Man.

Genki and I bought cans of Fanta—melon for him, orange for me— and stood against a nearby wall.

Genki pulled his phone out and it wasn't long before I had a new text. *Your parents aren't going to be angry if you're late?*

My dad will. I can deal with him, though. You?

My parents are too busy to notice if I'm around. He must have caught the sympathy in my eyes, because he added, *It comes in handy when I'm following clues all over Kansai with a strange girl.*

You think I'm the strange one? I raised an eyebrow at him and he mirrored my expression in return.

I drained the rest of my soda and walked back to the vending machine to throw my can away, Genki following with his own empty can. That's when I noticed a red soda can with a golden key painted on it in the vending machine I'd barely glanced at before. It was exactly the kind of strange and mysterious sign we were looking for.

My phone chirped. *Buy it.*

"You buy it."

I bought the train tickets.

Reluctantly, I counted out 150 yen and fed it into the machine. I pressed the button for the soda, but nothing happened. I tried again and still nothing.

"Hey!"

Genki gave the machine one desperate kick, but it was stubborn. No golden key soda for us. *Somebody was already here and got it before us!* He kicked the machine again and I put a hand on his arm.

"Genki? You're kind of freaking me out."

Sorry.

"Maybe it's the key, not the soda," I ventured.

What's the key mean? We need a lock?

My eyes fell on the Fushimi Inari Shrine tourism poster on the wall. The poster showed one of the stone foxes at the main gate in Kyoto, a large key in its mouth. "What we need is another train ticket."

〜

I'd been joking before about Purikura Man being a *yakuza*, but now that the sun was setting, it seemed like a real possibility. As we sped closer to Fushimi Inari, I became more and more restless.

Teach me something, I texted.

What? Like chess?

JSL. So we can stop talking to each other like this.

Genki smiled his first genuinely warm smile. Before he'd always smirked or grinned, but this smile was almost shy. He taught me my name first, then his.

And the most important sign of all.

Genki cupped his left hand and made a circular movement with his two first fingers.

I copied him. The movements reminded me of scooping rice out of a bowl with chopsticks. "Eating?"

He grinned and patted his stomach in affirmation. *Whether we get the prize or not, I'm taking us out for udon.*

I barely had time to register that Genki wanted to keep hanging out with me, let alone gotten a chance to ask him what he meant by prize, when our train ground to a halt.

〜

It was a five-minute walk to the shrine from the station, and the surrounding gift shops were closing for the day. Fushimi Inari rose up in front of us, and soon we were at the bottom of a long line of deep-orange *torii* gates leading up the mountain. In the day, walking through the gates was like walking to another world.

Lanterns had been lit now, but it only made the *torii* turn creepy and threatening. Genki didn't hesitate to start walking through the gates, but I turned around to take one last look at the more brightly lit main grounds we'd just left.

Marching uphill toward us was Purikura Man. He was watching his feet and hadn't seen us yet. I ran into the orange *torii* tunnel and pulled Genki aside to make him face me. He needed to read my lips perfectly. "He's right behind us!"

He cocked his head and curled his first finger and made an arc with it over his head. Finger question marks.

"Purikura Man. We have to call the police before he spots us."

Genki looked at me like I'd suggested we catch a train to Nara and find some deer to ride. He gestured at the rest of the waiting path through the *torii*. He wanted us to keep going.

While we argued, Purikura Man had caught up to us, and when he looked up from his shoes, he broke into a run up the path with Genki close behind. I was left standing there, not sure what to do.

My phone beeped and I dropped it in my rush to flip it open. It was a text from my father. He was angry I hadn't come home yet and demanded to know what I was doing.

What *was* I doing?

I sprinted up the path, orange *torii* flashing past. My thighs, calves, and chest screamed for me to stop, but I couldn't. Not when Genki might be in trouble. I kept waiting to turn a corner and see Purikura Man and Genki, but the only thing in front of me was more empty path and endless *torii*.

There was a break up ahead where the *torii* stopped, but the path only split into two tunnels. Purikura Man and Genki were wrestling, and Purikura Man was trying to pull something out of his pocket.

"No!"

I leapt onto the both of them, trying to pull what looked like it could be a knife out of his hand, but he held on tight.

"Get off me or I'm calling the police!" Purikura Man said, his voice strained as he fought off Genki and me.

His grip loosened and I saw he was only holding a cell phone.

There were footsteps and somebody emerged from the left path.

"Sango?"

I'd never seen her smile so widely. Me with a *salariman* and a strange boy didn't faze her.

"You're all too late," she announced. "I already won."

"What are you talking about?"

She wiggled a pair of tickets in the air.

Purikura Man shoved Genki and me off him. "It's for M. Night Shyamalan's new movie about a possessed boxing glove," he said. "We all won the first clue in an Internet raffle and had to figure the rest out from there. The clues lead to tickets to the Hollywood premiere."

"I've been running around all day for movie tickets?"

"What did you think?" Sango asked.

I gestured at Purikura Man. "That he was involved in something illegal," I mumbled.

He laughed. "Just an office drone who loves movies. I had to work today, so I got here later than I meant to, otherwise I would have had it." To Sango, he bowed and said, "Congratulations." He headed back down the way he'd come. I was feeling increasingly silly.

"And that's why you wanted to do *purikura*?" I asked Sango. "You thought there'd be a clue?"

"I'd been there earlier and I thought maybe the clue was weight sensitive, so I asked you and Yumi to come. I'm sorry I lied, but I would have been disqualified from the contest if I told anyone. I figured out to unplug it yesterday morning, but I got stuck with the '260 up' stuff." She flashed the tickets. "Until today."

Genki had kept a blank face this whole time because it had gotten too dim for him to read everyone's lips. He was trying to look like he knew what was being said and just didn't care. Reading him was getting easier.

We've been on a movie ticket scavenger hunt and didn't even win, I texted.

He looked disappointed, but nodded, as though he'd seen this coming.

I texted, *You didn't know, did you?*

He shrugged.

"You knew?!"

Sango looked back and forth between Genki and me, lost. I ignored her for the moment, waiting for Genki to text me an explanation.

It was the longest text I'd gotten from him all day. *My sister hadn't gotten the Internet invitation, and when I saw the* salariman *poking around the* purikura *booth, I had a feeling I knew what he was looking for. I just needed to figure out the clue he had been after, then follow the trail on my own to the tickets.*

"And you didn't think to tell me all that earlier?"

He mimed texting. I sighed and repeated myself in text, but with added angry-faced emoticons.

I thought you were after the tickets too, he answered. *That's why I didn't want your help finding them at first. What did you think all those clues were for?*

He had me there.

⤿

We said good-bye to Sango at the train station. "See you at school, Kana?" She discreetly waggled her eyebrows at me.

Once we were seated on the train home, Genki held his hand out to me and I knew this time he wasn't asking for my cell phone.

I ignored the offer and texted: *I've never felt so stupid in my life. This whole day, I thought we were doing something important.*

That's too bad, because I'm feeling pretty good right now, even without the tickets. I gave him a look, and he continued, *I got to chase hidden signs and golden keys with a very weird and very smart girl.*

Is that supposed to make me feel better? Calling me weird?

Genki shrugged. *I like weird.*

He still held his hand open for me to take.

Finally, I did.

Wings on the Wind

by Yuichi Kimura
translated by Alexander O. Smith

It happened at dusk.
The fox struck swiftly.

The cranes panicked—
One of their flock was gone.
A fledgling had lost his life.

In the twisting winds on the Mongolian plain,
the wounded flock spent the night in silence.

The hearts of the cranes wrenched tight with regret:
If only we'd taken flight sooner.
If only we'd seen the fox right away.
Their longing for the life lost
rushed round and round inside them and frustration welled
with no outlet for their grief.

 "Just before the fox came I heard someone flap," said one crane.
"When Kururu was feeding Karara?"
Kururu sometimes shared his catch with weak Karara,
who couldn't hunt on her own.
The rest of the birds began to speak, hurling harsh words.
At last their anger had a target.
"That's how the fox found us!"
"That was no time to feed!"
"You know, that always bothered me about you, Kururu. Always!"

I wasn't the only one who flapped, Kururu wanted to say.
The fox had his eye on us for a long time before he struck.
How could feeding Karara have made any difference at all?
But he knew it was no use.
He could tell which way the wind was blowing.

From then on, it was as if Kururu himself had killed the fledgling.
No one took his side. Even Karara stood with the others in silence.
Everything he had taken for granted—the flock, his friends—
had changed.
All turned their backs to him, and spoke not a word.
No one even tried to understand how he felt.

He couldn't trust his friends. He couldn't trust his flock.
All poor Kururu could be was alone.
He blamed himself.
Even the sound of his own wings on the wind
was ugly to his ears.
Why didn't I say something when I had the chance?
Why can't I get along with the others?
I hate myself.
I hate my beak, my legs, my wings. I hate it all.
It became hard for Kururu just to fly with the flock.

One morning, Kururu found he couldn't fly at all.
He flapped as usual, but remained earthbound.
All he could do was cower in a corner of the plain.

Winter was drawing near.
Winter on the Mongolian plains brought cold—
freezing, fifty-below-zero cold.
Before then, the cranes would cross over the Himalayas to the south,
leaving for the warmth of India.

A crane who could not fly when winter came was a dead crane.
But Kururu didn't care.
It seemed to him that sitting still and refusing to feed
Was the only way he could hold on to the last shred
of his bedraggled pride.
In time he saw one flock flying southward.
A second, then a third followed.

White flakes had begun to flutter around Kururu
when he spotted a single crane approaching from the southern sky.
It was Karara.

Karara settled down next to Kururu without a word.
If she had said, "Fly with me,"
or even if she had just flown away,
Kururu would have shaken his head and said,
"I know you don't need me."
But Karara said nothing.
She simply sat by his side
watching as the flocks fled southward.

Day by day the air grew colder.
But Kururu's heart had begun to melt.
She's ready to die here.
If I don't fly . . .

Just then, a fox appeared from the brush.
Fangs gleaming, he leapt at Karara.
"Look out!"
Kururu flapped his wings, pushing Karara aside.
She took off.

With a start, Kururu realized he too was rising into the sky.
Below them the fox remained, glaring longingly upward.

"I'm flying!" Kururu shouted.

He beat his wings with all his might, and felt himself soar higher.

The sound of his wings on the wind sent a pleasing rhythm
echoing through his entire body.
"I can make it! I can fly beyond those towering mountains."
Karara looked back and asked:
"You'll fly with me?"
"Of course," Kururu said
with a shy smile.

The two cranes headed southward, chasing the last of the flocks.
With powerful strokes, they beat their wings, flying on and on. . . .

Families and Connections

The Law of Gravity

by Yuko Katakawa

translated by Deborah Iwabuchi

"Don't cry. I'll cry for you so you can stop."

Five years ago these words changed my life.

Just so you know, my little sister Maika was the one who said them, but she didn't say them to me. She was talking to an elephant in the zoo.

It was right after I'd started junior high. I had fallen down some stairs and broken my right arm. My mother decided to take me to the zoo to take my mind off the pain. She said it would just be the two of us, but I did everything I could to avoid that. Mom always favored me—pushing me to do better and make something of myself. She made sure I had the best of everything—probably to make it easier for me to stay on the path she had chosen. But I hated my life. I didn't have a say in anything. Even worse, she didn't seem to think Maika would ever amount to anything, and it hadn't even occurred to her that her ten-year-old daughter might enjoy the zoo more than I would. But I refused to go without Maika, so Mom finally gave in and brought her along.

The idea of going out alone with my mom still sends shivers down my spine. I don't remember much from those days, and there aren't many good memories. I just recall wondering how I ought to end my life. At thirteen, I had made it through a long "entrance exam war," and been accepted to my first-choice junior high, but I no longer had the energy to go on living. It had all felt like so much work, and I was tired of it.

I had done what I had to do to get into the right school, studying late into the night. Dinner was always fast food or convenience store fare—whatever Mom picked up for me when she met me at the station to take my school satchel and pass me what I needed for evening cram school classes. The cram school teachers drilled it into our young heads to think of all the other test takers as enemies. Victory over our enemies would get us into the school that would guarantee our future. That was easy enough to understand, but things turned out to be more complicated. My new school was full of my former "enemies," and now, of course, we were expected to become friends for life.

Nothing made any sense.

By the time I fell and broke my arm, I had figured it out—life would go on in the same way. I would continue to act the way my parents wanted me to, get into the schools they picked, and pretend to be the perfect son they had always wanted.

But a perfect son would never get a chance to rebel or even have an opinion of his own. The more I thought about it, the more suffocating it seemed, until I couldn't come up with a reason to endure decades more of a life like that. If it was just going to be more of the same, putting a quick end to it all seemed the better option.

So that's what was going on in my head, but I was basically just a helpless teenager who couldn't think of any better way to change my life.

Then one day, someone pushed me from behind on a staircase landing at school, and I fell down the stairs.

As I fell, I turned around to see who had done it, so I could get back at him later. I should have just let go, because in that instant, what might have been a minor bruise ended up a broken arm—a worst-case scenario. What good was a student, a perfect son, without a right arm?

And all because of that hopeless idiot. The culprit was the guy who had been stuck in the number-two position below me back in cram school. We had both passed the entrance exam for the same junior high, and we had just finished our first midterms there, but he still couldn't pull ahead. Obviously frustrated to find himself still trailing behind, he had taken the simplest and stupidest route available to get rid of me. Even as I fell, I was disappointed that his motive was so obvious.

There was an instant between the hearing the bone break and feeling the pain. During that moment I wondered if he and I might be the same. Life was so ridiculous to both of us. The only difference was that I wanted to end mine and he wanted to hurt someone.

We were both idiots.

Then there was the trip home from the hospital. The way my mother behaved disgusted me. She was acting hysterical, trying to force me to get into a taxi. I used all the energy I had left to refuse. What would we talk about closed up together in the back of a cab? A train was definitely better. I knew it wouldn't be crowded at that time of day; my injured arm wouldn't be jostled around.

But it was on the train that I saw him: a photocopy of myself as I had been in the not-so-distant past, an empty-eyed boy whose mother had just put him on the train. He was still in grade school. He carried a bag filled with homework for cram school. His mother, on the station platform, held an empty fast-food sack and the kid's school satchel.

I gazed at the black satchel as the train pulled away. The whole scene made me sick. I realized that it was exactly the way I had looked before the entrance exams. My head had been completely filled with knowledge I needed to pass the tests and my stomach full of artificial flavors and colorings. Even then, I still had done everything I could to meet my parents' expectations.

That was when it hit me. This was how the future of our country was created. This was the life of Japan's youth. My life.

What was the meaning of a life spent doing nothing but fulfilling the expectations of our parents? What was so fun that anyone would intentionally choose it?

As we sat in the half-empty train car, Mom's next words just added fuel to the fire.

"He's just like you were, Kai. You've already got what you wanted, though. But you know, you can't relax just because you got into a top school. We've got plans for you for high school, university—I wonder where you'll end up working." She smiled just thinking of the possibilities. "You've got to keep at it!"

Shut up! The only reason I didn't say it out loud was because the blood rushing to my head made my arm hurt. The more I thought about it, the angrier I got, and my arm hurt worse than ever.

What do you mean, what I wanted? Who wanted it? It was you! Not me! What exactly do you mean you have expectations for me? Does it mean that anything Maika does is meaningless because you have no expectations for her? Here Mom was fussing over me, but what about the way she treated her daughter? Was Maika no more than an afterthought? *Can you really call yourself Maika's mother?* I wanted to scream.

I swallowed my words and went back to thoughts of how meaningless my own life was. I knew such thoughts put me on the same level as the idiot who pushed me down the stairs, but I was feeling I couldn't take it anymore. I could see myself going crazy. Wouldn't it be better to just lower the curtain on it all?

It was the next weekend that we all went to the zoo. I was still depressed and thinking morbid thoughts.

If I got into the lions' cage, would they rip me apart with their teeth? How about crocodiles? I was sure I'd heard that hippos could be violent. Giraffes not so much probably. Now elephants . . .

I stood staring at one of the elephants near us and thinking about what it might be capable of when Maika spoke up.

"Why is that elephant crying?"

"Is it crying?"

"Yeah, look. It must be sad. It's so big, it can probably see much more than I can. That must be why it's sad."

What was she talking about? I looked over at Maika; tears were streaming down her face.

I was so surprised I didn't know what to do. Then she spoke again.

"Don't cry. I'll cry for you so you can stop," she called out to the elephant in the cage.

My mother looked over at Maika and clucked her tongue in irritation. But my sister continued to cry.

I couldn't take my eyes off of her. I'd never known how beautiful tears shed for someone else could be. It was in that instant that I discovered something that I would happily live for. I would protect Maika. If my useless mother couldn't do it, I would be the one to stand by my sister. I'd be a good big brother.

And that was why I would have to play the good son—at least for now.

Maika cried for a while longer. Whether the tears were for the elephant, for herself, or for me, I didn't know. But it occurred to me that Maika had been leading a life as miserable as mine. While I was being pushed to achieve, nothing was expected of her. While Mom suffocated me with attention, Maika was dying inside for lack of it. It wasn't right. I might be the only one who knew it and the only one who could do anything about it.

Even with my arm in a cast, I threw myself into my studies as never before. It wasn't for my mother; I was doing it for myself. I had to make myself into a man who would always be there for his sister.

Studying for the first time ever because I wanted to, I realized I enjoyed it. Nobody was making me do it. I found I could work for hours on end.

By the time finals rolled around I was able to write again. After the teachers had finished grading, the school ranked all of the students in order by test scores and posted the results. I did better than the guy who had shoved me down the stairs. My scores were up and his seemed to be down. I was standing there when he walked up to look for his own position in the rankings and then mine. He went pale and quickly walked away. I was proud. I could finally say that I was different from him. Looking back now, I can't even remember his name or what he looked like.

∾

All these old memories came back to me the other night when Maika, now fifteen, knocked on the door of my room as I sat at my desk as usual, now studying for university entrance exams. Her eyes looked as sad as the day she had watched the elephant in the cage. She sat on my bed and began to talk about how she was ready to give up on life—just the way I had felt back then. She was devastated by the way Mom was still treating her. And what was worse, she seemed certain she'd never be anything but a failure. *What's the point of going on?* she said. She frightened me. I had to find a way to stop her thinking that way. Without Maika, I wouldn't have anything to live for. But how can a seventeen-year-old boy say that to his little sister?

In my confusion, I started talking about Isaac Newton. "Newton discovered the law of gravity. We can do the same; we can do anything." It was a line one of my classmates had famously used in grade school— not that I was sure if anyone else had been impressed by it or could still remember him saying it right before the annual class relay race had begun, when the runners were getting psyched up. I'm sure fewer than half the class even heard it.

But the words had stayed with me. I had mumbled them to myself just before junior high entrance exams began. Now I couldn't even remember the name of the guy who had said it, nor did I rely on those words the way I used to. But here, trying to encourage my sister, they just came out.

I could see I wasn't making sense to Maika, so I began to talk about the elephant we'd seen all those years ago.

"Maika, do you remember that day Mom took us to the zoo after I broke my arm?"

Maika shook her head.

"Well, we saw the elephants and you saw one of them with tears in its eyes. You were so sad that it made you cry. You told the elephant that you'd cry instead, so it could stop. You said it must be sad because it could see so much."

Maika nodded uncertainly. I had to make her remember.

"They're so big, the elephants. It's just like you said then. They can see far, far away. They can see things happening over the ocean. And of course the one we saw in the zoo saw you there—and it probably still can see you—and how sad you are. For all we know it's crying in its cage."

Maika smiled at me. She was fifteen, and we both knew she wouldn't believe a story like that, but she seemed willing to go along with my attempts to cheer her up.

"So the elephant can see me here, talking to you?"

"Exactly. You gotta feel sorry for the poor creature. So, stop crying. Try not to feel so sad."

"I don't know . . ."

"Maika, I know things are tough for you right now."

Maika looked up, maybe surprised that I even cared.

"Kai . . ."

"I'm not blind. I see what's going on with you and Mom. I want to be like that elephant, always keeping an eye on you."

Maika looked at me for a second, almost as if she wanted to believe me. Then she lowered her eyes and frowned. "Mom doesn't care about me. She'd never let you get away with that."

I thought about my mother and how, over the years, she'd managed to drive my sister to such desperation. But I didn't hate her as much as I used to. I was beginning to understand how childish Mom was and why she always took everything out on Maika.

"Maika, do you remember that time Grandma came to visit and she said that you reminded her of Mom when she was young?"

Maika nodded, "Yeah, there was that one time, wasn't there?"

"Grandma said Mom never did well in school and she was always getting scolded. Don't you see?"

"See what?" Maika frowned.

"Mom looks at you and sees herself—she never expected anything of herself either. It's not that complicated. Adults don't always grow up just because they get older. But you're not Mom."

Maika was paying attention now, so I went on.

"Right? It's true: Newton discovered the law of gravity. We're the same; we can do anything. No matter what Mom thinks or anyone else says.

"I am going to protect you until you figure out what you can do. One day we'll look back and laugh at all the awful things that have happened. So don't cry."

Maika wiped her eyes and smiled. She looked exhausted as she lowered her head onto my bed. I turned back to my books, and it wasn't long before I could hear her even breathing. She was asleep. Together we had smoothed over Maika's sadness. We had done it! And I was prepared to do it again, as many times as it took.

Then I heard her mumble something in her sleep. The words weren't clear, but it sounded like, "Don't cry. I'll cry for you. . . ."

The words that had meant everything to me. She hadn't forgotten them after all. Just knowing that was enough to make me happy.

The Mountain Drum

by Chloë Dalby

"*Hyaku-monogatari-tte, shiteru?*"

Her father sank his weight into his makeshift tree-trunk seat. Besides the haze of the sky above, their lantern was the only light on the mountainside. She didn't say anything. He asked again.

"*Ne*, have you heard of the *hyaku-monogatari*?"

She shook her head.

"It's a game everyone used to play. Laborers, aristocrats, everyone liked to get together and tell stories."

"What stories?" She cut him off. The trees that grew in a twined canopy over their heads gave little heaves side to side as a breeze picked up around them. The lantern's flame dipped and flickered, and the darkness that surrounded their illuminated circle crept inward.

"Ghost stories." he answered. "Legends about *obake* and *yokai*, tales about the strange, the supernatural."

"Hardly anyone still believes in *yokai*," she said, picking at her fingernails.

Her father continued as if he hadn't heard her. "Everyone would bring a single candle, and light them in a circle. As each person told a story, a candle was extinguished—until it was very late at night. After the hundredth story, when everyone was good and scared, the last candle would be extinguished."

The trees creaked *ten te-ke-ke-ke-ke* as a vigorous gust of wind swept up from the wide river at the foot of the mountains. The lantern's light bobbed wildly.

"And in that darkness you could expect to see something supernatural with your own eyes."

"Are you trying to scare me or something?" She asked as she stood slowly, trying not to slip on the dead leaves and branches under her feet.

"If I were trying to scare you, wouldn't I . . . do this?" He reached out to the lantern and, in an instant, snuffed out the wick.

⮌

Her screams and his laughter echoed through the trees as Junko and her father ran, slipping and sliding, down the mountain. They didn't stop until they were back in the house, their voices startling her mother, who had nodded off while sitting at the low dining room table. Junko headed for the stairs to her room, a little out of breath.

"Goodnight! We'll get started tomorrow?" Junko heard her father call after her.

"A new drum?" she called back from the top step.

"That's right. Oh, and be sure to turn off the light so you don't miss any ghosts or goblins."

⮌

Maybe that would scare me if I was, like, five, Junko thought to herself as she shook out a sheet on top of her futon. *We didn't even tell any stories.*

The creaks and groans of living lumber sounded in the breeze as the lonely mountainside settled into midnight. Just as Junko was drifting in and out of sleep, a clean rhythm cut through the forest air—*pon poko pon pon pon poko*—like the sound of a single small *taiko* drum. Junko turned over, and it began to rain.

By the time she came down for breakfast the next morning, her parents had long since finished. Her mother was going over inventory in the other room, and her father was drinking his instant coffee, watching the morning news. Reception was poor because of the mountainous terrain, and every so often the program would cut out and her father would swear mildly. Junko chewed on the pit of a pickled plum.

"There are reports of mudslides in the mountains above Shimozui, although no property damage has been reported. Please take extra caution in the next few days," the newscaster said.

"That's not far from here, dear," her mother called from the other room. Junko's father took off his glasses and wiped them with his shirt.

"You're right. We'll be careful." Junko nodded as he switched off the television. "Let's go."

⌇

Armed with trail markers, *onigiri* rice balls, and a thermos of tea, Junko and her father set out to find a tree big enough to fill their next commission. The Omura Shrine in Kochi Prefecture had ordered a giant *odaiko* drum.

To the left of their front gate, the paved road connected them to Shimozui, two kilometers downstream. To the right, the road continued on and up, following the curve of the river and eventually breaking off into wild mountainside. They headed in this direction. Cracked asphalt turned to river rocks, then gravel, and ultimately to slick leaves and earth. Though the going was not particularly rugged, the summer sun was rising and Junko felt the sweat run uncomfortably down her back as she maneuvered around a large rain-filled hole.

"*Ne*, Junko-chan . . . Did you hear anything last night?"

She shrugged. There had been something, but she was pretty sure it had just been a dream.

"I think the *tanuki* were having some fun," he continued.

She shook her head. "That was the rain, Dad. Anyway, no one's seen a *tanuki* around here in years."

"Ah, well. That's the question, isn't it? The blood-and-bone *tanuki* may have left these woods," he said, grabbing a low-slung branch to help him step around another pothole on the path. "But what about the *tanuki* who like to play tricks and appear in front of your eyes. Who knows if they've gone, too?"

Junko didn't respond immediately. The sun had reached high noon, and the forest air was thickening with humidity around them.

"Grandpa used to to tell me stories about them," she said quietly, "when I was really little. Didn't he say his parents settled here because there was a *tanuki* family living here too?"

Her father nodded. "There was no better place to build drums on this entire island. For a long time, *tanuki* and our drums were . . . well, you couldn't say one without thinking of the other."

"What do you mean?" she asked.

"In my grandfather's—your great-grandfather's—day, it was said that the *tanuki* would help them find the best trees to hollow out and build into drums. And I don't mean just little drums from forty- or fifty-year-old trees. We're talking big drums, from ancient trees."

Junko took a look up the trail. Many of the trees that lined the path were saplings, too slender to become drum bodies.

"How did they do that?"

"Oh, sometimes the *tanuki* would disguise themselves as tools." Her father rested his palm on the handsaw slung from his belt. "Tools that pulled whoever held them to the tree. Sometimes they changed the landscape to confuse even the best woodsman, who, when he got really frustrated, would find himself simply standing in an old grove. Sometimes they would help roll the trunks down the mountain, if they were feeling generous. You know, *tanuki* are known for their big, strong . . ."

"Dad . . ."

"Bellies. What did you think I was going to say?"

Junko rolled her eyes and laughed. The standing *tanuki* were known for their big male parts.

Though a little out of breath, her father began to sing:

> "Iiiiii'm the drummer of the mountain, a forest *ta-nu-ki*
> I beat my belly like a drum, so listen clo-se-ly
> *poko pon-pon-pon, poko pon-pon-pon*
> Come play along with me . . ."

"Jeez . . ." Junko laughed and combed her hair back with her fingers.

"Ask my grandmother, and she would tell you—every night before they would find a really, truly magnificent tree, there would be a ruckus in the forest."

Junko held a hair elastic between her teeth as she twisted her hair into a bun. "A ruckus?"

"Well, like a festival. Usually with lots of—"

"Drumming?" She ventured a guess just as the path hit a dead end. The left fork shot steeply upward, while the right fork meandered along a slight incline. "Yeah, I've heard that before. But have you actually *seen* one?" She asked, looking back at him. He shook his head and pointed to the left fork.

"No. Not yet."

⌒

The sun had sunk well past their horizon of sight before Junko and her father turned around to head home. It had been a disappointing day— many of the paths were impossible to cross because of the rains the night before, and they hadn't pushed very far into the forest. Her father's feet fell heavily on the path behind her. Yet despite the mud caked on her jeans and sneakers, Junko was in a surprisingly good mood. Even though her dad often annoyed her, and was always telling corny jokes around her friends, he had chosen her over her elder brothers to carry on their family's tradition of making drums. When Junko was still in preschool her brothers had moved away to find jobs and start families in the city. Junko felt she hardly knew them anymore. They rarely visited. Her father said it was just as well. They didn't have any interest in old traditions and had often complained of feeling trapped by the mountains around the house. Junko knew better. It helped that she had inherited her grandfather's sensitive ear and had a knack for craftsmanship. They were pretty isolated, yes, but the mountains hugged them from all sides, filled with life and creative possibility.

She took the lead, humming the *tanuki* song under her breath as she picked her way back down the mountain. "*Poko pon-pon-pon . . .*" It was hopelessly stuck in her head.

"Dad, what's that?" Junko stopped where she stood, and in a few steps her father caught up with her from behind. Off the side of the path stretched a deep, jagged chasm. The freshly upturned earth glistened with the disappearing tails of earthworms as Junko stepped off of the path and onto the firmest edge her feet could find.

Her father stooped forward and pointed down.

"Wow . . ."

At the foot of the chasm, its body sunk more than a few feet into the earth and still tipping forward, was a *keyaki* tree of such great proportions that Junko almost lost her footing. Its thick, tangled roots hung suspended from the base of its trunk, dirt clods still clinging to the tips.

Her father slid down alongside the fallen tree, a hand on its weathered trunk.

"How did this happen?" She called down to him, and reached out to one of the roots. It was oddly warm to the touch.

"Too top-heavy, I guess. This tree is old." He patted the closest bough.

Lush lichen and tree moss grew along its upper branches, many of which had the girth of a respectably large drum on their own. Her father stretched his arms around the base of the trunk in an attempt to gauge its diameter. Even sunk into the mud, the tree dwarfed him. Junko's laughter rang through the surrounding trees.

"Interesting isn't it?" She slid down to where he stood and leaned on his shoulder.

"What's that?"

"Just when you were getting frustrated . . ."

He smiled.

⤿

In the days that followed, the town was abuzz with talk of the monster *keyaki* up in the hills behind Junko's house. It was no easy feat releasing the tree from its muddy bed, and her father had to call in several favors from the men in town. They carted it down in pieces, first the upper branches and roots (which the men accepted as informal compensation for their help, since *keyaki* was so beautiful and rare) and finally the trunk. Night had fallen on the third day by the time Junko and her father at last sat down at the table, muddy and a bit bruised. Her father pulled out two small cups and poured them to the brim with clear sweet-potato liquor. As if on cue, her mother swept past and plucked up the cup closest to Junko, who opened her mouth to complain.

"I haven't made a drum this big since . . . well, before you were born." Her father raised his little cup. "To your first *odaiko*."

⤿

Shaping the trunk of a solid, aged tree was, traditionally, young men's work. Though her father had begun to teach her the craft of carving and planing, she fell back to watch as he wrestled to keep his tools steady. The outermost edge of the tree dropped easily from the blade as he circled the trunk. As his hands followed the curve of the tree's age lines—she tried to count them from the center, but her eyes blurred after two hundred—slivers of wood fell to the floor in thin curls. Every few minutes the plane would catch at a quick change in the direction of the grain. Beneath each layered cut lay a more exquisitely grained surface than the one above, down and down until his forearms bulged with the effort of guiding the plane and his forehead beaded with perspiration and dust. Only when the drum curved in near-perfect alignment, both sides sloping uniformly away from him, did her father stop to wipe his face.

"*Kirei ja nai ka . . .*"—isn't it beautiful? He sighed, and slouched back to join her.

They stood for a moment in silence, eyeing what had once been a living relic of bygone days up in the misty mountains. Now it sagged gently on its supports, rough-hewn and raw. The emptiness that filled her ears pressed in excitedly, mingled with her heartbeat, and though neither of them spoke she could almost hear a faint hum. Then, loudly, "Can you hear that, Dad?"

But he had already turned away and was carefully replacing his tools in their cloth cases.

$\backsim$

The next morning they pulled the lock off of the workshop door to find the drum squarely in the center of the room, as they had left it the night before. Yet its body, those streams and whorls of grain that had seemed so stark under artificial light, gleamed in the light of day. Had her father smoothed down the rough spots, rubbed it over with fine-grain sandpaper after she had left the shop? It was strange.

Her father didn't see, or perhaps just didn't acknowledge her puzzled eyes as they glanced back and forth from him to the drum shell. She wondered if he, too, didn't look a little sprightlier than he had just hours before. He handed her a small brush and a recycled candy tin filled with varnish, and they began to paint the shell in quick, broad strokes. As they worked, the varnish bloomed off of their brushes to fill in the seams of naked wood. Soon the entire body was covered, and after only one coat it shone with the same deep brilliance as the smaller, finished drums that lined the workshop. She peeked up from the bottom edge that she had been worrying with her brush and looked at the shell in astonishment. Her father chuckled and clapped her on the back.

"You see how it takes to the varnish? Incredible."

〜

On they worked, late into that night and early again the next morning. The drum almost seemed to build itself; the moment they finished one step, the next step was under way. Her mother phoned the head priest at the shrine to say that, in all likelihood, the drum would be finished at least a week ahead of schedule.

Junko's father sat back in the workshop, checking the hundreds of tacks that would be needed to nail the drumhead to the body. Since an entire cowhide was needed to accommodate the wide mouth of the drum, they chose a hide that needed only a little trimming at its edges. At this stage, Junko's father left it to her; she had finished practically all of the other drums in the workshop. These days it was on account of her keen ear that their drums were still sought after.

Being careful not to scratch the delicate surface, Junko tapped her fingers along the perimeter of the damp rawhide—*pon, pon, pon*—and bent low, listening for any shifts of tone or resonance. As she pulled away, she saw—or was it a trick of the light?—something whipping away suddenly in the shining varnish. Among the whorls of wood grain, she thought she could just make out the tip of a thick, bushy tail, before it vanished. She glanced over at her father, bent over the pail of domed tacks. A glittering smile tugged gently at the corners of his tired eyes.

That night as she lay in bed, below the lilting *pon-poko-pon* and creaking *ten ten tekke tekke* that swirled through the gusty air in the mountains beyond their house, Junko could distinguish the unmistakably deep, resounding *don* of a centuries-old drum.

Paper Lanterns

by Jennifer Fumiko Cahill

Michelle had been dead for three months and six days, and she still wouldn't shut up. Right when I woke up, there was always a moment before I remembered it had happened, like the weightless half-second on a swing just before gravity reaches up and yanks you backward and down in a tunnel of rushing air. Right then, just as I started to feel that pull, remembering she was gone, Michelle would start.

—*Seriously, is Japan always like this in the summer? Because this is like the jungle. I think I'm flashing back to Nam. I think I was in a tiger cage.*

—What, in a past life? You'd break in like a minute. You'd sell out your country for air conditioning.

—*Shut up. You'd break for spring rolls. Or pad thai.*

—Pad thai isn't Vietnamese.

—*Are you sure?*

—It has the word "thai" in it.

I puffed out a laugh into the tatami mat. Michelle's laugh was a light snort when nobody else was around, like a baby pig's. I inched my face off the futon to touch my cheek to the cool weave. The suitcases were pushed into the corner of the room, and Mom's futon was already put away. I could hear her downstairs, trying to light the gas stove and cursing in a rough whisper.

—*Mina, how can your mom want fire when it's this hot?*

—She's a tea junkie. It's a disease.

From the hot square of sun on the mat, I guessed it was maybe ten o'clock. Mom would have normally gotten me up hours ago to tough out the jet lag, but a week into our annual trip to my grandparents' house she was still letting me sleep in. It took a minute, but I remembered it was Friday here, and we were driving out to clean the family graves before the Obon festival in town.

∽

Mom slid the door open. She had on a T-shirt and her hair was knotted up high, the ends shooting out like sparks. At home she always had her face done, her hair all smoothed down like a black curtain for work. Coming to her parents' house was the only time she looked like this, like the girl she was in Obaasan's cellophane-covered albums.

"*Ohayo*, honey. How you doing? You want breakfast?"

"Okay. And yes." I smiled and tried not to look at her as she knelt down and touched my hair. Her worry face made my chest shrink.

"It's good to be here, right?" she asked. "I just thought it would be good to get away. And we were planning it already, so . . ."

"Yeah, of course." It was, actually. There was no weird curiosity here. When people in this town stared, it was because my light hair and my halting Japanese gave me away as *haafu*, mixed, and a foreigner, not because my best friend crashed her car and died in a stupid high school cliché. Nobody here was telling me how "things happen for a reason." And I knew my classmates back home were relieved not to have me drifting through their backyard parties and trips to the movies all quiet, like I had a stone in my mouth, ruining the summer you're supposed to have when you're sixteen. The truth was, they were handling it. Now that she was gone, everybody was always telling stories about Shell, something funny she said, or some shared moment, to keep her alive, like our school counselor Mr. Rhodes had suggested. And it was working in a way, building a group memory bank, their separate versions of her growing and evolving. I was the one who became a ghost, fixed and silent, trapped on this side.

∽

After breakfast, Mom sent me out to the garden with cold tea and a colander for edamame. Ojiisan and Obaasan were working in separate plant beds, stooping and plucking almost in sync. Behind the stepped beds, the woods were like a mirage of shade. The trees were a heavy apple-green, and beneath them it was as dark as early evening. As still as the forest looked, it rang with thousands of unseen cicadas. In English class we read a haiku about them, and the writer said their sound was "drilling into the rock." I felt like he nailed that one, but nobody in class was that impressed. You had to hear that sound to believe it. Sometimes it was so loud it felt like it was coming from inside your head. Shell would have said it was *insane*. She would have pointed at her ears and mouthed, *I can't hear a word you're saying.*

"*Do-o-mo!*" Obaasan took a big gulp with her eyes squeezed shut. Then she dumped an apron-ful of fuzzy soybeans into the colander and patted my arm. Her face was browned like the top of a pound cake, and she had rivers of creases around her eyes, despite her giant visor. Still, she didn't look old to me, just sunned. She was a photo negative of my freakishly pale mom, and Obaasan's wrinkles were probably the reason Mom slathered herself in sunscreen even on rainy days. She used the zinc-y stuff from Japan that made her look even whiter, and I sometimes called her "the Phantom."

"*Atsui!*" Obaasan gasped, and she took another drink.

Hot. I knew that one. Sometimes we could have little conversations without Mom as a translator, as long as we kept to weather and food. Even in Japanese, though, Ojiisan said little, and mostly he just smiled at me and gestured. Everyone said I spoke when I was little, that I babbled away in Japanese, and it was strange to imagine that tiny version of me chatting with my grandparents, pointing at insects and fruit, naming them as I went. Every year I'd wished I hadn't lost it, but this time it was kind of a relief.

In the kitchen, the fan was on and the lights were off. Mom took the colander from me gently and ran water over the edamame in the sink. She did everything carefully now, and always with the worry face. At the funeral, I just concentrated on her brooch, a little art deco arrow on her lapel. Watching Michelle's mother, Mrs. Frye, was easier. She seemed not to notice me at all. She was still and far away, like someone at the bottom of a frozen pond. Mr. Frye hugged me hard and cried when he smelled my hair, the same shampoo Shell used. I felt stupid for washing it at all, for doing something so vain on a day like that.

—*Don't worry about it. Can't come to my funeral with skanky hair.*

—Why, you think I might meet somebody?

—*Not with a snotty nose.*

I stifled a giggle with a crumpled tissue and caught a look from the woman in the pew in front of me.

—Um, can you please keep it down, this is a funeral, loser.
—Yeah, I know, I'm trying to mourn, thanks.
—Shut up and mourn then, snot girl.
—You shut up, dead girl.

Her snort made me shake in silent laughter, like it had in the same church months before for her cousin's ridiculous wedding with the rhyming vows. That day at the funeral was the first time we talked like that.

Mom shook the beans in the colander and dumped them into the pot of boiling water on the stove. Last time she scolded Obaasan for using aluminum pots because they gave you dementia, but now she didn't seem to care. Behind her, the table was already filling up with food for the trip to the cemetery. There was a pile of fried chicken laid out on paper towels, potato salad, and tightly packed rice balls. I could tell from the perfect rounded triangles that Obaasan must have made them. We used to marvel at how she could toss the steaming rice between her palms—it was like watching someone walk over hot coals.

"Do you want to talk, honey? To me? Or to somebody, you know, maybe somebody else?"

"I'm okay." One bean was clinging to the colander, and I picked it up. The fuzz was so fine, but sharp. It reminded me of a Venus flytrap we had at school in third grade. I'd fed it a little hamburger and its mouth had closed up, brushing my fingers. "Maybe I'll want to talk. Later."

"You can call Amy. I don't mind paying the long distance." Mom's worry face was back. "You girls used to talk, oh my God, for hours every day, about what I have no idea. I mean you just came from school all day together and you're still talking, but . . ." She waved her tiny hand.

"That was with Michelle, Mom."

"I know. It's just not, you know . . ." She smiled hard. "Maybe you should call Amy."

I dropped the bean into the water. "Maybe I will." I knew I wouldn't. The last time we spoke on the phone, I just lay on the couch mystified as she told me about her crush on her cousin's friend and her plans to go see colleges upstate. All I could think about was how every single thing that happened from now on was something Shell was going to miss. But I couldn't say that to Amy, not when she sounded so happy talking about dorms and sororities that no way would she ever pledge. I could have told Shell. There was nothing I couldn't tell her. I tried to fill the pauses in the conversation, to swoon with her at the possibilities, but it was hopeless. It was as hard as talking to my grandparents, with the vocabulary I needed beyond my reach, forgotten.

"So we're going to the cemetery around lunchtime, okay?"

"Okay. I'm gonna bike to the store. Do you need anything?"

Mom shook her head. "Be careful." Now it was her not looking at me.

"Yeah, I know."

It was about a mile of pitted dirt road to the little general store, but mostly under the shade in a tunnel of tall trees. If I pedaled hard and let the air blow through my arms, it would have felt like flying. But my legs were heavy and weak. I hadn't gotten any exercise in months. There were no more walks to Michelle's house, and even in the last few weeks of gym class, I just sat on the bleachers or at the edge of the field while everybody else did their drills and counted off into teams. I didn't have a note or anything, but Coach Volkman cut us both a break and didn't say anything. I was officially flabby, and still a little chubby, which seemed unfair to me, since depressed girls in movies always seemed to get thinner, and sort of chic in a sad-French-girl way, with dark eyeliner and thin gray sweaters falling from their pointy little shoulders.

—*Maybe you should talk to somebody. Because this is a little crazy.*

—I am talking to somebody. I'm talking to you. Just not out loud.

—*Okay. So much crazier. Like, bag-lady-putting-on-imaginary-makeup-at-the-bus-stop crazy.*

—It's not. Because I know.

That was true. I never asked her about death, and I still didn't totally buy the afterlife. I never turned to see her, even the first time. It was like talking on the phone, or during a movie when you're both watching the screen and passing popcorn back and forth without looking. Only her voice was inside, like headphones turned way down, smaller but clearer than the outside world.

—*You could talk to Mr. Rhodes. He has a degree AND a beard.*

—Yes, he does. And a vast collection of vests.

—*Vast vests! And he curses, so you know he's down with the kids.*

—And yet I think I'll hold off.

—*Until fall? When the leather vest comes out?*

—Yes. Because I like the idea of working through my issues with Han Solo.

—*Very retro-nerd. Not Yoda?*

—Yoda is too new age for me. And swampy. And unattractive. Is that shallow?

—*I think that's actually one of your issues.*

I parked the bike in the shade and walked around inside the little shop as long as I could without seeming weird. Everything on the shelves would have amazed Michelle—the yogurt chewing gum, the ramen-flavored potato chips, the little toy cars that came with the bottles of tea, even the miniature cans of Coca Cola with Japanese writing on them would have made her clutch them and gasp.

—I told you. Even the coffee is cute.

—*Is this flan candy? Is flan, like, its own flavor here? Hey, do you think they'd sell us cigarettes?*

I bought a can of sweet coffee and headed back to the house. By the time I got there, Mom was already packing the food into the car.

⌇

The cemetery was scorching, and I was grateful our plot was near the trees and there was a little shade. Ojiisan gave me a bucket and a brown-bristled brush, and we started in on the stones. They looked clean enough to me every year, but we scrubbed off the dust along the surfaces and in the grooves of the Chinese characters that spelled out the names of my great-grandparents, my great-uncle, and others I did not know. Ojiisan went over the names again with an old toothbrush when I was done. The granite was hot, and the swaths of black left by the wet sponge turned gray again in seconds. Mom and Obaasan weeded around the graves and set down the food on a blue tarp.

—*Graveyard picnic.*

—I know it seems weird. But it's a thing.

—*Not really. It's like an Irish wake, I guess. But you're not actually looking at the body, so maybe it's actually less creepy.*

—We're supposed to welcome their spirits back home.

—*Do you have to welcome all your relatives, or can you choose?*

—You can't choose. Just like when they're alive.

Everyone ate and talked in Japanese, which I didn't mind. Down the slope, a couple of other families were wringing out cleaning rags, opening and shutting coolers, just like we were. I thought about everybody at Michelle's house after the funeral, the women all unwrapping trays of ziti and carving ham on the dining room table while Michelle's mother pointed slowly to cabinets and drawers to tell them where they could find the serving spoons or extra bowls. The men moved folding chairs or stood in little groups eating or smoking outside. Mom said everyone needed something to do, and it seemed like they all knew what that was. It was like there was a plan, but I didn't have a copy of it. And here, under the shade, Ojiisan sat cross-legged eating fried chicken beside his parents' graves. He looked content to me, grinning at something my mother was saying. I wondered how it would feel to clean Michelle's grave in twenty years.

⌇

That night, the park over by the elementary school was strung with red and white paper lanterns that circled the rickety-looking tower in the center. The base was covered in red-and-white-striped cloth, but it just looked like Ojiisan's iffy homemade scaffolding to me. Nobody seemed worried, though, least of all the man up top beating the drum over the recorded festival music that played from the speakers. I always liked the slow circles they made with their arms and the crack of the sticks on the wooden edge of the drum, how it sort of hypnotized you. My mom and grandmother were taken up into the current of people dancing in unison around the tower. I watched for them to come around each time with Obaasan's cluster of friends, all old ladies who suddenly looked sharp in their stiff *obi* with fans tucked into the bows on their backs. Ojiisan was sipping a ridiculously tall can of beer next to me and looking regal in his striped, indigo kimono. Oddly enough, I stuck out most when dressed as a native. My heels hung off the backs of last year's wooden sandals, and I was sausaged into my *yukata*. The fabric was white with a pattern of straight irises that went crooked around my chest, which formed a lumpy shelf over the rigid yellow *obi*. Obaasan had clucked and laughed to my mother as she tried to get the lapels to lie flat, shoving at my boobs like she was punching down bread dough. By the time we were ready for a photo, my face was pink and sweating.

—*Should have brought a sports bra. This is the problem with inter-*

racial marriage right here. Your Italian boobs are like an invasive species taking over the Japanese kimono.

—Wow. Is that racist, sexist, or just bad science? How did you even pass Bio?

—*D. All of the above. Which is also how I passed Bio.*

—Shut up. Absorb some culture.

A little blue flag with the *kanji* for "ice" in red was swinging over the *kakigori* stall. Two little boys with buzz cuts were bumping against one another, watching the shopkeeper turn the cast iron wheel on an ice shaver that snowed into two paper cups. The mountains of white turned a nuclear green with the syrup, and the boys, suddenly still, dug in as soon as the cups were handed over.

—*Oh, my God. I think I have diabetes. By osmosis.*

—I think you can scratch that worry off your list. That and osmosis.

—*Get one! You know you want one. Get the lime. It looks like antifreeze!*

—It's not lime. It's green melon.

In minutes, I was drinking the melted, neon slush at the bottom, enjoying the cold ache in my molars. I knew Shell would have loved these even more than snow cones if she'd ever come with us.

—*This is insane. It's like honeydew on steroids.*

—Right? Wait till you try one with condensed milk. So good.

—*And it's so fluffy! Oh, my God. American snow cones are like licking a dirty snow plow. I'm never eating one again.*

I looked straight into the bottom of the cup, and pictured Shell next to me in a borrowed *yukata,* poking at her cup with a straw, her hair frizzing in the humidity. I focused hard on her standing there, her feet hanging off her sandals, like mine, and I pushed out the image of her in that white casket she would have hated, with the white satin lining and stupid lace pillow, and the brass railings all around it, like some tacky princess bedroom set.

Everyone was walking down to the river to watch the lanterns. As we inched down to the concrete embankment, we saw people lighting the tiny candles in the white paper boxes and setting them into the water. Mom asked if I wanted to do one, but I told her I just wanted to watch, so we waited by the railing and let my grandparents go ahead. This is when I would have gone all tour guide and told Michelle about how the lanterns are supposed to guide the souls back until next year. But it looked hard now in a way it never did before, sending them away like that, all the lights heading off and leaving the people on the banks in the dark.

—*What if you don't do it?*

—You have to.

—*But you're not. You could light one for me right now.*

—I know. Just not yet, okay?

—*Okay. It's so pretty. It's beautiful.*

—I knew you'd like it.

The lanterns spread out and clustered together like an ambling crowd of people as they were pulled downstream. Ojiisan and Obaasan lit one lantern each and pushed them lightly into the current, letting them drift toward all the others and float farther away until we could no longer tell them apart from the rest.

I Hate Harajuku Girls

by Katrina Toshiko Grigg-Saito

I am sick of Harajuku girls. I avoid the bridge in Tokyo where they con-
gregate on weekends, posing for pictures in their too-high heels, fiddling
with plasticky blonde ringlets, and lowering fake eyelashes in ruffled
Victorian doll outfits.

When I first get to Japan, I think it will be hilarious to take a picture
with one of them to send to my mom, but when I try, this girl pushes
my camera away and shakes money in my face. Like a picture with her is
worth twelve dollars. She should be paying me for a picture with an au-
thentic sixteen-year-old Amazon: I'm about six inches taller than pretty
much every Japanese person here (male or female), and can give a fierce
Maori *haka* look if people rub me the wrong way. She probably only
notices my darker-than-a-tan skin and crazy curly hair, but all she has
to do is look hard at the shape of my eyes to see that they look just like
hers. After the embarrassment rubs off, I'm angry: at myself for wanting
a picture, and at her for refusing one. It hits me how wrong it is that the
Harajuku girls dress like dolls and call themselves Lolitas. I don't know
which is worse: thinking they've never read Nabokov, or thinking they
have. I want to give them a brief history of the objectification and infan-
tilization of women, but—I don't speak a word of Japanese.

Just saying that chokes me up a little. I don't speak my father's native
tongue. He didn't teach me. I didn't ask him to teach me. Being the only
half-Japanese, quarter-Dominican, quarter-Scotch-Irish girl I've ever
heard of was hard enough in our little town of Barre, Vermont; I guess he
didn't want me to sound Japanese too. On nights when my mom worked
late, my dad would spin stories from his childhood. Our little apartment
would disappear, and we were inside the story, throwing crumbs to koi,
climbing inside giant Buddhas, or zooming through Japan on the bullet

train. "I want to go!" I would say when he finished. "It's too expensive," he would say, or "too far," or "what would you do when you get there?" and then I would recite things to do and places to see from his stories. "You have good memory," he would say, but we never made plans to go. I guess, because of the stories, I always felt more Japanese than American. And after I walked into a bathroom at school to see "Go home Sady you sneaky Jap" scrawled on the stall door, I imagined doing exactly that. There, I thought, I would belong.

After Dad died, I told my mother, "I have to go to Japan."

She kept washing dishes. Later, before bed, she said. "Honey, it's just that Japan's a tough place for foreigners. Your dad's family . . ."—she said *family* like it was a flawed theory, a gas, a myth—"cut us off when your dad married an American." She twisted one of her braids. "His life was *here*." I recognized this conversation ender, the mantra she repeats to friends.

But I knew his secret stories. I wanted to taste the foods he grew up on, to wear a kimono, to feel the human crush at Shibuya crossing. If I went to his favorite shrine would I find him there? I dreamed he was waiting for me, covered in mist, and I knew I had to live the answers to all of my questions, not google them, not guess at them. I had to be submerged in my dad's Japan.

Gary, my advisor at school, who I love, helped me find a program at an international school in Tokyo with a scholarship for kids who are part Japanese but have never been to Japan. I figured it was a long shot, but then the yes-envelope came in the mail. I jumped around a bunch before my mom got home, and then I told her.

"I'm going to Japan for a year." I had planned to ease into it, to give a speech about how enriching this experience would be, how I still loved her and would be back before she knew it, but I ended up blurting it out and freezing. Her shock resonated in the soft part between my ribs. Since my father died I've had the uncanny and irritating ability to feel what she's going through, rather than guessing it based on her still face. But she'd be okay, and I wanted this. "Colleges will love it," I added.

And here I am, regretting the day I decided to come here.

It isn't the school—the school is pretty awesome. The kids are sophisticated and open and from all over the world. A lot of them, like my best friend Oliver, went to Japanese schools before transferring and speak flawless Japanese. On field trips, Japanese kids always want to take pictures with him or practice their English. They ask if he's the guy from the *Twilight* film, which is half ridiculous and half plausible. He has the same enormous eyes and angular features, but his hair is too red and he's super skinny. I like walking with him, because we're about the same height and sometimes people stare at him instead of me. When kids mob him he tells them, "No, I'm sorry to disappoint you, but I'm not that vampire from *Twilight*," in near-native-sounding Japanese. This makes them go even crazier. I do not have this effect on Japanese kids. Usually they're not sure what language I speak, so they stare and run away. If people do talk to me they ask if I'm Brazilian or treat me like I'm a little slow. When I tell people I'm *haafu*, as in half, as in half-Japanese, they shrink away like *haafu* is a contagious disease. I look just as different here as I looked in the US. It's exhausting.

My dad always said that I was beautiful. He used to call me *otenba*, like he was really fond of me. I always thought the word meant something like "my favorite child" or "butterfly girl" or something really cool and complimentary. Right before he died, when we were home from the hospital, I googled *otenba*. Tomboy, it said. I checked again. *Otenba*, Tomboy. *Otenba*, Tomboy. Panic thumped in my throat. I ran into my father's room trying to keep the unsteady balance between crying and yelling, "*Otenba* means tomboy? Tomboy?" and even as sick as he was, my dad managed a laugh.

"Yeah, so what?"

"Dad, tomboy is not a good thing. I don't want to be a tomboy, I want to be a girl." My dad's laugh faded to a smile that told me how much he was going to miss me.

"No, no, you got it wrong." I can almost hear my dad's voice. Slippery like fish eggs, its l's and r's all mixed up. "I raised my girl to be *otenba*. *Otenba* mean strong, *otenba* mean know what you want." I unequivocally love my father's accent and his weird grammar. It reminds me of Yoda from *Star Wars*, his favorite old movie. Yoda's green and wise. Kind of like my dad at that moment. "I raised my girl to think for herself. I talk to her like adult, and she answer like adult. I'm proud of you, Sady, my *otenba*."

We had other talks before he died, but that's the one that stuck. I want to tell him that I'm trying, but I'm an *otenba* among Harajuku girls. My dad didn't warn me about them.

Instead he told me about the way the pebbles sound underfoot when walking down the long path to his family's shrine. They stand with thousands of other families, in the cold on New Year's Eve, waiting for midnight to hit and for the year to turn. His mother, wearing a heavy brocade kimono, fastens her *tabi* socks at the ankle, and slips on some *zori* sandals and a fur stole to keep her warm. His father wears an Italian suit and just-shined black loafers. My father, the youngest, holds his mother's hand and watches his brother and sister running off to see friends in the crowd. He tells me that even if Tokyo, this crazy city of fourteen million, reinvents itself, the sound of those pebbles would still be the same. I ask my mom if she remembers the name of the shrine, but she doesn't. I can't ask his family. I do extensive research, combing through my guidebooks and searching for his shrine in every part of Japan.

I look for koi ponds with fish that would remember his name.

I look for ramen shops with creaky stools and worn counters, cut from one slice of tree.

I look for stands that sell crispy hot cakes shaped like fish, with each fin articulated and sweet beans in the middle.

I look for little boys in my father's school uniform, the Showa hat with the red tassel.

I look for people reading Shakespeare, sounding out the English words the way my dad used to do.

I search for his brother and sister, look for his face in those around me.

But he doesn't surface.

↶

"Ok," Oliver says. "We've combed the shrines in Yanaka." That's a tiny little neighborhood with old shops and wooden buildings, almost like the Japan from Dad's stories. I was sure it would be there, but no go. If I can just find Dad's shrine, I can find the heart of Japan that never changes even though the crazy Harajuku girls are ruining Tokyo.

"Did you bring your guidebook?" he asks. I try to hand it to him, but he shrinks away like it'll give him leprosy "Not a chance, I will not be singling myself out as a tourist. Read me one we haven't tackled."

"Gokokuji," I say. We can usually fit in one a day, since we get out of school at three and most shrines close around five.

"Sady, that's a temple."

"What's the difference?"

"Buddhists, temples. Shintos, shrines."

"What's the difference?"

"Really, Sady, do you know nothing about your dad's country of origin? You said your dad went to a shrine on New Year's Eve, right? If he went to a temple, there would be gongs; a shrine, good luck toys." Oliver has a way of making me feel extremely stupid. I battle with the orphan tears that like to rattle in my chest and seep out of my eyes in moments like this. I try to focus on the memory.

"I'm not sure," I want to add, *and I can't ask him*. Ollie looks concerned and throws an arm around me.

"Sorry, Sades. I'm in for the hunt. We can go to every shrine, every temple you want. We can even go to that church on Omotesando." I punch him in the arm.

"So, Gokokuji?"

"Might as well give it a go. Yurakucho Line, car 10." Oliver is a secret subway nerd. He knows all of the stations and lines in the spidery map, and knows which subway car lines up with each exit. It's spooky. "Haven't been to that one."

I try not to breathe hard and I try not to lose him as I follow him through the transfers. His PASMO subway card is always ready. He taps it and spins through the turnstiles, expertly dodging businessmen in black suits and even helping a woman carry her stroller up the stairs.

"Here," he says, after charging up four flights of stairs. We're in front of an impressive gate and I cross my fingers. The road is concrete. No pebble crunch.

"Bummer," I say. "Well, might as well get my book signed."

I love the silence of temples-and-or-shrines. I love slinging off my shoes the way we did at home and tiptoeing into these dark damp spaces. I find the desk with the calligraphy monk and take out my accordion book. The old man opens it and says something to me in Japanese. I just nod, and I watch as he puts the heavy weight on one side of the book to keep it flat and steady. He inks up a square stamp in bright red, and centers it on the page. I think most people just drop their books off and walk around while he finishes, but this is the best part. After the stamp dries, he pulls the sleeve of his robe back and paints intricate black characters on top of the stamp.

"Look at this one," I whisper to Oliver.

"Right, lovely, what does it say, then?"

I give him my scary-*haka*-look. He knows that I can't read the Japanese *kanji* characters. "I might not be able to read, but I can tell you where every single stamp is from." Oliver raises an eyebrow. "Ok, here we go." I open up the accordion and tell him: every shrine-or-temple name, details about its unique architectural features, about the person who signed it. Oliver's impressed.

"Why haven't you got Meiji?" he asks.

"Meiji?"

"Yeah, Meiji Jingu. You know, the big shrine in Harajuku, on the other side of the bridge."

"There's not a shrine there."

"Not a shrine there? Meiji is only the most important shrine in Tokyo. Ah, at last! A crack in her stone memory! Meiji! The kryptonite to Miss Perfect's Encyclopedic Vault!" One of the monks shoos us out for being too loud, and I whisper as I tug my shoes on.

"Oliver, seriously, we never went to that one."

"Sady, seriously, we did. Don't you remember? Last year, Bao Yu and Luis tried to hammer on the huge drum in front and got chased out by the priests."

"Uh, last year? HELLO."

"Ah! You came *this* year. It seems like decades."

I roll my eyes. "You were saying? Meiji?"

"Yeah, it's brill, huge, though once you get inside, you still have to walk forever to get there."

"Walk?"

"Yeah."

"Ollie, remember? I told you my Dad's shrine has a long stone path."

"Right, but that was before I realized—Sades, it would make absolute sense. Your dad lived in Meguro, right? He'd just have to hop on the Yamanote, three stops and he'd be there."

"We have to go!" I start pulling Oliver toward the subway.

"Indeed . . . though it's closed now."

"I thoroughly and completely blame you for this wild goose chase we've been on."

"Blame accepted."

"How are we going to get in?"

"Sades, you're a loon, we can't just break in to Meiji."

"We can try!"

Oliver shakes his head. "You're trouble."

⌒

We walk all the way up Omotesando, the Fifth Avenue of Tokyo. I've walked it a million times, drooled over the shop windows and eaten terrible Japanese pizza at Shakey's. Once, Oliver and I even went on a sort of date to this crêperie. I say sort of date because he ordered for both of us, after which I launched into a tirade about feminism and equality and women having a voice. He listened attentively and then reminded me that he ordered in Japanese, a language I don't speak, that he'd been to France and knew what to order, and that I said that very day I liked surprises.

I said I was sorry. Basically Oliver is my best friend here, and I'm not about to ruin it by making out with him. Plus, Ollie loves food as much as I do.

We walk past the ramen place that has the fatty bone-marrow soup from up north, past the Choco-Cro that has amazing flaky hot croissants. Up the stairs to the overpass where he points to the treetops.

"That's not Yoyogi Park?" I ask.

"Nope." From up here, I see a white rolling fortress of fence stretched around a parking lot and in the distance a giant *torii* gate nestled in the trees. We head down the stairs to the bridge that's usually swarming with Harajuku girls. Tonight it's empty. We go up and rattle the gates a little.

We wander around the periphery, searching for some way in. Or really, we just wander around. I have no intention of actually going into the park after dark. It would be totally illegal. But I like when Oliver hoists me onto his shoulders to find "chinks in the armor of Meiji."

And then a voice below us whispers, "I know the way." From my great height, I see the ruffles of a Harajuku girl in a gingham Little Bo Peep outfit staring up at us.

I scramble down off Oliver's shoulders, ignoring his ouches. Was she following us? Sneaky. Heat flares in my belly. I am not going to be friendly with a Harajuku girl. "Whatever, we'll come back tomorrow."

Oliver switches to Japanese and I'm surprised that she doesn't fawn over him the way most Japanese girls do. She answers him in short gruff sentences.

"She talks like a boy," Oliver whispers and I glare at him.

"What did she say?"

"She says you can squeeze through a hole in the fence behind the station."

I get the creepy skin crawl feeling. The one I get when I'm home alone and the radiator bangs in our apartment building.

"Let's just wait until tomorrow," I say.

"Are you scared?"

"Yeah," I say.

"Oh, come on, it'll be an adventure."

"Yeah, getting deported is totally an adventure."

"At eight p.m.?"

"More likely eight p.m. than midnight."

"Okay then, we storm the gates at midnight." Oliver throws his scrawny arm into the air and I have to smile.

"Except the train stops running at midnight," I remind him.

"Well played."

Throughout this whole negotiation, the Little Bo Peep girl narrows her eyes and ping-pongs between us. I can't tell if she understands.

"Will you tell her thanks, though?" I say to Oliver.

"Meiji different at night," says the Bo Peep girl directly to me.

I still have the creepy skin crawl feeling and am not about to be pressured by Little Bo Peep.

"Thanks, but, I have to go," I say.

And then she says it. "*Hu-ri-ku guy-jean*." At first I don't understand what she's saying. "*Fu-rii-ku gaijin*," she says again and then I get it. She's calling me a freak foreigner. It's like being punched in the stomach. I don't know if I want to cry or punch back, so I grab Oliver's arm and break into a jog.

〜

The next day it's pouring.

The day after that I have to cram for an exam.

By the time three days have passed the whole thing seems like a dream, until Oliver passes me in the hall. "Chink in the armor at ten," he says.

"Sure," I say.

But I don't show up. And when Oliver asks what happened, I can't explain it to him. I can't explain that I never want that sucker punch feeling again of being called a freak, and that as much as I want to see my dad's shrine, I'm terrified of seeing the Harajuku girl again, terrified of her calling me out for the fraud that I am. It hits me that no matter how crazy they dress, they will always be Japanese, and that no matter how Japanese I feel inside, I'll never really look Japanese to anyone here. I also can't tell him how scared I am that it won't even be my dad's shrine, that I'll never find it, that I'll never find him. Instead I just say, "Oh, must have forgotten," like I am so over our friendship.

Oliver and I stop speaking.

I really hate the Harajuku girl.

〜

Sunday, our only day off from school, I get up early. I go to my favorite little mom-and-pop place that always serves the same Japanese breakfast special: a whole salty *sanma* fish, miso soup, pickled daikon, fresh rice, and my favorite, fermented *natto* beans with a raw egg. Most people think it's disgusting, but it was my dad's favorite, and I'm determined to like it. When I have these breakfasts I pretend I'm chatting with him on my cell. No one can understand what I'm saying anyway.

Today I tell him about Oliver being mad at me, and how I've abandoned the shrine hunt. I can't tell if it's his disappointment or mine, but I realize from his silence that I have to *ganbatte*—a Japanese word that roughly means, go get 'em. I have to visit Meiji.

I wait till after dark. If this even is my dad's shrine, and there's any chance my dad's ghost is going to show himself, I have to be alone. To avoid the Harajuku girl, I go the long way to the shrine, getting off at Shibuya and walking through the neon-craziness of the crossing, through the park by the Olympic stadium, past where the guys dress up as Elvises, to Meiji.

I snake around until I'm where she said the hole would be. And there it is, a neatly cut section of fence. I hesitate. I pretend to be bird watching, and then I slip right through. It's a little brambly, but a few steps away I can see the *torii* gate up front: two giant tree trunks ascending the heavens. My breathing shortens in my chest and my legs tingle, ready to run. I flip open my phone. "I'm scared," I whisper. No answer.

I take a deep breath and walk through the gates.

Everything goes quiet, like there's a force field around the grounds. The air is still, waiting. I breathe in the green forest, lush compared with the anemic topiaries in pots outside the gates. Above me I can even see a few stars.

And then I hear it.

The sound of pebbles crunching under my feet.

Tears spring to my eyes.

I know this is my father's shrine.

I walk down the long path, lit by the moon through leaves. The cicadas are going crazy and my heart beats a bass line. Being the only person here puts an electric grin on my face. I'm not nervous, not worried about being deported. Through the second gate and I know I belong here. This is my Japan, the Japan from my dad's stories, this is home. It's a long walk to the main shrine, but a magnet in my chest pulls me forward. Right before the main shrine, I wash my hands in cool water, then I walk through the last set of gates. The solid doors open up to a wide courtyard with a sacred tree where people have tied their wishes.

I imagine holding my dad's big rough hand, and listening as he points out the carved gigantic doors, "like a castle," and the giant drum, "I can see why your friends tried to play it," and the bad luck tied to trees, "Never give in to bad luck, just keep try and luck change."

I whip around—someone's coming. I pull into the shadows of the souvenir booth.

A security guard walks past, boots clicking, pausing for a moment to survey the grounds. I try to become one with the wood of the booth, only raising my eyes when I'm sure he's passed. A chill zaps through me as I catch a pair of shiny eyes gleaming in the darkness across from me,

Japanese, like my dad's. A finger raised to smiling lips. I'm yanked back in time to games of hide-and-seek with my father. That same gesture, a finger raised to smiling lips. I would refuse to hide alone and we'd sit in silence holding our breaths and smiling to the edge of laughter. I want to reach across to him now, but I can still hear the movement of the security guard. When we hid together I felt like I could hear his thoughts, or read them on his smiling face, *Mom's almost here*, and *shh, shh, shh*. Sometimes we would turn hide-and-seek on its head and leap out to scare her. I'd know it was time to jump just by my dad's widening eyes, *one, two, three*, they seemed to say. When we can no longer hear the click of his boots, the eyes flicker to the right and I notice a little side exit. *one, two, three*, they say and we're up. I scan the grounds, nearly running, trying to be sure we aren't spotted.

Shouts erupt from the main building. I break into a run and can hear my dad keeping pace behind me. I dart through the exit and am happy for that year on the track team. I don't look back as the footsteps slam after me. If they see my face, I'm a goner. No more visits to Meiji, no more hanging out with my dad in his favorite place. I hear a chorus of my dad's pebbles flying under my feet. His feet flying with mine. I've never run this fast. My breath is easy and strong. I hear the security guard mutter a curse as he trips, and am sure it's my dad's pebbles gathering up and pulling his feet from under him. I accelerate. Dad's hands push me through the hole in the fence and we speed around the corner.

I turn around to greet him, and am met by blue gingham ruffles. The girl from the bridge. I'm surprised by how quickly my heart adjusts. I guess I knew it wasn't him in there, and when she smiles I still see my dad's on-the-verge-of-laughing-smile. Giggles fly up my chest and sing out our mouths as we pound down Takeshita Street, laughing hysterically. People are staring at us as we catch our breath.

"You're right, it's different at night." I say.

And then she points to me, points to herself, and smiles big: "*Fu-rii-ku, ne.*" I smile too. Yeah. We're both freaks.

Peace on Earth

by Suzanne Kamata

According to the Prime Minister, Japan and the United States are best friends. So why are my parents always arguing?

Just this morning, my father made breakfast—*ojiya*, which is miso soup mixed with leftover rice and an egg. He said, "Isn't this better than hotcakes? All that sugar?"

Mom had made blueberry pancakes yesterday. She didn't say anything, but sighed loudly and then looked longingly toward the row of breakfast cereals on the kitchen counter.

"Taiga-kun, what do you think?" Otosan said, looking at me.

I shrugged. I'll eat anything and I like both kinds of breakfast—Mom's American ones, and Otosan's Japanese ones—but since he got started on this cooking kick, it seems like every meal is part of a competition between them. My sister Maya and I looked at each other across the table and rolled our eyes.

"Did you hear them last night?" Maya asks me later, as we ride our bikes to school.

"How could I not? *Urusakatta, na*,"—so annoying.

They'd been watching some DVD about World War II, and Otosan started going on about the atomic bomb. Then Mom jumped in and their voices got louder and louder.

"'I think you should apologize to Ueno-san,'" Maya says, making her voice lower like Otosan's.

Mrs. Ueno is our elderly next-door neighbor. She was in Nagasaki at the time of the bomb. She's pretty cheerful, but her voice is a little strange—high and squeaky. Otosan says it's because of radiation poisoning.

"'Why do you always hold me responsible?'" I imitate Mom. "'I didn't drop that bomb. I would have been opposed to it, if I'd been alive then. I married you, didn't I? Doesn't that prove anything?'"

Maya laughs, but then she gets serious. "What do you think other parents fight about?"

I shrug, letting go of the handlebar for a second. "Which professional baseball team is the best?"

"Or maybe whose turn it is to take out the trash?" Maya guesses.

"Maybe if Mom and Otosan were from the same country, they'd always get along."

"*So, ka na?*"—maybe.

⤳

That evening, the argument is about where to go for winter vacation. Mom wants to go back to the States to visit her family—Grandma and Grandpa, Aunt Ann and Uncle Brad, my cousins.

"We haven't seen them in almost two years," she says.

"We need to save money," Otosan says. "It's too expensive to go all the way to Wisconsin, but we could take a trip somewhere closer to home. Any ideas, kids?"

Me, I don't care where we go, or if we go or not. I'd be happy just to sleep in every day and hang out at the batting center with my friends. Or maybe I could get Chiaki, this girl in my homeroom, to go to karaoke with me.

"Hawaii?" Maya says. I guess it's because she loves watching our parents' wedding video. They got married on a plantation on Oahu, with a waterfall trickling down rocks and leis around their necks. They look really happy in that video. They're not fighting. Instead, they're feeding each other coconut wedding cake, dancing, and kissing.

"Hmmm." Otosan rubs his forehead.

"Why don't we go to Okinawa?" I suggest. Because of the army base, I know that there are lots of Americans there. Mom might feel sort of at home. And with all the palm trees and sugar cane fields, it's probably sort of like Hawaii.

"Okinawa," Otosan repeats, letting the idea sink in. He's a high school teacher, and he's been down there on school trips. The students at the school Maya and I attend usually go north to Hokkaido for skiing, so we've never been to Naha.

"Okinawa!" Mom says. "I've always wanted to go there!"

⌒

Mom likes to travel. Before she met Otosan, she'd been to half a dozen countries in Europe. She'd planned on spending a year or two teaching English in Japan before going on to Thailand, India, and various places in Africa. But she got stuck here, she says. She met Otosan and fell in love, and then she couldn't leave. So now she only gets to go someplace if we all go together.

She has her bags packed a week before we're scheduled to leave. I wait until the last minute, then jam a couple pairs of shorts, some T-shirts, boxers, my baseball mitt, and a couple of comic books into my backpack. Oh, and a bathing suit. Mom says it'll be too cold for swimming in the ocean—the main reason most people from other parts of Japan go to Okinawa—but that our hotel has an indoor pool.

I'm looking forward to going to Okinawa because it's home to the National High School baseball champions. Last summer, I watched every game they played, and I'm hoping that something in the air down there will rub off on me and turn me into a pitcher as amazing as their ace, Shimabukuro. Maybe the island food will make me stronger—all that bitter melon and ham.

⌒

On the plane, Mom thumbs through her guidebook. "Ooh," she says. "A&W! They have root beer in Okinawa!"

"What's A&W?" Maya asks.

"It's an American restaurant chain. I worked at one when I was in high school. Wow, it's been a long time. . . ."

"What's root beer?" I ask. I'm too young to drink alcohol, so it's not like I'll get to try it.

"It's a soft drink. Like cola, but different. We'll have to try root beer floats! At A&W there's a bell at the entrance. If you're happy with the service, you ring the bell when you leave."

And then wouldn't everybody be looking at you? How embarrassing would that be? I hope she doesn't go ringing the bell in Okinawa.

"We should go to the base, too," Otosan says, "so you can see for yourself how noisy those planes are."

My shoulders tense. When I came up with this plan, I must have forgotten. Whether or not the US military should be in Okinawa is the theme of another one of their arguments.

When an American army guy in Japan gets into trouble, it makes national news, and Otosan says, "Why won't the Americans get out of Okinawa? We can defend ourselves."

Then Mom says, "When you use that tone, it sounds like you despise Americans. The kids are going to feel negative about their Americanness when they hear you talk like that."

Luckily, Mom doesn't seem to hear him this time. Her nose is still buried in the guidebook.

"The snake museum!" she says, flipping eagerly through the pages. "Live music!"

~

When we get off the plane in Naha, the wind is soft and warm. *So this is the tropics. Nice!* It's not cold, like home on Shikoku, where we can see our breath in the hallway. I immediately take off my jacket.

We gather our luggage and then take a bus to the car rental service, where Mom chews out Otosan for not having reserved a larger car. "How are we supposed to jam all our stuff in here?" she asks. "Somebody's going to have to ride on the roof!"

"Well, you shouldn't have brought along the Christmas presents," he says. "We could have opened those when we got back home."

Somehow, we manage to cram everything in. With bags wedged between Maya and me up to the ceiling, there's no room in the backseat to move around.

The rest of the day is a blur of sightseeing. First, we hit up a red castle, once headquarters of the Ryukyu kingdom. We go through rooms filled with lacquered thrones and old scrolls. Whenever one of us falls behind, Otosan hurries us along. "C'mon, c'mon!" he says. "We only have three days in Okinawa, and we still have a lot to see!"

"Take it easy," Mom grumbles back. "This is vacation, not a packaged group tour."

My stomach is roaring by the time we get out of that place, but it's still an hour or so till lunch. Luckily, our next stop is Pineapple Park, where along with a pineapple grove and exhibits on pineapple cultivation and a little train shaped like a pineapple, there's a snack bar. Before Otosan can say anything about the harmful effects of sugar, I order a tropical fruit parfait with my own money.

Later, on the way to our hotel, we stop by the American Air Force base in Kadena. From the side of the road, we can see the rows of look-alike houses, all modest one-story structures. They're nothing like the houses you see in American movies. They're not even as nice as the house where my grandparents live. There aren't any people milling about either. The place is pretty subdued.

"It looks peaceful," Maya says. "*Shizuka na.*"

Otosan lowers the car window, but we hear no planes. The sky is clear except for a few puffs of white, and quiet.

"Huh." Otosan is clearly disappointed. "When we brought our students here on the school trip it was very noisy."

Mom shrugs. "They're probably on winter vacation, too."

Otosan starts up the car again and drives off down the highway.

⌒

Once we're checked in to our hotel, we finally get a chance to relax. In our room, there's a little tray of plastic-wrapped cookies—*chinsuko*. I'm starving again, so when nobody's looking, I scarf them down. Maybe housekeeping will bring more if we ask.

Otosan's tired from all that driving. "I'm going to take a nap before dinner," he says. "And don't forget, kids. We're signed up for glassblowing at seven p.m."

So that means we've got about thirty minutes of free time. I noticed when we came in that there's a game room on the first floor. "Hey Maya, wanna go play some air hockey?"

"Okay." She follows me to the elevator and down to the game room. We go past the lobby, where a woman in an evening gown and Santa hat is singing Christmas carols. Her voice rises to the ceiling: "Let there be peace on earth . . ."

Peace—that would be nice.

Maya, the mind-reader, says, "I wish they'd stop arguing."

"Yeah, me too."

The game room is empty. We've got it all to ourselves. We take our places at the air hockey table and I shove the puck her way.

Maya deflects my goal shot. "Do you think they'll get divorced?"

I sometimes wonder this myself, and it worries me. If they split up, would we have to choose between them? And if we chose Mom, would she try to make us move to America? Sure, we're half American, but we've never lived in the States. Who would we hang out with? How would we know if something was cool or not? And we don't even know the words to the national anthem. Not only that, but Japan is my home. And I'm the starting pitcher on my high school's baseball team. They'd never make it to the tournament final without me. But since I'm the older brother, I think it's best to keep my mouth shut. "Nah," I say. "They've always been like that, haven't they? They're used to each other now. If they were going to get divorced they would have split up long ago."

☙

On the following day, which happens to be the day before Christmas, we wake up early. Mom says something about needing coffee, but Otosan insists upon the Japanese breakfast buffet. I pile my plate with bitter melon fried with ham and eggs, and eat three bowls of rice washed down with guava tea. Then we're off to a famous aquarium about an hour from our hotel. We make it through in record time, and then we have lunch.

"Where are we going now?" Maya asks over a bowl of Chinese noodles.

"Himeyuri-kan," Otosan says. "It's an important historical site." He glances over at Mom. "It was a hospital during World War II."

Mom presses her lips together, but she doesn't object. Maybe the lack of coffee is doing her in. Or maybe she's actually interested in visiting this place.

☙

Otosan parks in a gravel lot next to a tour bus. We haul ourselves out of the car, past a souvenir shop with brightly printed shirts on sale, and up some stone steps. A group of high school students in uniform is hovering near some sort of shrine. Some people are praying, others are laying flowers and wreaths of origami cranes on the altar.

Otosan saunters ahead, then calls us over.

"Look at this, kids," he says. He's leaning against a railing, pointing down into a big hole.

"It looks like a tunnel," I say.

"Yes. This was the entrance to the cave. To the *hospital*."

Of course there is another entrance, now. We go through glass doors into an air-conditioned lobby where Otosan buys our tickets. And then we forge ahead, down the dark hallways that make up the museum. Along the walls there are exhibits. Photos. Artifacts: A dented canteen. Pages torn out of a diary. Primitive-looking medical tools. *Imagine having your leg cut off with a hacksaw! And no anesthesia!*

Eventually, we make our way to the main chamber. It's cool and dark. Before it was just a cave, damp rocks, maybe with some spiderwebs or bats hanging in the corner. But it's been fixed up nice. The walls are covered with black-and-white portraits. I look at the captions underneath: names, ages. Keiko Yamaguchi, fifteen years old, Third year, First Girls' High School. Noriko Saito, fifteen years old, First Year, Normal School. And on and on. There's one that reminds me of Chiaki from homeroom. Their eyes are kind of the same.

"Fifteen," my sister whispers. "Like us." She leans against me, as if she needs some comfort.

"Yeah." My mouth goes dry. "If we were living here back then, I wouldn't be playing baseball."

"You'd be a soldier," she says.

I try to imagine holding a rifle against my shoulder instead of a bat, warplanes zooming by overhead, bombs dropping all around. And Maya with a roll of bandages, or running around with bedpans and burying the dead. "You'd be a nurse."

I look away from the faces for a moment, back behind me, and spot Mom. She's reading something out of a big book on a stand at the center of the room. Maya and I go over to check it out. The books are filled with stories written by the survivors. Testimonies.

I skim over some of the titles: "A patient with no legs crawling in the mud." "Bloated corpses as large as gasoline drum cans." "I could hear maggots eating rotting flesh."

I read about how the nurses were warned that if they revealed themselves, they would be raped and killed. So when the US Army guys called for them to come out of the cave, they didn't move. They thought it was a trick to lure them to their destruction. Most of the nurses stayed down in the cave. When the American soldiers gassed the cave, many of them were killed.

I read a few sentences out loud. "It was so quiet you could hear a pin drop. So when you no longer heard someone's voice, you knew she was dead. One voice after another disappeared. First, Chinen-san, then Hamamoto-san, Ishikawa-san, Kanda-san, and Higa-san."

I imagine this cave filled with bodies—some dead, some dying, some just barely hanging on. I imagine the stench of rotting limbs. Those girls must have been hungry and lonely and scared. They must have thought the world was coming to an end.

Mom puts a hand on my shoulder. She puts her arm around Maya's waist. And then I feel another, heavier hand drop down on my other shoulder. I turn to see Otosan standing behind us, his arms around our whole family, as if he's trying to keep us safe.

"It was a terrible thing," Mom says, her voice all choked up.

We look at the portraits again, all those young faces.

By the time we emerge from the cave, back into the light, we are all sniffling and struggling to swallow the lumps in our throats. Just before we go out the door, we come across a guest book, a place to write about how we feel.

Maya goes first. She grabs the pen and scribbles a whole page, like she's writing a letter to someone. Then she wipes her eyes, turns to a clean page, and hands the pen to me.

I grab it from her and stare at the blank page for a long time. What should I write? I don't even know how to describe all these weird emotions going through my body. I feel a little bit guilty at having such an easy life. And sad, of course. And angry at the Americans who gassed the cave and the Japanese who told the nurses to stay down there. I'm feeling too many things at once, and there's not really enough time to process them, so I just write, "I'm sorry."

An elderly Japanese lady leans on her cane near the entrance. She thanks us for coming—Mom, Maya, Otosan, and me. I think she must have been one of the nurses, but even if she was, she doesn't seem to harbor any bad feelings toward Americans, or Japanese who married Americans, or half-and-half kids like me and Maya. She smiles at us as we go out the door.

This time when we go by the shrine, Mom stops and buys a flower. She lays it on the altar and puts her hands together in prayer. Then all of us go back to the car. I walk slowly, silently, my head bent down.

As we drive back to the hotel, we're each in our private worlds. I look out the window at the fields of sugar cane, the ocean in the distance, but what I'm really seeing is all those sad, dark eyes peering down from the cave walls. That girl who looked like Chiaki.

And then we go by a shop window that's all lit up with colored lights and I remember that it's Christmas Eve. It doesn't seem like the right time to be all gloomy. I'm glad that I saw all those girls on the wall, and I know that I will never forget, but right now we need to cheer up.

An orange-and-brown sign that I recognize from the guidebook looms into view. As if on cue, my stomach growls.

"Hey, Otosan," I say. "Why don't we stop at A&W for supper?"

I expect some resistance, but he pulls into the parking lot without comment. For once, he doesn't have anything nasty to say about Americans and their dominance of Okinawa and the evils of sugar.

We go up to the counter and order burgers and root beer floats. Then we settle at a table near the window.

A root beer float, I discover, is a scoop of vanilla ice cream bobbing in brown bubbles. It's fizzy and creamy at the same time. It tastes a little different from anything I've ever had before, but it's delicious.

Otosan seems to think so, too. He takes a sip and says, "Mmmm." And then Mom is humming along with him. For once, they are in tune with each other. I know that it won't last. Eventually they'll start bickering again. But for now, we can enjoy this sweet peace.

When we're done eating, we head slowly back to the car. We look around for Mom, expecting to find her right behind us, but she's not. And then we hear the bell clanging at the entrance. She's there, a huge smile spread across her face, ringing that bell and ringing it again.

Glossary

aragoto a style of Kabuki acting that involves exaggerated movements and speech

atsui hot

banzai a Japanese patriotic exclamation or shout of celebration

bara rose

bucho club captain

bunko or *bunko musubi* a way of tying a kimono *obi*

-chan suffix for a child's name

chanto shita done perfectly

chinsuko Okinawan sweet

chiyogami traditional block-printed paper

chotto kinasai come here

dokkiri shocked, startled

domo thank you

don sound of a drum beat

fukura suzume a way of tying a kimono *obi*; literally means "plump sparrow"

furisode kimono with long, draping sleeves

gaijin in Japan, a non-Japanese person

gaman endurance, perseverance

ganbare or *ganbatte* persevere, endure, hang in there

geta Japanese wooden sandals worn with *kimono* or *yukata*

Goku fictional character from *Dragon Ball* manga and anime by Akira Toriyama

haafu or *hafu* half Japanese person; person of mixed racial heritage

haka traditional Maori war dance from New Zealand

hakama skirt-like trousers worn by practitioners of various martial arts such as *kendo* and in some traditional ceremonies

hamaguri clams used in a soup to symbolize a happy marriage

hanami flower viewing, usually cherry blossoms in the spring

hanamichi in Kabuki, a raised walkway that runs through the audience from the back of the theater to the stage

haole in Hawaii, a word used to describe a Caucasian or white person

Harajuku an area of Tokyo especially popular with young people and known for street fashion trendy shops

himesama or *hime* princess

hiragana one of two phonetic syllabaries used in Japanese writing; the other is *katakana*, and they are sometimes called *kana* for short

hoihoi Hey!

honto ni really

hora hey

hyaku-monogatari one hundred stories, often of the supernatural, told as a sort of parlor game

ichinichi one day

inau whittled branches (usually willow or birch) that are decorated with wood shavings and believed to be popular with the Ainu gods

irasshaimase welcome; shopkeeper's call of greeting

itai it hurts, ouch, painful

jinbei traditional Japanese summer clothing consisting of a loose-fitting top and shorts

jingu Shinto shrine

joshiki common sense

kakigori shaved ice often served with sweet fruit or green-tea syrup or sweet azuki beans and condensed milk

kami a Shinto spirit or god, sometimes considered a deity, other times considered more like a spirit dwelling in nature, such as in a mountain or tree

kana Japanese writing syllabary

kanji Chinese characters adapted for the Japanese writing system

kankei nai doesn't matter, not related

Kannon goddess of mercy

kappa mythical water creature said to inhabit rivers and ponds

kazoku family

kendo a martial art based on traditional samurai swordsmanship

keyaki Japanese zelkova tree (*Zelkova serrate*)

kimon northeastern or unlucky demon gate

kirei pretty, beautiful

kodama a spirit thought to live in trees

kodomo child, children

maji de seriously, really

mata later; **mata ne** see you later

monpe simple Japanese pants for farming or outdoor work

nabe Japanese type of one-pot stew often cooked at the table

nagauta literally "long song," a type of music sung for Kabuki theater accompanied by the three-stringed *shamisen*

nakama close friends

natto fermented soybeans

nihonjin Japanese person

noren fabric divider often hung in shop doorways, between rooms, or to mark bathing areas

obake ghost or supernatural shape-shifting being

obaasan or **obaachan** grandmother

obi long sash tied around a kimono (*bunko, fukura suzume,* and *otaiko* are different ways of tying an *obi*)

Obon Japanese summer festival when spirits of the dead are believed to visit the living

ochazuke a Japanese dish of green tea over rice with various toppings such as nori, sesame seeds, salmon or *umeboshi*

odaiko large *taiko* drum

odango hairstyle in the shape of a dumpling made of mochi flour

ohayo or **ohayo gozaimasu** good morning

ohisashiburi it's been a while; long time no see

ojiisan grandfather

ojiya rice gruel with miso and vegetables

okaasan mother

okonomiyaki a Japanese dish like a pancake filled with vegetables and meat or seafood

omikuji fortune papers at shrines or temples

onesan older sister

onigiri rice ball or rice triangle, often wrapped in nori and containing a sour plum, salmon, or pickled seaweed

oniisan older brother

onsen hotspring bath

otaiko drum (*taiko*) or drum-shaped knot

otaku nerd or geek often obsessed with anime or manga or trains

otenba tomboy

otosan father

oyaji old man

purikura short for Print Club, meaning photo stickers

sake rice-based alcoholic beverage

sakura cherry blossom, cherry tree

salariman businessman

-san suffix for a name

sanma Pacific saury, mackerel pike

sayonara good-bye

senpai one's senior at work or school

SELHi Super English Language High School, a type of Japanese school in which some of the curriculum is taught in English

shamisen Japanese three-stringed musical instrument

shirabyoshi a style of court dance dating from Japan's Heian era; the dancers of that style of dance

shitteru do you know?; I know

shizuka quiet, peaceful

shogi Japanese chess

shoji paper and wood lattice sliding door

sugoi amazing, great

sumimasen excuse me, sorry

tabi traditional Japanese split-toed socks

tadaima words spoken on returning home

taiko traditional Japanese drum (*odaiko* is a large *taiko* drum)

taiyaki a fish-shaped batter cake filled with sweet azuki beans or custard

tanuki Japanese raccoon dog (*Nyctereutes procyonoides viverrinus*), portrayed as a trickster and shape shifter in Japanese tales

Takeshita-dori Takeshita Street—a trendy street in the Harajuku area of Tokyo

torii gate to a shrine

udon a thick type of noodle

umeboshi sour pickled plum

urusai/urusakatta is/was noisy, annoying

wan-chan dog or doggy

wan wan a dog's bark

warashi child

yakuza members of Japanese organized crime groups

yama no kami mountain spirit

Yamanote Line circular or loop train line that runs through Tokyo

yamete stop it

yokai supernatural ghosts or spirits

yoroshiku greeting similar to hello, hi; *yoroshiku onegai shimasu* more formal—nice to meet you

yukata lightweight, cotton kimono often worn in summer at festivals

yukar traditional Ainu tale

zashiki warashi a Japanese *yokai* that appears as a child

zori a type of flat, thonged sandal; dressy *zori* are worn with kimono

Contributors

Naoko Awa (1943–93, author, "Blue Shells") was born in Tokyo and lived in different parts of Japan. As a child, she read fairy tales by the Brothers Grimm, Hans Christian Andersen, and Wilhelm Hauff as well as *The Arabian Nights*. She published numerous books, including *Kaze to ki no uta* (Song of the Wind and Tree) and *Hanamame no nieru made* (While the Beans Are Cooking). A collection of her short stories translated into English, *The Fox's Window and Other Stories*, was published in 2010.

Deni Y. Béchard (author, "Half Life") is the Canadian-American author of *Vandal Love*, which won the 2007 Commonwealth Writers' Prize. *Cures for Hunger*, his memoir about growing up with a father who was a bank robber, is forthcoming in 2012, and in 2013 he will publish *Empty Hands, Open Arms*, a book about conservationism in the Congo rain forest. He has lived in Japan off and on since 2009. www.denibechard.com

Jennifer Fumiko Cahill (author, "Paper Lanterns") is a graduate of Columbia University's MFA writing program. She often visited Japan as a child and has lived in Tokyo for ten years with her husband and two children. Her poems have appeared in *The Southern Review, Greensboro Review, Prairie Schooner*, and *The Southeast Review*.

Juliet Winters Carpenter (translator, "Fleecy Clouds"), a Midwesterner by birth, is a longtime resident of Japan. Her many translations include mysteries, romance novels, haiku and tanka poetry, historical fiction, and works on Buddhist philosophy. Volume one of *Saka no ue no kumo* (tentative title: *Clouds Above the Hill*), her

joint translation of Ryotaro Shiba's epic on the Russo-Japanese War, is forthcoming from Routledge in 2012. She lives in Kyoto, where she is a professor at Doshisha Women's College, and on Whidbey Island, Washington. www.swet.jp/ index.php/ people/juliet-winters-carpenter

John Paul Catton (author, "Staring at the Haiku") is a British writer who has lived in Japan for fifteen years. He teaches at an international school in West Tokyo and is studying for an MA in Creative Writing from the University of Canberra. Japanese myths, folktales, and urban legends are a major influence on his work.

Yukie Chiri (1903–22, transcriber/translator, "Where the Silver Droplets Fall") was a linguistically gifted Ainu girl raised in a time of decline for the Ainu language and culture. She was in her mid-teens when she began preserving some of the *yukar* (epic tales) of Ainu oral tradition, transcribing them and translating them into Japanese. She died of heart failure at age nineteen, leaving behind an anthology of fourteen *yukar* published posthumously as *Ainu·shin'yoshu* (Collected Tales of the Ainu Gods).

Chloë Dalby (author, "The Mountain Drum") studies Comparative Literature and Japanese at Oberlin College. She builds *taiko* drums in her spare time. She recently returned from a semester abroad at Kansai Gaikoku Daigaku where she studied *obake* and *yokai*.

Liza Dalby (author, "Shuya's Commute") is a cultural anthropologist and writer whose career has focused on Japan in nonfiction (*Geisha, Kimono*), fiction (*The Tale of*

Murasaki, Hidden Buddhas) and a memoir (*East Wind Melts the Ice*). www.lizadalby.com

Deborah Davidson (translator-illustrator, "Where the Silver Droplets Fall") was born and raised in Japan, going on to earn a BA in Asian Studies and an MA in Advanced Japanese Studies from US and UK universities. Since retiring from a thirty-year career in Japanese-to-English translating, she has settled into a second career in the world of Japanese folk art. She resides in Sapporo, Japan. Her published translations include the works of novelist Miura Ayako and Ainu folklore. http://etegamibydosankodebbie. blogspot.com

Claire Dawn (author, "Ichinichi on the Yamanote") grew up on the Caribbean island of Barbados. She has been teaching English as a foreign language in Ichinohe, Iwate Prefecture, for three years. In her spare time, Claire writes young adult novels. Her work can also be found in the *Write for Tohoku* anthology. http://aclairedawn.blogspot.com

Charles De Wolf (author, "Borne by the Wind"), Professor Emeritus, Keio University, is a writer, linguist, and translator of Japanese literature, both classical and modern. His translations include numerous stories from *Konjaku monogatari*, a twelfth-century folktale collection, excerpts from *The Tale of Genji*, and works by Ryunosuke Akutagawa, Hyakken Uchida, Keizo Hino, Ryu Murakami, Haruki Murakami, and Akiko Itoyama. He has spent most of his life in Japan. www.sudaroan.com

Megumi Fujino (author, "Love Letter") is an Osaka-based author of children's and young adult literature, mysteries, and romance fiction. Her debut work, *Neko mata yokaiden* (The Story of the Nekomata Monster) was published in 2004. She is the author of the ongoing "Thief of Phantom and Darkness" series and recently of *Watashi no koibito* (My Boyfriend). home.att.ne.jp/apple/mogmog/

Andrew Fukuda (author, "Lost"), born in Manhattan and raised in Hong Kong, is half Chinese, half Japanese. After graduating from Cornell University, he worked in Manhattan's Chinatown. Author of the novel *Crossing* and the forthcoming *The Hunt*, he lived and worked in Kansai for several years and currently resides in New York. www. andrewfukuda.com

Alan Gratz (author, "The Ghost Who Came to Breakfast") is the author of a number of books for young readers, including *Samurai Shortstop*. His short fiction has appeared in Knoxville's *Metropulse* magazine, *Alfred Hitchcock's Mystery Magazine*, and the middle-grade anthology *Half-Minute Horrors*. He spent two months in Tokyo in 2010 teaching historical fiction writing at the American School in Japan. www.alangratz. com

Katrina Toshiko Grigg-Saito (author, "I Hate Harajuku Girls") grew up knowing Japan through her father's stories. Her essays and travel adventures about Japan and places all over the world have been seen in two National Geographic anthologies, the *Christian Science Monitor*, NPR, CNN-go, *The Japan Times, Skirt Magazine, Metropolis Magazine*, and *Tokyo Art Beat*. Her first children's book, *Ma, The Search for Silence*, is soon to be published by Little, Brown and Company. http://beinginlovethere.com

Sako Ikegami (translator, "Hachiro") can lay claim to various titles (clinical pharmacist, medical translator/writer, children's book reader), but best enjoys working with young adult books. She aspires to bridge her two cultures, US and Japanese, by translating children's literature in both. Her translations include Ryusuke Saito's *The Tree of Courage* and Angela Johnson's *First Part Last*. www. sakotrans.com

Deborah Iwabuchi (translator, "The Law of Gravity") made her first trip to Japan at age seventeen and took up permanent residence soon after college. She has translated, among other works, novels by popular Japanese authors, including *The Devil's Whisper* and *The Sleeping Dragon* by Miyuki Miyabe. Originally from California, she lives in the city of Maebashi with her family and runs her own company, Minamimuki Translations. http://minamimuki.com/en

Suzanne Kamata (author, "Peace on Earth") is the author of the novel *Losing Kei* and editor of three anthologies, including *The Broken Bridge: Fiction from Expatriates in Literary Japan.* Her short stories for young adults have appeared in *Cicada* and *Hunger Mountain*, and she is the recipient of an SCBWI Magazine Merit Award for Fiction. She has lived in Shikoku for over twenty years. www.suzannekamata.com

Toshiya Kamei (translator, "Blue Shells") holds an MFA in Literary Translation from the University of Arkansas, where he was the 2006–2007 Carolyn Walton Fellow in Translation. His translations include Liliana Blum's *The Curse of Eve and Other Stories,* Naoko Awa's *The Fox's Window and Other Stories,* Leticia Luna's *Wounded Days,* and Espido Freire's *Irlanda.* Other translations have appeared in *The Global Game, Sudden Fiction Latino,* and *My Mother She Killed Me, My Father He Ate Me.*

Sachiko Kashiwaba (author, "House of Trust") is a prolific writer of children's and young adult fantasy whose career spans more than three decades. Her works have garnered the prestigious Sankei Children's Book Award and Shogakukan Children's Book Award, among many others, and her novel *Kiri no muko no fushigi na machi* (The Marvelous Village Veiled in Mist) influenced Hayao Miyazaki's film *Spirited Away.* She has translated two fairy novels by Gail Carson Levine into Japanese. She lives in Iwate Prefecture.

Yuko Katakawa (author, "The Law of Gravity"), the author of six books, received a Kodansha New Writer in Children's Literature Award for her first publication, *Sato-san,* written when she was fifteen. Now in university, she continues to write while studying to become a veterinarian. "The Law of Gravity" is revised from a story she first wrote at age fourteen.

Trevor Kew (author, "The Bridge to Lillooet") has lived in Yokohama for three years, teaching Japanese and traveling extensively throughout the country. He teaches at Yokohama International School and is the author of three novels for children: *Trading Goals, Sidelined,* and *Breakaway.* "The Bridge to Lillooet" was partially inspired by the excellent Canadian NFB documentary *Sleeping Tigers.* www.trevorkew.com

Yuichi Kimura (author, "Wings on the Wind") was born in Tokyo, graduated from Tama Art University, and worked on children's magazines and TV programs before turning to writing. His picture book series *Arashi no yoru ni* (One Stormy Night) has won multiple book awards. His creations, comprising more than five hundred titles for children of all ages, are enjoyed around the world. www.kimura-yuuichi.com

Louise George Kittaka (author, "Just Wanderful") is a New Zealander living in Tokyo with her family and three cats. She is a freelance writer and editor for educational publishing, and also works with teens with special learning needs. She has co-authored two parenting books in Japanese about using English with young children. www.mamabaka.com

Hart Larrabee (translator, "Anton and Kiyohime") was born in New York State, majored in Japanese at Carleton College in Minnesota, and earned postgraduate degrees from the University of Pennsylvania and University of Hawaii. A full-time freelance translator, he currently lives with his family in Nagano Prefecture.

Misa Dikengil Lindberg (translator, "The Dragon and the Poet") grew up in a bicultural (Japanese-Turkish) home in New Jersey and has lived in both the United States and Japan. She was first drawn to translation studies while teaching at a bilingual Japanese-English school, where she fell in love with Japanese children's literature. She currently writes, edits, translates, and teaches in Vermont.

Leza Lowitz (co-author, "Jet Black and the Ninja Wind") is an award-winning writer and yoga instructor. Her work has appeared in *The Huffington Post, Shambhala Sun*, and *Best Buddhist Writing of 2011*. She has published more than sixteen books, most recently *Yoga Heart: Lines on the Six Perfections*. www.lezalowitz.com

Kelly Luce ("Yamada-san's Toaster") participated in the JET Program in Kawasaki and spent two years in Tokushima City. Her collection of Japan-set stories received the San Francisco Foundation's 2008 Jackson Award and was a finalist for the 2010 Bakeless Prize. Her work has recently appeared in *The Southern Review, American Short Fiction*, and *The Kenyon Review*. thecrazypetesblotter.blogspot.com

Thersa Matsuura (author, "The Zodiac Tree") is a longtime resident of Shizuoka, Japan, where she lives with her husband, her son and various dogs, cats and newts. Her collection of dark, mythical short stories (*A Robe of Feathers and Other Stories*) was published by Counterpoint LLC. www.thersamatsuura.com

Kenji Miyazawa (1896–1933, author, "The Dragon and the Poet"), one of Japan's most beloved writers, was born in Hanamaki City in Iwate Prefecture. Miyazawa's life and works were greatly influenced by his passion for nature, science, and Buddhism. In addition to writing poetry and literature, he devoted much of his life to helping improve the lives of Iwate's rural farmers.

Mariko Nagai (author, "Half a Heart") was born in Japan but writes in English, having grown up in the United States and Europe. The author of two books for adults, *Histories of Bodies: Poems* and *Georgic: Stories*, she has won numerous awards and fellowships from art foundations around the world for her writing. Her work has appeared in *Asia Literary Review, Foreign Policy, Southern Humanities Review, New Letters*, and *Prairie Schooner*, to name a few. She lives in Tokyo. www.mariko-nagai.com

Marji Napper (author, "The Lost Property Office") is a teacher and language consultant for businesses in Tokyo. She has a deep interest in children's literature. She has worked in high schools and colleges in the UK and in language schools in Italy and Japan.

Arie Nashiya (author, "Fleecy Clouds") was born in Tochigi Prefecture. She began her writing career with the novel *Deribarii age* (Delivery Age), which won the 39th Kodansha Children's Literature Newcomer Prize in 1998. Her novel *Pianisshishimo* (Pianississimo) was awarded the 33rd Japan Children's Literature Bungei Kyokai Newcomer Prize. Among her best-known other works are the novel *Surii sutazu* (Three Stars) and the short story collection *Shabondama domei* (The Bubble League).

Sarah Wittenbrink Ogawa (author, "One") has been teaching English and creative writing in Japan for twenty years, while also working in journalism and television. Her aspirations to become a senior high homeroom teacher at a Japanese school were fulfilled fifteen years ago, and her students continue to inspire her every day. www.kyotosarah.com.

Debbie Ridpath Ohi (author-illustrator, "Kodama") is a Japanese-Canadian writer and artist. She is the illustrator of the picture book *I'm Bored* and also the artist-in-residence at TorontoToJapan.ca, a Toronto-based fund-raising collective. Debbie writes and illustrates books for young people. DebbieOhi.com

Shogo Oketani (co-author, "Jet Black and the Ninja Wind") is author of *J-Boys: Kazuo's World, Tokyo, 1965* (translated by Avery Fischer Udagawa) and *Designing with Kanji*, and is co-translator of *America* by Ayukawa Nobuo, for which he received the Japan-U.S. Friendship Commission Award. He lives in Tokyo where he works as an editor and self-defense instructor. www.j-boysbook.com

Lynne E. Riggs (translator, "Love Letter") is a professional translator based in Tokyo. She is an active member of the Society of Writers, Editors, and Translators and teaches Japanese-to-English translation at International Christian University. Her fiction translations include *Kiki's Delivery Service* by Eiko Kadono and *School of Freedom* by Shishi Bunroku. www.cichonyaku.com

Ryusuke Saito (1917–85, author, "Hachiro") wrote original folktales rife with onomatopoeia in the musical cadence of the Akita dialect. In collaboration with his lifelong illustrator Jiro Takidaira, his award-winning short stories became classic picture books. Although a native of Tokyo, Saito fell in love with Tohoku and its people, as evidenced in his stories. His books include *The Tree of Courage* and *The Mountain of Flowers*.

Graham Salisbury (author, "Bad Day for Baseball") grew up on Oahu and Hawaii. He received an MFA from Vermont College of Norwich University, where he was a member of the founding faculty of the MFA program in writing for children. He lives with his family in Oregon. His books, including *Eyes of the Emperor* and *Under the Blood Red Sun*, have garnered many prizes. www.grahamsalisbury.com

John Shelley (illustrator, cover and part-title art) began his illustration career in London before an interest in Japanese art took him to Tokyo, where he lived for over twenty years. He has illustrated more than forty children's books for both Western and Japanese markets. Now based once more in the UK, he continues to produce illustrations for global markets. www.jshelley.com

Ann Tashi Slater (author, "Aftershocks") earned an MFA in creative writing at the University of Michigan and a BA in comparative literature at Princeton. Her stories have appeared in *Shenandoah*, *Gulf Coast*, *Painted Bride Quarterly*, and *American Dragons* (HarperCollins). Her translation of a Cuban novella was published in *Old Rosa: A Novel in Two Stories* (Grove). A longtime resident of Japan, she teaches American Literature at Japan Women's University. anntashislater.wordpress.com

Alexander O. Smith (translator, "Wings on the Wind") has been translating video games and novels from Japanese to English since graduating from Harvard University with an M.A. in Classical Japanese Literature in 1998. He is the founder of Kajiya Productions Inc. and is now based in Vermont's Northeast Kingdom. He received the ALA Batchelder Award for *Brave Story* (Miyuki Miyabe) and the Phillip K. Dick Special Citation for *Harmony* (Project Itoh). www.kajiyaproductions.com

Kaitlin Stainbrook (author, "Signs") is a recent graduate of Beloit College where she received a BA in creative writing and currently edits the *Beloit Fiction Journal*. She spent a semester abroad at Kansai Gaikoku Daigaku during her junior year and is now working on her first novel. www.disdainbrook.blogspot.com

David Sulz (translator, "Be Not Defeated by the Rain") is a librarian at the University of Alberta. He spent four years in the nineties in the JET program in Miyagi (Sendai and Towa-cho) and tries to return often to visit the kindred spirits there, who remain among his closest friends. Other translations include Jiro Nitta's *Phantom Immigrants* (*Mikkosen suian maru*), Kenji Miyazawa's *The Poison Powder Police Chief*, and lyrics from Miyagi friends' CDs.

Fumio Takano (author, "Anton and Kiyohime") is best known for works of alternative history with a science fiction twist. Her debut novel, *Mujika makiina* (Musica Machina), was selected as one of Japan's thirty best works of science fiction from the 1990s. Her latest project is compiling *Jikan wa dare mo matte kurenai* (Time Waits for No Man), an anthology of Eastern European science fiction and fantastica from the first decade of the twenty-first century that brings together twelve stories from ten countries, each translated directly into Japanese from its original language. homepage3.nifty.com/takanosite/indexEnglish.htm.

Holly Thompson (editor, Foreword) earned an MA from the NYU Creative Writing Program and is the author of several works that take place in Japan: the novel *Ash,* the picture book *The Wakame Gatherers,* and the verse novel *Orchards,* which received the 2012 APALA Asian/Pacific American Award for Young Adult Literature. A longtime resident of Japan, she teaches creative and academic writing at Yokohama City University and is regional advisor of the Tokyo chapter of the Society of Children's Book Writers and Illustrators. www.hatbooks.com

Wendy Nelson Tokunaga (author, "Love Right on the Yesterday") lived in Tokyo in the early 1980s. She earned her MFA at the University of San Francisco and is the author of two Japan-themed novels, *Love in Translation* and *Midori by Moonlight,* and the nonfiction e-book *Marriage in Translation: Foreign Wife, Japanese Husband.* She lives in San Francisco with her Osaka-born husband. www.WendyTokunaga.com

Catherine Rose Torres (author, "A Song for Benzaiten") is a Filipino diplomat and writer based in Singapore. She is a Palanca awardee

for fiction, and her works have appeared in *Ceriph, TAYO Literary Magazine,* and *The Philippines Graphic.* She takes part in Write Forward, an online writing course by Birbeck College Writing Programme and British Council Singapore. She stayed in Japan during a cultural exchange sponsored by JAL in 1999 and was an exchange student at the University of Tokyo from 2000 to 2001.

Tak Toyoshima (author-illustrator, "Kazoku") is the writer and illustrator of the comic strip *Secret Asian Man.* Since 1999, *Secret Asian Man* has been tackling issues of race with raw honesty, seeking to bring people together to work out these problems. Tak speaks at universities about his experiences and the importance of keeping tuned in to mainstream depictions and stereotypes of Asians in America. Raised in New York City, he now lives in Massachusetts. www.secretasianman.com

Avery Fischer Udagawa (translator, "House of Trust") grew up in Kansas and lives with her bicultural (Japanese-American) family near Bangkok. Her translations from Japanese include the middle-grade novel *J-Boys: Kazuo's World, Tokyo, 1965* by Shogo Oketani. Her writing has appeared in *Kyoto Journal* and *Literary Mama.* www.averyfischerudagawa.com

Acknowledgments

This anthology was a labor of love by many individuals on behalf of teens in the Tohoku region of Japan affected by the March 11, 2011 earthquake and tsunami. I am grateful to the authors for donating their stories, which together have created this rich collection of Japan-related tales. I wish to thank all of the translators for their incredible efforts under extremely tight deadlines, particularly Sako Ikegami and Avery Fischer Udagawa, who played key roles in seeking out Japanese-language authors, connecting them with translators, and ensuring that *Tomo* would include works originally written in Japanese. So many individuals have contributed along the way to *Tomo*'s success, including my agent Jamie Weiss Chilton; members of the Tokyo chapter of the Society of Children's Book Writers and Illustrators; members of the Society of Writers, Editors and Translators—especially Lynne E. Riggs; John Shelley, who donated illustrations for the cover and interior; Debbie Ridpath Ohi, who designed the *Tomo* launch graphic; David Sulz, who contributed his poem translation for the epigraph; as well as myriad friends and colleagues. I also wish to thank my ever-supportive family members for encouraging me through many months of this project. Publisher Peter Goodman of Stone Bridge Press has championed this anthology wholeheartedly from the moment I first mentioned my idea, and to him and the entire Stone Bridge Press team, I am deeply grateful.

H.T.

The Tomo Blog

For interviews with contributors to this book including cultural information relating to the stories, and for updates regarding the donations of funds raised through sales of *Tomo: Friendship Through Fiction—An Anthology of Japan Teen Stories*, please visit the Tomo Blog:

tomoanthology.blogspot.com